Timberline

by
J. D. Oliver

CCB Publishing
British Columbia, Canada

Timberline

Copyright ©2018 by J. D. Oliver
ISBN-13 978-1-77143-353-2
First Edition

Library and Archives Canada Cataloguing in Publication
Oliver, J. D., 1939-, author
Timberline / by J. D. Oliver. -- First edition.
Issued in print and electronic formats.
ISBN 978-1-77143-353-2 (softcover).--ISBN 978-1-77143-354-9 (pdf)
Additional cataloguing data available from Library and Archives Canada

Cover artwork credit: SelfPubBookCovers.com/Beverley

Disclaimer: This is a work of fiction. The characters, incidents and dialogues are products of the author's imagination and are not to be construed as real. Any resemblance to actual events or persons living or dead is entirely coincidental.

Extreme care has been taken by the author to ensure that all information presented in this book is accurate and up to date at the time of publishing. Neither the author nor the publisher can be held responsible for any errors or omissions. Additionally, neither is any liability assumed for damages resulting from the use of the information contained herein.

Publisher: CCB Publishing
              British Columbia, Canada
              www.ccbpublishing.com

To my wife Sharon,
she has shown infinite love and patience for fifty-six years,
and has also supported my writing efforts over the years.

Chapter One

The clackity-clack of the train's wheels on the iron rails had lulled me to sleep. I had been getting plenty of sleep ever since the train left St. Louis. But now the conductor's call of Louisville the next stop woke me from my dreams.

The thought of going home after all the years away made me excited and perhaps a little anxious. I had left, and again perhaps, not under the best of circumstances. I was fourteen years old and thought I was man-grown. Little did I know then how-much I had left to learn!

Home was in the Blue Grass country of Kentucky; down near Hodgenville, but some east of there. Now Hodgenville was where Abe Lincoln was born; some of his family still lived in the vicinity. But Pap's place was east of there. The closest town was called Helmsville. It was right in the middle of the best grass in Kentucky; blue stem it was.

Like I said, I was fourteen when I left; right before the war. It was called a Civil War. I never did see anything civil about it. We done fought that war to a standstill; the only thing all of that killing accomplished was that it sort of freed the slaves. I say sort of because what's freedom unless you have equality?

It was just coming on to spring; the trees were starting to leaf out and the flowers were blooming and the Ohio River was starting to rise with the spring runoff. The year was 1866 and I was coming home to a defeated land. Not the people; they weren't defeated; you couldn't defeat their spirit. You might quell it for a spell; but you would have to kill each and every one of them to defeat it.

I stood up and stretched, all six feet two inches of me. Of course, I was almost this tall when I left home. But now I had filled out some. But there wasn't any fat to speak of; unless of course it was between my ears. But I doubted that; because I had been thinking pretty clear of late.

My saddle and plunder were in the baggage car. In my bedroll I had my twin .44's as well as a brand-new Winchester. Of course, I had a Derringer and my Texas Bowie knife; that was on a rawhide string in a quick release scabbard down the back of my neck. A Mexican Vaquero had taught me how to use that knife. And a gunman down in Texas had got me started on how to draw fast and shoot straight.

In the seven years that I had been gone I had pretty much learned the ways and wiles of the world. I had been all over the west; from Canada to Mexico and lived to tell about it. I had fought the Blackfoot warriors in Montana Territory and the Apache and Comanche in New Mexico and Arizona. Now the Sioux and the Cheyenne were friendly to me; the Crow ran hot and cold, depending how the whisky supply held out.

I stepped off of the train to the hustle and bustle of a growing city. I claimed my saddle and plunder and walked through what I would call teeming crowds toward the nearest livery. The weirdest thing; I was never lonely in the middle of a desert, but here in this city with people all around me, I felt alone...

I saw several Union Soldiers here and there. Every one of them almost stopped dead in their tracks looking at me. I just smiled at them and they went on their way. They might have recognized me; since I was a Captain in the Army of the United States. I made Captain by a series of battlefield promotions.

But now I was on medical leave. I was sort of milking it, because I was as fit as a fiddle. My leave was sort of open ended, depending on me. All of my papers were in order all of the way back to Grant. I hadn't quite decided if I was going to go back to active duty.

At the livery I bought two Morgan Geldings and made the Hostler give me a bill of sale made out to me: Matthew Bodeen. It used to be spelled Boden; which is Celtic. But when I left home I added the extra 'e'. I also bought a pack saddle and had the hostler stow my gear until I was ready to leave; probably sometime tomorrow.

I had heard that the Carpet Baggers were as thick as fleas in the southern states since the defeat of the south. I spotted some of them that were sure enough Yankees. I don't know why those carpet baggers were here; since Kentucky was a neutral state. I fought for the Union but I was a dyed in the wool southerner. I just never could see that the making of slaves was the way to go.

2

I took my saddle bags and went to find a room for the night. There was a new Hotel; which looked like they might have a safe that I could stow my saddle bags in overnight. They did. Then I was sure enough hungry and I wouldn't mind a drought of some good southern whisky. Out west it was mostly rot gut and red eye; either one would kill you if you drank too much.

This hotel had a restaurant so that part was easy to find. Come to find out they also had a fancy Saloon; which I moseyed over to after I filled my stomach with steak. Now I was dressed pretty much like any rancher in the west would dress; which of course made me stand out in this hi-toned bar.

Yeah, you were right; the place was filled with Carpet Baggers. Those buggers were only out for the fast buck; whether it was legally made or not. I found an empty spot at the bar and ordered a bottle of Kentucky's finest. The glass was even clean...

The Yankee next to me turned and gave me a look and said to his companion: "Suddenly I smell a stockyard." And then he gave a sniff. I slowly turned to look at the crowd; but I hooked my foot behind his and gave a kick, his butt hit the floor with a bang, he had hit the spittoon on his way down and was covered with the slime....

"Oh, I am sorry, I'm afraid that you are quite clumsy, you were standing on my foot." I said and went to help him up. But being that he was slippery, my hand lost its grip and he fell face down in the muck and mire....

I wiped my hands on a clean spot on his back and picked up my bottle and went back to my room. I would have stayed and wiped up the floor with a few of them, but I didn't figure they were worth my effort. It wasn't too long before I got a knock on my door.

I dropped my Derringer from the holder in my sleeve into my hand. It was an officer of the so-called law. "Can I help you officer?" I asked, being quite polite.

"Are you the one who assaulted the gentleman at the hotel saloon?" he asked.

"I don't know about assaulted, but he was standing on my foot and I simply helped him step off of my foot."

He smiled and said: "I want to shake your hand; that Carpet Bagger was the head of the Reconstruction Office. Too bad you didn't kill him.

3

I guess I can stall him overnight, I'll tell him you lit out for the hills. You look familiar; are you one of the Bodens from down Helmsville way?"

"I reckon; I'm Matthew Bodeen; but the reconstruction office? What are they doing here, Kentucky was neutral?"

"I don't know; but hellfire man, I was led to believe that you were dead; killed in the war. I'm Chester Brown from Lebanon. Sorry to hear about your Dad, he was a fine man."

"What do you mean? Something happen to him?" I asked.

"Yeah, you didn't hear? I suppose not since you've been gone; he was bushwhacked last week. They found his body along the road to his place; shot in the back I hear."

"What about Ma and my little sister and brother, are they alright?"

"I didn't hear that they weren't, but I heard that carpet bagger that runs things in Helmsville is trying to evict them for nonpayment of taxes."

"Non-payment of taxes?" That don't sound like Pa, he was always the first to pay his taxes. I reckon I better head out tonight. Would you mind going with me to the livery? I don't want to kill any of your fine citizens this night; but first I have to get my saddle bags out of the Hotel safe."

"No, not at all, in fact that might be best; we'll just let them think I'm taking you to jail." Chester said.

I don't know what was going on in this state; but something was not right. In my way of thinking there should not be any necessity for any reconstruction, since there wasn't any war damage to speak of; since Kentucky was neutral and no major battles were fought in the state.

Chapter Two

Chester helped me saddle my horse and put the pack saddle on the other one and stow all of my plunder on the pack horse. I tied my saddle bags tightly onto my saddle horse and stuck my Winchester in the scabbard under my right knee. I also buckled my twin .44's on my hips.

It was a clear night with a full moon. The time was around eight, so I had the whole night to travel. It was an hour after dawn when I crested the last hill and looked down on Pap's ranch. There was breakfast smoke coming from the stove in the kitchen; but none coming from the hired hands cottages.

I came in from the back way and tied my horses under the trees so they could graze a bit. Taking my Winchester from the saddle scabbard I walked slowly to the back door of the kitchen. Looking through the window in the door I could see Ma sitting at the table and William and Caroline seated on either side of the table. Will and Caroline were fine looking teenagers, Ma looked haggard.

I stood there watching them for a bit; trying to figure out in my mind why I left in the first place. No sane answer came to me; unless it was the fact that Pa and I just never got along; you see those cottages that I called the hired hands cottages were in reality housing for Pa's slaves. My Pa believed in slavery and I didn't....

I knocked on the Kitchen door. Will come to the door; "What do you want? We don't have any food to spare for the likes of you." He said and started to close the door. I stuck my foot in the way and pushed him back inside.

"Damn, didn't Pa teach you any manners at all? You don't talk to people like that; and if I wasn't your brother I'd teach you some manners right now! I just might anyway." I said as I picked him up by his shirt front and sat him down in his chair.

Ma stood up and said: "Matthew, is that you? We heard that you were dead." She said as rounded the table and threw herself on me.

Then she turned on the tears…. Now, me being a man I didn't cry, like hell I didn't….

After the tears washed away the years; I looked at Caroline; she was sitting there like she didn't know what to do. "Well, little sister, do you remember me? You were just a little girl when I left."

"Yes, but you didn't look like you do now, with that beard and all." She said as she stood up and gave me a hug. I looked at Will setting there with a grumpy look on his face.

"Alright Will, I realize that you thought that you were the man of the house now that Pa was murdered. But you have to earn that title; it's just not handed down. Do you think your man enough to start on the path to manhood?"

"Damn right; I'm seventeen now and if you hadn't caught me by surprise I'd showed you!" He said standing there with his fists clinched. I handed Ma my rifle since I still had it in one hand.

"Alright Boy, do your worst." I said as he lunged at me. I just side stepped to the side a little and caught him in an arm lock as he came by. Then with my free hand I reached up on his neck and applied pressure to a nerve and he was out like a match in a blizzard. I learned that maneuver in the gold camps in California.

I looked at Ma, "Who's this boy been associating with?" I asked her.

"Ever since the south lost the war he's been fit to be tied. He runs around with a bunch that just runs wild. They are in trouble with the law all of the time." Ma said.

"Now what law would that be?" I asked.

"Those Carpet Baggers in Helmsville; I'm afraid he's going to get himself killed; especially since Pa was murdered. And they have been trying to kick us off of our place. They said we owed back taxes and I know that's not true. I've got the receipt for those taxes in our strong box."

"In the strong box, why not the safe?"

"Pa was the only one that had the combination and we can't get in; we're running low on money also."

"I know the combination; I'll open it later; I want to put my saddle bags in there. What about this boy; where do you want him?"

"Prop him up over there by the stove; it still gets chilly in these spring mornings. Will was right about one thing; we're running low on flour, salt, and sugar and such. The new man at the store said that we couldn't buy anything from his store. That we were blackballed." Ma said as she threw a ham steak on the fire for me.

"Is that right? Well don't worry about that I'll set things straight in town. Is there an Army presence in Helmsville?"

"Yes, about 24 or 25 soldiers I would say. The Lieutenant in charge is drunk most of the time; but his sergeant keeps the troops under control." Ma said.

"Do they have a telegraph office?" I asked.

"Yes, of course. But they don't let anyone send any messages except authorized people or so they said."

I turned to Caroline: "So, are you still in school?" I asked.

"Yes and No; Pa said it was too dangerous to travel to the school in Helmsville; so the school Marm has been bringing my lessons out here once a week and Ma helps me with them."

"Why that sounds fine Caroline; this must me your last year in school, am I right?"

"Yes, just one month left. Did you ever go to school after you left home?"

"Well not exactly, but I read every book that I came across and some people helped me along the way. I guess you could say that I went to the school of hard knocks. But I wouldn't recommend that school, the tuition is too high." I said with yawn.

"Ma, where can I put my stuff and maybe Caroline could help me with my horses; they need some oats and water. I rode all night to get here and I need a few hours' sleep."

"Why my goodness sakes; why didn't you say so. Your old room is still there, no one has slept in it since you left. You just go on in and get some sleep; Caroline and I will take care of your horses and bring your stuff in the house. Now go on, get to bed."

I checked on Will, he was still sawing logs. I rearranged him a little bit so he wouldn't fall against the stove. Then I headed for some sack time…

The bed had clean sheets on it; and they smelled fresh; looked like Ma changed them often. I stripped out of my clothes; including my underthings. Shoot, there was even water in the Pitcher. I poured some in the ceramic bowl and used a washrag and took what we called a spit bath. Now that sure made me feel a whole lot better. I was out as soon as my head hit the pillow.

My dreams started right away: I was in camp in the Rocky Mountains and old Pike was holding forth on many topics as per usual. We had made camp just inside the Timberline, one way was all timber and the other way was the rolling foot hills and wide-open plains.

Old Pike was saying: "Strange thing about being at timberline; you might say it's sort of a dividing line in your life. If you go into the timber and then continue on into the mountains; your life will turn one way; and if you go down into the plains you'll be a different man altogether. I call it a Timberline Moment, it's sort of a revelation you might say. Of course, you'll have many of those Timberline Moments, but there will be only one big one and you'll recognize it when it happens to you." And then he just turned over and went to sleep.

I awoke to a Mule Braying. Alarmed, I jumped up and into my pants and grabbed my rifle and ran through the kitchen and out into the yard.... Standing beside a mule was the most beautiful woman I had ever seen. She had freckles across her nose and dark auburn hair and in her arms, she had some books in one hand and in the other was a flintlock squirrel rifle. Our eyes locked.... Neither one of us blinked. The only thought in my mind was one word: TIMBERLINE. It was like I was being sucked right into those Emerald Green eyes.

"Uh, Matthew this is Hattie May the school Marm; she comes out every Saturday with books for Caroline. Hattie May this is my son Matthew, you know the one we thought was dead, he got home just this morning." We heard her; but neither one of us was willing to break our connection.

Hattie May handed the books to Caroline without looking at her; and then stepped toward me, I met her half way; we both had our guns in one hand, we embraced with the other and melted into each other. Her lips tasted of wild raspberries. I knew I would never let this woman leave my side.

We broke our kiss and I whispered into her ear; "will you marry me? She whispered back; "Why yes of course; what a silly question." And then we kissed again; only longer this time. I was going to step back, but I couldn't and she knew why; so I just turned her around and pulled her back in front of me and said:

"I would like to introduce my wife; Mrs. Hattie May Bodeen. Of course, it isn't official yet, but it might as well be." I said to a flabbergasted family. William must have woken up because he was standing there with Caroline and Ma; they were just staring at us with wide open mouths.

"Bodeen? Since when?" William said.

"Oh, I changed it; I added an 'e'. But that's not important, is it?"

"No, I guess not; but I want to apologize for my behavior this morning; Ma told me how out of line I was. You do know that Hattie May is from the Clinch Mountains down in Tennessee and those Clinch Mountain folks are a might clannish?" William said.

"Don't worry about them any; those brothers of mine know that I can whip them with one arm tied behind me and they know when I set my mind to something; come hell or high water I won't change it." Hattie May said.

Hattie May turned to me and said: "What now?" She had already felt that it had gone down and it was alright.

"Well, Ma needs some things from the store in town and we need to get married; so why don't we hook up the buggy and kill two birds with one stone?" I said.

"Alright, I'll go with Ma and get the list together; but maybe I had better hook my mule to the buggy; he goes where I go; he won't be left behind."

"I'll hook him up, that's no problem." I said.

"Well, he bits and kicks; I'm the only one he lets near him." Hattie May said.

"I tell you what, let me give it a try and if he won't stand still for me handling him; then you can; how's that?" With that I walked over to him; he turned his head and watched me. I stopped two feet short of him. I looked him in the eye and waited. He looked over at Hattie and then back at me. He walked forward and put his head over my shoulder and slobbered all over my naked back. I guess that meant that he liked me.

"I'll be hornswoggled; that's the first time in his life that he's liked anybody but me." Hattie May said as he followed me to the barn.

The buggy was a light one- horse surrey; it was only good for light trips; like to church. But I was sure Ma didn't need a whole wagon load of stuff. And she didn't. Of course, I had to wash the slobber off of my back and get dressed. I made sure I took my Army papers with me; I was sure I would need them.

Helmsville was only about six miles down the dirt road. Hattie sat close to me. She squeezed my leg and said: "How did you know it was me that you wanted?"

"Shucks, I could throw that question right back at you. But I'll give you a one- word answer: Timberline...."

"What does that mean?" Hattie said, a little taken back

I spent the next mile explaining it to her how old Pike went on about the paradigm switch. She looked at me and asked:

"Paradigm? How far did you go in school?"

"The sixth grade, why?"

"You sure didn't learn the meaning of that word in the sixth grade, what's the story? Hattie May said as she slipped her hand inside my belt and rubbed.

"Uh, if you want me to tell you; you'd better move your hand or I'll pull off the road into that grove of trees up ahead." She didn't remove her hand....

We lay there watching the clouds and listening to the birds in the trees. She rolled over on top of me and said: "So, what about that word; where did you learn it?"

"Everywhere, you know there are all kinds of educated men in the west. Some are punching cattle, some are in the Army. There is English professors swamping out saloons. Nobel men from Russia or even France; doing all sorts of things. And of course, I read all the books I can get ahold of." I said as she started to move again....

As we were getting dressed I picked up the blanket we were laying on; there was blood on it. I looked at her with a question in my eyes.

"You knew I was a virgin, didn't you? She said.

"Well yeah; but I guess I just didn't think about it; I would love you the same even if you weren't. How old are you anyway?"

"I'm nineteen; and I know you are twenty-one. Yeah and I know it's pretty unusual for a mountain girl to still be a virgin at nineteen. But they all knew I would cut their manhood off if they touched me."

As we got back in the wagon I asked her: "So how did you know I was the one?"

"I looked into your eyes and down into your soul and then I sucked you down into my very being; I know you from the time you were born." Hattie said.

"How can you know all of that?" I asked.

"Never mind; I just do, it runs in my family. You know how in the Bible it says that the two would become one? Well anyway, we're one and will be till the day we both die."

"Alright, if you know so much, look at these papers." I handed her the leather holder that held my Army papers.

"Yes, that answers a lot; I want you to know that I have always been against slavery. But that's no sign that I like those carpet baggers making a mess of our land." She said.

"Well I guess we agree on that; I don't like those Carpet Baggers either." I said.

As we reached town; Hattie said: "Turn down this street; I know where the Justice Of The Peace lives. We'll get hitched first and then get Ma's supplies." She said.

"Good, married first; but I need to go by the Army headquarters' before we go to the store. I need to let them know where the pecking order starts and ends."

Now that Justice of the peace knew Hattie May and he didn't give us one whit of trouble. By using the Justice of the peace we were able to get the official marriage license from the State of Kentucky. Hattie knew where the Army Barracks and Office was; she was driving; I had the feeling that I was going to be hitching my wagon to a Tornado. And that suited me; I liked things to be exciting....

A sergeant was setting at a desk in the reception area. "Can I help you Sir?" He said as Hattie and I walked in.

"I am Captain Bodeen on an inspection tour of all reconstruction offices and the troops as well." I said, showing him my papers. He looked at them and then up at me.

"How come you're not in uniform?"

"Look closely Sergeant, it says that I am undercover. I didn't have to let you know what was going on, but I also was an enlisted man at one time. Is your Lieutenant in?"

"Yes Sir, but I'm afraid he's drunk again and passed out at his desk." He said with his cheeks turning red.

"It's not your fault Sergeant; where is your telegraph key located?" He got up and motioned for us to follow him into the next room; the same room the Lieutenant was passed out in; he was passed out face down on his desk. I felt his neck for a pulse. "Sergeant, you had better get a detail together and get his body to the ice house because he sure enough is dead."

While the Sergeant ran to get the body moved I sat down at the telegraph key. It took a couple of minutes till I was able to get through to Grant's office. Luckily, he was in. I told him the whole story. He said he would get back to us before dark. The Sergeant came back with four men. They packed him out like a sack of grain.

"Sergeant, I need you to secure this office and not let anyone have access to the telegraph. General Grant will be sending us instructions. I want you to write down everything he says and tell no one else; is that clear? I'll be back tomorrow; hold down the fort till then...."

We didn't have far to go to get to our buggy; the Mule had it pulled right up to the door and he was pushing on the door with his nose trying to get in. "Jasper, you know that buggy won't fit in there. Now back up so we can get in the buggy." Hattie May told him. Then she turned to me and said:

"Can we go by my place before we get the supplies? I need to clean up a little bit."

"Yeah, I should of thought of that; I'm sorry I'm not used to being married. You'll have to teach me how to be a good husband."

"I think we'll both learn together; after all we are one flesh now. You know the store keeper is a good man; it's not his fault those Carpet Baggers have threatened him. They told him they would throw him in jail if he sold to anybody on the blacklist. Of course, I am not on that list; I guess they figure they need a school teacher or maybe it's because that jerk is trying to seduce me." Hattie May said, as she drove to the edge of Helmsville where her place was.

Her house was bigger than I thought it would be; a two-story brick house with a small barn and corrals'. "Do you own this or are you renting?" I asked.

"I own it; one of my uncles left it to me. He was killed in the first year of the war. I have a clear title; that is of course if those crooks don't try and pull a fast one. There is forty acres of good blue stem. I have been able to keep up with taxes; just barely. Come on I will show you what I like best about the place." She opened the door with a Skelton Key. We walked through the house to the kitchen that was in the back of the house.

"Look at this; I have running water, there is an artesian spring." She opened a faucet and a good stream of water ran into a sink. "I can plug up the drain and wash the dishes and then afterward I pull the plug and the dirty water runs outside to my flower garden; isn't that neat?"

"So where do you take a bath, in the sink?"

"No silly, come on there is a pool that the spring water runs into and then back into the creek. It's even warm; I'll get some towels, go out back I'll be right there." Hattie said and she rushed into kitchen.

I went to the pool, bending down I felt the water; it was warm. I took some in my cupped hand and tasted it; a mineral taste; but not that bad. In fact, it tasted pretty good. I could hear Hattie coming through the kitchen. She came to a stop beside me; I looked up; she was completely naked.

"Come on; I thought you'd have your clothes off by now; I suppose you want me to help you?"

"Uh, I guess; it would be faster, I guess." Those fingers of hers were very dexterous and talented. Later I asked her about her talents, she said she spent a lot of nights dreaming. The bath was a delight…

We walked back in the house with the towels draped over our shoulders. "I'll get a few clothes for the next few days. You do want to stay at your Mothers place, don't you?"

"Well for tonight anyway. But I'm thinking things are going to heat up here; that is as soon as I hear from General Grant. If it goes like I think it will; you wouldn't mind if we made our home here for a while, would you?"

"No, I wouldn't; that way I could still teach school; there is only one month left for the season." Hattie said as she dropped her towel and leaned into me- "Uh, honey, I think we'd better get to the store before it closes. I promise we can make love all night; I thought we'd use one of the cottages' tonight; that way we wouldn't disturb anyone. You tend to- uh, really enjoy yourself…

"You don't like that?"

"I didn't mean that I didn't like it; I do mean to tell you that I love it and I never want you to stop 'singing'. Otherwise how would I know if I was doing it right?"

"Oh, you were doing it right, but I just can't seem to get enough. Maybe someday it will get old and tiresome; after fifty or sixty years, but I doubt it...."

We got to the store with an hour to spare. The storekeepers name was August Kemper, he was a native Kentuckian.

As we walked in he said:

"Hello Hattie May, who's your friend?"

"Him? He's just my lover. We'll need some supplies you know how all of that lovemaking makes you hungry?" Hattie said all of that with a straight face. August Kemper almost swallowed his chaw.

Hattie handed him our list, "Sure Hattie I'll get right on this." He said as he hurried to fill our order.

"That was mean; he almost choked on his chaw. Of course, it was all I could do to keep from laughing, did you see his face?"

"Yes, I've wanted to shock him for a long time; he's a Deacon in the church and his wife is so self-righteous; they just turn my stomach. Now I suppose he will run to the school board and tell them I'm a fornicator. But don't tell him that we are married, we'll tell them all later; let them gossip."

I made a show of draping myself all over Hattie, if she wanted them to gossip I'd give them something to gossip about. He finished our order and I paid him. He stared at us till we were out of sight.

My beard was itching; I usually didn't wear one and I was ready to get rid of it, but the mustache I would leave on. "Does your beard bother you? You're scratching all the time." Hattie asked.

"Yeah, maybe I could get you to give me a shave tonight?"

"Yes, I'm pretty good; I always shaved my brothers and only one of them bled to death." She said as she gigged-up Jasper to move a little faster. Again, she said it with not only a straight face, but a dead-pan expression. I guess I'd have to get used to her sense of humor. At least I hope it was humor....

Ma was sure glad to get the supplies. "My, that's a lot more than was on my list; I don't know how I can pay for all of that."

"Don't you worry about it Ma; I have money; after we get all of this in the house I'll open the safe for you." I said.

"How come you know the combination; when Ma doesn't?" Will asked.

"Well, my bedroom was right next to Pa's office and that old combination lock makes a loud clicking noise; and I heard Pa get in it so many times that I just started counting the clicks one way and then the other way. So I tried it one time and sure enough I got it open."

"You could hear that in your bedroom? The walls are that thin?" Hattie May said.

"Yeah, that's why I said we should sleep in one of the Cottages tonight; and since you still have to teach school; it would be better if we stayed at your place; is that alright?"

"You're not going to stay here Son, you just got home? Ma said.

"Yeah, I know Ma; but I have some Army business to tend to; and of course, Hattie has a month left before the summer vacation. And I still have to find out who killed Pa and bring them to justice. Plus, we have to find some help for you so this place can get back on plus side-making money for you and the kids."

"This is your home too and you're the oldest." Ma said.

"Yep, I know that; but I'm not going to claim any part of this place; I figure I gave that up when I left when I was fourteen. I think those that stayed and worked the place deserve it more than me." I looked at Will; he had a big smile on his face.

Caroline was helping Hattie bring in the groceries; I heard her whisper to Hattie: "Did you do it yet?"

Hattie whispered something back to her, I couldn't hear, but Caroline's face turned red and she had a big smile on her face; then she looked at me and got an even bigger smile on her face. I reckon Ma would have to keep a close eye on that girl; her hormones were starting up full speed.

After supper I went to the office and opened the safe; Ma was looking over my shoulder. I pulled out all of the ranch ledgers. But setting on top of those ledgers was 1844 Navy Colt Revolver. I handed the ledgers to Ma. Then there was another bag of something stuffed way in back; I tugged at it, it was heavy. I got it out and set it on the floor; opening it was a surprise, it was full of Gold Double Eagles.

"Well Ma, it looks like you won't have to worry about money

anymore; but I wouldn't tell anyone else about this money; not even the kids at this time." There was one bigger envelope; in it was the deed to the ranch as well as a hand written will leaving the place to Ma and if she had already expired; I was the next in line...

Pa and I didn't see eye to eye, but I reckon he loved me despite all of the fights we had. Seeing the will made me more determined to see Pa's death avenged; not that I wasn't already going to bag the buggers...

Ma took a handful of gold coins and we put the rest back in the safe and closed it; turning the handle to scramble the combination; I said: "Did you memorize the combination?"

"Yes, I have it; my memory has always been top-notch. Can I pay you for the supplies?

"Nope, I have money Ma; I did some prospecting up in Montana and it worked out pretty well." I said.

"Are you sure you want to sleep in one of the cottages tonight? You sure are welcome to sleep in your old room."

"Ma, you know how thin these walls are, and us being newlyweds-well, we would probably keep you all awake." I said.

"Yes, I remember when Pa and I were newlyweds, I understand." Ma said with a flush in her cheeks.

Chapter Three

As we lay in bed; resting between bouts; Hattie rolled on her side looking into my eyes, she said: "So what do you see in our future?"

"Huh, what do you mean, like tomorrow or down the road?"

"Down the road; like where you see us, in say one year?"

"Well I don't see making the Army a career; but a lot will depend on what you want. I'm not going to make any decisions without your input." I said, tickling her belly.

"Well you sure know how to say what I want to hear; so, my input is, hurry and put it in…."

We almost missed breakfast; we would have except for Caroline waking us up, literally, she was standing at the foot of our bed, smiling. Hattie didn't seem to mind that we were laying there naked with no covers on; but I wasn't too happy as I yanked up the covers.

"Don't be such a prude Brother, Ma says breakfast will be ready in ten minutes; that is if you two have enough strength left to walk that far. And oh, by the way Hattie I didn't know you knew how to sing!" And then she ran out giggling.

"How are we going to be able to get there in ten minutes? We need a bath." Hattie said.

"There's a pump out back; come on I'll pump and you can set under and then we'll trade places." I said as we got up and ran out back of the cottage. The water was a little cool but it sure refreshed us. Hattie was giggling and looking at me; "Hey that water was cold, it's not my fault." I said, covering you know what with a towel.

We made it in ten minutes but Hattie was still combing her hair on the way to the main house.

After breakfast Hattie did get around to that shave. Oh, I could have shaved myself; after all I had been doing it at least once a year since I left home. But it sure was nice having a beautiful woman do the honors.

"Be careful of my moustache; I want to keep it just the way it is." I said. She finished and handed me a towel to wipe the soap off. She stood back and looked.

"Hey you have a nice strong chin; heck you're even handsome; how about that?" She said.

"Would you have married me if I wasn't?" I asked.

"Of course, we were meant to be together; ugly or handsome; but it sure is nice you turned out handsome." Hattie said as she straddled my lap and gave me a long kiss.

Caroline said: "Hey didn't you two get enough last night?"

Ma gasped and said: "Caroline, mind your manners; goodness sake child. I don't know what's getting into you lately."

Hattie was still setting on my lap; she leaned close and whispered in my ear: "It's not what's getting into her; it's what's not!" I kissed her and whispered back: "You sure don't have that problem."

"Not anymore I don't and I'd better not ever have that problem." Hattie said biting my bottom lip.

"I wish you children would stay longer Matthew; we haven't seen you for six years." Ma said.

"I know Ma, but Hattie has to teach school tomorrow and I have a few things I have to do; for instance, find out who dry-gulched Pa. And I suppose that Grant has sent me a message by now. And William, you have to be the man of the house; you know how to shoot, I take it?"

"Well of course I do. I can probably out shoot you!"

"Glad to hear that brother, I sure hope so. Just be sure what you're shooting at before going off halfcocked. Just remember those bullets are like words, once their said, or shot, you can never get them back. Anyway, trust no one, not even those that you think are your friends; because a knife in the back is sure hard to pull out. And just remember also, what's done in the dead of night doesn't get made right in the light of day."

"Huh? What in the hell does that last thing mean?" Will said, sarcastically.

"Why don't you ask some of your friends that you have been running with; I'm sure they will know what I meant."

"You just think you're so smart, don't you?"

"No Will, I don't think I'm so smart; because everything I have learned was pounded into me by doing and not saying. I can't tell you how many times I got knocked down before I learned to stay down and think things through. Even lying there in the dust, the Devil likes to take his boots to you. So, you see I'm not so smart; cause a smart man wouldn't of gotten in that pickle in the first place. He would of learned by other people's mistakes, not his own."

Chapter Four

I did leave most of the contents of my saddle bags in Ma's safe; just taking enough for expenses. Ma said that she wouldn't share the combination with the children. Not that we didn't trust them; but still being teen-agers, their brains hadn't fully matured. I was a good example of that.

We did pack the rest of my stuff on the second Gelding of mine. We didn't take a wagon; both of us weren't too fond of taking a buggy. I did have another good long talk with Will; I think he was starting to listen a little bit. Caroline was still trying to get more details from Hattie; what details? You know, don't you? I was starting to get more worried about her than I was about Will. When a girl starts to get that itch; it isn't long till some boy will scratch it.

As we were riding along I said as much to Hattie; about my fears about Caroline.

"Yes, I know. I gave her a bunch of home work to try and keep her mind busy. How do you feel about match making?"

"Depends on the match; I don't want some dumb yahoo who thinks with his penis and nothing else. I want someone with a brain and get-up-and go. Do you know anybody like that?"

"Might, I got a letter from My Pap. Ma died when I was born; so, he's single. No, I wasn't thinking of him. But I do have some brothers, they are as smart as a whip; my whole family is. Anyway, they were thinking about coming up this way. I guess those carpet baggers are running wild down there. And short of shooting those carpet baggers and starting a big feud; I suggested that they move up here; what do you think?"

"Yeah, how many brothers do you have?"

"There are four left at home; they range in age from twenty to twenty-five. Pa is about the same age as your Mom. Didn't you say that you were looking for some help to run the place with your Ma?"

"Yeah, are you sure that wouldn't be like tossing sheep into the lion's den?"

"Maybe, but I'm not sure who are the sheep and who are the lions?" Hattie said.

"When are they supposed to move up? And we'd have to talk to both your Pa and my Mother to see if it would work out, it might be sort of overkill, don't you think?"

"How do you mean?" Hattie asked.

"I mean I'm not sure the place needs all four of your brothers. And besides maybe they won't all want to stay there. I guess we will just have to wait and see." I said.

"To answer your question on how soon they will be here; in about a week, I'd say. And you only asked me how many brothers I had; I do have one sister, she's sixteen; she was adopted.

"Well, I would say that the plot thickens; wouldn't you?" But I don't think it will be a detriment; those cabins on Ma's place will be able to house all of them; and I'm willing to bet that your older brothers won't want to stay all too long." I said.

"As to staying too long; how long do you want to stay in Kentucky?" Hattie asked.

"Why, is your foot itching a little bit?" I asked her.

"Well, you have been around to different places; I haven't. And I'm thinking by your not wanting to lay any claim on your Ma's place; that you're not sure you want to light and sit."

"Yep, I think you've hit that proverbial nail on the head. And I'm betting that some of your brothers will be thinking the same thing. That country west of the Mississippi is big and wide and just beckoning us."

We turned one horse and Jasper out to pasture. Hattie wanted to get the house in order; she was a neat freak; good thing because I wasn't. Plus, she wanted to get her lessons together for school in the morning. I rode over to headquarters to see if Grant had sent his orders for me.

He had; he pretty much gave me a free rein to straighten things out. The good thing about it was that President Johnson had signed off on it also.

"Sargent." I said, as I turned to him: "You've read this of course, so you know the authority that I have. I want to speak to the men in the morning at roll call. So, what have you heard or what do you know about all of the problems that are going on?"

"Not much Sir, just rumors."

"Well, tell me all of the rumors; especially about the murder of Iden Boden; my Father."

"He was your Father? I'm truly sorry Sir. But the scuttlebutt going around was that the Carpet Bagger that runs the reconstruction office was behind the murder."

"Is there any proof tying him to the murder?"

"No Sir, but its general knowledge that he's been fudging the records at the Court House; and then foreclosing on delinquent taxes. Or so called past due taxes."

"Has anyone audited the county's books?"

"Not that I know of Sir; because he won't let anyone even look at the books."

"Thank you, Sergeant, I'll be back for roll call in the morning; please have the men fall out with rifles and side arms as appropriate."

I turned my horse out to pasture with the others and went to the house. Hattie was house cleaning. Now I remember how Ma used to dress when she cleaned house; with bonnet and apron and such. But I must say that I liked Hattie's cleaning clothes the best; or should I say the lack of them, since she was completely nude.

"Nice outfit, do you always clean the house that way? Or is it just for my benefit?"

"Oh, you think you're something special huh? Well, you're not; I always undress this way to clean house. I never could figure out why one would get more clothes dirty while cleaning." She said as she walked past me. I know women have a different walk than men, but her sway was not meant for that broom she was carrying. But I could play her game also.

I said, "Hey Honey is my bedroll in the bedroom? I need to get my uniform out and brush it for in the morning."

"Yes, it's on the bed, but I hung your uniform up in the wardrobe. Just a minute and I'll find it for you."

When she came in the bedroom, it turned out we had matching outfits on; or as close as matching as a male and female can get. I guess that uniform would just have to wait....

She was right; a person didn't need clothes on all of the time. But she did wear an apron when she made supper. That was the first time I ever knew an apron could be an aphrodisiac.... But I needed fuel to stoke the engine and build a full head of steam, so we calmly ate the supper my beautiful wife fixed.

The next morning the men were standing at roll call when I arrived. There were twenty-six of them; counting the Sergeant.

"At ease;" I told the men. I walked down the line inspecting each one; making comments as needed; which manly consisted of uniform violations. I did find a few dirty rifles. All of the violations I really didn't give a damn about.

"Men, how many of you have been in actual combat?" Five of them raised their hands. "Alright, that's good. I want the five men that raised their hands to each take five men to train in combat each afternoon the next five days. And in the evenings, you all can have leave to go to town; but I want each of you to keep your eyes and ears open. I want to know everything that you learn about the improprieties going on in this county. The Sergeant can tell you what those improprieties are that I am interested in."

"Sergeant, you can dismiss the men to their regular duties. Let's you and I ride into town and get us a drink; you do drink, don't you?"

"Yes Sir, but isn't it a might early to imbibe?"

"Depends on what you mean by imbibe, but yes, it is early for the hard stuff. The main thing I want to do is just let the town know that the Army is still here and there is a new Officer in Charge. Maybe we'll just get us some pie and coffee at the Café."

"Yes Sir, that pie and coffee sounds really good."

"We can dispense with the Sir, Kelly, when it's just the two of us. You can call me Matt. You see Kelly I don't know for sure how long I will be here, probably as long as it takes us to get things cleaned up and running right in this county. I for one can't understand why there are reconstruction offices even here in Kentucky; there weren't any big battles fought in the state. You see corruption is like gangrene, the only thing that cures it is amputation. And I'm afraid most politicians do not understand that cure."

"What about General Grant, does he understand that cure?"

"Oh yes, he most certainly does; that's why he gave me free rein.

But we're not sure about President Johnson; we both are of the opinion that he is a politician. That's why the details of this operation he is not aware of." I told Kelly as he saddled his horse.

As we rode into town, people stopped and stared when they saw the two of us riding together. I suppose it was mainly me with my Captains bars on my shoulders. Because, I suppose not many of them would recognize me as being the Matthew Boden that left over six years ago.

"Let's stop by the Sheriff's office first Kelly." I said as I pulled rein in front of said office.

"What's the Sheriff's name?" I asked Kelly as we tied our horses to the hitching pole.

"It's Jacob Rutger, but everyone calls him Fats. He came in with the Reconstruction people. He is a thoroughly disagreeable person." Kelly said.

"Where is your sidearm Kelly?" I asked him, just now noticing that he wasn't wearing one.

"I usually don't wear one, its back at the office."

"Alright, but from now on, wear one. Also, I want all of the men to wear a sidearm and Knife; hopefully they know how to use both of them, as well as you." I said.

I stepped through the door first, Fats was lounging back in his chair with his feet on his desk, smoking a cigar. He looked at us with a smirk on his face.

"What do you Jay Hawkers want, ain't no lollypops in here."

"No I suppose not, if there were they would be covered with smoke." I said as I leaned over and took the cigar from his mouth and dropped it in the overflowing spittoon.

"What the hell do you think you're doing; that cigar cost me fifty cents." He said letting his feet hit the floor and reaching for his hogleg." He stopped right quick, when he saw that he was looking into the bore of my .44.

"Listen close Fats, don't ever try and draw on me again or I'll put a bullet right through that stupid head of yours." I said, as I placed the barrel between his eyes. "Do you understand?"

His face was turning a sickly color of white. "Yes Sir, I do understand." He stammered out.

"Good, we just stopped by to see what you have found out about the murder of Iden Boden?"

"Who's he?" He said, still looking at my gun.

"He was the Rancher that was shot in the back the other day. I'm very surprised that you don't know his name, you being the Sheriff in this county." I said, still holding my revolver.

"Oh yes, I remember hearing about that." He said.

"I take it that you didn't investigate the murder?"

"Uh, no, I was told not to worry about it?"

"By who were you told this?" I said, twirling my revolver and tossing it from hand to hand.

"By Lester Dune, the Officer in Charge of the Reconstruction in the County."

"By what authority did he tell you this? Don't answer; we both know he has no such authority over the Sheriff's office. You have no business even being the Sheriff in this county, you are a disgrace." I said as I turned and put my .44 back in my holster. I have always had very good side vision; he was reaching for his gun again, I dropped to one knee and shot backward as I twisted, his bullet hit the wall behind me, mine drilled him right between his eyes, like I told him I would do.

Kelly stood there wide-eyed, like a school girl. "What's the matter with you; haven't you ever seen a dead man before?" I asked him as I shucked the empty shell and put a new one in, so there was a full six. Some guys kept only five in their guns, but not me; that sixth one might save your life someday.

"Yes, yes, I have, plenty in the war. But I have never seen anyone draw that fast and then hit what he was shooting at." Kelly said, as the door burst open and a man with a deputy's badge on came storming in:

"What the hell is going on in here?" He yelled, that is till he seen Rutger lying there with a third eye. Then he smiled; "About damn time someone shoot that asshole." He said.

"Yes, well someone did; that someone being me. You don't seem too perturbed at his demise?"

"No of course not; you see I was the duly elected Sheriff before that bunch of carpet baggers showed up."

"Well, how would you like to be Sheriff again? You see I am Captain Matthew Bodeen and I am declaring a modified form of Marshall Law. I say modified because I am going to appoint you

Sheriff again and I want you to keep enforcing the laws of this county; but run the major problems by me and the Sergeant here; Kelly O'Toole. I forgot to ask your name?"

"It's Edgar, Edgar Canutt; so, what about a Deputy? Can I appoint my own?"

"That depends; Edgar; let me think on that awhile. In the meantime, what do you know about that bushwhacking of Iden Boden?"

"I knew Iden, he was nice man, a little brusk in his dealings; but honest. As to who killed him, I think you just solved that mystery; your killer lies over there; bleeding all over my office floor. I heard him and that Lester Dune laughing about it. I am just one man and couldn't go up against that bunch..."

"Well, it looks like it's only partially solved. So, Edgar, don't say anything to anyone about how you told me what you heard. The Army will handle it from here on; you just keep the peace and if any of those carpet baggers say anything about that carrion lying over there, just tell them he drew on the wrong man. Tell them to take any complaints to the Army. Oh yes, you can get someone to bury him, can't you?" He nodded; as he bent over and plucked the Sheriff's badge off the dead man's chest.

We stopped outside the office; "What say we get something to eat, all that made me a little hungry?" I said to Kelly.

"Uh, yeah; I guess. That didn't bother you, killing him?"

"Nope, not in the least; I sort of figure that I didn't kill him; he committed suicide. A man should know who he is going up against before he pulls his hogleg."

"Hogleg? I never heard that term for a gun around here; where did you learn that?"

"All over the west; mostly in the gold camps. So where's a good place to get some Bearsign and coffee?"

"Huh, what's Bearsign?"

"Donuts, that's what the fur trappers in the mountains, call Bearsign. You don't get around much, do you?" I said, looking at him askance.

"I guess not; I'm from New York City." Kelly said.

"That's alright; I won't hold that against you." I said, slapping him on the back.

The little Café that we went to was called; Country Home cooking; anyway, that's what the sign said. Those Donuts tasted like they were freshly made.

"Kelly, I think we need more of a presence here in town. I think we should have at least two men, fully armed, in town at all times. They can make the Sheriff's Office their headquarters. You can set up a rotation schedule. Also when we get back to the Fort; if you can call our little Stockade a Fort, I want to send General Grant another telegram on the situation here in Helmsville. I think we need a few more troops; I want the people to know that the Army will not put up with any skullduggery."

I purposely spoke loud enough for those townspeople that were bending their ears to hear what I was saying; to come in loud and clear.

I had learned Morse code in my travels; it came in mighty handy at times. I sent that message myself; with a few added twists. I also sat in on some of the training that I had told the men in the morning to start in groups of five.

I was well pleased at how fast the men were in applying my suggestions. Maybe it was because the men were tired of just setting around doing nothing. Then in mid-afternoon I headed for the School House. I think Hattie was going to let school out early; the Kids all had a dose of Spring Fever. And the only cure for that was soaking their feet in the creek and wetting a line.

I arrived before she had dismissed the children. I walked in and the kids all turned to stare at me. "Children, I would like you to meet Captain Bodeen. He is in charge of the troops here in Helmsville." They all stared at me; I walked to the front of the room and turned to stare at them.

"Children, I am new here in your town and I need a little help; information mainly. You see, if you haven't already heard, the Sheriff committed suicide, and as such do any of you know of any person that would make a good Deputy Sheriff? You see Edgar Canutt is now the new Sheriff, but I need to appoint a Deputy for him."

One little girl raised her hand. "Yes, little girl, what is your name?"

"It's Mary Pickett and my Daddy needs work; he's very brave, he was in the Army and hasn't been able to find work since the war is over."

"Yes, that sounds fine Mary; which Army did he fight for?" I asked her.

"I don't know, but his uniform was gray, not blue like yours."

"That's fine Mary; could you tell him to come by Miss Hattie's house this afternoon and we can talk about the Deputy's job?"

"Yes, I will; thank you Sir. But why Miss Hattie's house, do you live there?"

"Uh yes, you see Miss Hattie and myself were married over the weekend; she is no longer Hattie May Beowulf, she is now Mrs. Hattie Bodeen."

The kids all rushed forward to hug Hattie. That is all but the older boys; they were a little disappointed; to have their hopes crushed by a blue belly. In fact, they were giving me dirty looks.

It's a strange thing about Kentucky; it being neutral in the war; some people were blue and some were gray; you just never knew which was which, just by looking. There is only one thing I knew about war and that was it was stupid; and this civil war was the stupidest one of all....

I went out and saddled Jasper for my wife while she finished dismissing the children. I had just finished when Hattie came in the barn with the older kids who had horses in the barn. The kids didn't waste any time in saddling their horses, while giving me dirty looks.

We were alone in the barn...Hattie smiled and came into my arms; giving me a kiss, while her hand sort of drifted south of the border while walking me backwards to the ladder leading to the hay loft. She let go and said: "Come on that hay is soft and inviting." Then she started up the ladder; I followed, I wasn't really surprised to note that she wasn't wearing any underwear.

By the time I topped the ladder she was standing there naked! She was right that hay was soft and very inviting....

We lay there in each other's arms enjoying the clean smell of the hay among other things. She gave me one of those kisses that would have started things up again; but she said: "What's that bull about the Sheriff committing suicide?"

"Well, I gave him every chance; I even let him get the first shot off. I don't enjoy killing but he gave me no choice. Besides, he was one of them that killed my Dad. I just saved the county some money by not having a trial."

"I'm not faulting you any sweetheart, but I knew that Bastard wouldn't commit suicide; the Devil's helpers never go easy; they need a little push. But you know you aren't done yet; there are several others that also need that little push?"

"Yeah, I know and that Lester Dune is one of them. But I hope to have the Army take care of that duty. I don't want to get the 'rep' of being a gunman; so I sort of set things in motion already."

"You did? How come I'm not feeling it?" Hattie said as she lowered herself unto me…

Chapter Five

We got a surprise when we got back to Hattie's house; her family was there. Good thing we took care of the necessities in the hay loft; because it didn't look like we would have the opportunity for a while.

Of course, they didn't know that Hattie had gotten married. And as such when we rode up and they saw me in my uniform; well you know what they were thinking.

"What's that blue belly doing with you?" Her Pa, Torr Beowulf said, as he leaned on his long squirrel rifle.

"It's good to see you too Pa." Hattie said as she swung down from Jasper's back.

"You didn't answer my question." Her Pa said.

"That's right, and I ain't agoin to till you get off of your high horse about my husband." Her speech was reverting to the vernacular of her childhood.

"Your husband! You married a Yankee?"

"He ain't a Yankee. He's from right here in Helmsville. Besides you've been after me for years to get myself hitched. And when I've done gone and did it, you're having a fit?"

"What's he wearing that blue belly uniform for then if he's from Kentucky?"

"Pa, you know Kentucky was neutral; anyway, the war is over." Aiken, the oldest boy said, as he stepped forward and shook my hand; "Welcome to the family." He said, as he plucked a bit of hay off of my uniform. He had a big smile on his face...

"Well hell, I guess the Coon is already in the well so the damage is done; welcome to the family son." Torr said as he also shook my hand. "Storm has supper about ready; it looks like you two have already worked up an appetite." Hattie's Pa said as he also plucked some hay off of Hattie's shoulder and then he hugged her.

Was it strange that Storm had started supper in Hattie's house? No, not in the least; I could tell that this family was just that- Family. Hattie told her Pa that she had already found work for them, if you could call it work- they were going to Ma's place and help out for a while.

I had plumb forgotten about Mary Pickett's Pa coming to our place till after supper I heard a buckboard coming down the lane. Hattie and I went out to meet them. Not only Mary's Pa, but also her Ma was in the buckboard.

"Howdy," I said, as Mary's Pa stepped down and shook my hand. Hattie howdy'd the Mrs. Also, her name was Ethel. They both were in their middle twenties or so.

"Did Mary tell you all about the deputy's job?" I asked him.

"Yep, she sure did; and if you think I fit the bill I'll sure take that job. By the way, my name's Doogie, Doogie Pickett."

"So Doogie, can you handle a side arm? I mean can you hit what you aim at with that gun you're packing?" I asked.

"Well, about nine times out of ten, I guess. But I'm damn good with a scatter gun. I heard how you shot the Sheriff; he sure enough needed killing."

"Good, your references stack up mighty fine." I said.

"What references?"

"Why, your daughter, she spoke highly of you."

"You mean you'd take a six-year-old girl's word as to my character?"

"Sure, there the best kind, kids don't lie, she loves you, that's good enough for me."

"Matthew," my wife said, "Ethel here was a school teacher back in Louisiana; she said she'd take over for me teaching school; what do you think?"

"Why I think that would be just fine; we don't need the money and they do. Besides that you have a lot to do with your family and all. Fact is you could take them out to Ma's place in the morning after you tell the school board about Ethel. And I'll take Doogie to his new job on my way to the Fort."

"No, I'm not taking them out to your Mother's place; you're coming with us. We'll just wait till you get done with your Army business and then we will all go together."

"Uh, yeah, sure that sounds like a better plan. It should only take me a couple of hours to get Doogie to the Sheriff; and then tell the

Sergeant what to do." I said as I glanced at Doogie.

"Welcome to the world of being married." Doogie said, while trying to stifle a laugh. I don't know what he was laughing about; because Ethel was giving him a dirty look.

As the Pickett family got in their buckboard and left; I was thinking about what Hattie said. And I didn't mind it one bit. In fact I sort of liked it; I was glad I didn't have to make all of the decisions anymore. Hattie was not just my wife; she was my partner.

As we were lying in bed later that night Hattie asked me: "Do you reckon Pa and your Ma will be taken with each other?"

"What do you mean taken?"

"Well, you know maybe get hitched? Even if they are both you might say are still be grieving?"

"I don't know too much about love; except that I love you. But old Zack, a mountain man friend of mine, once told me that-"Love was an obsession that might wane but would always be there."

"You mean if they were truly in love with their deceased spouse that they wouldn't want to get married again?"

"No, I don't think he meant that; I think their love for their dead spouses would 'wane'; but would never completely go away. And I think if they both realize that then their new marriage would work." I said.

"Yeah, that sounds about right. Do you want to make love again?" Hattie asked, as she held on to my hickory.

"No, but if you want to we can?" I said.

"No, not right now." Hattie said, while she still held on.

"Uh, are you sure; you're still holding on pretty tight."

"I was last night also; didn't you notice? I'm a little embarrassed to say this, but it's sort of like a security blanket for me; do you mind?"

"No I don't mind; in fact I'm flattered. When did you discover this obsession?" I asked.

"The first time I saw it; I never wanted to let go of it and don't think I will ever want to let go of it the rest of my life."

After her telling me this; I changed my mind; I did want to make love again....

When we awoke the next morning, we were both lying there with the covers thrown back and a soft spring breeze was blowing through the open window. I watched as Hattie slept; I do believe that all five-foot ten of her was all muscle. There was not a bit of fat anywhere; I reached out and took one breast in my hand; I could swear that was all muscle, but I knew better, even though it felt full and firm.

She opened her eyes and said: "Didn't you get enough last night?"

"I don't believe I'll ever get enough of you; but for now, I'm completely satisfied. I didn't know we left the window open last night." I said, without taking my hand off.

"What does it matter about the window; it feels good on my skin?"

"Uh, well, you know how sonorous you get; you're quite vociferous also. With your family here and everything…."

"My, what big words you use just to say that I get loud during sex. But you do also, maybe not quite so loud." Hattie said as she squeezed a little harder.

We could smell bacon frying; Storm must be up and fixing breakfast. I guess she was used to doing the cooking for her Pa and her brothers.

They were already at the table when we came in. Some were giving us sly looks and some were trying to ignore us. But Aiken said; "Did any of you hear that Panther scream last night? I heard it several times. I was about to get my rifle and shoot it; but it finally went to sleep or something."

Brother Alden said: "Yeah, I did get up. Hattie, I didn't know you kept a pet Panther, but that noise was sure coming from your window."

Alfred and Arthur were snickering and trying to keep from laughing; till Storm said, "You all better shut up or you won't get breakfast; what Hattie and Matthew do in the night is none of you all's business; you all just wish that you had a Panther to pet."

Hattie's Pa didn't know what to say; he had no idea Storm knew anything about sex, from the way he was staring at her.

"Boys as soon as you eat your vittles you had better hitch up the wagons and saddle the horses so we can be ready when Hattie and her man get back from town."

So I was Hattie's man? I guess I had aways to go in earning Torr's favor. That was alright; I didn't fault him none; cause I suspect I would be the same way with my daughter, when we had one anyway.

When we got to the school the Pickett's were already there. Doogie and I rode to the Sheriff's office. Edgar Canutt was sitting behind his desk.

"Edgar, I brought your new deputy. Meet Doogie Pickett, he's hell for leather with pistol or shotgun; I think you two will make a good team." Edgar stood up and shook hands; they both were in a little pissing match. Trying to see who would quit squeezing first. I think they both came to the realization that if they didn't give it up that they wouldn't be able to use their right hands for shooting criminals.

I rode on to the Fort and checked with Kelly. Training was coming along fine. And there were two troopers in town at all times.

"Captain, we got word that the other troops will be arriving in a day or two. A Lieutenant Twedle will be in charge of them."

"Oh, I guess I'd better get in touch with Grant and make some more arrangements." I told Kelly and then I went to the telegraph key. I sent a long message and it wasn't ten minutes till I got a reply. I wrote it down and then reread it, just to make sure.

"Sargent that Lieutenant Twedle won't be coming with the troops. We need to promote one of our troops to Sargent; you pick which one. And oh, by the way, you've been promoted to Lieutenant. Have you received any more intelligence about the scuttlebutt going around in town?"

"What did you say?" Kelly asked.

"Which part didn't you understand?"

"About me being promoted to Lieutenant?"

"Yeah, you heard right; I recommended you and Grant agreed. I didn't want some other officer coming in here and messing with my troops. Especially someone named Twedle. What about the other part? You know, about any information coming from town?"

"It's general knowledge that Lester Dune and his gang have been breaking a lot of laws. There has even been some raping going on."

"Is that right? Well hell, has the victims come forward a made a complaint to the Sheriff's office?"

"Yes, I guess so; but the Rutger fellow wouldn't do anything about it. But maybe now since you killed him and there's a new one in office, something will get done."

"Yeah, the new deputy is named Doogie Pickett, he's an ex Reb;

from Louisiana. His wife is also teaching school; their nice folks. I want you to get with the Sheriff and go over the records and see if any of those victims will come forward and press charges now. Just maybe we can clean that gang up and hang a few of them."

"I didn't know rape was a hanging offense?" Kelly said.

"It is now because I say it is; Grant also gave me authority to proclaim martial law; if I see fit. Don't blab it around; I haven't made up my mind yet. So, carry on Lieutenant, I have some things to take care of in the country."

When I got back Hattie was already home. "So how did it go?" I asked her.

"Fine, I had to convince the school board; they were a little upset about her being black; but they knew times are changing. You have to admit it's a little strange to have a white man married to a black woman; and him being a Reb and all."

"Yeah, but that's why I like both of them; they're not afraid to go against the stream." I said.

Aiken came over and said: "Matthew, Hattie has told me about everything going on here and how you are sort of in charge of things here in Helmsville; well anyway, I think both you and Hattie could be targeted for that reason; so Alden and I are going to sort of going to stick close to the two of you; we don't want anything to happen to our sister and her husband."

"Well that's good of both of you. But I could get some of my troops to do that also."

"Nope, they couldn't stick as close as we can; they ain't family…if you know what I mean?"

"Whoa, you aren't planning on being in our bedroom, are you?" I said, alarmed.

"Heck no; we don't want our hearing drums busted." Alden said, "We sort of will be with the two of you; sticking closer than ticks on hogs."

One thing about all of Hattie's family; they all went well armed; rifles, pistols, knives-the sharpest that I had ever seen. Hattie said that the 'tinker' made them. I had heard of him-he was also a friend of a lot of those hill folk in Tennessee. Hattie had two of those knives; she had as yet to give me one…

Hattie and I rode ahead of the rest; so we could talk. "So, what's the story on Storm? Why did your folks name her that?" I asked Hattie.

"They didn't; her name was Jessica Sue; that was her given name. But you see she was found on our doorstep on the night of a big storm... Now that normally wouldn't of been enough to name her after that storm. But the way she was howling up a storm, they gave her that nickname. And it sure enough fits her. Folks have to be careful they don't get her riled; she's libel to cloud up and rain all over them. You noticed how the boys settled right down when she got on them?"

"Yeah, I was wondering about that; you answered that well enough. I suppose that you have noticed that my brother and sister's ages sort of fit with your youngest brother and Storm?"

"Yeah, I've thought of that; Storm is sixteen and William is seventeen. And Arthur is seventeen, he was adopted also, and Caroline is sixteen. I can see that they are going to fit together or they will fight together." Hattie said.

"Oh, I don't think there will be much fighting between the kids; but the fight will come to keep them from sneaking off and making out. Our parents are going to have their hands full." I said.

"Oh, I don't think that a'tall; when it comes to Storm nobody is going to lift her skirts up till she's good and ready; and the same goes for Caroline. I sort of pity those boys."

"Well I sure don't, those two girls are worth waiting for; just like you and I waited for each other. Oh, it wasn't because I didn't have the opportunity; I just didn't have the inclination till you came riding up on Jasper."

"It was the same with me; some of those boys' tried just about anything to get my bloomers off. What they didn't know was that I didn't wear any and I still don't; you want to see?"

"Sure, but not now, I think your Pa would see."

"No he wouldn't." Hattie rose up a bit in her stirrups and gave a little tug on her skirt; sure enough she wasn't wearing any bloomers. She left her skirt that way till we got in sight of Ma's place...

I asked her just before we got to Ma's place: "Why are you gritting your teeth and standing in your stirrups?"

"I'm trying to keep from singing; and you know what I mean; so get that smirk off of your face."

36

"Yeah Honey, I do. I'm not going to laugh; because I know what's good for me. But maybe the next time a padded pair of bloomers would be in order."

"Yes, but I've rode this way before and never had this problem. Maybe it's just because you're riding with me…"

"Now I'm flattered. I think ever one else is too far back to have noticed. Just pull your skirt back under you. I love you babe…" I am sure glad I married such a sexy wife…

Ma and the kids had heard the wagons coming and were standing in the yard. William had his rifle with him. That was good; be prepared was my motto. But I don't think any of the three of them were prepared for the Beowulf family…

"Ma, this is Torr Beowulf; Hattie's Pa. And Torr this is my mother, Louisa Boden." Now I wouldn't say that they were took with each other right away; but I guess I could; cause they were sure staring at each other. I went ahead and introduced the rest the family to each other.

Arthur and Caroline were standing there red-faced staring at each other; as were Storm and William. Aiken, Alden and Alfred were just standing there leaning on their rifles, smiling at the bunch of them. "Well hell boys," I said as I walked up to them, "looks like you all will have to go peach picking, I know there is a lot of ripe ones just waiting to be plucked." They just looked at me and smiled some more.

Storm pointed at William; "You come on, I need some help in unloading the wagon." I guess she had already staked out her territory. Caroline was a bit subtler; she said to Arthur: "Do you need some help?" He stammered around and finally was able to get out a "Yep".

"You all can take your pick of the cabins over yonder." Ma said, and then turning to Torr she said: "Perhaps you would like me to show you around?" Torr just nodded and followed along like a love sick bull. Storm called out: "Where do you want your stuff put Pa?"

Ma looked at her and said: "Just bring his stuff in the house." I guess that settled his goose…Hattie and I looked at each other and smiled. And then she added: "William you move your stuff to one of the cabins; Storm can take your room and Torr can take Matthew's old room; that is till we get hitched." All of us turned to look at her; she just fluffed up her hair and jauntily turned her back on us…

37

Well so much for love taking a long time to wane; life was too short to mess around mourning. I really didn't think that Ma was overly in love with Pa anyways, not in the last few years; he was sure one hard one to live with.

We stayed for supper; it didn't take long for all four women to whip it up. Aiken and Alden were going back with us. Alfred was going to stay on for a while anyway. We figured one more rifle around the place was a good idea for a spell; one that wasn't all love sick and could think straight.

Now Hattie changed her riding habit; she went to wearing pants. Now that I didn't mind so much; because they fit her right smart. Some of the ladies in town frowned at her; I think out of envy more than anything else.

Things had sort of settled down; with more troop presence in town; that helped. But I knew Lester Dune's gang was just biding their time. We did have some of the rape victims lined up to testify, but I wanted a few more to come forward. At least they weren't out there raping at the present time.

I didn't wear my uniform much anymore; there were enough uniforms parading around the county now. The four of us rode together; it seemed that most people gave us a wide berth. That is all except a few widows that had set their caps for the boys. I guess there was a neighbor of Ma's that was sweet on Alfred also.

There were more women than men in the country now; war widows and young girls with not enough young men to go around. But if they wanted a husband all they had to do was go west. Which; I had been thinking of talking to Hattie about things in New Mexico.

Lieutenant O'Toole came by the house and said: "Between the Sherriff's Office and us we have six women that will testify. All that we need now is an honest Judge. I don't think the jury will be any problem; most people in the county are fed up those reconstruction people."

"What about Judge Volker; what's the word on him?" I asked Hattie.

"Well he was a Judge before the war, but I hear he had been taking payoffs from Dune. Might be he was just afraid for his life?" Hattie said.

"Alright Lieutenant, you set things up with the Sheriff's Office, we'll take care of the Judge. Be sure and keep those women's names secret till the day of the trial; I don't even want the Judge or court officials knowing their names."

"That's bit irregular isn't it?"

"Yeah Kelly, it is. But it is necessary so as to keep them alive. The day before the trial I want your troops to round all of that gang up and keep them at the Fort and bring them to the court house that morning. I'll have the Sheriff's Office have the women there."

Some later said that it was a Kangaroo court. One reason was that the twelve jurors were relatives of the six victims. But hell, the truth was the truth. We ended up hanging three of them, of which Dune was one. The other seven we gave them a choice; lite a shuck and never come back or they would be shot on sight. Now that wasn't my idea; I never liked to give Rattler's a second chance to bite you again.

It was coming on to the middle of summer and things were sort of lazing along. Torr and Ma were raising Tennessee Walkers and Thoroughbreds; along with mules and Morgan's. And oh yeah, they did get hitched.

Those two widows had roped the boys and were fixing to throw and tie them. But the Boys were sort of kicking at the traces and watching those wild geese flying by. That was till I told them that four could fly as easily as two; then they sort of quit kicking and let them tie the knot. Now those two ex- widows was sisters; that made it a sight easier.

Their names were April and June. Named after the month they were born in; I don't think their Pap had much of an imagination or was just lazy. But they sure weren't lazy; they could cut wood faster than a buzz saw. They were both pretty in a lanky sort of way; pure Kentucky through and through. They matched Aiken and Alden just fine.

The sisters moved in our house with their new husbands. Now as singers go, those two and my wife made quite a chorus at night. I told them the first morning after that they should get together and work on their harmony…My wife threw a frying pan at me; the sisters just glared at me. The boys just smiled all the bigger. I never could figure what the sisters were mad about; I thought it was a compliment. Compliment or not; I had to apologize to just smooth their ruffled feathers.

Later that night as we were letting the warm summer breeze blow over us as we lay in the rumpled bed. "Uh, Honey;" I said, "Kelly brought me a telegraph today. I think I forgot to mention it, till just now. Anyway, it was from Fort Union…"

"Fort Union; where's that?" Hattie interrupted me.

"It's in New Mexico Territory. Anyway, it was from my partner-" She interrupted me again….

"You have a partner? Why didn't you tell me this before?"

"Well, I'm trying to; He's a Spanish Don; I saved his life and I guess his ranch. He was so damn grateful that he deeded me half of the ranch. Anyway, there is more trouble; I was only supposed to visit my folks and then come back, but I sort of got sidetracked. Anyway; since the war ended in the states here, there has been a lot of men and people at loose ends; they are moving west; some honestly looking for work and such and others to just steal what they can find. I guess there is an outfit that is trying to say that his Spanish Land Grant isn't legal anymore." I said and stopped to take a breath.….

Hattie jumped up standing on the bed and was still jumping; it was quite a sight. "How soon are we leaving?" She almost yelled.

"Well, at least not till you get some clothes on. But seriously, it will take a week or two to get everything all gathered up. And I thought I would ask Aiken and Alden to come along and of course their new wives. And then there is your place here; what about that?"

"No problem with that; I can get Alfred and his new girl, Leah Jane, to move in here; they need a place they can get away from Pa." Hattie said as she stopped jumping and sat cross legged on the foot of the bed facing me…Which was not a position to elicit chastity….

The next morning as all six of us sat around the breakfast table; I broached the subject: "So, how would the four of you like to go on a little adventure?" I asked.

"Adventure huh, what do you mean by a 'little' adventure?" Aiken's wife April said.

"Well, I guess it's not so little; Hattie and I own half of a ranch in New Mexico Territory. And there are some unscrupulous people who are trying to take it away from the Spanish Don who owns the other half. It's a long nine hundred miles down the Santa Fe Trail; and it's not for the faint of heart." I said.

Alden's wife June spoke up. "Who are you calling faint of heart? It better not be April and I."

"Whoa, don't get your dander up; I simply meant that it will be rough on all of us. In fact we'll be moving pretty fast and dresses aren't going to cut it; riding astride; do you three women have any pants and such to wear?"

"I have buckskins. Hattie said, "What about you two?" Hattie said looking at April and June.

"No, we don't; but we know some Indian women who can make us some in short order." April said. Now that word *short* didn't quite apply when it came to April and June; they were both almost as tall as Aiken and Alden. And I bet they were just about as tough. I knew for sure that Hattie could whip her weight in wildcats; and I bet they could also.

"So I also reckon that the two of you can shoot?" I said looking at them.

"Yeah, we can shoot. We grew up hunting the meat for our family to eat." June said.

"Well that's good; then there will be six rifles to speak for us. Because I know that your husbands and Hattie can shoot a fly off of a frog's ass at a hundred yards." All of this time Aiken and Alden hadn't said a word; they just nodded from time to time. They probably figured that their wives were doing a good job in palavering and that they couldn't improve on it.

Aiken and Alden and their wives left to see about those buckskins for the women and probably some new ones for their selves. Also, they were to see about acquiring the Mules and Horses we would need for the trip. I told them to see Ma about getting in the safe and giving them some of the money that I had left in the safe. Hattie and I were to go to the Fort and telegraph Santa Fe and also, I needed to talk to Grant, so to speak.

Grant was all for the trip; the Army was sending reinforcement to Fort's along the trail and Grant wanted me to be in charge of the column. And since there was already a Captain with those troops he promoted me to Major. I don't know why he liked me so much; I only saved his life two or three times. Oh well, I guess it wasn't mine to reason why, but to just get the job done. One other favor I asked him for; that he appoint Aiken and Alden scouts for the trip. I did explain that he would be getting two for one, so to speak, since their wives were plenty handy also.

One thing I did know, that going with the Army, it would make the trip a lot safer.

When we had got those extra troops here in Helmsville they had also brought a shipment of those new Henry *yellow boy* Repeaters with them. They held fifteen shots and were .44 caliber; the same as our pistols. I appropriated six of them. That shipment was just for the Army to try them and see if they worked out alright. The Regular troops still were equipped with the single shot .45-70 breach loaders.

I stored the repeaters in our bedroom for now and then Hattie and I headed out to see Ma and Torr; I suppose that Ma would be mildly surprised that I hadn't told them about the place in New Mexico. I suppose that meeting and marrying Hattie had filled my brain clear up...I guess I had been doing a lot of supposing lately.

"So are Alfred and Leah Jane living out to the ranch also?" I asked my wife.

"Yep, they sure are; didn't I tell you that they got married the other day?"

"Nope, I guess not; so, are you going to ask them about moving into your house?"

"Hey, it isn't just my house anymore; or don't you remember we done got hitched?"

"Yep, I do seem to recollect standing in front this old guy and saying I do. But I do know that some married people don't include property in them there I do's."

"Well I ain't one of them. Besides, I heard you say that 'Hattie and I' were part owners of the hacienda down in New Mexico. So I think its tit for tat." Hattie said, while leaning over in her saddle and giving me a kiss; it just so happened that we were passing that same grove of trees that we stopped at the day we first met...It was just as good this time as it was the first time....

The ranch was a bustle of activity, which was good to see. Ma came out drying her hands on her apron as we rode in. "Land Sakes, it's nice to see you two; you're just in time for the noon meal. Torr is out irrigating the alfalfa, he should be in shortly."

"Yeah, we are a might hungry; we stopped and made love on the way here; you sure work up an appetite." Hattie said.

"Goodness sakes, I was wondering why your cheeks were so rosy; maybe I'll have a grandchild soon?" Ma said.

I looked at them both and just shook my head; I don't think I'll ever figure women out. "I wouldn't count on it too soon Ma, we been trying, but so far nothing's took." I said.

"Well, just don't give up." Ma said, just like we would stop having sex.

"Oh, we won't." Hattie said. "We do have some news to tell you all; but it can wait till after we all are fed and happy." She added.

The seating at the table was about just like I thought it would be: William and Jessica Sue were seated side by side; as well as Arthur and Caroline. Of course, the newlyweds were billing and cooing so much they didn't take time to eat; that was the newlyweds Alfred and Leah Jane.

Now Ma and Torr weren't far behind, but at least they were more discreet. We were drinking our Arbuckle Coffee when Ma asked: "Well what's the big news you wanted to tell us?"

"Well for one thing I was wondering if you had any riding Mules for sale, as well as pack Mules?"

Torr spoke up, "Yep, the boys have been working a few head and they're coming along just fine; what you want them for?"

"Well," Hattie answered, "We'ens are going to Santa Fe. That is Matt and me, as well as well as Aiken and Alden and April and June. And we need some reliable mounts for the Santa Fe Trail."

"What in the world are you going there for?" Ma asked.

"For one thing the Army wants me to command a column of relief troops to Fort's along the Santa Fe Trail. But that's not the only reason; you see Hattie and I own half interest in a big ranch down there; a Spanish Land Grant. I did a few favors for a Spanish Don and he was so grateful that he made me a partner in the ranch. But now he needs help against some high binders that are trying to take it away from him."

"What about your place here; are you just going to let it go to weeds?" Ma asked Hattie.

"No, I was thinking about asking Alfred and Leah to move in there and work the place; of course, they could live there for nothing and keep all of the money from any crops. But I don't want to sell it at this time; we may want to come back." Hattie said.

"What do you mean; are you planning to stay down there forever?" Ma asked, plainly a little disturbed.

"Well, we aren't really planning on much of anything; I've found out that life has enough forks in the road as it is; it just depends on what fork you want to follow…" I said.

"We don't want you to worry Ma;" Hattie said and then added; "whatever trail that we follow won't take us away from where we started."

Torr cleared his throat and looked at me and said: "How come a fellow as young as you are, came up through the ranks so quick in the Army?"

Hattie spoke up; "He saved General Grant's life a few times; and the General took a liking to him. Plus, he's pretty smart and might handy. And also, Aiken and Alden and April and June are going with us. Matthew got the boys hired on as Scouts for the trip."

"Scouts? That don't make much sense; they have never been down that trail; although they are pretty handy with a gun or a knife. But what are they going to do after they get down there?"

"I figure to hire the four of them on; you see there is trouble a brewing for the ranch; they will earn their pay." I said.

"The four of them; you mean April and June also?" Torr asked.

"Yes, Pa. Those girls are also good with guns and knives. Almost as good as me; I reckon between the six of us we make up a small army." Hattie said.

"Well don't beat your drum too loud; cause every time a person does, someone else comes along and shoots it full of holes." Torr said.

"Yes Pa; I didn't mean to brag; I know pride goes before a fall. But I guess I was just stating a fact. To change the subject, what about those mules and horses; you said that you have some for sale?" Hattie asked her Father, not letting Torr's drum roll dampen her spirit; as if anything could.

"I reckon I could let you have ten mules and six Morgan's; say fifty dollars a head for the mules and seventy-five a head for the Morgan's.

Is that too much?" Torr said, mellowing out a bit; that is after Ma gave him one of her *looks!*

Hattie looked at me; I nodded. Fathers; sometimes it takes them a while to warm up to their sons-in-law. "Yes Pa that will be fine; can you have them delivered to our place in three days?" Hattie said.

"Yep, I'll have the boys deliver them."

"Hattie my saddle bags are still in Ma's safe so she'll have to get them out for you and you can count out what we owe them. We need to take them with us anyway." I said. Hattie and Ma went into the office and came back with said saddle bags.

Hattie counted out nine hundred and fifty dollars and handed them to Ma. That amount didn't make much of dent in those saddle bags. I didn't know for sure just how much I had in those bags. But I was sure Hattie would count it out when we got back home.

"Yes, and we'll need bills of sale for all those horses and mules; don't want to have any trouble on the trail about the proper ownership." I said.

"Sure and we wouldn't have it any other way; we have to keep our books accurate." Torr said with a scowl at me. He sure had a burr under his saddle when it came to me…That's alright; my own Pa acted the same way about me. I guess I just rub some people wrong.

On the way home Hattie was some quite; then she looked at me and said: "I want to apologize for my Pa; I have never seen him act this way before. If I didn't know better I would say that he was jealous of you."

"Yeah well, forget about it; I married you not him. You see sweetheart we have no control over the way people act; the only control we have is how we react and I choose not to." I said.

"Not to what?"

"React; your Pa will come around; he loves you, don't he?" I said.

"Sure, he does; he always said I was the apple of his eye; but now he's acting like you're a worm that spoiled his apple." Hattie said.

"Well I guess so; since I have bored pretty deep into his apple. Some people just don't like to share their perfect fruit." I said.

"Well you're going to have to keep boring; you haven't reached the core yet." Hattie said with a wicked grin.

Later on, that night I was pretty sure I reached her core; how? By the way she shook the house…

"You two alright in there? I think we just had a small earthquake." It was April pounding on the door.

"Yeah, we're alright; that was sure some quake wasn't it?" Hattie said breathlessly.

"Well I wasn't sure with all of that screaming and all." April said as she went back to bed.

The next day we found out that there was really a small earthquake last night. Talk about a coincidence!

Chapter Six

At breakfast we made our final plans on moving everything that we would need to St. Louis; including the horses and mules that we just bought from Ma; plus, those two Morgan's that I had bought earlier.

While Aiken and Alden and their wives gathered things in Helmsville; Hattie and I went to the Fort to send some telegrams and finish the details in turning over my command to the new Lieutenant. There was an Ambulance wagon that was never used. I commandeered it.

We used our saddle horses to pull it over to the blacksmith shop. Where I had the blacksmith install one-eighth inch plating on the inside; that armor would stop most rifle shots and arrows from penetrating. Of course, it wouldn't stop a cannonball. But then again, I doubted that any of the Indian tribes had cannons. Of course, that platting would add about two hundred pounds to the wagon.

I was talking to the Blacksmith about that problem and how it would be a dead giveaway to what was inside if I had to use a six-horse hookup to pull the thing.

"Well Major I just might have the solution to the problem. You see right now you have fixed bearings that take frequent greasing to keep it rolling and still there is friction. My brother back east sent me some different type of bearings; they have what is called ball bearings. Here let me show you."

The ball bearings were in a round case that would fit over the axle. I held it in my hands and worked the bearings. I looked at him; "but these would still need some kind of lubricant. I don't think the common grease that we use now would work, would it?"

"No, he also sent this wheel bearing grease it has carbon fibers mixed in; so, it sticks longer and better."

"Well you have sold me; install them. I don't care about the cost." When you say something like that you had better be prepared to pay the piper; I was. When I tried them out two days later I was sure that I could get by with just two horses. But since most ambulances were pulled by four-up; I figured I had better stick with four mules. Oh yeah, I had him also install some rifle ports that could be locked from the inside; they slid sideways to open, there were six of them; two to each side and one on the front and back. The ambulance could be driven from the outside or the inside; since I also had the blacksmith make allowances so it could be. One thing though; if someone was driving from the outside seat; he had better lift his legs if someone had to shoot out the front rifle slot.

We had most of our supplies in the converted ambulance; with just a few to be put on pack mules. We were going to leave the next day, but first we, that is all of us; were going out to the ranch and say goodbye. Alfred and Leah had already moved most of their stuff into Hattie's house. They weren't sleeping there yet; till we all left anyway. I don't think Leah Jane liked the six of us all that much; she thought we were a bit wild in manner and dress. I think every family had a prissy.

One thing about traveling together like we all were going to; you had better not be a prude. I sort of wondered about April and June. Found out though that they were not prudes. Why? Cause on the way to Ma's place it was hot and April asked if there were any swimming holes on our way.

"Sure, I know of one; did you girls bring anything to swim in?" I asked with a grin.

"I think the question is did you boys bring anything?" June grinned back. I looked at Hattie, she winked at me and said: "I'm game; my brothers have seen me naked a time or two and it looks like April and June don't mind my husband seeing them in the all-together so it just remains for Aiken and Alden; what about it boys?"

They looked at each other; not sure about what the other would think. Aiken spoke up: "Well, it's bound to come up sooner or later on this trip; might just as well get it over with."

Turned out it was no big deal; as soon as we got there the women stripped in nothing flat and dove in. They turned on their backs and floated saying: "Come on now, don't be babies get in here."

Of course, they gave a running comment as we reluctantly took our clothes off; hooting and laughing as each garment came off. I think the three of us were beet red as we dove into the water. Just maybe Leah

Jane was right; maybe we were a bit wild in manner and dress.

I think everyone was wondering why our hair was wet when we got to the ranch; we passed it off as perspiration. But I think Ma knew different; she looked at Hattie and Hattie winked at her. Ma winked back. I think there was still a little bit of a wild spirit running around inside of Ma.

After supper was over and we were getting ready to leave we were all standing around feeling awkward; William and Jessica Sue were standing together as well as Caroline and Arthur also were. I looked at them and said: "I don't know how long we will be gone; but I do suspect that the four of you will be married and have children before we see you again." Jessica Sue (Storm) and Caroline looked a might embarrassed; but Arthur and William were all smiles at what I said.

Ma spoke up: "Just how long do you figure you all will be gone?" I looked at her and how Torr had his arm around her smiling.

"Well Ma, I don't rightly know. It's going to take a while getting over those nine hundred miles of the Santa Fe Trail for one thing. But we have some business to take care of with the Ranch and all; I suspect maybe three years."

"Three years? That seems like a long time." Ma said. Torr hugged her a bit closer and said:

"Don't you worry Ma; those years will go by right fast, I'll see to that." Then he gave her a kiss and she sure enough blushed.

"And remember if you have to get ahold of us for any reason, just go the Fort in Helmsville and have the Lieutenant send us a telegram." I said as we mounted up and left.

There was a note pinned to the door when we got back; the Lieutenant had delivered it; seems the troops that were supposed to be in St. Louis were already at Fort Leavenworth. I was glad about that; it would save us a lot of time.

The next morning we left before the cock could crow. The wagon moved along smoothly on its new bearings; not a squeak or squawk out of them. Being that we left so early I hoped to get into Louisville before dark.

The first person we seen as we rolled into Louisville was Chester Brown the Marshall. He was just crossing the street and stopped and stared at us. I had my uniform on.

"Matt is that you?" he said.

"Yep, it sure is; Chester I would like you to meet my wife: Hattie May and these two are my Brothers–in–law, Aiken and Alden and their wives, June and April." After all the hand shaking he looked at us and said:

"Looks like you guys have enough guns to start a war."

"Well, that's because we're going down the Santa Fe Trail. Right now, we need to get our horses and mules to the livery and get us a hotel room for a couple of days, till we can make arrangements to get our outfit to St. Louis and then down the river to Fort Leavenworth.

"Alright, follow me and I'll get you settled with the Livery and then we'll go to the Hotel. There are a lot of people in Louisville right now, most just moving west. But a lot are staying and making a new life for them. That stupid war sure messed things up. That's quite an Ambulance you have there; are those gun slots?"

"Yep, it's better to be safe than sorry; or that's how that old saying goes anyway." I said.

"How about a stich in time saves nine?" Chester said, "That's sure an oldie."

"Yep, I reckon we could stand here all-night swapping clichés, but to use just one more- we're burning daylight."

Hattie looked at us and said: "You know I'm a school teacher and how much I hate clichés; so, knock it off."

We got all of the horses and mules fed and watered, and in their stalls and I also locked the Ambulance and I looked at the Hostler and said: "That Ambulance and stock are Army property and as such if anyone messes with them you'll have the Army down on you. So, keep a close eye on them." I told him that they were army property to put a scare into him; of course, they weren't.

We didn't have any problems getting rooms at the Hotel. Three separate rooms far enough apart so they couldn't harmonize. We had water sent up so the women could take a bath before dinner. I wasn't going to; but Hattie sure looked comfortable in that tub and a bit lonely, we were the last ones down to supper…I don't think I would ever get tired of riding that saddle; it sure was accommodating….

The Hotel was a fairly new one; it was the same one I stayed at before. The boys had ordered for us; steak and eggs and beans; food that would stick to your belly. The boys and I stood at least a head taller than most of the men nowadays; since the average was about five-foot eight and we all stood over six-two. So, we sort of stuck out a might.

Our wives had changed to dresses; but of course, they filled them out in just the right places; the men were staring at them and the women were giving us men the eye. I had left my uniform on; since we were on a mission for the army.

Chester Brown was setting a few tables over with his wife; he got up and came over. He squatted down beside my chair and said: "Say, the duffus that you dumped in the spittoon is in the bar; he's been drinking and giving everybody a hard time; I just wanted to warn you in case he recognizes you. He is worse than ever lately; I sort of wish someone would dump him in the river. I just wanted to give you a heads up."

"What was that all about?" Hattie asked, so I explained how I sort of put the head of the reconstruction office in Louisville on the saloon floor. I always hated to leave a job half finished; and letting a rattler wiggly off without killing it, was a job half done.

April and June were enjoying themselves; this was the first time they had been in town that was bigger than Helmsville. No one in Helmsville had given them a second look; being that they were married and all; the men in Helmsville respected the marriage vows. You could tell here though that a lot of men didn't; the way they were ogling them. Yeah and they were enjoying it. Aiken and Alden were just watching and not saying anything....but Hattie was noticing; she said:

"Come on girls lets go powder our noses." She gave me a wink as they started to leave. I stopped her and said: "Since we have finished eating the boys and I are going to the saloon to get a drink; perhaps you had better take the girls to our room and talk some sense into them." She nodded.

Chester Brown followed us into the saloon. I motioned him over; "Chester let me buy you a drink in appreciation for how you helped me last time I was here."

"Sure, but do you think it's wise? Since that blowhard Frank Stool is here."

"As far as I know it's a free country." I said and left it at that. I got my whisky and turned my back to the bar and looked around. Frank

Stool and three of his accomplices were setting at a table drinking and trying to play cards; but I think they were doing more drinking than playing cards. He looked this way and seen me. You could tell by his eyes that he recognized me. I nodded to him.

The four of them put their heads together talking; once in a while they would look my way. I undid the tie downs on my .44's. Aiken and Alden did the same. I said to them: "Follow my lead; let them start the party and we'll finish it."

"Chester why don't you take your drink down to the end of the bar and stay out of this; it's their party let them pay for it."

"Yeah but, it's the four of them and only three of you." Chester said.

"I know it's a little unfair on my part; tell you what I'll only use one of my .44's, will that be more to your liking?"

"I didn't mean unfair on your part, on theirs is what I meant."

"Oh, alright then, I guess I can use both of my guns." I said.

Chester took his drink and wandered down the bar stopping and talking with different ones as he went. "Boys", I said, I called them boys all though they were older than me. "I don't know how fast you are with those guns but just take up any slack that you see; I'll be able to get three of them for sure; maybe all four."

"You think you're that good?" Aiken said.

"Well, I sure hope so or I'll be eating crow won't I?" I said.

Frank and his boys got up and pushed their chairs back under the table; real neat of them I guess. They turned and started our way. But two more got up from the adjoining table and came with them. Well hell, six of them.

"Well boys, I guess you'll have your time to shine also; I sure hope you can shuck those guns right fast and shoot straight." I said as I put my drink back on the bar. Those two that came with the four, looked like hired guns. In fact, I'd swear one of them was a back shooter from down Santa Fe way; he was a Mexican with pock marks on his face; I forget his name, don't matter much I guess.

I whispered to the boys: "Those two are hired guns, I'll take them out first; you two shoot Frank first, those others might just turn tail and run."

There wasn't any bluster and wasted talk; they knew what they wanted to do; kill us; and they thought with two to one they were sure to win…they made a little semi-circle about twenty feet from us. Everyone in the saloon was hunting a hole to hide in. We stepped one step forward from the bar and they started the ball rolling. That Mex was fast, but not fast enough. He just cleared leather when a hole appeared in his forehead.

In the heat of battle my reflexes took over. My hands had a mind of their own; and they wouldn't stop till there were no more targets.

I stood there looking through the smoke, not seeing anything more to shoot at; I holstered my left hand gun and started ejecting shells in my right hand gun and putting new cartridges in and then did the same with my left hand gun. I felt a hand on my arm; I looked and Hattie was standing there.

"Come on Matt, it's all over, their all dead." She said.

"Are the boys alright?" I asked her.

"Yep, not a scratch, Chester said they started it, it was self-defense." Hattie kept her hand on my arm and led me out. Last, I remember was her undressing me and lying down on the bed with me and then I was out.

I awoke slowly; I could hear Hattie talking to someone at the door. "Yes, he's alright, he's still sleeping; he was exhausted." I heard Chester answer:

"That's good. I was afraid he wasn't the way he was just standing there staring through the smoke reloading his guns. And then he stood and didn't move till you came and got him. The coroner declared it self-defense. I also wanted to tell you the train will be ready to load all of your horses and mules and other baggage in the morning." Chester said, and then he left.

"Oh, I see that you are awake; I will ring down and have the bath water sent up. You have been sleeping for twelve hours. It's almost noon. Do you go into those trances after each gun battle?"

"No, I never did before." I said.

"Well I have an explanation, I didn't notice it at first because it really didn't bleed that much, but a bullet glanced off of your skull, you have one hard head. I think Chester is getting anxious to get us gone from his town. The town thinks the three of you are some kind of killing machine. All though they are happy that Frank Stool and his

53

bunch are gone. I guess there is no pleasing some people."

There was a tap on the door and our four cohorts came in: "Well I see you are awake; we were just going down for lunch are you up to it?" Aiken said.

"I think so, but Hattie wants me to have a bath first; so you guys go ahead." I said as I threw the covers back; but I forgot I was naked. I just ignored it and so did they. But April was the last one out the door she turned and gave a low whistle and winked.

"Did you talk to those girls?" I asked Hattie.

"Yes I did; but girls will be girls; they are just experiencing their first taste of freedom; they'll be alright, they both love my brothers all of the way. But not as much as I love you; so get out of bed before I jump your bones." I didn't get out of bed; that is till the bath water came….

"What about the train? Did all of the stock get loaded?" I asked.

"Yeah, it's due to pull out this afternoon, so you had better get a move on or we'll leave you to mutter and stew in your own juices." Hattie said.

Oh yeah, like you would leave that." I said, pointing down.

"You think you're the only guy with one of those?"

"No, but I think you think that." I said with a hopeful grin."

"Well smarty, it just so happens that's exactly what I think; so you don't have to worry." Hattie said, and then almost started things going again, but pulled away and smacked me on the butt. "Come on get going." She said and handed me my pants.

The train was a special one; with only the Engine and coal tender and one passenger car and one stock car and one flat bed car that held our Ambulance and of course the Caboose. I guess Grant had all kinds of pull….

That wound on my head hadn't bled all that much, but it sure was sore. Hattie had put some kind of salve on it; good thing it was below my hat line. I wore my uniform with my oak leafs on the collars. Hattie said that I cut quite a figure; I guess so by all of the female looks I was getting. But not near as many as the women were getting in their skin tight buckskins…..

We would only be stopping for wood and coal and of course water. But we would be stopping at St. Louis before heading across the State of Missouri. The jumping off point for the west was now Kansas City. It used to be Independence.

The carriage car had seats bolted to the floor; so we sat about unbolting some of them and making three different sleeping areas with blankets separating them. We didn't have to worry about the windows since they had shades that could be lowered.

For beds we used the abundance of saddle blankets that were new and unused. This was luxury compared to what we would encounter on the trail. Of course, we did cover the saddle blankets with flour sacks otherwise we would itch to death. Yes, we did use empty flour sacks....

At both ends of the car were coal stoves that were used for heating in the winter; being that it was summer we would just use them for cooking.

It took us three days to get to St. Louis; being that we were unscheduled, we had to spend some time on sidings to make room for the regular trains. That was alright; it gave the women a lot of time to work on their 'harmonizing'. Our motto was to make hay while the sun shined; because there wouldn't be much time for love making on the trail. At least I didn't think there would be...

St. Louis was a buzz of activity; Aiken and Alden took one look and said that they would stay with the train and guard the stock and our plunder. April and June though they were another thing; their eyes sparkled as they gazed at the city.

I had to take all three women with me to resupply some needed things. As well as I had to go by the bank where I had some of my money stashed. There were a lot of rough necks; I guess you could call them; loitering around hither and thither. I took the tie downs off of my .44's. I guess I wouldn't have had to; because the women were plenty capable of handling anything that might come up; they were armed to the teeth and knew how to use those weapons. Shucks, maybe they could protect me...

The women were carrying their Henrys in the crook of their arms as well as they had revolvers strapped to those lovely hips. As we went into the bank we got alarming looks, but the clerks recognized me and they calmed down.

I filled my money belt that was under my shirt and then gave the women each a hundred dollars to buy what foofaraw that they wanted. I also secured a letter of credit for the bank in Santa Fe. Now, a hundred dollars would go a long way; but in St. Louis not so far as in Louisville.

April and June stuck their hundred dollars in an empty shell holder in their cartridge belts that crisscrossed their ample bosoms. Wasn't much anyplace else to stick the money; those buckskins fit mighty tight.

Hattie just stuck hers inside the ankle on her Moccasins'; all of her shell holders were full of shiny new cartridges. I would have to speak to April and June about keeping their belts full; didn't matter all that much here in the so-called civilization, but where we were headed it mattered a lot.

When we entered the bank; I had noticed a few men loitering about here and there watching the bank. They were also watching the women and snickering between themselves. Now these just weren't the run of mill hangers around; but were sure enough hard cases. One or two still had gray Rebel Caps on. I thought I recognized one or two that had rode with Quantrill.

How would I have recognized Quantrill's riders? I fought them a time or two and I have a good memory. Not counting a scar across my right shoulder from one of their bullets. I thought about Quantrill every time the weather changed and that shoulder ached some.

I had heard that the main band broke up; but some of the riders stuck together and were raiding here and there. I walked with the women to one of the respectable Mercantiles in town and left them to do what shopping they wanted; I was going by the Sheriff's Office and let them know that the bank was about to be robbed; after all I still had money in that their bank.

I knew the Sheriff; his name was Willie Mack. He was an ex-reb himself, but an honest man; as most of those who fought for the south were such.

Willie was setting at his desk with his feet up smoking a big cigar. He dropped his feet down and said: "Bodeen, when did you get back to town?" Then he stood up and held his hand out to shake.

"Just a little while ago; we came in on that private train. I hate to disturb your rest Willie, but you are about to get mighty busy, some of Quantrill's riders are fixing to rob the First National Bank. Do you have enough deputies to handle them?"

"Yeah, I reckon, this town is mighty rambunctious; so, I have ten of them to help me keep the peace." Willie said and then he turned to one of them told him to roust out the rest.

"Are you sure it's some of Quantrill's riders?"

"Yeah, I recognized Pete Tolliver and maybe one other; didn't see Quantrill though."

"You probably wouldn't see him, he's a coward. I know most of them that rode with him. I rode a spell with them; till I couldn't stomach their blood thirsty ways. Where did you see them?" Willie asked.

"Over by the bank; are you sure you don't need help?"

"Naw, we'll just round them up on general principals and run them out of town; might have to kill some of them just to let them know we mean business. So how long are you staying in town?"

"Probably pull out this afternoon; we wanted to let the horses and mules stretch their legs some before we load them on the Stern Wheeler and then head on to Fort Leavenworth and then down to Fort Union down near Santa Fe."

"So, you're going down the Santa Fe Trail; I hear some of the tribes have been doing some raiding along the trail. You might want to hang on to your hair real tight."

"Yeah, I've heard the same thing; but I'll have Calvary Troops with us; but don't know how many yet." I said.

"Who all do you have with you?"

"There are five very qualified Calvary Scouts that can shoot a hair off of a flea's ass at a hundred yards. Plus of course yours truly."

"Well I can testify to how good you can shoot; I've still got scars to prove it." Willie Mack said.

"Yeah, I'm sorry about that; but at least it got you out of the war alive and you didn't even have to spend time in prison."

"Yeah, I want to thank you for keeping me out of prison. I would have probably died in there. You even went out of your way to get me home so I could recuperate. I owe you big time for that."

"Yeah, well, maybe someday you can return the favor, but I'm not holding my breath. Just keep on keeping the peace here in St. Louis; that's a big enough favor for me." I said in leaving....

I went back to the mercantile; the women were still wondering around looking at this and that. Hattie looked at me and said: "There isn't much here; that we want anyway. I did find a nice stiletto; we each bought one; they only had three of them. The Tinker made them, I saw his mark. They didn't know what they had or they would of cost more than three dollars.

I looked around the store it was full of foofaraw that most women would die to have; but these three couldn't find anything but a knife. Granted they were the best that could be had; I guess they knew what was important and what was not.

But they did buy something else; it was a bolt of soft absorbent cloth. "What's that for?" I asked.

"Really, you don't know?" Hattie said and then leaned close and whispered in my ear. My face turned red. April and June thought my discomfort was real funny. Well, I guess they were wise in buying the cloth; otherwise they would have had to use moss; like a lot of Indian women did. Hattie handed me the bolt of cloth to carry; since they had their rifles and I just had my twin .44's.

I don't think I had ever seen St. Louis as full of nondescript people as it was this day. Now I say nondescript people to describe those of questionable character. And some of those were giving us the eye and snickering. Three of them were following us and making comments about the little solider boy letting women protect him. Now I could of dropped the package and turned around and shot all three of them; but it would be good practice for the women to take care of them.

Hattie winked at me and slowed down to let them catch up. One of them reached forward to pat Hattie on the posterior; his hand never reached the forbidden territory. Hattie simply raised the butt of her Henry up and backward and caught him square in the jaw. He went down like a poleaxed steer.

The other two stopped and reached for their guns; they didn't even clear leather before April and June shot them off of their hips; and then finished the job by kicking them both in their gonads. Every one standing around got a good laugh out of that. We just turned our backs and started on our way when we heard shots being fired over by the bank. That gave the crowd something else to wonder about and they forgot about us and headed for the bank. We did not; we went back to the train.

Aiken and Alden were standing by the river boat looking our way; "What's all the shooting about?" Aiken asked.

"Oh, the Bank's being robbed; or I guess I should say they are trying to rob the bank. But Willie Mack and his deputies are thwarting that endeavor." I said.

"Yeah, but what about the shots that we heard over by the General Store?" Alden asked.

"That was your wives taking care of a little problem; no big deal for us; but two guys will have sore nuts for a while." Hattie said in her rather direct and to the point style.

"They shot them in the groin?" Aiken said incredulously.

"No, they shot their guns off of their hips before they could draw and then they kicked them; hard." Hattie said again.

"Well what about you? You laid one out with a broken jaw." June said to Hattie.

"She broke someone's jaw with her fist?" Alden said.

"No, silly, with the butt of her rifle; she just swung it up behind her without even looking." April said. Aiken and Alden looked at me. "Don't look at me; I had nothing to do with the whole thing; I was just standing there holding this bolt of cloth; when that jerk tried to feel up Hattie's behind; big mistake for him." I said while leaning over and giving Hattie a kiss; which was heartily returned by the way…

Chapter Seven

We had the whole state of Missouri to cross and I for one was going to take advantage of the down time; for I knew the Santa Fe Trail would allow no time to lolly-gag around. We ran pretty steady through the night. It must have been the boat that acted like a lullaby for us; cause we all slept like babies.

We awoke when the boat stopped for fuel and water just as the sun was painting the hills with her gold glow. The small town that lay outside our window was called Kingdom City; someone's imagination must have run away with them, sure didn't look like much of a Kingdom to me; but to each their own I guess.

Hattie was already up when I joined her at the window; I had come up behind her and kissed her on her bare neck; heck, she was bare all over. And some of the dock workers were staring at her. I reached up and pulled the shade down.

"Aw, what did you do that for? I was having a staring contest with that guy." She said.

"Well, I think he done won that contest; there was no way he was going to blink; in fact, he may never blink again. And that was mean of you; you spoiled him for any other woman, and if he is married think what will happen when he looks at his wife and compares her with you? Now aren't you ashamed of yourself?"

"Nope, not in the least; I feel so alive and I love walking around with no clothes on; don't you? You're still naked. Hey, I know, let's run through that sleepy little berg and wake them all up?"

She probably would of done that; but the boat took a roll and she fell into my arms; that got her mind off of that nonsense and onto something else and you know what that was!

And that's the way it went all the way across the show me state; the sound of the waves against the hull and us trying to keep up with their rhythm. Fort Leavenworth had grown since the last time I saw the place. After all it was the supply depot for all of the Forts to the west.

There was a sergeant standing on the dock to welcome us. I walked down the gangplank and he snapped to attention and saluted. I returned his salute.

"Welcome to Fort Leavenworth Major, what can we do for you?"

"You weren't expecting us?" I asked him.

"Uh, no; should we have been expecting you?"

"Yes, we are under orders from General Grant. I expected the base commander to meet us. Get your superior officer here on the double." I said, he gave another salute and hurried away.

Hattie and the others had just walked down the gangplank as the sergeant's fanny went around the corner of depot.

"What's up Honey?" Hattie asked me.

"It seems we were not expected; but don't worry I'll straiten everything out. I know that Grant had informed them we were coming. But you know how the army is; they seem to run on snafus. Colonel Beauregard is supposed to be the Commander of the Fort. I know a little about him, and it's not all that good; but we will see, won't we?" I said.

The Sergeant came back with a 1st Lieutenant following close behind him. The Lieutenant slide to a stop and gave a nervous salute.

I returned his salute and said: "Lieutenant what's this about you not expecting us?"

"I don't know Sir, I wasn't told anything about it. What is it that I can do for you?"

"First off, I need our stock and our Ambulance unloaded. I want stall space for our stock and feed them a bait of oats. And then we need billets for the six of us in Officer's quarters. And then tell Colonel Beauregard that I want to see him within the hour."

"I can take care of the stock Sir, but as to space in Officer Quarters, that would be up the Captain Percival and then nobody ever gets to see the Colonel; his adjutant would have to handle that."

"Who's his adjutant?"

"The Captain is Sir."

"Get him here on the double. Tell him Major Bodeen, the liaison for General Grant wants to talk to him pronto." As the Lieutenant was hurrying away the Sergeant was already seeing to the stock.

As the Sergeant led two horses by I asked him: "Where is the

Telegraph Shack?"

"It's in the depot at the far end; but you have to have the Captain's permission to use it."

"I do huh? Thank you, Sergeant, don't forget to feed and water all of them." I motioned Hattie to come with me as I went to find the Telegraph; Aiken, Alden, April and June went with the horses.

"What's going on?" Hattie asked me.

"Seems there is a little problem around here; but don't worry that is one thing General Grant wanted me to scope out and let him know."

There was a Corporal seated by the telegraph key; he looked up and stood up and saluted.

"Move aside Corporal, I need to send a message to General Grant."

"But Sir, I'm not supposed to let anyone near the keys unless the Captain gives the order."

"Like I said, move aside or I will have your stripes and perhaps give you a few more; if you know what I mean." He did.

I sat down at the key and started tapping away. General Grant had a special receiver in his office so it didn't take long after I had finished my message till the telegraph key started banging away with the return message. I looked at the Corporal standing two steps away and said to him:

"Set down here and write out his reply and don't try and change any words, cause I will know if you do."

As soon as he finished he looked up and said: "I'm sorry Sir, I didn't know who you were; it says here that you are now the Commanding Officer of this fort; that is till you get the problems fixed here."

He had just finished talking when the Adjutant came running up and slid to a stop. "What's going on here? Who are you?" He finally got out between gasping for breath.

He was short and on the pudgy side; a bean counter if I had ever seen one. "Corporal, let Captain Percival read the telegraph from General Grant." He grabbed the message out of the Corporal's hands and as he read it; his face went from flushed to pale.

"I...I, don't understand; what problems do we have?" He said.

"You would know that better than I; but perhaps not a skunk never smells his own stink. But it could be I am judging you too harsh. So,

Captain, if you will, please escort my wife and me to Colonel Beauregard." I said, as I reached out and took the telegraph from his numb hands.

"Corporal, please make a copy of this and post it on the bulletin board. And then make sure the other copy gets filed in the proper place." As we followed along Hattie said in a whisper:

"Weren't you a little hard on him; calling him a Skunk?"

"Perhaps, but I thought it was better than calling him a Rat; but time will tell, won't it?"

As we walked along all of the other soldiers were giving Hattie the once over. Perhaps she should of changed out of her buckskins and put a dress on. I suppose it didn't matter much; she could of worn gunny sacks and her sexuality would still have shined through.

It seems our good Captain was getting more and more nervous as we approached the Forts Headquarters; he kept giving nervous glances at us. I could feel his animosity rising. I whispered to Hattie: "Get ready, something to going to happen, I think this guy is crazy in the head." She nodded to me. Another thing that bothered me; two or three soldiers were following along behind us; I didn't like the looks of them.

I leaned close to Hattie and said: "When we get to the office door, you unlimber your Golden Boy and keep those three outside; if they give you any trouble perforate them." She nodded again.

Our little Captain opened the door and rushed inside; "Kill him," he yelled at somebody inside. I had palmed my twin .44's and stepped in and to the side. A shot just missed me, but I didn't miss; there were two soldiers inside and they were both trying to get me in their sights. I killed the one, and shot the other one in the shoulder, he dropped his Spencer. I jumped forward and clipped the Captain upside of his head and he went out like a short wick in the wind.

Outside I heard the thunder of Hattie's rifle, once twice and then she said to the last one, "Just drop it, kick it aside. That's a good boy, now get face down in the dirt, yeah that's right; get yourself a good mouthful, if you look up that will be the last thing you ever see."

The one I shot in the shoulder was starting to whine like a little girl. "It wasn't me, it was the Captain, he poisoned the Colonel; I didn't have anything to do with it."

I put my .44 up to his ear, "Who else is involved?" I asked.

"Just the Captain and the five of us; the Captain has been selling our supplies and charging the townspeople for protection services and I don't know what else, he's evil, he's the devil." He said and then he passed out; that was after I twisted his bad arm....

I looked out of the door, a crowd had gathered; in the crowd I seen a few officers, the highest rank I saw was a Major. I motioned him forward.

"Do you know anything about this?" I said.

"Yeah, a little bit, I knew we hadn't seen the Colonel for two months and we all were getting worried. Where is the Colonel?"

"That little bean counter killed him; I suppose he would have buried him somewhere. But right now I need a detachment to gather up the dead and get this Sergeant in here to the medics and throw the Captain and this other one lying in the dirt to the stockade and lock them up. And Major, I need you to take over in the office and try and see what all this trash has been up to; use any personnel that you need; and one more thing; who is in charge of the billeting?"

Hattie went with a Lieutenant to secure our billet and get our entire luggage stored in said billet. After the bodies were removed I sat down with Major Miller in the late Colonel's office and filled him in on everything that I knew. Then I asked him if he knew anything about the regiment that I was supposed to escort to Fort Union.

"Regiment? There is no regiment; it's the dependents of the 10th that need to be escorted there."

"Dependents? What do you mean, how many of them are there?"

"About fifty of them; women and children. I think only about ten are children. The women range in age from teenagers to about thirty years old. I have been in charge of them; physically they are in good shape. But they're sort of in the dumps missing their men and fathers."

"How many companies of Calvary are stationed here?" I asked.

"Six, but four of them are out on patrol due to all of the Indian problems that have cropped up. To tell you the truth Sir, the moral of the fort is at the lowest that I have ever seen. We all knew something was wrong; but we didn't know what to do about it."

"Do you think that the fort could spare a company to help escort them?"

"I don't see how Sir, we need all of the personnel that's left to just run the day to day stuff around here. You see we have a high amount of personnel in the stockade; if I didn't know better I would think that they are using us as a federal prison."

"I understand, what about supplies, is there any shortage of them?"

"No, in fact we seem to be overstocked, that bean counter, as you call him had been selling things to the people going down the Santa Fe Trail. So whatever you need I'm sure we can supply."

"Good, I think right now you should concentrate on straightening out the problems that the Captain did; and then getting this fort back on the straight and narrow." I told the Major. He was about forty-five years old and I found out later he had been in the Army ever since he was sixteen years old. I think I had found the man to take over as Commanding Officer of Fort Leavenworth.

"And oh yeah Major, see if you can find out where the Captain had been stashing his ill-gotten gains. That money belongs to the Army." I told him as we left to find those dependents of the 10th.

That Sargent that had met us when our train pulled in was standing outside. "Sir, can I be of any assistance?" He asked.

"I don't know Sargent; maybe, do you know where the dependents of the 10th Calvary are billeted?"

"Yes Sir, they have tents set up at the far end of the Parade Ground; it's this way Sir." He said as he turned and Hattie and I fell in alongside of him.

There were two tents; one large one that held their sleeping cots and one mess tent. I looked at the Sargent; "how come they aren't billeted on better quarters?" I asked.

"That's what the Captain wanted; he said slaves didn't deserve any better."

"Is that what you believe Sargent?"

"No Sir, I'm from New York; I fought for the Union; I don't hold with slavery. But we really don't have any permanent quarters available for them."

"Alright, but I want individual tents for each family and also different latrines for the sexes; and also, facilities for bathing. And I see that they are dressed in clothes that have seen better days. Have the quartermaster issue uniforms for every one above thirteen years old."

"But Sir, they're all women and children; you want uniforms for them?"

"Yes Sargent, I do. We have nine hundred miles to transverse, with Indians waiting to take our scalps. Also I want them trained in fire arms and make sure they all know how to ride. In fact Sargent I am putting you in charge of their training. And oh, by the way, you have only two weeks to accomplish that task. So you had better get going."

As we walked away Hattie said to me: "You really don't expect him to accomplish that entire task in two weeks?"

"Nope, your brothers and their wives are also going to help as well as you, that is, if you want to; you see I need you to get to know each and every one of them and appoint leaders. Call those leaders whatever you want to; but we need them to be ready to fight and shoot straight when needed. Or none of us will get through to Fort Union."

Our quarters were nice enough; we had three adjoining rooms in the Officer's Quarters. And we would eat in the Officer's Mess. I told them to get some sleep tonight; because I wanted them to start training our charges first thing in the morning.

"And just what are you going to be doing?" Hattie asked.

"I have some recon to do. I want to know everything that has been going on here in Fort Leavenworth. So I will be sticking my nose in places that they probably don't want me to see. General Grant wanted a complete report."

My first stop the next morning was to see Major Miller; he was hard at work going through all of the files and reports.

"So Major I am going to be doing a lot poking around on my own; but I would like an escort so to say. Maybe that 1st Lieutenant that helped us yesterday would be available?"

"You mean Lt. O'Brian?"

"Yeah, if that's his name; it would make things a little faster having someone who knows the Fort."

"Alright tell the Corporal on the front desk to have him report here to you." Major Miller said.

I poured myself a cup of coffee while I waited. It wasn't as strong as I was used to, but it was decent. It didn't take long and he rushed in and saluted.

"Lt. O'Brian reporting as ordered Sir." He said.

"At ease Lieutenant; I need you to show me around the Fort. Also, I want you take notes as we go. The first place I want to see is the Armory; who is in charge there?"

"Captain Fontaine is; he usually doesn't let anyone inspect the Armory; he thinks it belongs only to him."

"Oh, does he now? Well I guess it's time to change a few things with his attitude. Because in the Army nothing belongs to the individual; everything belongs to the Army; including his soul." I said as we went toward the Armory. I was still getting funny looks from the personnel that we passed. I guess they had never seen a Major with twin .44's strapped around his hips, what were also tied down as gunfighters wore them.

"I will knock; Captain Fontaine doesn't want anyone to come into his office without his permission." Lt. O'Brian said as we reached the Armory door.

"No, don't knock; I will do the honors." I said, as I kicked the door off its hinges. Well I could see why he wanted his privacy; He had a half-naked woman bent over his desk and he was quite busy banging her.

"What the hell!" He yelled as he whirled around. "Who the hell are you?"

"I can see that you didn't read the bulletin board. I am the Officer in Charge of this Fort and as such I am ordering you to put your pop-gun away and stand to attention. He did neither; he just stood there with it standing straight out. I unhitched my right hand .44 and cold-cocked him up beside his head.

The woman bent over the desk hadn't moved; she just glanced around at us and said.

"Do either of you want to finish what he started? Because somebody owes me ten dollars; no use letting 'it' go to waste." She said as she wiggled her behind.

"Lieutenant, if you would be so kind as to go through his pockets and pay the lady with his money; never let it be said that the army cheats working ladies." I said, "And then set him up in that chair; no don't bother pulling his pants up; just leave him that way. But do tie his hands behind the chair back."

"Now then Miss; if you would be kind enough to cover the merchandise; I would appreciate it very much. Is your brothel in town or do you live here at the Fort?" I asked her as she pulled her dress down. It was apparent that she didn't wear underclothes.

"I live here at the Fort; my husband is out on patrol and yes he knows about the Captain; and I'm not a hooker. My husband owes a poker debt to the Captain. I'm paying it off one screw at a time. Otherwise the Captain said that he would make sure that Danny meets with an accident. And I really didn't mean it when I asked if either of you two wanted to finish what he started. I was just embarrassed."

"Well you were bare-assed that was for sure. You can consider your husband's debt paid and more so. But you may want to consider a different husband; one that will not let his wife pay his debts."

She gathered up her money and left. "Well Lt. let's inspect the Armory while the Captain sleeps."

There were not only racks of the 45-70 Single shot Springfield rifles but also crates of the new Henry Golden Boy Repeaters. "Lieutenant, are the troops equipped with these new repeaters?"

"No Sir, they have the Springfields. I have never seen these new ones."

"Alright, I want Fontaine ensconced in his new quarters; that is the Stockade. And then get that door fixed and a padlock put on the door; and then bring me the key, do you understand?"

"Yes Sir. Do you want me to finish showing you around the Fort?"

"No, I will look around on my own. I will see you at the noon meal and get that key." It looked to me like Fontaine and Perceval were in cahoots. They were probably selling the new guns. I hope they weren't selling them to the Indians.

I didn't run into any more real problems; but the quartermaster had a large supply of stores. This was good because we would need clothes and groceries for our trip down the Santa Fe Trail.

At the stables I was happy to see a good supply of horses; because we would need over fifty head for our trip. Everyone seemed to be honest here anyway.

I went over to see how things were going with the rest of my family. They had been interviewing the women to see what they were capable of doing in our new company. I dubbed them Charlie Company. Why that name? Because, I had always liked the name of Charlie. I guess one reason is as good as the next when it came to what people do in their lives.

I told Hattie about what happened at the Armory. "Did you get her name?" She asked me.

"Nope, I didn't, but her husband's name was Danny and no I didn't ask his last name. Why do you want to know her name?"

"I just wanted to talk to her; it seems she could use a good friend. Did you ever think that she might love her husband is the reason she did that?"

"Hell no, I didn't; it didn't even enter my mind. You weren't there you didn't see how she waved her tail at us. It seemed at first she actually wanted us to finish what he started."

"Hum... that is interesting. Never mind, I'll talk to her. Did you see about the supplies that we will need; clothes, guns, horses and such?"

"Yep, they have an overabundance here; more than they would ever need in fact. I think that Perceval was selling things out the back door."

"That's good that they have more rifles than they need; because I figure that we will need at least fifty of those Golden Boys." Hattie said.

"I'll tell Lt. O'Brian to give you the key to the Armory and you can issue what you want for Charlie Company." I said.

"You know of course that we will need several wagons to transport those that can't ride and also the supplies? Hattie added.

"Yeah, I'll go by the Blacksmith Shop and make sure that we will have what we need. Say, I just had a thought; make sure the women cut their hair that same length as the men. I want them to appear to be men from a distance; some tribes are always looking to capture women."

"Alright, but I'm not cutting my hair and I'm sure that June and April won't cut theirs either." Hattie said with her hands on her hips; daring me to contradict her.

"Of course not; but maybe you could tie it back someway under your Calvary Hats." I said in a very conciliatory tone. I may walk around giving a lot of orders lately; but I know better than to order my wife around.

Chapter Eight

It did take us the next two weeks to get us all set up for the trip down the Santa Fe Trail. General Grant promoted Major Miller to Colonel and gave him command of Fort Leavenworth. Altogether there were fifteen men who were court marshaled; and they were serving their time right here in Fort Leavenworth. Captain Perceval was condemned to death and was shot by a firing squad.

I was kept busy with all the paperwork and sitting on the panel for the court marshals. So, I didn't get to participate in the training of Company C. But I had full confidence in Hattie and her brothers. We had a full-dress drill on the parade field; I was very impressed with them. In fact, I couldn't tell that they weren't regular troops.

They did some patterns that I had seen seasoned troops mess up on; I just hoped that their marksmanship was a good. Hattie told me though that they all qualified. All fifty of them; the women were all fit and trim. There were about five or six teenage boys counted in those fifty mounted troops.

There were some older men and women; parents I suppose; they were driving the wagons; six wagons all told; not counting our armored ambulance. I did a double take; driving the ambulance was that young woman that Captain Fontaine had raped. I turned to Hattie:

"What the hell! What's she doing driving our ambulance?"

"She's going with us; her husband Danny was killed over a week ago. She had no one around here; so I told her she could go with us. That's alright, isn't it?"

"I suppose; as long as she keeps her legs together. Can she shoot?"

"Yes, not as good as April and June, or me; but she'll do. Her name is Becky." Hattie said.

"I see you have the 10th Regiment's Colors flying below Old Glory; is that a bugle that young Sargent is carrying?"

"Yes, and he knows how to play all the Calvary commands also. And do you see that Older Man with the Lieutenants bars? Well, I

70

figured we needed a black officer or it wouldn't look right; he's the Father of one of the men at Fort Union. And he also knows what he's doing; so, if you have any orders to give Charlie Company, tell him."

"Good Idea; but you know they're not really in the Army, don't you."

"Yes, of course, but the Indians don't know that. And I think at times they don't know that either. But you know I think they should be; because I've never seen regular troops as good as these." Hattie said.

"I think it's all in the want to; not the have to. But you know, I think when we get on the trail that I will change into my buckskins and just give advice when it's needed. What's the Lieutenant's name?"

"Henri Gascon; his former owner was French. So, he knows French, Spanish and of course English. He sort of ran the plantation; so he knows how to give and take orders."

"Alright, tell him to be ready to ride out at first light; I have to telegraph Grant one last time and say goodbye to Colonel Miller. But before I do, do you have the names and ranks of each person in Charlie Company?"

"Yes, I have a complete list of all of them; including even the babies."

"Good, I will need that list to draw their pay." I said.

"What do you mean, they are getting paid?"

"Yes of course; the Army pays its troops; as well as its scouts. Why don't' you want to be paid?"

"Yeah, I guess so; but I wasn't expecting it."

"Hey, we're not just play acting here; we have nine hundred miles of some of the roughest country and the driest there is; plus, when we reach the Comancheria; that's when the fun really starts." I said.

"What's the Comancheria?"

"It's a vast area of Colorado, Kansas, Oklahoma, Texas and New Mexico that the Comanches more or less rule; plus, the Kiowa also run with them at times. The Comancheria covers almost 250,000 acres. We are trespassing, they say, and they have an agility and hardiness peculiarly their own that makes them very hard to kill. The settlers of Oklahoma and Texas have been in open warfare with them for years. I've been in several battles with them. They give no quarter and neither did we."

"Well, hopefully they won't bother a fighting force like us."

"Along with that hope you had better do a lot of praying and even that doesn't work at times." I said as we went to get that list.

Grant gave me the authority to put Charlie Company officially on the payroll; that is, they were in the Army now. And that's what I did, was have headquarters fill out the paperwork and officially swear them in. I don't think Colonel Miller liked it all that much; true equality had a long way to go I fear. I told Hattie about it."

"What about Becky, is she in the Army also? And what about my brothers and their wives?"

"Yep, she's a Corporal now. And no, it doesn't include them as being in the Army; they are hired contractors as well as you; I didn't want the Army to have any permanent hold on my loved ones."

"What about you? They got you by the short hair, don't they?" Hattie asked.

"Nope, Grant and I have an understanding; I serve at my leisure. That means that at any time I want to pull the hitch pin and let my wagon roll free I can." I said as we got to our quarters.

"Free huh? Well Mister you're not free; I not only got you by the short hairs, but also by these." Hattie said as she reached down and grabbed the family jewels. Of course, she had to let go in order to unbutton my pants; while I was returning the favor....

* * * * *

The sun was breaking the horizon as Charlie Company jingle-jangled out the main gate of Fort Leavenworth. The extra noise didn't matter too much right now; but I would have to make sure that all of the trace chains were covered in burlap to mask some of the noise as we got further down the Santa Fe Trail. Those bell like sounds from those trace chains could be heard for miles in the clean quite air of this unspoiled land.

Henri Gascon was riding at the front of the column as he should have been; his beard was gray as well as his mustache; he was quite imposing in a fatherly way. You could tell that all of Charlie Company looked up to him.

I was in my buckskins as were all of us scouts. Most of the people really didn't know me; they knew that Hattie was the unofficial leader; you might say. I left it that way; Henri knew who I was and showed the proper respect of my rank. The rank was respected; the man had to earn it....

The wagons were interspersed between the columns and as such were protected. They were not allowed to lag behind and as such become easy pickings for Indian or outlaw. The Remuda also was kept close to the side of the column; horses and mules meant the difference between life and death.

I hadn't mentioned to Hattie but there was also the Comancheros we had to look out for; they were made up of the dregs of the west and were totally unscrupulous. They ran guns and alcohol to the Indians. As well as sold white women to them. I had never gave them any quarter and never took prisoners. If there weren't any trees nearby; a firing squad took care of them.

Does that sound brutal? No, justice is never brutal; that is if the punishment matches the crime. There was one more thing that I had never told her and that was about Quanah Parker; I must do that before we reached the Comancheria; he hated my guts.

I didn't push very hard, this first day on the trail. The stock needed to get use to the trail and also we humans had to work into sort of slow also. I guess we made about twenty miles; which everyone, including the stock was glad of. I knew the trail and where the water and grass were the best; some of them had seen no visits for years. This first stop was one of those.

I was surprised Henri had his troops set the camp up according to the military way; I asked him how he came to know about that.

"I don't Sir; I just figured it worked best this way. Do you want to set the guard or should I do it?" Henri said.

"By all means, you set the guard; consider Charlie Company to be your baby; if I see anything that you should be made aware of, I will advise you. Hattie and I are going to scout ahead; we should be back in about two hours; save us some chow would you?"

"Yes Sir, of course we will; will the scouts be eating with us all of the time?"

"Yes, I think it will be easier that way. I see no reason that we should eat separately, do you?"

"No Sir, I surely don't." Henri said with a slow smile lighting up his face.

Aden and Akin were setting up our three tents. We walked over with our horses trailing us.

"Henri is expecting all of us to eat at their fire, is that alright with you four?" I said.

"Of course," April spoke up. "They make the best food I have ever tasted; my mouth is watering already."

"Good, Hattie and I are going to scout ahead aways, Henri said he would save some chow for us. And oh yeah, tell Becky what's going on. Keep an eye on her also." I said, shaking my head.

We headed out at a mile eating trot. When I led us toward this camping spot I left the main trail to get here. I wanted to check out what kind of traffic was on the trail. It was always a good thing to know who was ahead of you and most certainly who was behind you.

We sat just below the ridgeline in a Juniper Bush watching the trail. We had sat up our camp two hours earlier than normal, so now most travelers were just pulling off the trail and setting up their camp.

I had a field glass that Grant had given me for a present; it had my name and all engraved in the brass. There were six wagons in this group; with about fifteen men; hard cases by the looks of them. Ammunitions' Bandelier's were crossed on their chests. I handed the glass to Hattie.

"Whoa, would you look at that." Hattie exclaimed.

"Yeah, I just did. What else do you see?"

"They just pulled four females out of the back of one of the wagons. Young women by the way; one of the girls tried to kick him, he slapped her and she fell down. What are we going to do about them?" Hattie asked. She had a very pissed off expression on her face.

"Nothing right now; we'll go back to our camp and get your brothers and the girls. And then after dark we'll sneak in and get those girls and kill a few of those Comancheros."

"Just a few? Why not all of them?"

"Well, it depends on them, doesn't it? I mean what if they give up and beg for mercy?" I said.

"I bet those girls begged for mercy and that didn't keep from getting raped and sold to the Comanches." Hattie said, with a little rise in her voice.

"Hold it down; they can hear you. Sound carries a long way in this dry air." I said.

"Shit, they did hear me; look! They….. Most of them are looking this way." Hattie said.

"Do you have a full magazine in your rifle? Good, wait for them to get closer. Looks like all of them are coming up the hill. When I tell you, you shoot the ones that are the closest, I'll take the ones down the hill; and don't miss." I said.

"You worry about yourself, I never miss." Hattie said. She waited till they were about a hundred yards off and started shooting; I never seen anybody work a lever action that quick. I started picking the ones down the hill off. When the smoke cleared; there was no one moving. The girls by the wagons had crawled under them, scared out of their minds.

Now you're probably thinking that we were cold blooded murders. Well maybe, but I knew what they had done and would do again if we hadn't killed them. There was no law this side of the Missouri; that is except us.

We got our horses and rode down the hill. The girls were still under the wagons. Hattie got off her horse and said: "Hey you're safe now, come on out. It's alright now they are all dead."

They crawled out; they were a sorry looking lot; they looked to be between thirteen to sixteen years old. Looking at them made me glad we killed every one of those low lives.

There was a spring at this camp sight. Hattie took them over to it and had them take their clothes off and wash up. I looked into the wagons. There was rifles and whisky kegs; Just about everything that they could steal or kill other travelers to get. I opened one of the trunks; there was women's clothes'; I yanked an armful out and took them over to where the girls were standing there naked washing themselves. Handing them to Hattie I said:

"Do you girls know how to drive a team?" They looked at me and all of them nodded. "Good, try these clothes on; we have to get underway, there is not much daylight left. Come on Hattie let's rope those dead bodies and toss them in that sink hole over there; people have been tossing garbage in there for years." I made sure we stripped everything of value off of those bodies before we tossed them.

We tied our horses behind the wagon that Hattie drove. There were six wagons and six of us which came in handy. It was just after dark when we got back to our outfit. It caused quite a stir when we pulled in. Henri had some of his troops unhitch the wagons and gave a bait of oats to the horses.

It turned out that all of the girls' relatives were murdered by those Comancheros. But at least all of the women in our troop took them in like long lost relatives; especially Becky. Two of the girls were twins; their names were Ethel and Myrtle Ward and they were but thirteen years old; Becky took them under her wing.

One of the other girls was older than she appeared to be; twenty-one and the Comancheros had not only killed her parents but also her husband and their three-year old child. Her name was Ruby O'Rourke and she was fighting mad; I suppose she took her grief out in anger. She had strapped two of the bandoleers across her chest and two .45's on her hips and was carrying a Winchester. She took over one of the wagons as her own.

The other girl was seventeen and was of a mixed race; white and Lakota I learned later. Her and Hattie seemed to hit it off; her Indian name I couldn't pronounce but she said to call her Selena. She also wasted no time in confiscating arms and ammunition to suit her taste. Said she didn't want to ride in any wagon; even though she could handle a team better than any teamster that I had ever seen. Hattie let her have one of our Morgans; and I guess also let her become one of our scouts.

Those four wagons held all kinds of useful supplies; plus, also arms and ammunitions and gold and silver and some union greenbacks. Hattie said that the gold and silver and the greenbacks would be split between all four of the girls. You would think that I let Hattie make decisions that the husband would normally make; but I knew if something would happen to me that she would need to know how to handle herself in a man's world; which we seemed to be living in this particular slice of history.

Henri assigned some of his troops to drive the excess wagons; of course, Ruby drove her own wagon. Selena and Ruby slept in the wagon at night. And the twins were with Becky in the ambulance. Oh, one other thing, in one of the wagons we found a Gatling gun. It was stamped U.S. Govt. Property. I was becoming more at ease with the killing all of those Comancheros.

I had sat down and figured if we made about forty miles a day we would traverse the trail in about twenty-two of twenty-three days; of course, the Santa Fe Trail had its own ideas about keeping a schedule. And I knew for sure I was being optimistic about the forty miles a day. Do you remember what I told you about having 'timberline' moments? You see that's another thing the Trail had plenty of; and that's life changing decisions'.

I know I was speaking about the Trail as if it were a living thing; well, I'm not too sure it wasn't a living thing, just lying in wait to devour the unwary. I had been over it several times and knew it was a chameleon; changing its colors to match the traveler.

Chapter Nine

The Trail

One thing about the Army it was trying its best to protect travelers on the Santa Fe Trail. In 1864 they established three new posts: Camp Nichols in the Oklahoma Panhandle, one at Fort Dodge and Fort Aubrey (formally called Camp Wynkoop), in Kansas.

The Army had also set up a schedule to escort the caravans going up and down the Trail. On the first and fifteenth day of each month, troops would escort caravans from Council Grove, Fort Larned, and other military posts on the trail. They prohibited any wagon train from leaving between those dates. Their schedule did help reduce causalities due to Indian attacks somewhat.

But of course, it did not apply to us; we were a force unto ourselves. When we had left Fort Leavenworth we had headed cross country and hit the trail just below Westport Landing; that was where we found those Comancheros; that Hattie and I had dispatched.

I figured that the next stop should be Willow Springs; there wasn't too much there the last time I was there; but now you could never know what could have sprung up. Willow Springs set about a half mile northwest of the trail. Which gave enough room for the caravans to spread out; without stepping on each other. But what a lot of people didn't know was that there was another spring about a mile further northwest than that of Willow Springs. That's where we stopped.

Someone had set up a Tent Bar at Willow Springs. A tent bar consisted of a tent and a plank set on two barrels for the bar. You would think that people who were intelligent enough to get this far on the trail would have enough sense to not drink that rotgut. We could hear the goings on a mile away.

Hattie said that we should go down there and smash that operation; for the good of the people. But I knew when you got in between people and their so-called pleasure; you turned into the bad guy. Everybody had a different way of going to hell…and who was I to stop their slide?

"But, what about the women and children of those drunkards? It's not their fault." Hattie said.

"Oh hell, alright get your horse and rope and see if Alden and Aiken and their wives want to join us; we'll pull down their tent and trample the whiskey into the ground. But you had better unlimber your hog leg cause their sure to be downright put out. We'll come out of the dark hit them fast and get our butts out of there. Hopefully they'll be so drunk they will think that Indians did the damage."

"You four hang back; Hattie and I will rope either end of the tent and spur forward and hopefully bring that tent and whisky down together. If anyone tries to shoot us; well you know what to do." I said. It was dark with a lamp hanging in the open end of the tent. The bar was set up right in front of open tent flap.

As our ropes settled over the tent poles we gave a loud war hoop and spurred our horses. The tent came down right on the whisky plank and the lamp fell into the spilled whisky with a loud burst. We shook our loops loose and spurred away yelling and whooping. Our backup wasn't needed.

The next morning Charlie Company rode down to Willow Springs; we stopped at the burnt out tent.

Henri asked: "What happened here; somebody drop a match?"

"No way, no thanks to you Army guys some Indians came by and destroyed all of my whisky. I thought the Army had them Indians under control?" The owner of the burnt-up whisky said.

Henri shifted in his saddle and spit tobacco juice at the fellows' feet. "Nope, we just shuffle them around some; ain't nobody can control an Indian." And then said: "Charlie Company forward at the trot."

There were now thirteen wagons in our outfit; the six we had commandeered from the Comancheros and the six we already had plus of course our armored ambulance. As we passed the teamsters caravan; plus of course a few emigrants' wagons; all eyes watched us go by. I heard one guy say: "Hell, would you look at that; most of them are black; including their officer in charge; what's this world coming to anyway? And hey, would you look at that: them's women, not men!"

I could of told him what this world was coming to; but he wouldn't have believed it. Just like the Indians didn't want to believe what was happening to them. I figured it would take about thirty years before they fully came to understand the magnitude of the invasion.

That's also what most white people didn't understand; that they were an invading force and as such were at war with the native inhabitants. They just figured the Indians were outlaws and murders; and should be dealt with as such.

It was about fifty miles from Willow Springs to Council Grove; I knew of a good spot to stay overnight just a few miles short of Council Grove; the spot was about a mile south of the trail in a grove of trees with a small spring; along the Neosho River.

Council Grove was becoming a small community; by now I suppose it had grown some since I had last been there. I wanted to stay away from camping too close to populated areas. I didn't need any prejudiced bigots causing any trouble. I knew Charlie Company wouldn't react violently; but it was us so called white people that might; especially maybe Ruby O'Rourke would be the one to plant bigots. And I wasn't too sure about the rest of the women, either.

I could see dust rising from Council Grove about two miles before we got there. Of course, we weren't going there anyway. Hattie and I rode ahead to a low hill that we could see Council Grove from. There were wagons' and caravans' camped all around it.

Strange thing about people; they liked to flock together; I never could figure that out. Now me, I'd ride miles out of my way to just get away from them. Funny thing about that though; damned if I wouldn't set up camp and sure enough there would come some pilgrim along and he'd want to camp right next to me....

The camp spot was some ideal; Plenty of shade and was right next to a spring, as well as the river. The best part about it was that no one had been here in a while; probably too far off the beaten path for most of them.

Henri had circled the wagons right around the spring; so even if we were attacked we would have water. The Neosho River was only about fifty yards away. The stock was unhitched and taken to the river to drink. The Horse Wrangler had already started watering the Remuda.

We; the six of us put our Army tents up close to the Ambulance and Ruby O'Rourke and Selena's wagon. We didn't have to worry about cooking; we ate at the general mess that Charlie Company prepared.

And I must say the food was down home delicious.

Henri's troops took turns bathing in the river; upstream from where the stock watered. Of course Henri had set the watch; sentries where needed. Now he didn't stand them out in the open he set them up in trees, behind bushes, anywhere they wouldn't be seen. A WestPoint man would have stuck them out like sore thumbs. I could see that Henri would make a fine frontier commander.

After supper Becky and the twins wanted to bath; well really all of the women did; that is all the ones we rescued from the Comancheros and of course Hattie, April and June. Alden, Aiken and I went along to watch; uh, that is not watching them; but to watch out for them....

Now when I was younger; I always thought that women were the shy retiring types. But this bunch was anything but that. They wasted no time in yanking their clothes off and jumping in the river. Now we; the three of us were not perverts; but I defy any red-blooded man not to sneak a look now and then. But I guess we shouldn't of bothered because they, in no uncertain terms, said for us to get our butts in the river; that they were tired of smelling our sweaty selves.

That water wasn't that cold, how could it be? It was a long way to the mountains from which it originated. But it sure enough was pleasant. Especially when Hattie plastered herself up against me....

The river mellowed every one; the music of the south was pleasant to hear again. I can remember growing up hearing their music. In fact, at times I wished I could live with them. I think that was one of the reasons I left home; I couldn't stand the way they were treated. Don't get me wrong; my Dad didn't treat them worse than any other slave holder did; but owning other humans just wasn't right. That's why when the war started I volunteered to fight for the Union.

After the evening meal or should I use the vernacular: Chow; we sat around the fire drinking our coffee; when April asked:" You haven't explained the details about that ranch in Santa Fe; we need to know more; like what's this Don's name?"

"His name is Javier Santiago; he sort of thinks of me like I'm his adopted son or something."

"Why would he think that? You save his life or something?" June asked.

"Well, yeah I did; you see he has this Spanish Land Grant that a lot of Gringos would like to take it away from him. I had stopped to water my horse and he being gracious invited me in for a cool drink. While I was there, it just happened that some of them stopped by to kill him; there were three hired guns with them; along with this so called rancher that had a few acres on the other side of the river; all told there were six of them. Between Javier and two of his vaqueros' we killed five of them and sent this rancher packing. I had no place I really wanted to be so I stuck around for a while and helped. I guess he took a shine to me."

"So how many of the five did you kill?" April asked.

"Why, does it matter? But they all said that it was me that got those three hired guns. Anyway, right now I think we had better be aware of what's coming on down the trail. You see we have just reached the outer edge of the Comancheria and Quanah Parker; he doesn't like me so much."

"Who's this Quanah Parker?" Selena asked.

"He's the main war chief of the Comanches. And ever since we rescued his white mother and his little sister from the Comanches in 1860 he has been a little pissed."

"So why is it just you that he is mad at and not the rest of your group?"

"Oh, he's mad at the rest of the Texas Rangers also; I was the one who grabbed his little sister and spurred away before he could shoot me. But you know if I had to do it over again, personally, I would of left his mother and sister with the Comanches. His mother didn't want to be rescued."

"Then why in the world was she; when she didn't want to be?" Selena said.

"Policy; you see its standard policy with the Texas Rangers that anytime they run across any white captives with the Indians that they liberate them." I said.

"Let me get this straight, you are not only in the Army, you were a Texas Ranger also?" Ruby asked.

"Yeah, I was till the war started then I joined the Union Army; I never did hold with slavery."

"You seem to have accomplished quite a bit for as young as you are." Becky said.

"I suppose you could say that; I like to keep busy. I figure as long as the fire is still hot you might as well heat as many irons as you can; you never know when some maverick needs branding."

"Well come on Honey, I think, this, maverick needs branded by your hot iron." Hattie said as she grabbed me by the hand and led me to where we had our bed roll in the trees. Of course, we left a lot of snickering behind us. Now when I made that crack about branding and mavericks; I sure wasn't talking about sex; but I guess if she took it that way, well….. Use your imagination, mine's busy…

The next morning we were well on our way before the Sun woke up enough to rub the sand from its eyes. I wanted to get on the trail before any of those pilgrims that were camped around Council Grove could kick dust in our face.

We could make better time than most of those freight wagons because they used oxen, while we used mules and horses; and also, we had a deep Remuda. Having a large Remuda also gave us a leg up over any wagon trains. We could change out a tired team in no time. Two days later we were deep into the Comancheria.

Sometimes, some tribes used smoke signals to communicate; or anyway that's what some people thought. I have never seen them use smoke; nor drums. But I have seen them use light flashes from polished metal or even small mirrors. They learned how to do that from the Army; I don't think they used the Morris Code as such, but they probably had a code of their own. I knew Quanah Parker was smart enough to figure something out. Otherwise I think that they had a sixth sense.

I never considered the Indians to be savages as the newspapers from back east called them. It wasn't the Indians that started the practice of scalping; it was the white man who put a bounty on Indian scalps. I never under estimated the intelligence of the Indian; especially in battle.

We passed Stone Corral, Cow Creek, Plum Butte and camped at Great Bend on the Arkansas River. We had been moving fast and had not stopped to take time to bath in the little creeks along the way. So everyone was anxious to wash the sweat and dust and grime from their bodies. I figured on the morrow we would bypass Pawnee Rock and stop at Fort Larned; where we would rest for a day and make repairs that were needed to wagons and tack.

Hattie and I searched out Henri to have a little confab about Fort Larned; we wanted to prepare him and his command about certain things. We found him setting around his campfire with his troop leaders.

They scooted over a little to make room for us; we squatted down Indian style and I said: "Henri, when we get to Fort Larned we're not going inside the compound; I mean the whole bunch of us. Why? Is because I know the Officer in Charge and he doesn't like me; and he would do anything to cause me trouble; even going so far as trying to enlist the whole bunch of you into his command. So, there is a good spot to camp along the creek just before the creek enters the Fort. We'll camp there military style; with the proper pomp and circumstance; complete with posting the flag and the playing of taps and reveille. Then you and I will pay a courtesy call on the nice Major."

Henri thought a bit and then said: "This creek that feeds the fort; is that the only water supply they have?"

"Uh, what makes you ask that?" I said.

"Well, how easy would it be to divert that creek from entering the fort?"

"I suppose it could be done; but it would have to done out of rifle shot of the stockade. But why would you ask about that?"

"Well, I was just trying to gage the intelligence of the Fort's Commander. If he didn't dig a well how long do you think they could last under siege?" Henri said.

"I don't know if they have dug one since the last time I was there, but maybe they have by now. As to how long, that depends on if they have any storage tanks. I really don't know; the last time I was there I wasn't thinking about things like that; you see when I was there last I was still a Texas Ranger and I had traced a herd of stolen longhorns from Texas to Fort Larned. You see I was out of my jurisdiction, being this Fort was in Kansas; anyway to make a long story short Major Whipple knew they were stolen and he bought them anyway; with the intention of selling them to the Indian agent for a profit."

"So what happened, did you arrest him?" Sergeant Tilly Field asked.

"Nope, like I said, I was out of Texas, so I couldn't. But I did tell him that he'd better not ever get caught anywhere in Texas. But I did get the herd back; Whipple was so mad that he told me if he ever seen me again he would have me shot."

"What did you say to that?" Tilly asked.

"I didn't say anything; I just knocked him out and sat him in his chair and I found a bottle of whisky in his desk; so I poured some down him and the rest all over his uniform. On my way out I told the sergeant at the front desk that he'd better see to Whipple that he'd passed out at his desk. The sergeant said: ", "Not again!""

"So what year was that?" Tilly asked.

"Just before the war started; when I got back to Austen I resigned and went north to join the Union. So I really don't know what happened to Whipple after that."

"So you came up in the ranks very quickly then; I hear that you are a friend of General Grant's?" Tilly said.

Yeah, I reckon you could say that; I was with him on the march to Vicksburg in 63. That advance took us six months through mud and muck; and then we lay siege for six more weeks; till they surrendered to Grant on the 4th of July." I said.

"But why would he like you more than his other officers?"

"I don't know that he did like me more than the rest; but maybe he appreciated that I saved his life a couple of times."

"Was that all?" Tilly kept pressing for more.

"Nope, I guess he liked the way that I could get things done; you might say if he had some task he could call on me; I suppose I was his trouble shooter; for instance, what we are doing right now."

"You mean it was General Grant that gave the order to help us get with our husbands?" Tilly said.

"Yep, it sure was; otherwise it sure wouldn't of got done. There are a lot of bigots in the world; being free is only the start of true equality, I'm sorry to say."

"Don't we all know that; but it's sure good to know that there are people like you and General Grant in the world." Tilly said.

"There are more of us than you might think Tilly; it just takes time for them to realize it. Anyway, I think it's time for taps; which will not be played due to the fact we are deep in Indian country." I said.

"Hey," Hattie said, "I don't feel like sleeping yet; so as soon as the camp quiets down, what say we go for a little night time swim?"

"You sure; there will be the sentries posted you know?"

"So who cares; there hasn't been any privacy on this trip anyway. Heck fire you can't even take a leak without someone seeing you."

"Yeah, I guess that's some my fault; I'm the one that gave the order that when you needed to do your business that you go in bunches of four; that way while two were doing the necessary, the other two would keep watch for hostiles."

"Yeah, you know that's a pain in the butt, literally, don't you?"

"Yep, but at least your alive to complain about it."

"So does that mean if we go swimming that we have to take two more with us?" Hattie said.

"Well, I don't know, I guess we could break the rule one time." I said.

"Nope, we're not going to; I'll ask Ruby and Selena to go with us." Hattie said with a smirk on her face."

"Uh, are you sure; there won't be any messing around if they come?"

"We'll just see about that, won't we?" Hattie said.

"Alright, you get them and some towels and you all meet me upstream of the camp by those big cottonwoods. Don't forget your rifles; we shouldn't have any problem seeing with that full moon."

That moon was a bright one; almost as bright as a cloudy day. I walked a ways upstream just to be sure our bathing area would be secure; looked alright, but there was some drift wood floating downstream; made one wonder how it came to be floating without any rain upstream.

I heard the women coming; they were giggling about something; which did not bode well for me, I was sure. They had taken their buckskins off and were wearing some kind of a short dress or under garment; I never could figure out the name of some of those things that women wore under their dresses.

They had their rifles and Selena also had her bow with a full quiver of arrows. Ruby and Hattie put the towels on a log and laid the rifles against said log. Selena did the same with her rifle; but kept her bow and walked over by me and stood looking at the river.

"That's not right." She said looking at me.

"I'm glad you seen that too; I think they are foreshadowing what is to come." I said to her while I glanced at Hattie and Ruby who were already naked and stepping into the water.

"Hey you two, stay near the bank; I think we're about to have company." I said, as Selena notched an arrow and stood there staring at each piece of driftwood as it floated by. Hattie and Ruby had stopped about knee deep in the river; they seen us checking the driftwood as it floated by; they both got out of the water and retrieved their rifles. Selena took off her shift and slung her quiver full of arrows over her naked back. Now there was a sight to see; three naked women ready to do battle; I had to pull my eyes away from them and watch the driftwood.

Selena raised her bow and let fly an arrow; it hit right behind the piece of driftwood; a yell went up and an Indian flapped around in the water. Hattie and Ruby and I started shooting at the remaining pieces of driftwood.

The results were good; we knocked the driftwood out of the hands of the Indians that were hiding behind them; they dove under the water and we couldn't get a good shot at them. Some more shots rang out back toward the camp; evidently they were trying to get at the horses and the sentries were doing their job.

The one that Selena hit wasn't dead; the arrow had taken him in the shoulder; the current had brought him close to shore; I waded out and clipped him behind the ear with my .44. And drug him up on the bank. The arrow was sticking out of his shoulder, so I broke it off and pulled the arrow back out of him.

"Why don't you kill him?" Selena asked.

"Naw, I don't think so; I don't kill to just be killing. Besides he's a Kiowa and if he survives I want him to go back and tell the others what they are up against so they won't mess with us again. You see even after that thunk on the head I gave him he's starting to come around."

He looked at me and then he looked at the women; his eyes opened wide staring at them. "Hey Hattie, tear off some of that dress or whatever it is and make a bandage for his shoulder so we can stop that bleeding."

After Hattie bandaged him, he could see that we weren't going to kill him so I asked him in what little Kiowa that I knew; "Do you understand English?"

He nodded his head and said: "Naked women warriors?"

"Yep, that's right. Heap strong naked women warriors they like kill Kiowa; but I say no; let this one go home and tell heap big Chief how strong we are and to leave us alone or we kill all Kiowa." He looked around at us all; because Aiken and Alden and June and April had arrived and told us that they had driven off the attempt to steal the horses.

"How come they not naked?" He said, indicating June and April. I thought fast and said:

"They have their bleeding time; not good drop blood all over." He nodded, "Are you strong enough to go back to your people?" I asked. He nodded again. So, I gave him back his knife and his bow and arrows which we had taken off of him so he wouldn't get any ideas about trying to use them. He got up and disappeared into the night.

"Do you think he believed you?" Ruby asked me.

"Maybe, but one thing for sure he either believed me or he thinks we're all crazy; either way maybe they will leave us alone."

"Hey, I don't know about the rest of you, but I still want my bath." Hattie said stepping into the water. Selena and Ruby joined her. And of course, April and June were stripping down also. The boys and I sat down on a log to watch, oh, not at the women, but watching for any more hostiles. Yeah, right…

"So, boys", I said to Alden and Akin, "what exactly happened at the Remuda?"

"One of the horse guards was the first to spot them coming out of the river; I think she said that she drilled him dead center. At the first shot the four of us was right there; I figure we accounted for at least three more dead; they all floated down the river." Akin said.

"So how many do you figure there was altogether?"

"Rough count at least ten; they should have waited for a darker night to make their move. How many did you have here?"

"At least six; I really don't know for sure, we shot the drift wood they were holding onto and they just ducked under water and disappeared. But we did get that one that Selena put an arrow in; we bandaged his wound and told him to tell them the next time they tried anything like this that we would kill all of the Kiowa. Yeah, I know that's bragging; but he was some impressed by our naked female warriors. And I don't mean just because they were naked; I think they think they are some kind of super warrior."

"Well they are super warriors; I don't know of any other women who can do what these women can; not just our wives but all of the women here." Alden said.

The women got out of the water and dressed, sorta; Hattie had to make do with trying to wrap her towel around her; account of, she used her shift as a bandage for that Kiowa. She had to make do with either the top or bottom, cause the towel wasn't big enough for both. I didn't mind one little bit.

We didn't have any more excitement the rest of the night; well that's not entirely true; any night with my wife was exciting. But that's beside the point. It was an easy trip past Pawnee Rock and into Fort Larned.

When we got within a half mile of the Fort, I had our Bugler play Boots and Saddles to just get the Fort's attention; then we rode to the creek just outside of the Fort and proceeded to make camp. I guess they heard our Bugler; because there was a Lieutenant and a Sargent that rode out to meet us.

Henri and Sargent Tillie rode to meet them; I hung back; just close enough to hear what was being said.

The Lieutenant said: "What the hell outfit is this?"

Henri gave a salute and said: "This is Charlie Company of the 10th Regiment on our way to Fort Union. With whom do I have the honor of addressing?"

"I am Lieutenant Peter Fram, who are you?"

"Lieutenant Henri Gascon at your service sir and who may I ask is the Commanding Officer of the Fort?"

"Captain Dary is the commanding officer. Why are you making camp out here instead of coming inside the compound?"

"Orders Sir; Major Matthew Bodeen gave us orders to make our camp outside of the walls of the Fort." Henri said.

"So where is this Major or is he a figment of your imagination?" He said sarcastically.

I gigged up my horse and rode up to them. "Lieutenant, I am Major

Bodeen and I don't think I like your attitude; you will apologize to Lieutenant Gascon right this second or I will put you on report."

"Oh yeah, where is your uniform smart ass." He said. My horse was standing close to his so I simply took my foot out of the stirrup and kicked him out of the saddle. He hit on his shoulder and head, it didn't knock him out, but he was a little woozy.

"Sargent, please collect your Lieutenant and return him to the Fort and inform Captain Dary to please have himself available at 1500 hours; Lieutenant Gascon and myself will be making a courtesy call on him at that time."

Our camp was set up complete with sentries posted. We even put up our mess and cooking tent; since we would be here for two days. There was plenty of grass and water for all of our stock; they could use the rest also.

I put my complete uniform on; with all of the pomp, including Sabres for Henri and me. We also had Sargent Tillie and a squad of troops to go with us. We rode in with a flourish. Captain Dary met us on the steps of his headquarters. Lieutenant Fram was not in evidence.

He stood there staring at us; then glanced at me and said: "I don't understand what's going on; I have never seen Negro female troops before. You say you're Charlie Company of the 10th Regiment heading for Fort Union?"

"Yes, Captain that is correct. And you are in the Army, are you not?"

"Why of course I am."

"Well then I believe it's customary to salute a superior officer." He snapped to attention and gave a proper salute and said:

"Forgive me Sir; it just surprised me so much, I am truly sorry."

"Apology accepted Sir; and this is Lieutenant Henri Gascon. We are in need of a few repairs on our wagons and tack; Lieutenant Gascon might call on your blacksmith for needed material and such, please afford him every courtesy."

"Uh, I hate to ask, but may I see your orders Major." He said, his face turning red.

"Why of course you may." I said as I dismounted and reached in my saddle bags for the orders General Grant gave me."

He stood there reading them; his face went from red to pale. He glanced at me and handed them back. "I'm sorry Sir; I didn't know that you were General Grant's personal representative. The whole Fort is at your disposal."

"That's fine Captain; we'll try not to bother your command as much as possible. Did you know Captain that the Kiowa are looking to steal horses? They tried while we were camped at Great Bend last night. We repulsed their attack with no losses of our horses or personnel; while they lost several braves. You might want to take precautions so you don't lose any of your livestock. Feel free to visit our camp this evening and meet the rest of our company." I said as I mounted up and gave a nod to Sergeant Tillie.

Her troops were in a horizontal line behind us; she gave a nod and they did a perfect spoke maneuver; Tillie being the hub and the outside rider backing her horse around with the others following like a spoke on a wheel. I didn't know they knew how to do that. It looked pretty neat. All of the Fort's troops were standing around there with their mouth open.

Chapter Ten

At 17:00 hours Captain Dary and Lieutenant Fram rode into our camp; as you will remember I invited the Captain to come and visit and to partake of the evening meal with us. I always believed in forgiveness and that would apply to Lieutenant Fram also; but as to forgetting, that would depend on if the Lieutenant had learned his lesson.

Our camp was perfectly laid out military style; if Charlie Company had graduated from West Point it couldn't of looked better. As soon as they dismounted Private Ula appeared and led their horses away.

I had changed back into my buckskins; like the rest of us scouts were wearing; that is all except Becky; she was wearing a skirt and blouse. And the way they fit her; I was sure she was wearing nothing underneath. You remember Becky was the woman that was getting 'raped' back at Fort Leavenworth? Anyway, I wasn't really sure that was an actual rape. Also, her husband was killed. Anyway, I think she was on the hunt, if you know what I mean.

As I was introducing Captain Dary to our group Becky was the last in line; but certainly not the least in the Captain's eyes, I could tell by the way he took her hand and kissed it. I turned to Hattie and whispered: "Looks like we lost an ambulance driver."

"That's no surprise to me; I could tell that she was going to jump the first available man she came across; I think she is what they call a sex addict. But that's alright; that Captain Dary looks like he can handle her. I guess Selena can take over with the twins. Those twins need someone to look up to for a role model; Becky sure isn't one."

Lieutenant Fram was trying to shine up to Ruby; but she didn't want any part of him. Ruby was some down on the male part of the human creation; couldn't say that I blamed her; after what she went through with those Comancheros. I didn't want to lose Ruby anyway; she knew how to use the Gatlin Gun.

Becky didn't let loose of her Captain all evening; literally. But she had to when Private Ula brought their horses. As she was telling him goodbye, I walked up and said:

"Do you have a Chaplain at the Fort?"

"Huh, uh, yes of course we do." He stammered.

"Good, we'll bring Becky and her belongings to the Fort in the morning and you can have the Chaplain ready to marry you two; say at 10 hundred hours. Is that alright"

He looked at her and she nodded. "Yes, it's quite alright major; I guess it was love at first sight between us." I thought to myself; more like lust, but heck fire, they both start with the letter 'L'....

It wasn't that I really wanted to unload Becky; but when this opportunity arose; it was sort of like a bird in hand beats two in the bush. I figured a Captain in Fort Larned was better than a private at Fort Union.

We weren't even half way to Santa Fe; the next stop would be Fort Dodge; around sixty miles as I remembered; give or take a few miles. I didn't plan on stopping long there; probably just over night. One thing about this time being on the Santa Fe Trail; there sure was more Army presence then the last time. One reason was that the different tribes were finally realizing that they were losing their land. I really didn't blame them; I guess I would be doing the same as they were; fighting to save their way of life. Of course, they had one more realization to come; they didn't have a chance of a snowball in hell.

The wedding didn't take long; good thing because they both high tailed it out of the commissary as soon as the Chaplain said: "I now pronounce you husband and wife." Like I said; they both start with the letter "L."

I guess our lay over at Fort Larned accomplished two things: We got all of our tack and wagons repaired and the wheels greased and made two horny people very happy. We were on the trail as the sun rose at our backs the next morning.

Alden and Akin and their wives were riding flank and drag this morning; while Hattie, Selena and I were scouting ahead. We were well into the Comancheria; and I have to admit I was a little apprehensive. Why? Because I was having that feeling that someone was watching us; of course, I knew the Indians were always watching everyone that used the Trail. But this was more personal. Whatever it was, was watching me.

Hattie was riding Jasper, her esoteric mule this morning. His ears were almost whirling in a circle he was flicking them so quick. Hattie looked at me and said: "He is trying to tell us something; the last time he did that I had to shoot one of the Swartz boys that tried to jump me along the trail one night."

"Well, one thing I have learned is to trust what your mount is trying to tell you; especially if your mount is a mule. So how many of them does he think there is?"

"I don't think it's how many; it might be how dangerous whoever it is that's out there. Like I said the last time he did that there was only that one Swartz boy. But hellfire, one bullet will kill you just as dead as a hundred." Hattie said with an excited grin. One thing that I had learned about Hattie was that she loved action.

We were so busy watching Jasper's ears that we were surprised when they stopped flicking and were pointed straight ahead. We looked up and there was a lone Indian setting on his horse looking at us; or should I say looking at me! It was none other than Quanah Parker!

I was somewhat relieved; One Indian setting in the trail was better than two in the bush. That's not to say that there wasn't a hundred hiding in the bush; but Quanah Parker counted himself as honorable. If he wanted to kill me he would just do it, not ride out to talk about it. Selena gave a low whistle of surprise. She said: "Well he sure isn't ugly, is he?" She knew who he was right off.

"Simmer down Selena; he probably has ten or more wives and they would make mincemeat out of you." Hattie said.

"Don't worry; I was just making an observation. When I take a man, it won't be a man that is liable to get killed. I want a man who will be with me for life."

I didn't tell Selena but I had a hunch that Quanah would be around for a long time. He was one smart Comanche. Like right now, he knew that I wouldn't shoot him; you see I had a chance when I rescued his mother and sister but I just looked him in the eye and spurred off.

As we rode up to him and stopped; neither of us said a word. Quanah looked first at Selena and then Hattie and then he said to me: "Bodeen, you not a Texas anymore; but now in the Army, are you?"

"It's good to see Quanah and that he still lives." I didn't need to answer his question about being in the Army; being that it was a rhetorical question; he knew full well I was in the Army, even though I was not wearing my uniform.

"Have we killed so many that the long knives have to use women warriors?" Quanah said while studying Hattie and Selena. That was another question that I did not need to answer; he knew that the long knives were as the sand of the sea; too numerous to count. I didn't say anything so he finally said:

"How many horses you want for woman?" All of the time he spoke he was looking at Selena.

"Woman not for sale; she is my sister. Her name is Selena and this one is my wife; her name is Hattie. They both have killed heap many men."

"Maybe I take woman and give you nothing."

"I would advise against that; woman would cut off your baby maker and stuff it down your throat. She mucho bad; she like kill very much." I don't know whether that turned him off or made him want her even more; but he changed the subject.

"How come you have so many black white women?" Most Indians considered the Negro race to be the same as the white people but with a black skin. I guess we could learn something from that...

"They are Army warriors the same as the black white men are; they also mucho bad; they would not only cut off your baby maker they would also gouge out your eyes and then you would not be able to find your way to the happy hunting grounds. And you know this to be true for Bodeen does not lie." Showing the white part of him; Quanah just laughed.

There was a Crow flying around and squawking; we must have disturbed some carrion that he had been feeding on. Anyway, Selena had not only her Henry rifle but had also brought her bow. She pulled an arrow out of her quiver that she had slung on her back and shot that crow out of the sky.

Quanah sat there thinking; he gave a huff and said: "I have enough Squaws anyway; don't need trouble maker like her." Then he turned his pony and rode away.

"What's does he mean 'Squaws'? What's the name mean?" Hattie asked.

I looked at Selena; she just shrugged and tossed the ball back at me.

"Well hell, I never use the word; but the first time I heard it was when I was with some mountain men up in the Rockies. They applied it to any Indian woman. But since then I have learned that it is a derogatory term for a woman's private parts. It must have rubbed off on the part of Quanah that is white."

"What, what was that all about; what did he want?" Hattie asked; while she was looking at both Selena and me.

Selena answered and said: "He was just like a big dog; he was marking his territory; and also, he was serving notice on the Major that he hasn't forgotten the kidnapping of his Mother and Sister. He blames your husband. He wants revenge; he plans to kidnap me and perhaps you too Hattie."

"Do you think he'll do anything right away?" Hattie asked me.

"Nope, he wants us to fret and worry; he's a sly devil. From now on Jasper stays close to our sleeping area and also you ride him during the day; you saw his reaction when he spotted Quanah." I said.

"What if he sends some of his warriors instead of doing it himself?" Hattie said.

"He won't; oh, he will have some of them with him; but he wants to be the one to do the deed. Of course, I'm just surmising here; he might have changed his mind and figure his mother and sister are better off where they are at now."

"Do you really think so? You could be right; I didn't get the feeling that he was all that mad at you." Hattie said.

"Yeah, if he was really pissed at me, he would have just waited in ambush and finished me off with an arrow. I think what he was trying to tell us and he wasn't shy about it; that he was going to try and get some of the women; probably starting with the two of you. But what he doesn't fully realize is that the women in our outfit are plain mean; along with being dangerous." I said with a smirk.

"Yeah, and don't you ever forget it, smart ass." Hattie said.

"I won't, that was one of the reasons that I married you; I love danger and baby you are it in a nutshell. But enough foreplay; let's ride back and let the column know about our little meeting with Quanah."

Selena leaned over and asked Hattie; "what's foreplay?"

"I'll explain it later." Hattie said, with red cheeks.

"Oh, I bet I know; it's something to do with sex, you two are always going at it." Selena said, with a smile of her own.

Hattie and I exchanged smiles; hers was sort of sultry; all of this talk must have got her libido going. Me? Naw, it didn't bother me at all....

We had no more than got our horses turned around then about a dozen Comanches jumped up out of an arroyo on our left, yipping and yelling and spurring hard after us. We didn't try to run; instead we just hopped off our mounts and knelt down and went to shooting; we didn't want Jasper to get killed as well as the other two horses. I noticed right away that Quanah was not with them.

We only had to kill eight of them before the rest got the hint to either run or die. They must not have believed Quanah when he told them to leave us alone and wait for a better time. That's what happens when stupidity over rules common sense. But of course, they probably thought that four to one odds were pretty good. Which if everything was equal that would have been great odds. But of course, our three Henry Golden boys held fifteen shots each and we didn't miss.

Selena headed toward the bodies with her knife out. "Hold on there Selena, don't scalp them; let them go to their hereafter with their hair; no use pissing them off; maybe they will just chalk it up to a learning experience. After all we were just defending ourselves. Let them gather their dead and the ponies they rode in on. We'll head back to the column and give them time to do so."

We didn't get but about a mile back down the trail when we met Alden and Akin and their wives galloping toward us. "What was all that shooting about?" Alden said, sliding his mount to a stop.

I started to tell them; but a thought just hit me: "Damn, get back to the troops; they're going to be attacked; that Quanah is a sneaky one; he just sacrificed eight men as a ruse."

As I was talking the shooting started back down the trail; Akin said: "Don't worry they're prepared. We thought as much when we heard the shooting you all were doing. The wagons are circled and the Remuda is in the circle."

"Good, where are the Comanches shooting from? What kind of cover? Can we hit them from the rear?" I fired the questions at the four of them.

"Yeah," April said, 'that is if Ruby doesn't cut loose with that

Gatling gun; I wouldn't want to be anywhere close to those Indians if she does."

"We're not going to be fighting them hand-to-hand; we'll be far enough away if she does." Hattie said.

The shooting continued as we rode toward the fight; most of it sounded like the Golden Boys were doing most of the singing. We slowed down and when we got close we hobbled our mounts and proceeded on foot. We topped a little rise and looked down on the festivities.

The Comanches had given up on riding around the wagons and shooting at them; might be because a lot of them were already laying out there dead. They had pulled back to cover and were shooting into the wagons. I knew if that kept up they would be hitting some of our troops. We were above and behind where they were shooting from. So the seven of us spread out and started sniping at them. It didn't take long till their casualties started to mount and they took notice and high tailed it out of there. As we were walking back to our mounts I asked:

"Who gave the order to circle the wagons and Fort up?"

"Not us, it was Henri; you should of seen him you would of thought that he was General Custer or something the way he was tossing around orders." June said.

"I knew he was a good officer and now he just proved it; he probably saved a lot of lives, including ours." I said. I made up my mind as soon as I reached a telegraph I would put him in for a medal and a promotion.

Henri saw us coming and moved a wagon tongue so we could ride in the circle. "How many casualties did you take?" I asked him.

"A few minor wounds, nothing big." He said, then added; "I seen how many there are lying dead out there; how many did you all kill?"

"Eight, they were trying for a diversion; which I suppose worked to a certain extent. What they weren't expecting was how well trained and disciplined Charlie Company is; and of course, our firepower." Hattie said.

"I'm glad Ruby didn't unleash the Gatling gun; I prefer to keep it a surprise." I said.

"She wanted to; but I told her no; I'm surprised she listened to me; she's a headstrong woman." Henri said.

"Good, but let's get everything together and move out; that will give them a chance to recover their dead; I'm sure Quanah will appreciate us letting them have their dead. And I think he will think twice about attacking us full force again. But that's not to so say he won't sneak up and try to steal the horses and maybe slit a few throats." I said.

"I will double the guard." Henri said, as he gave the order to move out.

That night we camped just short of Fort Dodge at a sweet flowing spring I knew about; it was less than a mile off of the beaten path. As soon as we made camp Henri was as good as his word and doubled the guard.

After the evening meal Hattie said: "Hey, let's go for a little walk." She grabbed my hand and pulled me up; she had a blanket over one shoulder. I sort of knew what she had in mind. We went past the spring up on a little hill that overlooked the camp. I was a might uneasy being just out of sight of the guards. I looked around, it was just past twilight and the campfires were sparkling. I turned back toward Hattie; she was standing there stark naked looking at me.

She was in stark relief with the full moon behind her; she slowly turned in a circle; she stopped with her legs slightly apart; the moon highlighted her female attribute. I couldn't stop staring.

"Is that all you're going to do, is just look?" She said as she slowly moved her hand down over her belly toward where the moon shined the brightest. I was torn between the show she was putting on and the need to join the cast. The need to join the cast won out.

As we laid there looking at the stars; I asked her: "Where did you learn to do that?"

"What, make love to you?"

"No, that little show you put on?"

"Oh, that. It just comes natural; sometimes when I was younger I would go out at night when the moon was full and dance around naked dreaming of you."

"You didn't know me when you were younger."

"Didn't I? Why do you think the second I saw you at your Mother's place, I knew it was you? And what about you, you never dreamt about me?"

"Well, yeah, I guess. But I never could quite put a face to you. Sometimes I almost could; take for instance your eyes, I seen them in my dreams. And, and, I feel embarrassed about saying it; but your hair down there, the color, the way it curls into, into you know, don't make me say it."

"You mean it's just like you dreamt about it? Oh, I bet you had a lot of wet dreams about me."

"Hattie! Really, what if someone heard you say things like that, what would they think?"

"They'd probably think we were just two normal people deeply in love."

"Well, yeah, you're right about that, I am deeply in love with you." I said as she rolled over on top of me and sat up and started to move...On the way back to camp we stopped at the spring and washed up; the sentry's probably seen us, but we didn't care....

The next day when we rode into Fort Dodge; we found Bravo Company of the 10th Calvary stationed there; or what was left of them....

I had put my uniform on before we got to the fort; as such Henri and I rode in front of the column. Of course they had seen us coming and the gates to the stockade were open; we swept in with a flourish and executed the same maneuvers that we did at Fort Larned.

The Commanding Officer of the Fort was standing on his headquarters steps. He was a Colonel that I had never seen before. He stepped down and walked over.

"A little bit of a Smart Alek, aren't we?" he said, then said: "What the hell, those troops are women!"

"Yes sir they are." I said while looking around myself. "What's happened here, it looks like your outfit has been rode hard and put away wet?"

"We were attacked by hundreds of Indians. There were Comanches, Utes and Kiowas; they hit us in broad daylight just before noon yesterday. If it weren't for Bravo Company they would have overrun us. As it was we lost most of the troops in Bravo. And they laid siege to us over night. They only rode away just before your column came in sight."

"Did you recognize the Chief in Charge?" I asked him, although I already knew who it was.

"Yes, my Sergeant did; he said it was Quanah Parker, whoever that is. And why the hell are those women in uniform?"

"I'll explain that later; right now, would you please muster the troops of Bravo Company that are still alive; I believe some of these women would like to know who is alive and who have been killed. My second in command will take care of the details; by the way this is Lt. Gascon, soon to be promoted to Captain." Henri looked at me, somewhat surprised, I nodded to him.

"You're pretty free with the orders aren't you Major; what's your name anyway?"

"Oh, I'm sorry sir, my name's Matt Bodeen and I didn't catch yours?"

"It's Colonel Alvin Shepard and I didn't give it; I'm not sure I like this whole thing."

"Well perhaps we can talk in private and I'll show you my orders from General Grant." I said as I dismounted and dug my orders out of my saddle bags. "Henri, would you please see to the camping arrangements for Charlie Company?" I said as Alvin and I walked toward headquarters.

After we got settled in his office I handed him my orders, he read them three times. I thought to myself he must be a slow learner. He looked up; "Uh, it says here that you are doing an inspection of the forts on the Santa Fe Trail; is that right?"

"Among other things; yes; in line with that I would like to know the number of white troops stationed here permanently and the number of Bravo Company dead and alive. Oh, also the number of white troops you lost in this last battle." He called his clerk and told him to get the numbers.

"Yes sir, I know the numbers without looking, there are six hundred white troops and there were one hundred black troops; now there are 27 black troops uninjured and three in the infirmary. That would make seventy troops of Bravo Company dead; while ten white troops were killed in the initial attack."

I said, "Thank you Corporal," as he left the office. "So, Alvin, did you get a count of the enemy dead?"

"Not really, but I can ask my Sergeant."

"That won't be necessary; I'll have my Lt. find out."

"Well Alvin, do you see anything out of kilter about those numbers?"

"I would appreciate it Major if you would address me by my rank."

"Humm, well Alvin I think I'll just call you Alvin for a time. Please answer my question."

"No, I don't. It's not my fault they put themselves out there to be shot."

"All right, I'll leave this point to be discussed after I gather more facts. Where have you been serving before this post?" I asked.

"I taught at West Point and then in Washington." He said, rather haughtily.

"Yes, I see, what did you do wrong to be sent to the frontier?"

"What! Why you little upstart I can crush you." He said jumping up.

"No, you couldn't; now shut up and set down and tell me the truth." He slowly sank into his chair.

"I had an affair with President Johnson's sister."

"Why didn't you marry her?"

"She was already married." He said looking at his hands.

"Alright I know how you got here; but the question is do you want to stay in the army?"

He looked up; I could see his gears going around. "Yes, I think I really do want to stay in the army; it's the only thing I know how to do."

"Good, then Colonel what I want you to do is think back to what you used to teach at West Point, then throw everything you learned and taught in the garbage can and listen to your 1st Sargent. Being he was the one who knew who Quanah Parker was and is; he knows a thing or two."

I didn't see any reason to brow beat him further, so I said: "Come on let's go see if Henri has everything under control."

When we walked out of the office door Hattie and her brothers; Aiken and Alden as well as their wives April and June were lounging on the front steps waiting for me to come out. Alvin almost tripped over his chin when he seen them. Why because of course the three women were wearing their buckskins. Not only were the women wearing pants offensive to his back-east protocol, but of course those buckskins left nothing to the imagination.

"Shut your mouth Alvin before you trip over it; these are official army scouts; the best in the business. Also, this is Hattie my wife and these are Hattie's brothers, Alden and Aiken and their wives April and June. And all of them can shoot a tick off of a Buffalo's ass at two hundred yards." I had just finished telling him that when Selena, Ethel, Myrtle and Ruby O'Rourke walked up; they also were wearing their buckskins; but Ruby had a habit of letting her breasts show a little more than the other women. "And yes, these women are also part of our team; and yes, they are just as deadly as the rest. So, I would suggest you tell all of your men to stay away from them; we don't need more casualties of your troops."

Ethel and Myrtle were youngsters, but they had been taking some lessons from Selena and they were quick learners. Hattie had been teaching all of the women her expertise with the knife and stiletto. And I knew they had no compunctions against harvesting family jewels of any would be rapists.

One thing that I probably forgot to tell you was that all of the women; Hattie, April, June, Ruby, Selena, Ethel and Myrtle had taken those bandoliers that we had taken off of those Comancheros and were wearing them crossed over their breasts. Of course, they also had .45's belted on their hips. Why I mentioned this was because all of the white troops were staring at them with trepidation in their eyes. As well they should. They didn't wear those bandoliers all of the time when on the trail; but I suppose they specially did it this time to keep any amorous individuals from approaching them.

I whispered to Hattie; "perhaps it would be wise to post a guard on our wagons. We don't need anyone poking around in them and finding out what arms we have; especially the Gatling gun."

"I already have, Sergeant Tillie and Private Ula are watching all of the wagons. How long do you plan on staying here?"

"Not long, I have to telegraph Gen. Grant and do any repairs to the wagons that are needed. We're going to take the surviving troops of Bravo Company with us when we leave; the wounded will ride in the ambulance of course. It's time these white troops quit hiding behind the black troops and do their duty."

General Grant didn't have any qualms about promoting Henri to Captain; he did have a few harsh words for Col. Shepard though but gave him another chance before demoting him. As soon as we left the next morning I changed back to my buckskins; I left the running of the command to Henri.

The traffic on the trail was at its peak; we weren't far from the Point of Rocks and the Cimarron crossing; after that the trail would split. We would be taking the Cimarron Cutoff or the Dry Route. It was the shortest one. I hoped to make it to Fort Union in four days. There were no more Forts on this route; Bents Fort was on the other one. Most of the wagon trains that used Oxen would use the other route where there was more water. We would be moving fast between the springs and the natural rock tanks (Or Tinajas as the Indians called them) that held rain water.

I made sure that all of the water barrels were full on all of the wagons. I really wasn't worried about water all that much. We would be passing two different forks of the Cimarron River; plus, also various springs along the way.

It was just past mid-morning and we had already passed two freight outfits with about thirty wagons each; we didn't stop to palaver, we just waved. It was sort of funny how they all did a double take looking at us; and not just because of our racial make-up; I think it was because of armament; each trooper not only had the old Springfield's but also the new Henry repeaters. Plus, I guess also our women in buckskins with those crossed bandoleers.

Each day we pushed further than we had been doing; we changed out our teams a little more often also. We reached the Wagon Mound rock on the fourth day with about twenty miles left to go to La Junta; where the trail went on to Las Vegas and Santa Fe or northwest up the other trail to Fort Union.

It was about two in the afternoon when we set up camp about a mile out of La Junta; I seen no reason to go into the small town. Henri was a little puzzled by our stopping so early.

"How come we are stopping here?" He asked.

"Well Henri I think we'll part ways here; I want you to take your command on to Fort Union in the morning. I'll give you the needed documents to show the Fort Commander. Sergeant Tillie and Private Ula wants to go with us; since they have no loved ones alive anymore in the 10th Regiment. The wounded soldiers in the Ambulance are doing better now and they can be transferred into one of the other wagons. If you have to get ahold of us we'll be at the Hacienda of the Don Joaquin Santiago; I am part owner."

"Just where is this Hacienda?"

"A little east of Las Vegas between and including the Gallinas River that runs into the Pecos River and the Conchas River that runs into the Canadian River. We're going to head down the trail for few miles and then there is a trail that leads right to the Santiago Hacienda. We will cover part of the distance today yet."

Chapter Eleven

There were twelve of us that would be branching off; along with six wagons and thirty head of horses and mules besides the ones that were four up on the six wagons, giving us fifty-four head altogether. April and June volunteered to wrangle the Remuda. It wasn't more than twenty miles to the Hacienda anyway; but I wanted to make most of the way before dark and then scout out things before we rode in. I had learned a long time ago to never ride in hot and unexpected; especially when one knew there was trouble already afoot.

The cut off was in-between La Junta and Las Vegas; I didn't want to go into either town, thereby announcing our presence. We were well within the Santiago Land Grant when we stopped near a spring to camp for the night. The grass was plentiful and still mostly green; the stock settled down like they were trail savvy, which they were. We did set the guard though; even when things seem peaceful it didn't mean they were.

After we had all eaten we had a confab; "Hattie, I want you and Selena to get Jasper and you and Selena can ride double while I run alongside; it's not more than a mile or two to the Hacienda. It's a dark night with very little moon; we need to scout everything out before we ride in come morning."

"Why don't we all take a mount?" Selena asked.

"Because Jasper knows when to be quite; and not even break a branch when he walks." Hattie said.

"Yep, that's exactly why. Also, be sure and wear your moccasins; and take your weapons of the night; I have a feeling that they may be needed, then again, maybe not." I said as an afterthought.

"We always have what we need with us." Selena said while holding up a two-foot length of piano wire that she had unwrapped off of her one ankle while demonstrating in the air how it was to be used. Of course, she also had her bow and quiver of arrows.

Hattie looked at me and said: "I hardly ever hear you second guess yourself. What's up?"

"Strangest thing; remember I told you about how that old mountain man told me about 'timberline moments', well he just popped up in my mind and said *timberline* right after I said that we may need our weapons of the night. Don't ask me to explain what it meant; maybe my sub-conscious is trying to tell me something."

As I remembered the hacienda sat in a little low spot with a spring within its fortified walls; those walls wear at least two feet thick around the whole perimeter of the compound. The main house itself was at least three feet thick. The whole thing was way over a hundred years old; it was built to withstand Indian attacks. There were low hills around here and there; but they were not high enough to see into the compound itself, but if one wanted to spy on the place they were high enough for that, plus they also had Juniper and pine trees for cover.

All of that was running through my mind as we took the well beaten track or road I guess you could say that led toward the compound. Jasper headed right out, like he knew where he was going. Funny thing about Mules was that they took the best parts of the horse and the donkey and they were more intelligent than either one of their forbearers.

"Do you smell that?" Selena said in a whisper.

"Yep, we do, and Jasper does also." Hattie said. What we smelled was wood smoke; someone had a camp fire going.

"Alright, let Jasper take the lead, you two slip off of him and we'll follow where he takes us."

Jasper headed toward the highest of those low hills. Now I just thought I would mention that being that we had been on the trail for almost two months; Hattie and I looked pretty much like we were sure enough Indians ourselves. I had my hair braided down my back the same as Hattie and Selena; and of course, we were wearing our buckskins. I was telling you this to just set the stage for what happened next.

Jasper was moving slow; picking his way through the trees; I almost laughed out loud; he looked just like a big Hound Dog sneaking up on a coon. The closer we came to the fire the slower Jasper went; we stopped when we were about ten feet away.

There were three of them with their backs to us staring into the fire.

Now that's a stupid thing for a person to do; it destroys their night vision. We stood there waiting; finally, Jasper got tired of waiting and stomped a hoof in annoyance.

They jumped up and fell over themselves turning around; still not able to see us standing in the dark like we were. "Who's there?" The biggest one cried, literally. Crap! They were kids…

All four of us stepped into the fire light…They were kids alright; two boys about ten and eleven years old and the girl must have been about twelve. They were all dressed in homemade clothes; after the war a lot of people were migrating west; that's who these kids probably were.

"Don't scalp us, please we weren't doing anything." The girl said.

Selena looked at me and said in Lakota: "Do you want me to scare them?"

"No," I said back in Comanche, "I think their scared enough." Then I said in halting English- "You have any food? We are hungry."

The girl looked toward the fire, "We have a few beans left from supper is all."

"No want beans, meat, you have meat? Where your horses, we kill eat meat."

"Please don't kill Daisy, she's old and we love her." The girl said starting to cry…

"That's enough, you two, stop scaring the kids, shame on you!" Hattie said, stepping up and hugging the girl. "Don't cry they were just having fun with you. We will not hurt you kids."

"You're not Indians?" The girl said.

"Nope, not Matt and I, but Selena is and she won't hurt you. What in the world are you kids doing out here?"

"We're supposed to be watching the fort down there and keeping track of anybody leaving or coming and tell the man in town. He's paying our parents a dollar a day. He says then our parents will get some land when he takes over."

"That man is lying to your parents; this land belongs to Joaquin Santiago and my husband, Matthew Bodeen and me. My name is Hattie, what's yours?"

"I'm Elisabeth Nottingham and these are my brothers Billy and Bob, they're twins. My parents' names are Oliver and Ruth

Nottingham, we're from England."

"Why would your parents let you kids do this on your own?" I asked.

"My Mom is sick and we ran out of money. Dad said we didn't have any choice."

"Well, don't worry about it tonight. Gather your things and get your horse; you're coming with us; we have a camp about a mile back that way and then in the morning you can come to the Hacienda with us." Hattie said.

"The Hacienda, where's that?"

"Down there, what you called the fort; then when we get settled we'll take you to your parents, how's that?"

"Alright, I guess; but there is supposed to be someone coming out tonight and get our report."

"Really?" I said. "Selena get Jasper back in the timber, that way. Lizzy, can I call you Lizzy? Good, you guys set back down by the fire we'll pull back in the timber and wait for them; don't tell them that we are here, just give them your report and wait tell they leave; alright?"

"Yes, some of those men are creepy, I don't like them." Lizzy said.

We didn't have long to wait till we heard a horse coming, just one. He rode up and swung down and said, "There's my little girl." Then he looked at the two boys, "Why don't you two make your selves scarce, I want to talk to your sister alone."

"No," they both said in unison.

"Alright then you can watch and then when I'm done I'll save a little for the two you." He said as he swung back toward Lizzy. He reached out to grab her and before I could even move an arrow came out of the dark and struck him in the throat. Selena walked forward and started to pull the arrow out.

"No, leave it in him. Was that one of your arrows?" I said.

"No, I picked up some Comanche arrows when we had that dust up with Quanah." Selena said.

"Good, we'll take him out to the cutoff, off of our land; they'll think a Comanche got him."

"Then we'd better scalp him, do you want to or shall I?" Selena said.

One of the twins stepped forward, "Can I help? I will if you will show me how."

"Why would you want to?" Hattie asked.

"He was the one who hurt our Mother. Mom was pregnant, she lost the baby." The other twin said.

"Then you have every right, Selena you take him, tie him on his horse, you can take Jasper and the boys. Take him out where I said; then come back to camp. We'll take Lizzy and her horse to our camp."

We had Lizzy mount her horse Daisy and we ran beside. It didn't take us but twenty minutes to get back to camp. About an hour later Selena and the twins rode in on Jasper.

Selena said: "We would have been earlier, but we stopped to wash up. The boys wanted something special, so I showed them how to carve the symbol of the Thunderbird on his chest."

Ethel and Myrtle had taken charge of Lizzy; the boys followed Selena, she showed them where to sleep under her wagon. Hattie said, "What does that symbol look like?" I bent down and drew one in the dust. I looked up at her; "I don't like that, it looks evil, is it?"

"It didn't used to be, but I'm afraid in time people will come to hate it." I said.

"What do you think about those boys? They could be scarred forever." Hattie said.

"Well sometimes you have to grow up before you want to. Look at Selena she's been fighting and killing before she was ten years old and she's still pretty level headed." I said, Hattie looked at me funny and let it go. I thought to myself, well maybe not all that level headed, but then again neither am I."

"Explain to me again about this *timberline* thing?"

"Well it's simple and then again it's not; but I have been thinking about the last few days."

"Oh, what about these last few days? I know you've been pushing us to move faster the last four days; like you had a burr under your tail." Hattie said.

"Yeah, well I did feel an urge to get here; I can't really explain it, but on the timberline thing; it's simple a word to describe what path you're going to take. Or a decision that you make; it could be a major decision; for instance, like getting married or a minor one like throwing a length of rope away because it's too short and then later you find that-

that piece of rope might save your life.

For instance, like us not going with Henri to Fort Union and coming here tonight; that *timberline* was very important; we saved three lives; if we hadn't of been there he would of killed all three of them to keep them from telling. But I guess we had better go to sleep." I said.

"I would but you're on top of me." Hattie said with a smile.

"Yeah, but you're the one doing all of those fancy moves." I said.

"Just shut-up, I'm almost there......"

The next morning when I woke up my beautiful wife was setting on top of me; the sun was just coming up. "Good Morning." I said.

"You've heard that term 'waste not-want not?' Well you had one of those big nocturnal things; and I certainly was not going to let that go to waste." My wife said as the sun and we all came together! My wife was ever the connoisseur of the nocturnal.

The sun had been up for over an hour before we broke camp and headed for the Hacienda. June and April had the Remuda out ahead of the wagons. Alden and Akin were bringing up the rear behind the wagons; just in case. Hattie and I were out ahead of the Remuda.

We came out of the hills in a rush and circled the Remuda on the grassy meadow just outside of the compound. There was two vaqueros' standing on the wall beside the big gate; they had raised their rifles, but at the last moment they recognized me. Juan and Pedro were long time hands of Joaquin's.

"Senor Bodeen welcome." They called out together.

"Where do you want these horses?" I asked them.

"Turn them in the south pasture; there is plenty of grass and a small stream runs through there." Juan said.

I showed April and June where it was; while I was doing that they got down and opened the gate for the wagons. The walls around the compound enclosed twenty acres; where the main house, barn and other adobes were situated. The horses that were pulling the wagons and our saddle stock were turned into the main corral that was hooked to the south side of the barn; a small stream also ran through the barn and then through the corral. Our wagons had been put under a group of cottonwoods that also sat beside that same stream. That stream originated in a spring that set inside of the compound.

When we were at Fort Leavenworth I had sent a message to Fort Union for the Don, a messenger from the Fort Union had delivered the message over a month ago. I had told him how many would be coming give or take a few; so I was sure they had accommodations ready for us. Which they did.

Joaquin Santiago was a man in his late sixties; by the looks of him in fair health still. His first wife had died in childbirth twenty years ago; he had never remarried. His only son was standing beside him; Jose was his name.

I rode up and dismounted; along with April and June. Hattie and the rest of group were already there and introductions had already been made. I introduced April and June as Aiken and Aiden's wives.

I had better take a moment here and explain the favor I did to earn Joaquin's gratitude; so much that he gave half interest in the Spanish Land Grant. I saved his only son's life; Jose. It was interesting about both of their names: Joaquin means 'God will establish' and Jose means 'God adds.'

But how did I save his life? Well he had been taken captive by the Apaches'. They were always raiding and still are; that's why the Hacienda had been built like a fort. Jose thought that he was invincible and he often rode by himself. I was still in the Texas Rangers and was chasing a murderer from Texas; borders didn't mean anything to me; just an imaginary line. Anyway, when I caught up to the murderer, the Apaches had both of them staked out over an anthill. There was only time to save one of them or risk getting caught myself; as soon as it got dark I crawled on my belly and cut Jose loose; he was a little stiff but was able to crawl away with me. Why didn't I take the other guy also? My horse could accommodate only two people. The murderer was pretty far gone anyway; he didn't even know that I was there.

Joaquin gave me a hug and said: "Welcome home." Jose stepped up and gave me a man hug; you know what that is, a one arm hug while patting me on the back with the other one.

Jose wasn't giving me his full attention; I looked where he was looking; it was at Selena…I said to Jose: "Be careful Jose, don't play false with her or she will cut your cohunes off; if she doesn't like you she might cut them off anyway, just for fun." Of course, being who he was, he wouldn't pay any attention to advice.

I turned my attention back to Joaquin; we both said at the same time: "We need to talk."

"Right," I said, "Would you see to it that my entire bunch gets settled into their accommodations?"

"Yes, Jose will you see to that?" Joaquin said to his son. By Jose's expression he didn't want to do his Father's bidding; but by the look on Joaquin's face he knew enough not to cross him.

"Good, I want my wife Hattie and Selena to set in on our confab." I said as I motioned for them to come with us.

We were still dressed pretty much as we were last night and as such we were armed to the teeth. All of the women and children of the Hacienda were staring at us; the children hiding behind their mother's skirts. The main house was quite large with walls that were at least three feet thick and as such it was cool inside despite the temperature being at least in the nineties outside.

We went into Joaquin's office, study, library, den; whatever you want to call it; we sat in the big hide covered chairs. We had just got settled when a woman brought in a large jug of lemonade. By the looks on Selena's face she had never had any before.

"So, Joaquin fill us in on what's been happening," I said.

"There is much to tell since I seen you last Senor Bodeen; most of it not so good, I am afraid."

"Call me Matt Sir, we know some of it from what happened last night. Did you know that you have been under surveillance?"

"Yes, we have been losing some stock also; and every time we go to Las Vegas we have trouble. A lot of Gringos have moved there and have scared the people. They have even installed their own Marshal of sorts."

"Hattie why don't you and Selena tell the Don what happened last night while I quaff some of this lemonade down."

After they finished telling him all about it, he said: "Did you get his name?"

"No, I'm sorry I did not." Selena said, and then added: "But I have his scalp, would that help?"

Joaquin's face turned a shade paler. "Yes, perhaps I could tell who it was if I seen it."

"Excuse me and I'll go get it, the boys have it, and I'll tell them you'll give it back after you see it." She got up and left the room. Joaquin cleared his throat and said:

"Why do the boys have it?"

"It seems that the former owner of that scalp hurt their mother and she lost a baby due to that injury." Hattie said.

It didn't take Selena but a moment or two to get back. Joaquin looked at it and said: "I'm afraid that scalp belonged to the Marshal of Las Vegas, his name was Wes Simple; a very bad man; he liked to hurt people; I don't think anyone will care too much about his death. But of course, his employer will."

"A man named Curt Talent; he likes to be called Colonel Talent. He says he was one in your Civil War. He has many men who claimed to have ridden with him in that war. I believe he was a Confederate."

I looked at Hattie and she nodded. "Yes, we know him and he did not fight for the south; he was one of Quantrill's raiders; He was a neighbor of mine in Tennessee" She said.

Selena got up to leave; "Just a minute Selena, are you going to return that scalp to the boys?"

"I was thinking about it."

"Uh, do you really think that is a good idea? I mean that scalp holds a lot of hate."

"What do you mean a lot of hate, it's just a scalp."

"Yes, to you; you could care less; you didn't bear any malice against him; I mean he was just another bad man to do away with. But to the boys that hated that man because he hurt their mother it's another story. You see every time they look at that scalp more hate will build up in their heart; and it will eventually eat them up. Hate only hurts the man that cradles it in his bosom."

Selena stood there for a moment and then said: "I know what to do with it; we'll hold a burning ceremony. I'll tell them the Great Spirit wants to burn the memory of that bad man so that he won't be able to hurt anybody ever again; even though he's going to hell. I'll make a big to-do, with dancing and throw in some chanting."

"What's the reason for the dancing and chanting?" Hattie asked.

"No reason; it will be something like I seen one of those traveling medicine men do, just a lot of smoke and mirrors; just for show."

Selena said as she walked out.

Jose came back and said: "I showed everyone their rooms, what else do you want me to do?"

Joaquin looked at me for an answer. "Good then you can help me get the wagons settled somewhere that they won't be bothered." I said.

"Bothered? How do you bother a wagon?" Jose said with a smirk.

"Well I know quite a bit about being bothered and your attitude is starting to bother me; and it's not the wagon so much as the contents that I don't want disturbed, like you're disturbing me right now." I said as I motioned for him to follow me.

He dropped his smirk right quick when he seen my hand on the butt of my .44. Not that I would have actually shot him for being disrespectful; but he didn't know that.

"I think there's room in the barn for the six wagons; I might have to move a few things around though." Jose said.

"Good, Hattie why don't you go to our room and do whatever you need to do; while Jose and I do the wagons. If you want anything out of them they'll be in the barn."

We had covered the weapons and ammunitions with tarps inside of the wagons. Jose looked in and said: "What's under all of those tarps?"

"Things that will keep us safe from the people that would like to kill all of us and take this land; that's what in those wagons. How many of your men can be spared to guard the wagons?" I asked Jose.

"I don't know you'll have to ask the foreman, Ricardo Sanchez."

"What, do you not know that you are third in charge now, after your Dad and me? And as such you should know everything that goes on the whole land grant. From now on you are in charge of the day-to-day operation of the ranchero. When you're Dad or I ask you a question we will expect an answer."

"I'm sorry; I didn't know that; I'll ask the foreman."

"Good, then see Sergeant Tillie and Private Ula and they will set a schedule for the guard duty." I had found out a long time ago with difficult young people that if you give them a responsibility that they will step up and meet it; most of them anyway. I started to walk away, then I had a thought: "Tell Ricardo to see me, I want to talk to him." I told Jose.

I went back to the main house and found our room. Hattie was setting in a large brass tub filled with soapy water. "This sure feels good; there's room for you in here also; that is if you want to join me?"

"If I want to, you have to be kidding. Of course, I do." I said, tearing my clothes off. She was right it sure did feel good…When we got out we were a little wrinkled; but totally satisfied.

All of us met in the main dining room for the evening meal. "Do you eat like this every night or is this just a special meal for us?" I asked Joaquin.

"It's the first opportunity that we have had to lay out a fancy meal." Joaquin said.

"Well thank you for that; but thank also your kitchen staff; they've outdone themselves." I said as I glanced around the table. Jose was just picking at his food while stealing looks at Selena. If he kept that up, picking at his food, he would starve to death. Selena finally looked over at him and said:

"Will you stop acting like a love-sick calf and come over here and set beside me; that is if you can behave yourself."

The twins weren't too happy that they had to scoot over and make room for Jose; but Selena smiled at them and they melted. They also weren't too happy when Selena told them about the Burning Ceremony; which would take place right after dark.

Speaking about that-Selena had already sat up the wood for the fire in the main courtyard. She had also told Hattie and April and June what their part would be; but Hattie hadn't said much about it to me. So right after the meal was done; the four of them retired to their rooms. The rest of us went out to the courtyard; along with most of the people of the Hacienda.

When we got their Ruby lit the fire and when it was going well; the four women came out. A gasp went up from most of the attendees. Why? Because they were dressed in skimpy outfits; that didn't leave much to the imagination.

Selena had that scalp in one hand and a decorated lance in the other. Oh, by the way Jose was standing there with his tongue hanging out. Our three wives also had lances. You could tell by their smiles that they were enjoying their display; if you know what I mean.

They started to chant and dance around the fire- Hi-yi-ya. The chanting matched the stamping of their feet. The flames reflecting off of their near naked bodies were mesmerizing. They finally stopped with their backs to us; which by the way was a lovely view; Selena raised the scalp over her head and when she did her top fell down. Another gasp came, and then she threw the scalp into the fire. She must have loaded it with gun powder because the flames reached far into the air; they all turned to face us. And wouldn't you know our three wives had somehow let their tops down while everybody was watching the flames. Then they all run off toward the house.

Ruby stood up and said: "That was the burning of evil ceremony and it required partial nudity for it to work; so don't be shocked." Then she winked at me. Both of us knew damn well it didn't require nudity; but what the hell they all sure looked beautiful; in fact, there was no such thing as that ceremony in any of the tribes that I had ever seen.

When we got back to the house they were clothed, more or less, and laughing their heads off. Alden and Akin had big smiles on their faces; they knew what they would be getting this night. As well as me I guess. But poor Jose just had to grin and bear it…. Marriage has its privileges.

Chapter Twelve

The moon was shining in our window making patterns as it shone through the leaves of the big cottonwood trees that were undulating in the cool night breeze. The best part of those patterns was that they were cast in my memory as they shone on my wife's naked body. I don't think I could ever get enough of watching her sleep; even if she wasn't naked.

I was having a really sexy dream when I woke up with Hattie setting on top of me and she was smiling as she was slowly moving; "I was wondering if you were going to wake up before I was done." She said.

"Well, I was having a nice sexy dream with a beautiful woman till I was interrupted." I said.

"Oh, and just who was that woman?" She said as she stopped moving.

"Alright, alright, don't stop; it was you of course."

"Don't worry, I won't; you see I woke up and it was just there; so, I sure wasn't going to waste it; you know waste not-want not!" Hattie said. The only thing I could think of to say was: "I'm sure glad you're so thrifty."

Reality came back with breakfast; when Selena said: "Lizzy and the boys are worried about their parents; what are we going to do about them?"

"Well what do you propose we do?" I said.

"Go in there and whip ass; that's what I would do." Selena said.

"Well, that is one option. Hattie what is your opinion?"

I do like what Selena said; but perhaps we go in there like a wolf in sheep's clothing; hiding our club behind our back so to speak."

"Alright, what does this sheep's clothing consist of?"

"How about we put our Army uniforms back on and set up an Army Post, again so to speak. We say the Army has sent us in to restore order;

like Marshal Law?"

"Um, yeah, that would be another option. But perhaps we should be a little more circumspect, you might say. We could save the big club; that is the Army for later. How about we just go in with a wagon; like we're emigrants'?"

"What about the kids? Are we taking them with us?" Selena asked.

"Yes, we say we ran across them on the trail and they were lost and they said that their parents lived in Las Vegas. So, we were just returning them to their parents. But of course, our big stick would be what is in Ruby's wagon; if it was needed."

"Oh, that is a big stick." April said, then added; "who's all going?"

"Selena and Ruby will be in the wagon; the six of us will be outriders; with full armaments."

"Won't that be a little bit contradictory? What emigrants wear bandoliers?" Adin said.

"Well perhaps not many; but we do. I don't want them to think we're push overs; and then we will have to kill them, just because they think we are weak Willys."

"What's a weak Willy, I've never heard that before?" June asked.

"I just made it up; I guess it could mean a weak coward." I said.

Selena turned to the three children; "Come on, I'll help you get your things together and then we will take you home to your parents."

"But, what if they have killed them?" Billie asked.

"Don't worry I'm sure they're all right." I said. And then I turned to Ethel and Myrtle; "While we're gone you two work with Ula and Tillie to boost defensive capabilities around here and don't make them too subtle."

"What do you mean, not too subtle?" Ethel asked.

"I want anybody that thinks they are going to attack us, to know they are in for one hell of a butt whipping."

As Selena was walking out she stopped and said: "What about my leech, can he come too?

I looked at Jose and said: "No, this time you stay here and help the girls with their task; we don't want them to know that we are part of the ranch yet; otherwise you could come because you would be good bait."

"What do you mean by that-good bait?" Jose asked.

"I'm sure Colonel Talent would like to shoot what he thinks is the heir to this land grant. But for some reason Selena thinks you might be worth saving."

Selena looked at me with her face turning red and then followed the children out of the dining room.

Joaquin hadn't said anything while we were discussing the day's events but now he said: "Yes, I think Jose should stay here also; anyway, till it is well known that he is only one of the prospective heirs; perhaps then he won't be bear bait any longer."

Joaquin pushed his tea cup away and then said to me: "Perhaps Senor Matthew it would be a good time now before you leave to go over the paperwork?"

"Yeah, we have some time while the wagon is getting prepared; Hattie you come also; you're smart at this sort of thing." I said as we three retired to the ranch office.

Joaquin knelt before his safe and worked the combination; pulling a leather folder out he sat down at his desk. We sat across from him. He handed us a sheaf of papers; Hattie took a few moments looking them over. She lifted her eyes to Joaquin.

"You will see Senora that I have given your husband fifty one percent of the land grant. And also, you will see the territorial seal from Santa Fe is embossed over my signature. All of this transaction has been filed there."

"Yes, I do see that; but you have only given your son twenty percent when you die; that leaves twenty nine percent?" Hattie said.

"Yes, that is true. I have not yet decided what to do with that. At one time I thought of leaving it to the Church; but of late I have become quite disillusioned with the church and their greedy ways. Perhaps if I marry again, but I do not know."

"Well, you certainly have a lot of good years left to you; why not marry again?" Hattie said.

"Well, we will see. Is the woman Ruby, single?" Joaquin asked with a blush.

"Why yes she is; her husband and children were killed by the Comancheros."

"That is a shame; perhaps she is still mourning them and would not be interested?"

"Well one thing I know about Ruby she is a very level-headed woman and knows what can be changed and what can't. And death, at this time cannot be reversed; and life is for the living. So, give it a shot Joaquin, you have nothing to lose."

Joaquin looked some cheered up at what Hattie had just told him; so we took our leave and went to join the rest of our party; who by the way were waiting for us.

Selena was leaning against the wagon with a cloud on her face. "Do you two know what starting early means?"

Hattie said to her with a sly smile: "Honey if you had a man like mine you would still be in bed."

"That's a bunch of bull; if he was my man I would have had him wore out by mid-night." Selena said.

"Hey, you two I'm standing right here; and you know those children can hear you?" They both clamed up; and they had sheepish looks on their faces. Hattie's brothers were enjoying her discomfort. But they all knew better than to look at Selena; she had a short fuse at times. I thought to myself that she needs a good husband to settle her down; or anyway one who had staying power. I didn't know whether Jose was man enough for her; but I guess we would find out.

Joaquin and Jose were standing there and Selena went over to talk to them; I suppose to tell Jose goodbye. But it looked like she was talking mainly to Joaquin. They both turned their heads when Ruby stepped on the wagon wheel and swung into the wagon seat. And Selena smiled at Joaquin and nodded her head. As she turned to leave she punched Jose on the arm; like a school kid would do with someone they were sweet on.

As Selena got in the wagon the three kids were already in the back. I heard Ruby tell them to keep away from her Gatling gun. I didn't know it was hers, but I guess I did now. I was sure learning a lot about women; one thing was that I didn't know snuff about them....

I really didn't expect any trouble on the trip to Las Vegas; but isn't that usually when the big dog sneaks up behind you and bites you on the butt? So, knowing that fact Hattie and I scouted the trail ahead. Hattie was riding Jasper her mule; Jasper could sense trouble ten miles away, I was sure.

It was a beautiful sunlit day with just a few clouds scudding by. We would be on the Ranch's land for the next hour or so; so logically we should be safe to lollygag around; but I hadn't lived this long by lollygagging. Or even by watching my wife's beautiful derrière bouncing softly in her saddle. We weren't riding on the trail but skirting it; I was on one side and Hattie and Jasper on the other side; we were both about a hundred yards away from the trail in the trees.

I heard a Meadowlark give its distinctive call, I didn't think much of it; but then I remembered that Hattie had fell in love with its song on the trail. Back in Tennessee and Kentucky there weren't any western Meadowlark's around. Hattie had mastered its call; that I did remember.

I cut over the trail and came up behind Hattie; Jasper and she were stopped. Hattie was dismounted and peeking through the underbrush at something.

She looked at me and held her finger to her lips. "Quite." She whispered. "There's a camp about a hundred yards ahead; Jasper alerted me."

"How many?" I asked.

"Don't know for sure, but Jasper said there were three or four; I'm thinking three."

"Alright, we'll leave the mounts here; Jasper can watch my horse. We'll sneak up and see what they are doing here on our land." I said.

"Our land! That sounds good doesn't it?"

"Yeah, I guess, but it means a lot more responsibility than just drifting. But we're getting off the point; right now it looks like we will have to do some fighting just to keep it."

Hattie went back to peeking through the trees and brush. "Hey, it looks like there are three of them alright; but it appears that the one leaning against the tree is tied up; and it looks like a woman."

"Well it's a good thing that Selena isn't with us right now or those other two would be dead with arrows in them. Let's see if we can't take them alive." I whispered to Hattie.

"You know of course it would be a lot easier to just kill them; after all they are trespassing." Hattie whispered back.

"You're kidding, right?"

"Yeah, yeah, I'm kidding, but sometimes I wish I wasn't. Come on I think I see a way we can sneak up on them." Hattie said, sometimes I think Hattie was more Indian than Selena.

Hattie bent low and headed off on a circuitous route. I had no trouble following her; because I couldn't take my eyes off of-you know what. It took a lot of will power to look beyond those buckskins.

I had learned the hard way to move through the trees without making noise; but I wondered how my wife learned to move like that, so when she paused I asked her.

"I told you I used to hunt for meat as a little girl and we were poor and couldn't afford much shot and powder. So, you can put two and two together." I think sometimes my wife thought I wasn't that smart; but come to think about it, I think most wives think their husbands are a little slow at times. It's not that we're slow but we have a hard time keeping up with the female brain. Anyway, she eased her comment by giving me a quick kiss.

What Hattie had seen was an old dry creek bed that ran close to where they were; it had a lot of brush around it and we could belly crawl almost on top of them. They weren't paying much attention to anything besides bedeviling their captive.

One of them was saying: "Well little Momma, you didn't find your kids did you; you know the Indians got them and probably ate them; but don't worry we're not going to eat you; that is not till we're done with you. You think you can steal a horse and get away with it?"

After he said that he bent over and tore the top of her dress exposing one breast, the other man said: "Hey, not till we get something to eat, the bacon is almost done. We'll have more energy to take turns on her." They both laughed and turned their backs on her. She was crying; but she had spirit, her eyes were fighting mad.

Hattie crawled up behind the tree where she was tied. "Don't move or even blink, I'm going to cut the rope; stay still, we'll take care of them, when we start you roll to the side and get behind the tree."

They both were armed with belt guns and they had laid their rifles against a fallen tree close to where the woman was tied; which I thought was a silly thing to do. I always kept my rifle close to hand. The woman never raised an eyebrow when Hattie cut her rope.

Hattie looked at me and mouthed; "stand up together."

Now when we both stood up the men looked at us. Here's where things took a different turn; instead of the woman rolling behind the tree, she reached out and picked one of their rifles and jacked a shell in and shot one of them and then jacked another shell in and shot the other one. She looked at us and said: "I'm not sorry; those two bastards have raped me before." Then she shot them both again and again till the rifle was empty.

I looked at Hattie and said: "Well she saved us some lead anyway; what is your name woman?"

"Geisel Nottingham, they not only have raped me they stole my children and now the Indians have probably killed them." She started crying again.

Hattie put her arm around her and hugged her. "Well we have good news for you; your children are not dead; they are with us and we were just heading to town to reunite them with you and your husband." As Hattie was talking; crashing through the timber was her brothers: Alden and Aiken.

"What the hell went on here?" Alden exclaimed. Geisel was belatedly trying to cover her breast. But it was torn so bad; she gave up on it and glared at the boys. She said: "I shot them and good riddance; and I would do it again but the rifle is empty."

"Hattie said, "She is the kids mom; ride back and stop the wagon and get a shovel and then come back and bury this trash. I'll whistle for Jasper; I think I have a shirt in my saddle bags for Mrs. Nottingham, we'll bring her along and surprise the kids."

"Really? The kids are with you, and, they're not hurt? We all thought the worst when that trash of Sheriff was killed by Indians." She started bawling again.

"Where is your husband? How come you came looking for your kids and not him?" I asked.

"He's in Jail; they are going to hang him tomorrow for stealing a horse. He tried to go looking for them yesterday. I took a horse last night, but those so-called Deputies must have followed me; can I have their badges?"

"I didn't see any badges they must have put them in their pockets." I said. Hattie rolled them over and searched their vest pockets. In fact, she cleaned out all of their pockets and handed everything she found to Gisele. She took the stuff and then asked: "Can I have their guns also?"

"Sure, what do you want them for?" Hattie asked.

"No one is ever going to take advantage of us again. We only had a shotgun; we're farmers not killers; but no more, I will shoot first and ask questions later from now on. You see we are Quakers or should I say we used to be Quakers. No more." She said wiping the last of her tears off of her cheeks. I think a sheep just transformed into a tiger…

Jasper came trotting into camp with my horse following him. Gisele put the shirt over her dress and then packed all of the loot on one of the three horses. Looking at us she said: "Can I have their horses also?"

"I reckon, but someone might ask questions about them." I said.

"Let them ask; it'll be the last question they ever ask." She said. I just nodded. She stood there looking at us; "Who are you people? The way you're dressed it looks like you are prepared to go to war or something."

"No, not war, that is unless someone makes war on us; we're right peaceful folks; most of the time anyway." Hattie said. Then she stepped close to me and whispered: "We can't take her with us to Las Vegas; what if we sent her back to the Hacienda with Selena, Ruby and her children?"

"Yeah, you're right; turning her loose on that town would be wrong at this time."

"I'm glad you agree with me Sweetheart; the six of us can go in and get her husband out of jail."

"Out of jail, just how do you propose to do that?" I asked.

"I don't know, maybe burn the town down." She said with a smile, and then added. "I'm kidding; I wouldn't burn the whole town down, maybe just the jail."

"I have a better idea; why not just ride in and play it by ear?"

"Well of course there is always that; but if worst comes to worst, can we at least think about burning the jail down?"

"What is with you and the fixation of burning the jail down?"

"Not just the jail; I was hoping that maybe we could put that Curtis Talent in the jail and then burn it down. You see I know him; he is completely evil and it would be only logical to burn the Devil in his own flames."

"What in the world did this Talent fellow do to you that makes you hate him so much?"

"Not to me, exactly, but to a friend of mine." Hattie said just as Alden and Aiken got back with the shovel. "I'll tell you later; come on we'll take Gisele to the wagon."

Hattie went to help Gisele mount her horse; she was wearing a dress like I said before, when she swung her leg over her dress rode up- she wasn't wearing any under garments. Hattie had her stand up in the stirrups and then tucked her dress underneath her. Hattie came over to where I was standing and whispered: "She needs a bath."

I gathered the reins up of the other two horses and followed Hattie and Gisele on my horse. I looked back and told Alden and Aiken: "When you get done, we'll be at the wagon waiting for you."

When we got to the wagon they were all standing outside of it waiting for us. When Gisele seen her children, she started to bawl and the crazy look in her eyes disappeared; to be replaced by the joy of seeing her children alive and well. She gathered the three of them in her arms; looking back at Hattie she said: "Thank you, I thought I would never see them again."

Hattie explained things to Selena and Ruby; "take her back and get her cleaned up and fed and keep an eye on her; she killed both of those Deputies and then emptied the rifle into them. Make sure she doesn't get all depressed about killing them, they deserved what they got."

"What are you guys going to do?" Selena asked.

"We're going on to town and get her husband out of jail; we might stay overnight; but if we're not back by tomorrow night, come looking for us." Hattie said.

It sure was nice to have a wife and partner like Hattie; I didn't have to do all of the thinking anymore; not that I was so good at it, mind you. Gisele got in the wagon with the kids. Selena took the reins of the two horses I was trailing and then went to swing up on the horse that Gisele was riding; but she wrinkled her nose and swung up on one of the other two. I looked at Hattie, she just shrugged her shoulders.

The six of us waited till the wagon and Selena turned around on the trail and headed back toward the Hacienda.

"I know a shortcut to Las Vegas that way we won't have to take the main wagon road, since we don't have the wagon with us we can make better time. Also, I have a hunch that they won't be watching this trail. The way the kids were talking they must monitor the main road watching what emigrants that they can hassle." I said.

"Yes, that Curt Talent is evil; as my brothers can testify to; but like all evil men they have one flaw: They think they're smarter than everyone else and will never get caught in their lawless schemes."

"When we get there, I know a little Cantina that we can stop at and get the lay of the land, so to speak. It's run by a man and his family that know me. I did a few favors for them one time. Besides, the food there is great." I said.

The land grant lay between the Gallinas River and the Conchas River and was well watered by tributaries of both rivers. We didn't have to cross the Gallinas River to get to Las Vegas; we would come in from the southwest; as such we would stay off of the main wagon roads leading from Santa Fe and the one coming in from the east.

We came across large herds of Elk who just looked at us and went back to grazing. All of the wildlife was the same; including herds of Deer and a Griz or two. Their conduct was synonymous of not being hunted.

We sat looking down on the town. I took my Army issued filed glasses out of my saddle bags and took a closer look. I was right about the road being watched. I could see that they had some wagons stopped that were coming in from the east. Probably trying to exact a toll from them; if the wagon master knew his salt he would put the run on them. I could count about twenty wagons; more than enough to protect themselves. A wagon coming in by its lonesome wouldn't stand a chance; that's what probably happened to the Nottinghams.

"Look there on the edge of town; you can see the Cantina I was talking about. There are corrals as well as a barn where we can get our horses out of sight. Senor Paco Delgado and his family owns the business and land; last time I was here he had six children; but no doubt he has many more by now. There is a back door to the Cantina that leads to the barn and corrals; that's where we will head for."

We took a circuitous route so no one from town seen us rein up by hitching rack in back of the Cantina; that is all except the young man that was forking manure out of the barn. He stopped working when we rode in; I motioned him over. "Do you speak English?" I asked him in Spanish.

"Si Senor I do."

"Does Senor Delgado still own the Cantina?"

"Si, he is my father, do you know him?"

"Yes, Paco is a friend of mine. Would you see to our horses; perhaps some oats or corn and then keep them out of sight. What is your name?"

"Alfonso, may I ask why all of you are so well armed?"

"Yes, you may ask, no harm in that." I said, as we handed him the reins and I winked at him and then we left him with a confused look on his face.

He was right; we were better armed than most; all six of us wore two pistols as well as we had our Henry Rifles and our crossed bandoliers. And of course, our Bowie Knives.

We stopped just inside the door and let our eyes grow accustomed to the inside light. Of course, everyone turned to look at us. Paco was tending the bar; at first you could see the fear in his eyes; then he recognized me- "Senor Bodeen," he exclaimed, "welcome, it's been years; I heard you were killed in the war; but I see that you are very much alive and that makes me very happy."

"Come, all of you are hungry of course, set over there at the big table." He said, and then called for Rosetta to wait on us. The table was a good choice, we could see both the front door as well the back door; and our backs were to the wall. Paco came over with a coffee pot and filled our cups.

"You don't know how glad I am to see you Senor Bodeen, there is much trouble. We heard that the Don had sent for you; how long can you stay?" Paco asked.

"Well Paco, it looks like we are here to stay; this is my wife Hattie May, and this is Aiken and April and this is Alden and June. The boys are Hattie's brothers and their wives."

"Oh, I am very happy to hear that Senor Bodeen; things are so bad that I can't let my daughters even go downtown."

"Please call me Matt; I always considered you a friend Paco. Tell me who is running things in Las Vegas now?"

"A gringo named Talent came to town a few months ago and started to buy up whatever he could; if they didn't want to sell he scares their customers. The only ones that come here are the Navajo and the Latinos like me. There was a Sheriff named Simple, but he was killed by Indians, they say he was scalped. He was a very bad man also; he liked to hurt people."

We were interrupted by Rosetta and her sisters bringing large platters of enchiladas and frijoles' and rice. It had been so long since I had good Mexican food that I thought I had died and gone to heaven. Of course, I didn't believe in heaven, like the Church tried to tell everyone, but that's another story. I sorta liked it here on earth…

After we had licked the platter clean Paco came back over and sat down. "So, Paco, is the jail still in the same place?"

"Why yes, they use it to keep innocent ones in; the bad ones walk around free. Right now, they have a poor man in there; no one has seen his wife and children for three or four days."

"We have the wife and children; they are safe at the Ranchero. We have come to get Mr. Nottingham. Do they keep a guard at the jail?"

"Yes, usually one or two men; there are about twenty or so bad men hanging around altogether."

"Well, right now we are just after the one man; but we will try and whittle the odds down on those twenty plus bad men. Don't worry Paco we have every intention of making Las Vegas a nice place to work and live in; where everyone will feel safe. Do you mind if we hang around here till after dark?"

The cantina didn't start to get busy till around 7 that evening. Like Paco said it was mostly Navajo and Mexicans. I said mostly because I counted us Gringos in the total. We got a lot of stares. But there wasn't any unfriendliness'; in fact most of them came over and introduced themselves and told us how happy they were to have us there. Of course, just like Paco, they knew that the Don had sent for us; well maybe not the whole bunch of us, but me anyway.

It was full dark now; so I got up and went to the back door and looked out. The moon wasn't up yet; which was good because I figured we would leave the horses here and go on foot. We had all brought our moccasins; they were in our saddlebags.

Paco was at our table when I got back. "Paco, we are going to leave our horses here till we get back from the jail, would you make sure they are ready to go, you know all saddled with their cinches tight. We might be in a little hurry. And oh yeah, just in case could we borrow a horse and saddle. I might bring one with us from the jail for Mr. Nottingham to ride, but I don't know for sure."

Si Senor Bodeen, no problemo. Do you want some food to take with you?"

"Yes, I suppose that would be a good idea; and would you put fresh water in our canteens?" I dug in my pocket and gave him a twenty-dollar gold piece and then on second thought gave him another one.

"Oh, that's too much Senor Bodeen." Paco said.

"No, it's not, and please call me Matt, Paco; I don't think you have been taking in many Pesos with that bunch around here; but don't worry I think things will be getting back to normal pretty soon."

"Si` Senor Matt, with you here now we all have much hope."

"Well, have faith Paco; it will happen." I told him as we went out the door. You see Hope is the precursor to Faith; and faith is the assured expectation of things hoped for, and it's the evident demonstration of realities though not beheld. Of course, there are always those who say 'if I can't see it; it ain't real.' I sort of feel sorry for those type of people; because they lack imagination. And believe me most of the time my imagination is a lot more fun than reality.

And what we were about to do this night was real; and we couldn't afford to be caught gathering wool right now. All of the saloons in the main part of town were doing a bang-up business; or at least it sounded like it. We skirted around them; keeping to the shadows.

When we got close to the jail we could see there was a lamp burning through the window. I stopped and we had a little confab: "I don't know what you all have in mind; but I was thinking that maybe you five could spread out and keep an eye out for anybody that might come this way; while I look through that window and see who is all in there. And then if nobody is there, or say just one of them, you all could watch my back as I go in and get Mr. Nottingham."

"Oh, you want us to stand around and you go in and have all of the fun? I don't think so; what if the three of us girls go in and get Mr. Nottingham and you three watch our backs?" Hattie said.

I gave it some thought and said: "Alright, but first let's look in the window and if there is only one or maybe two in there then you three hell raisers can do the deed."

Hattie and I crept forward and looked in the window. We were in luck, you might say, because I really didn't believe in luck, just chance and circumstance. Anyway, there was only one and he was asleep at the desk. Hattie was looking all around the office; and she pointed to the wall behind the desk; there was a set of keys hanging on a nail. We stepped away from the window.

"I think I can sneak in there and get those keys without waking him up. But just in case you come along in there and watch my back." Hattie said to June and April.

He wasn't asleep, he was drunk and passed out; they just walked up and got the keys and unlocked the cell door. "Who are you?" Nottingham asked.

"Quiet, come on if you want to see your wife and children." Hattie told him and then locked the cell door again and hung the keys back on the nail.

When they got outside I explained who we were; he nodded his head and said: "But they have my wagon and all our stuff, even our horses and my guns, I need my guns so I can kill that Bastard." He was starting to get worked up so I gave him a little tap on his head and knocked him out; Alden and Aiken picked him up and we started back to the Cantina.

"He was just coming to when we got back. "Wha, what happened, who hit me?"

"I did, you were making a fuss; you have to be quiet. Have you eaten supper?"

"No, they only feed me once a day. Did you say you were taking me to my wife and children? How is she, is she alright? And my children, I haven't seen them in days."

"Take it easy, they're fine now, we'll get some food for you and then we will ride most of the night to get home."

It took us only a few minutes to get some food for him; Paco's son Alfonso had a horse all saddled for Nottingham. I didn't know his first name, so I asked: "Lafayette," he said, then added: "Everyone calls me Lafe."

"How come an Englishman has a French name?" June asked him.

"My mother was French, but I don't answer to it. I was in the British Army, a Major I was. And if you would supply me with firearms

I will kill that Bastard, Talent I believe his name is."

"Slow down, we'll take care of him later, now's not the time." Hattie told him. "Now we have to get going, we don't want anyone to know we were here, yet that is." She added.

Like I said, it was dark and it would be a little trouble following the trail. But Hattie had Jasper, so we just let her take the lead and I would ride drag. Some people didn't like to ride at night; but I always enjoyed it, different it was. The shadows played tag with the spirits of the night. And it was up to you to figure out who was who. Of course, if you had a spooky horse it wasn't too much fun if they spooked at every little imaginary monster. But we had all trail wise horses; about the only thing that would spook them was a Mountain Lion or a Bear or a Wraith, I've seen a few of them, a might scary they were. If you see one of those you had better get to praying to the Almighty and then those Wraiths will leave you alone; they were scared of the Almighty.

We didn't have much to do but let the horses follow the leader. Now me, I always preferred to ride drag, that is in back of everyone; why? Because then I could see that they were alright; if I was riding point I would have to be turning around in my saddle to check on them. Yeah, there was another reason also; I had been up and over many the mountain and if anyone was going to pick anyone off they would more than likely pick off the straggler or the last in line. And me being me, I sort of felt responsible for every one of my family members; after all it was due to me that they were here anyway.

The moon was full and looked like you could almost touch it. I could see Hattie up ahead and she was letting Jasper set the pace; but she was turning around in her saddle and looking back along the line; I guess we sort of thought alike, or maybe it's like the Bible said: we had become one flesh....

Lafe was riding right in front of me and you could sure tell he used to be in the British Army; his back was ramrod straight; but he still sat a good saddle. But like a lot of those that were coming west in their straight-laced ways clashed with the reality of the frontier. One reason was that they expected everyone to be civilized; and I think that was a few years off yet.

After three hours on the trail Hattie called a stop so we all could take a break and eat something. The horses also took advantage of the lush grass that grew alongside of the small stream.

Hattie, June and April walked a few paces away and pulled down their buckskins and watered the lilies so to speak. Lafe looked at them and said: "Well I never seen anything like that; don't they have any decency?"

"Yep, they do, but common sense overrules decency at times; we are in wild country and those shadows are deep and I would advise you to not go very far when you relieve yourself." I told Lafe as I stepped behind my horse and did my duty.

The moon went behind a cloud and just at that time a Mountain Lion decided to let the moon hear his displeasure at being disturbed by our presence. If you have ever heard a mountain lion scream in the dead of night then you know what effect it had on Mr. Lafe Nottingham.

"What was that? Was that a woman screaming?" He asked with a tremble in his voice.

"Nope, it was a mountain lion and that is why you stick close to do your business. By the sound of him we disturbed his hunting. Don't worry though; he won't bother us, because there are too many of us. But if you had wondered off too far from the group you would be a snack for him."

When we got back on the trail, he was a little different man; he wasn't sitting up so straight. Of course, it could have been that he was just a little tired. It was a funny thing about life on the frontier; it could either beat you down to a frazzle or it could refine the impurities out of you and make you a man. A lot of prideful men left the west with their tail between their legs. And then again, a lot of them that looked like they didn't have in starch in their backbone became men that other men looked up to. I guess the jury was still out on Mr. Lafe Nottingham.

When we got back to the Santiago Land Grant we found Selena setting beside a small campfire waiting for us.

"You're right on time, almost; maybe a half hour late." She said.

"How did you know when we would be getting back?" Hattie asked her.

"I dreamt it; so I got up and rode out here to see if it was true."

"What exactly did you dream?" I asked.

"That I was setting by this campfire when you all came along...It was a good thing I had that dream because there were some way layers waiting to ambush you all. I killed one of them; the rest run off."

"What did you do with the body?"

"I tied him to his horse and sent him on his way to hell."

"Any ideas where they come from?"

"I suppose they were some of that bunch from town; I don't think they were waiting for you exactly, but just anyone from the ranchero."

"Oh yeah, Selena this is Gisele's husband. Lafe this is Selena, she is one of us."

"What do you mean one of you?"

"Just that, she is one of us and we are one of her; or I guess you could say a member of the body."

Hattie whispered: "What the hell does that mean?"

"Well, do you have a better answer?"

"I guess not, we sort of belong to each other now. Birds of a feather, I guess."

It was still a couple of hours before dawn when we rode into the Hacienda's yard. Juan and Pedro were waiting for us.

Juan said: "We were just about to ride out looking for the Senorita; she said if she wasn't back before dawn to come looking for her."

"Thank you, Juan, Pedro but as you see, we are back. Perhaps you can take Senor Nottingham to where his wife and children are sleeping?" Selena said.

"Of course, Senorita and then we will take care of the horses." Pedro said.

When Hattie and I got back to our rooms I started to undress, but Hattie said: "Not so fast, we're not getting in that bed without taking a bath; come on grab a towel and we'll take a dip in that warm spring by the creek."

"But, what if anyone sees us?"

"Don't worry, they are all asleep; and anyway, what are you a prude?"

"No, well maybe at times; but I do think we need a bath."

"Good, but let's leave our clothes here and just wrap our towels around us; we'll be back before you know it." Hattie said as she dropped her buckskins to the floor.

We left by the side door where the path to creek was. The path was worn smooth with no stones to bruise bare feet. And there was no one there; as per what Hattie said. We hung our towels on a bare branch and stepped in the lukewarm water. It sure felt soothing on our sore muscles.

There was some kind of minerals in the water that helped one to float without any trouble at all. Hattie was floating beside me when we heard: "Hey, do you mind if I join the two of you?" I hurriedly let myself sink below the surface.

"No, not at all; the more the merry I guess." Hattie said to Selena. The moon was still up and also the stars seemed brighter than usual. So, Selena stood out in bold relief, as she hung her towel beside ours.

"I seen you two leave the hacienda, so I thought I would join you. Besides I wanted to talk to the both of you." She said as she waded in till those puppies were floating by their selves.

I stood up and pulled Hattie over in front of me. Why did I pull my wife over in front of me? Really, you don't know....?

"What I wanted to talk about was Jose, what am I supposed to do about him?"

"What do you mean? Has he been bothering you?" Hattie asked.

"No, not in that way; but he said he wants to marry me. But I'm not sure about him; he seems a little immature at times; and when I get married I want a husband I don't have to raise up to be a man. I want a husband like you have Hattie." Selena said as she looked at me.

"Even though he's hiding behind you right now; and yes, I know why, but I don't see why he's self-conscious about it; it's a perfectly normal reaction to two naked women. In fact, if he wasn't having one of those then there would be something wrong with him."

"Well you can be sure there's nothing wrong with him. But to your problem, I think what you should tell Jose is that he has to court you; with flowers and the whole bit. Just like you were a fancy Senorita in Spain." Hattie told her.

"But I'm not one of those, I prefer buckskins and such."

"Yeah, I know; but why not get yourself some skirts and blouses and fix your hair like you were one of those. I'm sure some of the girls around here would help you."

"But where would I carry my guns and knives?"

"You can strap your knife to your thigh and also that little .32 to the other thigh. That should be plenty of protection around the hacienda. And when we go somewhere else you can change back into your buckskins. How would that be?"

"What about my bow and arrows? Can I keep them with me?"

"Well, you could stash them somewhere you could get them quick in an emergency. How many bows do you have?"

"You mean besides the one I brought with me tonight?"

"Yes, of course. If you have more you could stash them in different places."

"I have four more in the wagon; plus, about one hundred arrows. Yes, I see where that could work. How long is he supposed to court me?"

"Till you fall in love with him or get tired of him; it's your choice."

"How long did Matthew court you?"

"Uh, we didn't exactly court; maybe one minute or less. I rode up on Jasper and we took one look and fell in love. And we're still in love and will stay that way; that is if he stops jabbing me with that thing."

"Hey it's not my fault, you keep moving around when you gesture with your hands; fact is I'm going back to our room and you two can finish this conversation." I said, and then went around them and got out and dried myself off and I didn't care if they were looking. And they were, because Selena gave a low whistle and Hattie said: "Hey don't do that, his ego is big enough anyway."

As I made my way back to our room dawn was just starting to break in the east. I hadn't realized how tired I was, that is till I had soaked in that warm spring water. The towel kept slipping down so I just tossed it over my shoulder as I groggily walked to the room. I just threw the towel on the floor and flopped on our big bed and fell instantly asleep.

I woke up hours later with my wife draped over me. I pushed her hair back from in front of her eyes and gave her a kiss on her beautiful nose.

"Hi honey," she said as she slowly came awake. "How did you sleep?" She asked me. "Fine, how did you sleep?" I asked her back. She just kissed me and snuggled closer.

"I slept fine too, that is if anyone cares." The voice was coming from the other side of Hattie.

I raised my head and looked over Hattie; Selena was lying there, naked as a Jay Bird; just like Hattie and I were. I dropped back and looked at my wife.

"Oh, don't get your nose all bent out of joint; the Nottinghams took over her room for the night; we'll make different arrangements for tonight. I don't see why you're so upset; you are the one who paraded through the halls naked in front of all of the servant girls."

"What? I didn't see anyone last night."

"Well they seen you, it's no big deal, but they sure thought it was and for the life of me I can't see why." Selena said as she got up and pulled a dress over her head and stomped out.

"Come on get dressed I think we'll be in time for the noon meal, I'm starving." Hattie said as she reached down and pulled me out of bed.

"What's wrong with Selena, she seemed mad?" I asked.

"Oh, she just needs her own man, she's getting that itch, and you know how it is."

"Yeah, I reckon; I remember how it was with me the first time I seen you ride in on Jasper."

"Yeah, well you weren't alone on that; but right now I'm starving." Hattie said as she pulled a gaily colored blouse and skirt on; neither Selena nor Hattie had bothered putting on any under garments. But I did, and as a consequence they were already eating when I got there. In between bites Hattie was busy answering questions about our trip to Las Vegas and back. I kept my mouth shut; being a teacher Hattie could spin a tale better than Charles Dickins, I do believe.

Joaquin turned to me and asked: "So Matthew what happens now?"

"Now I think we have to concentrate on securing our borders; you might say. We need to put scouts out to let us know if anyone is trying to squat on our property. And also, we need to tighten our efforts on defending the hacienda; you never know they might even try and attack us, thinking they can kill you with one quick strike. Not knowing that we are even here."

"But," Hattie said, "that isn't all we need to do; Matthew and us, have been discussing the fact that 'offense is the best defense.' Of course, we have yet to solidify our strategy; and we are open to suggestions."

"Uh, yes that is right; but instead of just blurting your idea out why not just write it down and give it to Selena and she will share it with the six of us and then we will let Senor Santiago have the deciding vote." I said while looking around the table.

I let all of the hubbub settle down and then I said: "On the defense of the hacienda I think Ricardo Sanchez and Private Ula and Sergeant Tillie can see to that; also, Ricardo can be the one to send out scouts periodically. And Jose you can be the overseer to make sure it's done." I looked at Jose, he had a big grin on his face; I hoped that I had not created a monster.

One thing that I had learned while in the Army; a good officer shares the load. I didn't see any reason why that wouldn't work here. Also, responsibility builds character. Give a man a job to do and he will rise to the occasion. At least I found that true most of the time....

I noticed when we left the dining room that Jose had run over to Selena and was bending her ear. That was good I guess; because Selena would keep him in line. I motioned for Alden and Akin with their wives to follow us, they did.

We stopped under a big Ponderosa Pine tree; "What's up?" April asked.

"Well I just wanted to find out what you'all were thinking we should do now?"

"I don't understand; you're actually asking for our input?" June said.

"Well sure, we're all in this together. But I think I do understand that I've been sort of been making most of the decisions. Anyway, any thoughts?"

"Uh, yeah, you've looked at the map of this land grant; just how big is it anyway?" Alden asked.

"About as well as I can figure it's about a hundred and twenty square miles. Why what did you have in mind?" I asked, while checking their mood.

"Well," Akin spoke up. "Are we going to sort of get some of that land to make a ranch of our own?" I looked at Hattie and nodded; in essence putting her under the gun.

"Yes, that's the long-range plan; it wouldn't hurt if we started to scout out the whole land grant; but it all hinges on fighting to keep this land whole and intact. I believe when it's all said and done we all will have earned some land of our own."

I was some proud of Hattie the way she laid it out; that you had to fight to earn the land. Free is fine; but free is easy come easy go; if you have to work for something you appreciate it and will take care of it. I do believe we had a fight coming. Not just a physical fight but a legal one. And on that point, I knew we had to make a trip into Santa Fe; to the territorial courthouse.

We had no more than finished our conversation when Pedro rode up in a lather and hopped off his horse; "Senor Bodeen there are some squatters on our land." He said.

"Alright, take it easy and tell us about them; where and how many?"

"Over by the Gallinas River Senor; there are three wagons with women and children. But also, many armed men."

"How long have they been there?" Hattie asked Pedro.

"Not long, I think Senora, perhaps just a few days."

"Where is your sidekick, Juan?" I asked.

"He stays, to watch them; I tell him I go get you."

"Alright, go get yourself some food and then gather up a few more men to go with us; also pack some food on a pack horse; we might stay out longer than overnight."

Selena had seen Pedro ride in and she came over while we were still talking. "I'm going along also, don't try and stop me." She said glaring at me.

"Who put a burr under your saddle; I didn't say you couldn't go. We all need to get our gear and change into our buckskins." I said, and then whispered to Hattie; "What's wrong with her?"

"You haven't noticed how every time it gets close to her time of the month she gets this way; just walk easy around her, she'll be alright."

"Well, she isn't just going to start killing people, willy-nilly is she?"

"No, of course not, she's always selective." Hattie said with an evil grin. And that made me wonder if she wasn't in the same condition. And again, that made me wonder if that condition wasn't catching or something?

Pedro had gathered up eighteen men along with three pack horses with food and such on them. So, that made a total of twenty-seven; counting Pedro and Juan and the seven of us.

Hattie looked at all of them and said: "Do we need this many men? Isn't it sort of overkill?"

"Yeah, I didn't know he was going to get that many men; but who knows; we might just need them." I said.

Selena rode up; she had her bow and a quiver full of arrows. I noticed that the arrows were the Comanche ones that she had liberated. Of course, she had her Henry Golden Boy plus twin .45's around her hips. We all had that and more of course; not the arrows, she was the only one that could hit the broad side of a barn with arrows anyway.

"That Jose wanted to go also; but I told him he had a job here to do and that he had better make sure he did it or he would answer to me..." Selena said, as she pulled her Bowie Knife out and checked to make sure it was razor sharp. I pity the fool that got on the wrong side of her...

Selena had an accent; a cross between Indian, Spanish, French, English. All I knew was that it could be alluring or deadly; depending on her mood. She scared the living daylights out of me at times.

I had Pedro take the lead; since he knew where we were going. Selena rode with him. Hattie and I dropped to the back of our little column. The sun was hanging at around two in the afternoon.

"Do you have any idea what you are going to do with those squatters?" Hattie asked.

"No, not really, that is till we get there and see how many and who. If they are really emigrants it's one thing, but if they are some of Talent's men then it's another." I said.

The shadows were reaching into the next day when we got there. We had stopped well back from where Juan was watching on a hill overlooking their camp. We had about a half hour of light left when Pedro, Selena, Hattie and I crawled up beside Juan.

Juan looked at me and said: "There is something not quite right about those women, Senor Bodeen. They not move like women; they walk like men. Also, I think there be a lot more men back in those trees."

I had brought my filed glasses. He was right, they were men in women's dresses; and the children were not children; I had seen dwarfs before and that is what the small ones were; there were two of them. I glassed the trees and Juan was right. Altogether there were at least thirty men down there.

"It's a trap, they are just waiting for us to show up and tell them to move on and then kill us from ambush." I said.

"So then, what do you have in mind?" Selena asked.

"Right now, we're going to fall back and have a cold supper and then as it gets full dark we're going to even the odds."

It was full dark with just a sliver of a moon with a few clouds. I had a plan in mind; but you know how that goes when you four headstrong women in the party.

"We need one man to take the pack horses back about a mile and make camp; Pedro you can pick the man for that. Alden, Akin and your wives along with seventeen men will circle the area of their camp; but stay back at least two hundred yards. Pedro and Juan will take their original positions on the hill. Hattie, Selena and I will infiltrate the wooded area and take the ones hiding there out of the picture. If any escape it will be up to the outer circle to make sure they don't escape; I don't want anyone to get back to town. After we get that done we will pull the circle tight around their throats. Any questions?"

"So, you think it will be just that simple huh? And then what do you mean pull the circle tight?" April asked.

"No, it's never that simple; but that's why you all have a brain; you might have to use it. What I mean about the circle is: we'll press into their camp from all sides at once. So, don't shoot unless you have a sure target; use your knife or a tree limb." I said.

"Uh, honey can I make a suggestion?" Hattie asked.

"Sure, I'm open to anything."

"Well why don't we wait till morning on pulling the circle tight on the camp itself? They won't be going anywhere we have them boxed; that way we won't be taking a chance on any one of us shooting one of us. And also, that way they can surrender if they want to."

"Yeah, that does sound good. I guess I was thinking about war tactics. Some of the people may be there against their will. But those in the woods are just there to kill anyone from our outfit; but you know what? I just had a Timberline moment."

"You remember I told you about them? Anyway, maybe they're not just there to kill us; we don't know for sure. Getting back to Timberline; we have a decision to make on what path we're going to take; become callous killers or only kill when there is no other choice."

"Well honey isn't that what we've been doing; only kill when they shoot first?"

"Yeah, more or less; but maybe sometimes I get a little trigger happy; it's been worrying me. Do you know how many men I've killed since I left home at 14?"

"Are you counting those you killed while in the Army?"

"They were men, too weren't they? But yes, I know how many and they all hunt me in my dreams at times."

"Yes, I know what you mean; my numbers have been adding up also. But they have all been very bad men and have deserved what they got." Hattie said.

"Yes, yours have, but in the civil war they weren't. Some of them might have been cousins, or even brothers. Or even went to the same Church that I may have attended. It just wasn't right; even though it did set the slaves free-which was good."

"Alright, you've made your point; we'll try to think more before we shoot; but remember to know your enemy is your enemy and they will shoot before putting much thought into it." Hattie said.

"Say, Hattie, didn't you say that Jasper could more or less understand what you were saying? I asked her.

"Yeah, so what do you have in mind?"

"Well, when the three of us, you and I plus Selena get in that timber back there; do you think that you could talk Jasper to go in there with us and sort of, be our eyes and ears, it's going to be very dark and he could warn us where they are hiding.

"I have been listening to what you two have been saying; I'll tell you one thing I will not let any one of them Sons of Bitches get the first shot; they are all cut out of the same cloth; and that's raping, killing children, murder, you name it; they all deserve to die." Selena said and then stomped off to get her horse.

"What the hell got into her?" I asked Hattie.

"I'll tell you later, but if you had been in her moccasins you'd be just like her."

142

"I'll take your word for that; did you talk to Jasper?"

"Yes, I think he understands; but he did have a wicked smile on his face." Hattie said, and then added: "He doesn't want to be saddled, so I'll ride one of the other horses."

"You do know that he's not human, don't you?"

"Yes, smart ass, I know that because he's smarter than the average human, because he doesn't talk back." I took the hint and kept my mouth shut.

It must have been close to mid-night when the four of us started to infiltrate the timber in back of their camp; Jasper went in first with the three of us following on foot; we had tied the horses far enough away so their stomping and snorting wouldn't tip them off.

There was a moon coming on to full that played tag with the clouds that gave us just enough light to see where Jasper was from time to time. We would hear a thump and then Jasper would come back and find us and we would go and tie his victims up. They were in four different spots in a semi-circle that would have given them a clear shot at us that is if we were stupid enough to approach the main camp in the daylight. Their intent was definitely murderous; we could hardly carry all of the guns and ammunition that they had.

Jasper had an artful kick; all six of them were still breathing when we left; most times if you got kicked in the head by a Mule it would kill you…We got back to our camp in time enough to get a little sleep before dawn.

It was just breaking dawn when I walked my horse to the timbers edge at their camp. I sat there watching them getting up and starting to make breakfast. No one took any note of me and my Morgan horse setting there quietly watching them. I had my rifle ready just in case one of them done something stupid.

Hattie and Selena were on either side of me; but back in the timber enough they couldn't be seen. The rest of our party was in a Simi-circle ringing their camp. I must have set there ten minutes before anyone noticed me.

"Who the hell are you?" One of the men dressed as a woman said.

"I could be the angel of death or the angel of mercy; depending on you. You see you all are on private property and building a cabin like you think it belongs to you. No need for you to look for any help from those six you had back there in the timber to ambush us we took care of them last night."

"You must be crazy just one man; I don't see anyone else to help you." The fellow said, as they spread out like they were going to take me on. But then Hattie and Selena showed themselves along with rest of us.

"Just drop all of your weapons in a pile there in the middle by the campfire." I said. Why does there always have to be just one stupid one? The one I was talking to brought his rifle up to shoot me…Selena put an arrow through his throat. I was hoping to get this business taken care of without killing anybody.

"Alright does anyone else want to die?" I asked, they didn't. "Just load everything in your wagons; including the dead one and those that are tied up in the timber there. Leave all of your weapons and ammunition and tell that Talent fellow if he sends anymore claim jumpers on our land that I will come after him and hang him to that big oak tree in the middle of town."

Selena rode her horse over where her arrow had passed through his throat and picked up her arrow. And then tossed it in the fire; she looked at me and said: "We don't want them to know that the Comanche arrow came from us, do we?"

We sat our horses watching them do as they were told. Now if looks could kill we all would be dead; just before they left one of them asked, "Who should we say that you are?"

"The owners of the Santiago Land Grant, is all that you need to know; now get and don't let me ever see your faces in this territory again; I have a good memory."

I had Juan follow them till they left our land. The rest of us buried the fire and threw dirt over the blood stains. They had almost finished the cabin; I was thinking it might make a good line shack when all of this was settled and in the past.

We went back to our camp and cooked up some breakfast; while I was eating I was thinking, sort of. Hattie noticed that I was distracted and asked me: "What's on your mind?"

"Well I was thinking that is always best to get ahead of trouble before it bites you in the butt; what do you think about you and me riding up to Fort Union and having a confab with the commander. I was thinking of maybe having a detachment of troops stationed in Las Vegas; maybe declaring Martial Law for a spell. What do you think?"

"Yeah, I think you're right. It's long overdue; that jerk Talent has been taking the law into his own hands too long; killing, raping, kidnapping, stealing, etc. We could leave from here; we could take one of the pack horses with food and needful's with us. Selena and my brothers could take care of everything back at the Hacienda."

"Yeah, but you had better talk to Selena; knowing her she would want to go with us. Also we had better include my brothers in that conversation." Hattie had just finished saying that when all of them came up to us.

"Just the people we were talking about; we wanted to let you know that Hattie and I are riding up to Fort Union to see if we couldn't get a detachment of troops to declare martial law in Las Vegas. And before any of you say that you want to go with us, we need all five of you to stay home and take care of the home front. Just in case anything happens to us; Selena you should marry Jose, that will secure you a share in the land grant. And of course, Alden and Akin, you will inherit Hattie's and my share." Selena started to protest, but I shut her down:

"Another reason we want you to stay Selena is that you are a leader and as that is true you will have to take the lead; of course, along with you four." I said indicating them.

"How long do you think you'll be gone?" Alden asked.

"I would think it shouldn't take over a couple of weeks at the most." I said.

"Two weeks; why so long?" Selena asked.

"You know how the Army is; everything in triplicate. Besides we may have to go with the detachment that goes to Las Vegas and get everything set up." I said as Selena came up close to us and in a lower voice said:

"I'll tell you one thing and that's for sure if you're not back in two weeks I'm coming to find the two of you and you had better hope you're dead when I do find you or there will hell to pay." Selena said as she stomped off and got on her horse.

"Umm, what is she trying to say?" I asked Hattie.

"Maybe that we're going to hell?" Hattie said.

"Well, I don't believe in those Bible Thumpers so called version of hell; so I don't have to worry about that." I said.

"Yeah", Hattie said, "if even there were a hell, I don't figure I'm that bad; or take for instance their version of heaven, I'm not that holy to be going there either; so, I figure I'll just stay right here on earth."

"I'm with you sweetheart; I'll stay right here with you." I said, as I tightened the cinch on my horse's saddle. We both mounted up and along with our packhorse we hit the trail.

The trail I took was an old Anasazi trail that I had found years earlier that bypassed not only Las Vegas but also La Junta and took us within a mile of Fort Union. Hattie asked me how I found this trail. I explained how a Navajo friend of mine showed it to me.

"Navajo? Where are they now? I have heard of them of course; but isn't this their land north of here? And for that matter who are the Anasazi?"

"The Indians of today call them the old people and as far as to where they are you can blame that illiterate Colonel Kit Carson; well really he was just the tool the Dept. of the Interior used."

"You see the Army couldn't defeat them by regular means so they destroyed all of their crops, land and sheep herds in order to starve them to defeat. They even killed their horses. Finally, in January 1864 they cornered them in their sacred Canyon de Chelly. To make a long story short they starved them into submission and first they took them to Fort Defiance in Arizona where they were fed little and clothed less; but that wasn't the worst of it all because in March they were marched three hundred miles across mountains and deserts to Bosque Redondo which is 180 miles southwest of Santa Fe."

We rode for aways while she thought about what I told her. Then I added: "But that isn't the worst of it. I hear conditions there are worse than you can believe. I've been talking to Grant about it, but so far he can't get anything done; but he told me he hasn't given up. All of the Indians are getting a bad deal I think."

"Of course, they are; but I'm not going to let them kill me just because I feel sorry for them and at the same time I'm not going to kill them for no reason; like some people do." Hattie said.

"I never have either; I believe all people were put on the earth by the creator and as such basically are brothers and sisters. But the greater number have forgotten and consequently turned into animals; and at the slightest provocation will turn and tear each other apart." I said.

We rode for aways in silence; or mostly in silence anyway; Hattie was moving around in her saddle like she was uncomfortable. "What's wrong?" I asked her.

"I think I'm getting a blister on my butt, or something, is there a place we can stop and take a bath?" She asked.

"Yes, I remember a spring on the Conchas; it's not too far from where we were on the Gallinas; do you think you can make it?"

"Yeah, maybe, do you think it could be a tick?"

"Hell, I don't know; but when we get there we'll check each other for ticks." I said, as I gigged up my horse into a fast trot. The land we were on was still in the Land Grant; wild life was abundant and could be seen looking at us as we passed by. The terrain was hilly with Ponderosa Pine and grass belly high to a tall horse.

It didn't take too long to reach the spring on the Conchas, maybe an hour. Hattie was standing in her stirrups trying to keep her hinny from touching the saddle. It was starting to worry me.

The spring was well hidden in the trees about fifty feet from the river. Hattie jumped off Jasper and ran for the spring; while shedding her clothes. I told Jasper to keep a watch out for anything that would happen by. I tied my horse and the pack horse to a tree; of course, Jasper didn't need tied; he wouldn't get too far from Hattie.

Hattie was totally nude by the time I got to her. She turned her back side to me and said: "What do you see? How many ticks are there?"

"Bend over and let me look." I said, as I gave her the once over. "I don't see any back here, turn around and let me look in front." Ticks were notorious for hiding in dark warm places; so, I checked under her breasts and armpits first, then I moved down… "Spread your legs so I can check there." I said; as I knelt down to get a better view.

"I don't see any; uh, is it alright if I check the crevasses?" I asked her while slowing glancing up across her beautiful belly to her full breasts. She was smiling!

"Please do, and take your time doing it." She said. What did she mean by that?

I looked back down and checked through her triangle; no ticks there so I moved down a little bit more and checked between the folds of skin. "Oh yes, there that's it, you've found it, finally, I didn't think you ever would; keep rubbing till I tell you to stop." So, I did.

As we were soaking in the warm spring she gave me a kiss and said: "I didn't mean to trick you like that; but there is more to love making than just inter-course. I was hoping you would find it on your own; but you never did."

"Well, you know I never had much experience with women, I told you that; you should have said something before. If there is anything else I should know be sure and teach me?"

"Oh, you may be sure I will sweetheart; as soon as we get home."

"How come you know so much about love making?"

"I'm a woman, and women talk to each other."

"Who? Selena perhaps?"

"Among others; my Mother gave me a talk when I turned thirteen; I thought it was all gross at that time; little did I know how much fun it would turn out to be. Do you want anything more or should we get dressed and hit the trail?" Hattie said.

I told her I could wait; but Hattie had found a tick on me; so, I guess it was a good thing she was so horny… We tightened the cinches on Jasper and my Morgan Horse, also on the horse that we were using for a pack horse. When you're using a pack horse it is always best to keep a watch on how tight the cinch is anyway. I've seen some guys that paid no attention and ended up scattering their plunder all over the trail.

"Will we make to the Fort tonight?" Hattie asked.

"No, I don't want to reach there all tired out. I figured we'd stop in the hills just outside of La Junta; I know of a nice spring with grass enough for the horses. It's just, a three-hour ride from there to Fort Union."

"How can you remember where all of these springs are?"

"How can you not? Is the question; you see water is the life blood of the west; there have been more battles fought over water than anything else and will continue to be fought over. Men and animals can go longer without food than they can without water. And even the food that we eat needs water to grow. Every Indian knows where to find water; and if the white man wants to survive he had better take lessons from the Indian."

"Oh, is that what you did?"

"Damn straight; I kept an open mind while keeping my mouth shut. You'd be surprised what you can learn that way."

"Humph, are you trying to tell me something or what?"

"What? No, no I wasn't meaning you sweetheart; but just the opposite you already know all about that, you being a school teacher and all; you know how kids can't take in knowledge if it's all spilling out of their mouths as fast as it comes in their ears. It's got to sit in there and percolate a while."

"Well thank you for your homespun wisdom; but you are right; that's why you have to have a tight rein on those kids; their just like a young colt; if you let them have a free rein no telling where they will end up."

"What are you trying to say Hattie, that's what happened to me?"

"Yep, exactly; but in your case you were fortunate that you found me and because of that we live happily ever after."

"Are you trying to say that I am prince charming?" I said.

"I think that's stretching it a little bit, but close." Hattie said with a sexy grin.

I didn't know whether that was an invitation or not; but if we stopped every time we got the urge we'd never get anywhere; because between the two of us, that would be every ten minutes. But we controlled ourselves and kicked our horses up to a trot.

Chapter Thirteen

We left our camp at La Junta just after dawn; and we came in sight of Fort Union around nine in the morning. We stopped on a hill overlooking the Fort and gave the horses a blow and let them crop some grass.

"What do you think?" I asked Hattie; since she had the telescope and was glassing the activity.

"Looks normal, I guess. I see the tenth regiment is billeted away from the rest of the troops; what do you think that means?" She said.

"Same old crap; they're good enough to fight and die; but not to live too close to. Bigotry dies hard I guess."

"Yeah I expect; I need to tie my hair back before we go down there; also I need to check the loads in my .45's and you should check your .44's." Hattie said as she combed her hair and tied it back in a ponytail.

"Are you expecting trouble when we go down there?"

"Maybe, something about that place rubs me wrong." Hattie said as she ejected the loads from her pistols and put fresh loads in.

We were still wearing our buckskins; because that's all we brought with us. As I told you before Hattie's fit skin tight and with her guns around her waist and the bandoleers across her breasts she was quite the sight. Of course, I was dressed the same, but at the same time totally different; if you know what I mean.

The sentry at the gates was a young black from the 10th. We reined up and looked at him. He smiled and said; "I know who you are Sir, you're Major Bodeen."

"That's right son; and you are?"

"Private Trevor Howard Sir."

"Well Trevor can you direct us to Captain Gascon?"

"Yes Sir, That first tent over there; if he's not there he's probably over to the stables."

We thanked the boy and rode over to his tent. All the while the white troops were staring at us. Henri wasn't at the tent, so we rode

150

over to the stables. We dismounted and tied our three to the hitching rack.

Henri was in there; he was directing the cleaning of the stalls. He looked up and seen us and his face lite up in a big smile. Hattie gave him a hug.

"I wasn't expecting to see you all. What are you doing here?" Henri asked.

"We have some business to discuss with the Commandant; but that can wait. How are things going for the 10th?" I asked him.

"It could be better; since the new fellow took over, not so good."

"New fellow, what do you mean?"

"The new Commandant; he showed up last week and he doesn't like us. We've been on stable duty ever since."

"What's his name?"

"General Samuel B. Lewis; he's a one star general. The scuttlebutt was he was he was a decent guy; but that wasn't true."

"Is that him walking over there?" Hattie asked, while pointing out the stable door.

"Yep, that's him. He never goes anywhere without those three men with him."

"Uh, I know General Lewis; and that's not him." I said.

"Yeah, I don't know General Lewis; but I know who that is." Hattie said.

"What you know who that is?" I said.

"Yeah, that's Talent's cousin; Zeke Talent, he's worse than Curt Talent."

"Henri, we need to get to the telegraph shack; can you point it out?" I asked.

"They have it under guard all the time; he's got two of his men there around the clock. They know you're here, look their coming this way." Henri said.

"Henri, go out the back and get some of your men and flank them." I said.

"I have twenty men here right now and they have their rifles with them."

"Alright, you back us up; I think Hattie and I can take the four of them; but if anyone else tries to butt in, take them out."

Hattie and I stood in the shadow of the entrance to the stables; waiting till they came closer. When they were about ten feet away we stepped out and Hattie said:

"Hello Zeke, where did you bury the real General?"

"Hattie Beowulf, I'll be damned. Didn't I rape you one time?"

"No Zeke, you tried, that's where you got that scar on your neck; I'm only sorry that I didn't hit the juggler vein. And it's not Beowulf anymore, I'm Mrs. Mathew Bodeen; Major Bodeen that is. If you all will drop your weapons we won't kill you."

"So, you must think pretty high of yourselves, or else you can't count, there are four of us and only two of you." Zeke said as the four of them started to fan out.

"Stop right there Zeke, you all take one more step and it'll be your last." I said.

"Like hell it will," Zeke said and started to draw....

Now I'm fast, but I didn't get the first shot...Hattie did. She drilled one right between his eyes. I got two of them before Hattie got the last one.

Henri and his troops came out. "Henri, were these four the only ones?"

"No, those two at the telegraph shack came with them."

"Alright, Henri, take your troops and secure those men; try and take them alive; we need to know where the General's body is buried. Also, who is the next officer in line that can take over the base?"

"There was a Colonel and a Major, but one retired and the other transferred to Fort Larned."

"I guess that leaves you. As soon as you get those two bring them to the Commandants office. And have the bugler sound assembly as soon as you get those men. And please have these bodies taken care of."

"Uh, Major, did you know that you are bleeding?"

"No, but maybe I had better get my arm looked at; where is the infirmary?"

"Over there, but I just remembered the doctor is a Major; but he is retiring; his replacement is already here. Perhaps he would stay awhile and take over as commandant?" Henri said as he scurried off to his tasks that I gave him.

"Come Honey," Hattie said, "I will go with you to get that wound looked at."

"I never noticed it, till Henri drew my attention to it. I guess that's what adrenaline does. Crap, now it hurts." I said, trying to play on her sympathies.

"All of a sudden you turned into a big baby, huh? That's alright; I always knew you were one anyway."

"You mean I'm not your knight in shining armor?"

"Of course, you are Honey; but hold your arm out; you're getting blood on your buckskins."

The bullet had just grazed my arm; just enough to make it bleed. The doctor poured some pure alcohol over the wound and slapped a bandage on it; and yes, he agreed to stay on and be the commandant.

We had him change out of his smock and into his uniform and then all three of us headed to the commandant's office. Henri met us there with those two that were left of Zeke's band of murders. The two of them were more than happy to tell us where the General and his aides were buried; that is after Hattie used her stiletto to interrogate them. While she was engaged in said endeavor, the bugler sounded assembly.

While the new commandant explained to all of the troops what had transpired, Hattie and I made our way to the telegraph shake and I sent a message to General Grant.

General Grant made the entire changes official; plus gave us permission to institute martial law in Las Vegas. By the time we got done with all of the click-clack back and forth the Major had already sent out a detachment to retrieve the bodies.

It was two days before everything settled down with the burial and all before we could leave with the detachment for Las Vegas. It was made up of half of the 10th Regiment and half of the 3rd Regiment. Therefore, it was half black and half white. But Henri was in charge of all of them.

Grant wanted Hattie and I to go with the troops to make sure everything was set up right in Las Vegas. We hadn't brought our uniforms with us so we drew new ones from the Quarter Master. We stowed our buckskins in our saddle bags; but of course, we still kept our bandoliers' on as well as our pistols.

Hattie was always sexy in her buckskins; but that Lieutenant's uniform was just as sexy. You may be thinking that it was against Army

Regs for a woman to be in the Active Army; well yeah it was; but Grant made an exception…

An emigrant wagon train had arrived the night before we were to leave and the troops who were escorting them had to head back to Fort Larned. The trail from Fort Union to Santa Fe was considered to be relatively safe; so, no troops usually went on from here. But I decided it would be a good thing that we would act as their escort into Las Vegas, or anyway to just a few miles short of Las Vegas and then let them go in on their own. *Welcome to my nest said the spider to the fly!*

There were only eight wagons in their train; small enough that the Talent gang would think that they would be easy pickings. Their wagon master was a pulpit pounding preacher; I didn't know which denomination and I didn't care. I was having thoughts of just letting the Talent gang shoot him. Of course, Hattie said that wouldn't be Christian of me….?

Now that, that made me sit down and think a mite. 'Christian of me'. Just what did I believe? Well I knew that God Almighty, whose name was Jehovah, had sent his first-born son down to become the messiah. And I didn't believe in heaven, which is not for us common folk, maybe for the Apostles and such; and I sure didn't believe in their so called fiery hell. What kind of a god would burn people alive forever and ever? It sure didn't fit the God I knew Jehovah to be. I guess time will tell who is right, the devil or me….

As we rode along I could see that most of the people on that train were scared of that P.P. (pulpit pounder). I also noticed there were several young people of the opposite sex in the families. And they were eyeing each other; as the hormones were raging; I hoped they wouldn't ignite before we got shut of this wagon train.

That night we set up the Army camp separate from the wagon train; but close enough to be able to watch over them in case of an attack. I really didn't expect any; because of the hundred troops camped nearby. Of course, I didn't take into account the internal combustion of the situation.

The peace of the evening was shattered by screaming and yelling coming from the wagon train camp. Henri had started some troops heading that way; but Hattie and I passed them by.

The scene was somewhat unsettling as we raced into the camp;

there was a young girl with her hands tied to a tree branch and her top was down to her waist. And the so-called wagon master had a bull whip and was about to start whipping her naked back.

"This is what a hussy gets'; nine lashes, even if she is my own daughter." He raised the whip up and while it was still behind his back and starting the forward stroke; I grabbed the end of the whip and jerked back.

I heard a crack; it was his arm breaking. The sudden cessation of his forward motion and me jerking the opposite way; something had to give and it was his arm. He let go of the whip and dropped to the ground, writhing in pain.

Hattie rushed forward and cut the girl down and pulled her torn top over her breasts as best she could. Henri had arrived with some of his troops; he instructed one of them to get their medic.

I looked at the crowd and said: "What the hell was that all about?"

A middle-aged woman stepped forward; "My husband caught our daughter kissing her boyfriend; I tried to stop him but he wouldn't listen." She said with tears running down her face as she ran to her daughter.

The medic had arrived and was splinting his broken arm. I walked over to him and said: "You're one lucky bastard, did you see that the Lieutenant was about to put a bullet through your brain pan? When I grabbed that whip it saved your life. You are no longer the wagon master; I am going to appoint someone else in your stead. And you had better thank your God for my kindness in not killing you myself."

He cut loose with a string of cuss words; some even that I had never heard. It just goes to show you what lies under the façade of those that are overly self-righteous. I stepped forward and clipped him behind his ear with my .44. Then I told the medic: "Now you can finish splinting his arm, he won't be moving around for a while."

"So, who are you going to appoint to be the wagon master?" Hattie asked me.

"Hell, I don't know; you find someone and if anyone doesn't like your pick let me know and I will take care of them." I said.

"What do you mean that you will take care of them?"

"Just what I said; and you can tell them what I said; maybe even embellish it a little bit; let me know who you picked when you get back to camp." And then I stalked off.

That comment of Hattie's about being a good Christian kept gnawing at me; just what was I? Like I said, I believe in the Bible, I just don't believe in people's goodness all that much. Now don't get me wrong I believe most people are trying to do right things; but greed and selfishness always seem to interfere. And of course, there are those that would tell a lie even if the truth would serve them better. Take those pulpit pounders, they know most of the things they are preaching don't come from the Bible; they twist the truth to suit themselves and tickle the ears of their flock. Someday it will catch up with them; I don't know when; maybe a hundred years from now, who knows?

I shook my head and brought my thoughts back from lala land to the problems at hand; which were mainly how to stay alive in a lawless land, mostly lawless anyway; the army was the only law in most of the territories; which isn't saying much.

I cleared out debris and clutter under a Ponderosa Pine and laid down fresh pine needles before I spread our bedrolls while I was waiting for Hattie to come back. It didn't take long before I heard her coming.

She said as soon as she seen me: "Hey I found a spring back away from everybody; do you want to wash up before we go to bed?"

"Yeah, but I think I know that spring and it wasn't very big the last time I saw it."

"Well it is now; big enough for two people anyway and it has a lot of willow trees around it; if you know what I mean?"

"Really, you're in the mood, after all of that ruckus? Who did you appoint as wagon master?"

"His wife, Effie is her name, and the son and daughter he was going to whip; all three of them. You should have seen them smile; I don't think he's the head of the family anymore. Are you trying to get out of taking a bath with me?"

I got up and headed for that spring, I looked back at her and said: "What's keeping you?"

"I was just getting the towels, you want to race?"

"Nope, I will save my energy for you know what-----?" She sure did know what.....I had the best night sleep I've had in a long time; must have been the minerals in the water? Not!

156

As we were saddling our horses and of course Jasper I asked Hattie: "Well just how do you think we ought to handle things when we get to Las Vegas?"

"What do you mean?"

"Well, just ride right on in with the wagon train or hold back and see how it goes?

"I think we should camp just short of town tonight and go in fresh in the morning; we'll put two of the troops in each wagon and you and I will dress as emigrants and be in the first wagon and if they start something we'll end it. How's that?" Hattie said with a lovely smile…

"Well it certainly shows that you have been thinking about it a lot. And I like it; remind me to never get cross ways of you. I think also that I'll put one black trooper and one white trooper in the wagons. So, they can share the risk, besides they need to start working together as a team." Hattie and I, quite frequently one of us would lay out the major plans and then the other one would fill in the details. Isn't that what all husbands and wives do?

The day went as smooth as I hoped it would. We camped about two miles out of Las Vegas in a grove of trees with a small stream running close by. There was good grass for the stock.

Looking around at the country side it always amazed me; how so? Most of this land hadn't been claimed yet, you would think those clowns that were trying to take away the Spanish land grants would just take what was available and not try to take someone else's land. I guess they didn't know the meaning of the word 'covet' and the consequences'. But I am sure they will come to know….

After supper Hattie and I were setting beside our fire watching the stars come out to play; when I said: "I was thinking about us dressing up as emigrants, I don't think I will; I mean you can set up there with Effie, but I think I will ride along on my horse; I never was a wagon man."

"Well hell, if you aren't going too, neither will I. I like to fight from horseback also. I'll have one of the white troopers ride next to her and her husband can ride in back. You and I will wear our buckskins; and if that Jay Hawker Talent wants a fight I'll ventilate his britches."

"What do you mean by that?"

157

"I mean I won't shoot him in his head; not that head anyway, the one he sits on I mean."

"Yeah, I had forgotten that he had tried to rape you back in Tennessee."

"Yeah, even though he didn't succeed I still feel violated; just the thought gives me the creeps." Hattie said as she shuddered and then shook herself as if she could rid herself of the memory.

I pulled her into my arms and held her close till her shaking stopped. Then she crawled into our bed role as I put the fire out....

I held her close as she drifted off to sleep; I lay there thinking: How sometimes it's hard to tell the difference between right and wrong; how sometimes I do the right thing and it still turns out wrong, but when I do the wrong thing- it's always wrong, of course I guess it depends on who's doing the judging, man or God...

Chapter Fourteen

The next morning, we split Henri's troops up; half were to go on the side street on the north of the main street and the others to go on the side street on the south. Hattie and Henri were to go with the troops on the south; while I went on the north.

It was just breaking dawn as we infiltrated each side and took up our positions.

The wagon train was only about fifteen minutes behind us; they were to make a lot of noise on their way into town, so the people were awake.

All of the noise the train was making didn't bring out the general populace; but it sure brought out the ones we were hoping for. Oh, a few of the people stuck their heads out and went right back in their abodes; like frightened rabbits. Really you couldn't blame them; fear is a mighty inducement to keep your head down.

There were about twenty of them; like wolves waiting to pounce on their prey. And Talent was there; he looked like his cousin; I was tempted to cut off the head off that rattler but knew better than to encroach on Hattie's revenge.

Turned out neither one of us got our wish. Because Henri's troops stepped out of the shadows right behind them; heckfire, us on the other side of the street couldn't fire because of the chance of hitting them. But we didn't need to, when they seen fifty troops wanting to blow them to hell, they just dropped their guns like good little boys.

Hattie hadn't stepped out with Henri's troops; she was standing in the shade of a building; as I likewise was. I motioned for her to join me at Paco Delgado's Cantina; she stepped back and went to get Jasper, as I likewise went to get my horse where I had him tied.

As we tied up at Paco's hitching rail, I asked Hattie: "I thought you wanted to kill the sidewinder?"

I stood there looking at him and it came to me that revenge when cold makes a poor stew. Besides, I have a feeling that I'll still get my chance, with a snake like him he always finds a hole to hide in; and when he sticks his head out I will be there to blow it off."

"You sound like you expect Talent to escape Henri's custody?"

"Yep, I sure do; Henri's a good man, but he's no jailer. What should be done is quick justice; say a firing squad at dawn before he gets a chance to slither out a hole somewhere." Hattie said with wicked grin.

Paco had heard us ride up and he opened the saloon door. He waved us in.

"Senor, Senora, I have been expecting you. The birds this morning told me you were close, come breakfast is ready." Paco said with a welcoming smile.

"So, the birds talk to you, do they?" Hattie asked him.

"Oh, not in so many words; but they seemed very happy this morning, just like last time you were here. I have heard that you brought the black white men troops with you?"

"Yes, we brought the 10th Regiment as well as a few white troops; Captain Henri Gascon is in charge of the troops. We will be declaring Marshal Law, till we get the lawless element controlled."

We will be appropriating all of Sheriff Talent's property and assists. You might want to tell Captain Gascon of any property that belongs to him or any of his men; but if any of their property was stolen from any of the town's people it will be returned to them."

"Yes, I know of several that need to be returned, some that belongs to me." Paco said with a big smile pasted across his face.

"Can you get Alfonso to take care of our stock, I think we will be staying the day and then Matthew and I will be leaving this evening to ride back to the Hacienda; we have pressing business that cannot wait." Hattie said, I looked at her, she gave a slight shake of her head that told me she would tell me later why we leaving this evening.

We spent the morning visiting with the towns' people that came by to see us; and then we went to see how Henri was doing; he had all of them locked securely in the jail, it was a might crowded, but who cares.

"Where are you going to billet your troops?" I asked him.

"Part of them in the Hotel, it belonged to Talent, the rest will be camped around the towns perimeter; I will switch them out every week."

"Oh yes, Henri, Matthew and I will be leaving this evening for home; you will be in charge from here on, we know that you will do a good job."

"What will I tell Fort Larned?"

"Tell them we are taking an extended leave; I don't know when we will be back. You can have them tell General Grant that we will contact him in the future. Remember Henri that you are in charge now; don't take any guff off of anyone." Hattie said just before we turned away. I looked at her with a dumfounded look....

"What the hell Hattie?" I asked.

We stopped in the shade of a big Ponderosa Pine Tree; she faced me and said: "Timberline...."

"Huh?"

"You remember what you told me about a Timberline moment; that you can either go up or down the mountain and that decision would change your life?"

"Yeah, but I don't remember having any decision to make."

"Well really, we haven't yet; but when Paco talked about the birds this morning I got a premonition about how we had to start home this evening; don't ask me why I don't know, but I have never had a stronger premonition in my life."

"You think there's something wrong back at the Hacienda?"

"No, not necessarily; but it just said to start home."

"It..."

"Uh, yes, come to think of it, a voice said that, in my head."

"Are you feeling all right, you didn't hit your head, did you?"

"No, of course not, you have been with me every minute, did you see me fall off Jasper or something?"

I turned her face to me and looked into her eyes; nope there was nothing wrong with her; to me she was perfect in every way. I leaned down and kissed her; she tasted good too.

We went back to Paco's to see if he had the stock ready and also to get some food for the ride home, he did, the stock I mean. We did eat a meal before we left around four in the afternoon. But before we left I reached into my saddle bags and gave Paco a hand full of double eagles. He protested that it was way too much. But I just reached into the bag again and gave him another hand full of double eagles. Hattie looked at me and smiled and nodded.

161

Why did I do that? I just had a feeling that they weren't as important as I used to think they were. Weird huh? But I had a feeling that the weirdness was just starting.

Chapter Fifteen

As we headed out Jasper took the bit in his teeth and pulled to the front; Hattie looked back at me and shrugged. It looked like he was heading in the general direction of the Hacienda; so why not set back and enjoy the ride.

After about an hour riding, Hattie said: "Hey I think I know where he's going; remember that one lake that has a hot spring feeding into it?"

"Yeah, I do. We had a very good time there; do you remember that?" I asked.

"Of course, I remember every time we have made love; don't you?"

"Sure, but that lake was special; wasn't it?"

"Yes dear, it was." Hattie said as she gigged Jasper up to a trot."

It was pleasant thinking about that, but for some reason I don't think that was the main reason Jasper was taking us there this time. It took us about three more hours to get there and the sun had about one finger left before it would set.

The spot we camped at the last time looked like no one else had used it; the grass was still high and green. We unpacked the pack horse and took the saddles off the rest. We had an extra horse because we had used up the supplies off of that horse.

We built a small fire in the stone fire ring and Hattie cooked our supper while I laid our bed rolls in the same spot that we did last time.

As I finished up eating the last of the side pork and beans Hattie said: "Hey the last one finished eating has to wash the utensils."

"I have a better idea, why don't we both wash them and take a bath at the same time. The moon's out so there is plenty of light, how about it?" I said as I looked over at her. She was just shucking the last bit of her clothes.

"So, what's keeping you slowpoke." She said as she ran for the water. I was a little bit slower; cause I had to pack the dishes with me; I must have been quite the sight, a naked man trying to balance dirty dishes, without dripping grease on you know what!

Hattie was floating on her back watching me; as I scrubbed the frying pan with sand before dipping it in the hot spring water. "Hurry up, or I will start without you?" She called as she splashed water my way. I ignored her as she swam closer, then I dove in the water and came up under her...she didn't start without me...

There was a warm breeze blowing that dried us off and then we lay on our bed roll watching the stars come out to play. We played a game on nights like this; to see who the first one to spot a falling star.

Hattie was the first to spot one; "You know," she said, "they cannot be stars falling; if they were it would be a lot bigger flame trails. I think they are some kind of rocks or something falling toward earth and burning up, what do you think?"

"I think you are awfully pretty with the moon beams playing across your naked body."

"Stop it, I'm serious; what do you think they are?"

"Yeah, come to think of it, it must be something smaller. You know I left school early so I never did make a study of the universe; but I've seen a lot of those things streak across the sky. But I have a question for you: Do you think there are other people out there?" Hattie turned on her side and looked at me.

"Yes, yes I do. We would have to be pretty egocentric if we didn't; wouldn't it be logical for the all-powerful creator to have created more worlds than just ours?"

Hattie turned on her back again and then exclaimed: "Look, there is a big one now." She said while pointing.

She was right, but this one seemed closer than usual. We kept watching it, but it wasn't burning up; and then a smaller piece split from it, while the bigger one kept on its route. It seemed like they were right above us.

"Hey, what the hell, that small one looks like it's coming right at us." Hattie said as she jumped up. I jumped up and grabbed her and pulled her back under the tree with me. Jasper must have seen it also, because he came and stood in front of us, but he didn't seem to be all that shook up about it.

It seemed the closer it came, the slower it seemed to move through the night air; till it was right in front of us…it looked like a fat cigar, as it fell into the lake. We looked at each other as it slowly sank out of sight. We started toward the lake, Jasper stopped us. And then the object came to the surface and floated about 80 feet from shore. Jasper moved out of our way; he looked at us and nodded. I guess he wanted us to swim out and get it. It looked to be about fifteen feet in length and three feet in circumference.

We dove in together and swam to either side of the craft; craft I said, because I didn't know what to call it. We pushed it to shore and then we stood beside it in about four feet of water. We heard a click and the top part started to open, we stepped back a little bit. Jasper walked out beside me and stood there looking with us.

Some kind of lights were glowing from inside of the lid, illuminating the interior of the craft. We peered inside; laying there was a woman with her eyes closed.

Hattie stepped forward and reached in and touched her shoulder. Her eyes snapped open. She looked at Hattie and then looked at me and Jasper. She looked back at Hattie and said: "Hi, would you give me a hand out of here?"

Hattie helped her over the edge; while I steadied the craft. She was just a tall as Hattie and naked like she was also, or so I thought. I pulled the craft forward to where it was resting on the sand, and then we came out of the water and stood looking at each other.

"Oh, I thought everyone here wore clothes?" She said.

"Yes, we do, but I see you are naked also." Hattie said.

"Oh, this is my skin suit; I can take it off and then I'll be nude just like you two. How's this?" She said as she touched her throat and the invisible suit contracted into a ball the size of her fist.

"Uh," I said. "Who are you and where did you come from and how come you speak the same language that we do?" I said as I was looking her up and down; she was humanoid all right. But what was weird was that she looked enough like Hattie to be her sister.

"I know you must have a lot of questions; I did come here looking for the two of you; but not like this. My ship malfunctioned and I had to use the escape pod, otherwise I would have landed my exploration ship instead of the pod."

"Did your other craft crash?" I asked.

"No, I hope not, it didn't want to land here; sometimes that AI can be so stubborn, he wanted to land further south, I told him I was going to have him updated with a female AI, he was just pouting."

"What's an AI?" Hattie asked.

"Artificial Intelligence; It's just a super computer."

"What's a computer?"

"Oh my, just a second." She tapped her left temple, and then said: "Yes, I forgot we are in your nineteenth century, never mind right now. Would you help me get my bag out of the pod?"

I reached in a got it; it felt like it held a lot more than clothes.

"So, Hattie said. "Where you're from do you wear clothes or not?"

"Yes, at times and then other times it's alright to go without; it depends where you are at in my world; and also, who you are."

"What do you mean 'who' you are?" Hattie asked.

"Well, the real rich like to go naked and then the poor in warmer climates go naked. But most of us wear clothes at least down there." She said pointing at my neither regions and giggling.

"What about you, are you self-conscious being naked around us?" I asked.

Her face flushed a little and she said: "Not too much, but that thing of yours keeps pointing at me. That's why I giggled."

Hattie and I both looked down, "Hey, that's not my fault; he's just like your AI, stubborn and quite naughty at times." I said, turning red myself.

"So, I guess it's time we introduced ourselves; I am Matthew Bodeen and this is my wife Hattie May. And yours is?"

"I already knew your names; my name is Fiera Castillo."

"Fiera, What, kind of a name is that?"

"It means 'wild beast' or go-getter, hustler and demon for work. Take your pick."

"How come you knew our names?"

"Why shouldn't I, she's my sister, well half- sister anyway. You see one of our scout ships had to land for some repairs and one of our men fell in love with a married woman and she wouldn't leave with him when the ship was repaired and she was pregnant. The child was you Hattie and the Father was my Dad and he wanted to know what has happened to his earthly daughter; so, I volunteered to find you. Oh yes, and you will be happy to know that he didn't leave without leaving someone to watch over you and that someone was Jasper; you have noticed that he was always by your side?" Jasper just gave a loud bray….

That was almost too much to believe, but being she was here and came from outer space, I guess it was true. Hattie's sister? I looked down, he believed it anyway because he had made a hasty retreat…I told him, yeah, you should be ashamed of yourself…

We stood there looking at each other; the silence was a little bit awkward; so I said: have you had anything to eat?"

"Yes, I have; but I see you have made your bed under that tree; you do know that it is going to rain tonight?

"Oh," I said, looking up at the stars; it looks clear right now."

"Yes, well it is going to rain, would you mind if I made a shelter big enough for the three of us?"

"No, I don't mind." I said with a smile, or maybe a smirk; doubting her ability to perform such a task.

She reached into that bag of hers and brought out two round balls about the size of a fist. She took one and spoke to it: "Shelter for three please." And then walked over by our bedrolls; "this area would be fine if you would pick up your bedding?"

Hattie walked over and rolled them up and put them aside. Fiera tossed the ball under the tree; before it hit the ground, it turned into a round dome and settled into place.

"What color do you want it to be, or do you want it to be transparent?"

I looked at Hattie, not knowing what transparent meant; Hattie said: "Yes make it clear so we can see through it; one never knows if someone will sneak up and try and kill us in our sleep."

"Alright, so what about the horse and tack shelter; you want it clear also?"

Again, Hattie answered, "Yeah, make it clear, they like to see what's around them also."

Fiera tossed the other ball over beside the horses; it turned into a three-sided shelter big enough for the four of them and also space for our saddles and stuff. The horses followed Jasper and stood facing out of the shelter; just like they were used to being inside of it.

This was starting to get spooky, Hattie noticed my expression and put her hand on my arm, "It's alright Honey, and somehow this feels natural to me."

Well it sure didn't feel natural to me. I looked at the lake and her craft, what the hell ever it was, and said to her: "What about your little space boat, you going to just leave it floating around in the lake?"

"No, I wasn't," She looked at it and said: "Close the hatch and settle yourself in the deepest part of the lake; I'll be back; but I don't know when."

It did like she said, the hatch closed and it backed off of the beach and sank out of sight.

I turned and looked at the two sisters; they looked almost like twins; I mean everything was almost identical and I mean everything; this was starting to really freak me out. I walked over to the shelter, thinking I would put our bedrolls in it.

"Oh, you won't need those." Fiera said. "You can store them in the horse shelter; our shelter has everything we'll need."

"Everything we'll need, you mean blankets? Hattie asked.

"Much more than that, you'll see; come on I'll show you."

She was right about there being everything; the raised bed was big enough for three people; plus there were a couple of things I didn't know what they were. But I was sure she would tell us. She bent over and pushed a button over next to the wall; I don't know why she didn't kneel down instead of bending over with her backside toward me; I looked at Hattie, but she wasn't looking at me; she was looking at some kind of thing appearing out of the wall. Then she glanced at me and seen I was red in the face. I pointed to Fiera's hind end.

"Uh, Fiera you are embarrassing my husband." Hattie told her. Fiera looked at me and just wiggled it all the more. Oh yeah, this was going to be fun. (That was sarcasm by the way.)

She finally stopped waging her butt and said: "This is the toilet; you don't have to go outside."

"What do you mean you just go right there in front of everyone?" I asked incredulously.

"How does it work?" Hattie asked.

"It vaporizes the molecules and exhausts them outside. And look over here, this is a dry shower, it cleans all the bad bacteria off of you, let me show you."

She took the 'wand', as she called it, and waved it back and forth across her body. I said: "I don't see anything falling off of you."

"Oh, the bacteria are so small that you can't see them, but the wand not only kills the bad bacteria but also gives you a massage as well."

"I want to try it." Hattie said as she took the wand from Fiera and ran it over her body. "Yes, it feels so good." Hattie said with a small moan.

"Is that hurting you?" I asked her.

"On the contrary; it feels so good...." She moaned again, I went out to check the horses; I don't think I liked all of this new stuff.

The horses were backed into the shelter; Jasper gave me a small bray. I rubbed him behind his ear; "So what do you think about all of what is going on?" He shook his head and then nodded his head. "Yeah, I guess you're like me, not too sure about any of this crap."

As I stepped out of the shelter a drop of rain fell on my head. I looked up; the clouds had blotted out the stars. I guess she was right about the rain. I walked over behind a pine tree and took a leak; I'll be damned if I used that thing inside. As I finished, the rain had picked up. And when I got back to our shelter I was soaked; I stepped inside and shook myself like a wet dog would do.

"Hey," Hattie said, "you're getting us all wet."

Fiera said: "That's alright, just stand there the dryer will do its work."

I felt a warm breeze coming from somewhere, she was right I was dry in short order. "I wonder how long this rain will last." I said out loud.

"Well, I did see a hurricane building off the California coast; so I suppose it could last for a few days. So we might as well use this time to get to know each other."

"Well I don't know how much more we could find out about each other; all three of us are bare-assed naked."

"For one thing we need to find out why you are so cantankerous." Fiera said.

"Well I'll tell you...it's because.... hell, I don't know why; it's maybe because I find out my beautiful wife has a doppelganger that's a space alien. And the first thing that I know she'll probably want to run off to some god forsaken planet and leave me all alone."

"Our planet is not God Forsaken. It's called Terra and it's a lush paradise. And I am sure Hattie would not leave you behind; our family always marries for life."

"Hey, who says I want to leave earth? This is our home; oh, maybe I might like to see your home, but Matt will be with me, that's for sure."

The rain was coming down harder and the wind had picked up; sounding like a mountain lion in heat; but the strangest thing was that the shelter we were in didn't even ruffle a feather so to speak.

Hattie held out her hand to me; "Come to bed and hug me, this storm sounds really bad." I was going to lie on the outside of Hattie, but she pulled me over her so I was between the two of them. And I wasn't hugging them they were hugging me. Heck I guess things could be worse...

I couldn't figure out why Fiera was scared, so I asked her; she said: "We don't' have storms like this on Terra; oh, it rains that's for sure, but not hard with the wind blowing." Just then the thunder cracked and she tried to crawl inside of us, or so it seemed, anyway she was lying on top of us. Well I guess Hattie having a twin wasn't so bad.... We were still cocooned like that when I went to sleep.

I woke with a smile on my face; I had been having all kinds of sexy dreams; I wondered why, because I usually didn't. But I looked down and seen the reason. Hattie and Fiera were still asleep with one hand each around my nocturnal appendage.

"Uh, Hattie," I said, as I tried to wake her. She opened one eye and looked at me and gave me a big smile, while moving her one hand. Fiera woke also and joined the movement.

"Uh, you two had better stop that or you're going to have a big mess any second now."

Hattie looked at Fiera and said: "What do you think, should we stop?"

"He's your husband; your call." You could sure tell they were twins; they both had a mean streak; they didn't stop....

As the three of us were standing under that molecular clean up thing; I said: "You know the two of you are twins, not just half-sisters; half-sisters don't look alike; would you like to explain that Fiera?"

"Sure, but I lied a little bit, when I said your mother didn't want to leave you and stayed behind, because you were told that your mother died at your birth; she didn't die, she had twins, you and I... She didn't love your father any more. But he had a big fit and was going to shoot the three of us; that is till they struck a bargain and she had to leave one of us behind. You see your mother is still alive along with our father."

"Do my brothers know this?" Hattie said, somewhat flabbergasted.

"No, they think she died when you were born; didn't you ever notice that you don't look much like your earthly father? Also, how you are able to see things that other people can't? How different you were than other girls?"

"Yeah, I did; but I didn't think I was an alien."

"Half alien, we are; our mother was an earthling after all."

Hattie stood there enjoying the molecule clean and pondering what Fiera had said.

I decided to change the subject; "it is still raining pretty hard I would like to put on my clothes and do that, but I don't want to get them all wet."

"Oh, I have skin suits for the two of you, let me get them out of my case." Fiera said, as she stepped over there and bent over to get them. Now she could of just squatted down and picked them up, but no she had to flash us big time. I looked at Hattie and she just shrugged.

She handed us each one, they weren't any bigger than what could fit in my hand. I hefted it and said: "How do you put in on?"

"Just hold it above your heads and say 'on." We did it and they flowed down over our heads clear to our toes; we had to lift each foot up so they could complete the flow. I was surprised we could breathe without any trouble. Fiera said:

"If you don't like it over your face just tell it what to do."

"Uh, does the same thing apply if you have to pee?"

"Yeah, just tell it that you have to pee or number two, if that be the case; but you could do that right here in the commode, you don't have to go outside." Fiera added.

"No, I'll go outside with the horses; Hattie will do what she wants though, she always does." Not meaning any sarcasm, just fact.

I stepped out of the shelter, I bet that rain was coming down an inch an hour; but that suit really worked; it felt like it was climate controlled also. I went over and stood on the lee side of the horse shelter and said: Pee. My thing popped out and the suit sealed around the base. I wondered to myself as I was going: Just who invented this thing? I bet it was a woman....

The rain didn't stop for two more days and then it took another day for it dry enough so we could hit the trail. You know with all of that rain the lake didn't rise more than a foot; I asked Fiera about that and she said: "It would off, but the pod took care of the runoff by enlarging the spillway as needed."

"Why did it do that?" Hattie asked.

"I told it to keep the level of the lake within a foot of normal; I didn't want it to be washed down-stream or that the lake would dry up enough to expose the pod."

"Flood and drought control, you'll be right popular around the west." I said.

"Oh, you can't tell anyone about all of these things; it would change history."

"Maybe history needs to be changed." I said.

Before we got ready to go, I asked Fiera if she had any clothes that would fit in with our time period. Of course she didn't; so the only extra clothes Hattie had was her Army Uniform. Of course it fit Fiera the same as it fit Hattie, explanation enough...

We kept those skin suits on under our buckskins. They were pretty neat; especially when the sun rose on high. We didn't give Fiera a gun, but she did have my .50 Calber Sharps in the rifle boot.

I asked her if she ever shot a gun before. "Well no, not exactly, but I did read up on them, they seem pretty simple." She said, as she pulled the sharps out and took a bead on a pine cone in the trail about a hundred yards ahead; she hit it dead center. She started to put it back in the boot.

"Hold on, eject the spent shell and reload a new one." I told her; she did have a bandolier of .50 Caliber shells around her ample breasts.

"Good thinking," she said, "You never know when you will have to kill a bad guy, huh?"

"Uh, no I usually use that gun for big game; you know Elk or Moose and sometimes a Grizzly."

"You kill them; aren't they on the endangered list."

"What the hell is an endangered list?"

"Oh wait, I've pulled up the wrong century; here it is now, yes I see there are no laws as yet protecting animals. Such a shame, I feel sorry for the Buffalo, they shoot them almost into extinction."

"What? How could they there are millions of them, well maybe not now. Yes I guess you could be right." Hattie said.

I looked at Fiera and asked her: "Didn't that kick of that Sharps hurt your shoulder? And you said you pulled up the wrong century; from where?"

"No, the skin suit absorbed the kick. And I have an inter-face to my ship; you know the ship that Alfred my AI ran off with; well he didn't really run off with the ship, I told him to take it and hide it."

"What in the hell is an inter-face?" I asked her.

"It's an electronic digital signal to the main computer in the ship; it's a small chip imbedded in my skull. I know this must sound pretty foreign to you; but if this was a hundred and fifty years in your future you would understand some of it; not all though."

"Well it isn't a hundred and fifty years in the future; so when we get around other people don't mention any of this gobbledygook. I don't know how to explain you suddenly showing up as Hattie's twin; you two had better cook up a good story about that." I said giving them both a stern stare. They just looked at me and started giggling.

"And another thing, aren't you afraid someone will see your spaceship; even though you had your AI hide it?" I said, still red faced about their giggling.

"No, it's got a cloaking device." Fiera said and then added: "Matthew, sweetie, you worry too much; people are really more open minded than you realize." Fiera said.

I looked at Hattie while mumbling under my breath-'I'm not your sweetie."

Hattie said: "What did you say honey?" "Nothing, I'm going to check the trail ahead; so you two can talk about me all you want." I said while spurring my horse into a run.

Fiera looked at Hattie and said: "What in the world is wrong with him?"

"Nothing really, but maybe it has something to do with our teasing him this morning, maybe we should of let go of his thing we he told us to?"

"Oh really, he didn't enjoy that?"

"Oh, he enjoyed it all right; I think that is part of the problem, he feels guilty."

"Why would he feel guilty about that?"

"Well in our society it just isn't done; you know three people, uh, doing that."

"Well what about you, do you feel bad about it?"

"I don't know, I didn't at the time, but now, maybe we had better take it easy and not embarrass him." The two of them rode on in silence....

Chapter Sixteen

I dropped down to a walk when I got far enough ahead of them, trying to make sense of everything that was going on; an alien, spaceships, even Hattie being half alien. Everything that I thought I knew about the world had just been turned upside down. And then what they did this morning; with not even a twinge of conscious? I was going to have to talk to Hattie about that, I love Hattie not her sister…. oh, Fiera was alright, I guess, but there was going to be no more of that kind of stuff…

My horse's ears bent forward, he heard something, I pulled up and stepped off and put my hand to his nose, so he wouldn't nicker. Then I heard the lowing of cattle. We were on our home range. It could be just the vaqueros moving our cattle, but for some reason I didn't think it was that. You know how you can just tell when something is just not right? Well, I knew it for sure….

I stood there till the girls caught up with me; Hattie seen me standing there, she laid a hand on Fiera's arm, signaling her to be quiet. I could tell by the sound of the cattle that they were moving north. Those cattle moving north put a clincher on it; some of our stock was being rustled.

Hattie knew it also, she got off of Jasper and went back to the packhorse and pulled a pistol and belt full of shells out of the pack and handed it to Fiera; "You know how to use this thing?" She asked her.

"Yes, I think I can; what's going on?"

"Some of our stock is being rustled; do you think these skin suits will stop a bullet?" Hattie asked her.

"Well we never tested it on lead projectiles, but they will stop a laser beam so I am sure they will." I started to ask her what the hell was a laser beam, but, figured now wasn't the time.

I started to lay out a plan on how catch those thieves, but Fiera stopped me.

"Wait, let's send Jasper to look things over first and then we will know how many and what they have for armament." She said.

"What, how will he be able to tell us all of that?" I said.

"Well, you probably didn't know this but he has an inter-face installed also, and he can send back a report to my inter-face."

"What, is that so?" Hattie exclaimed.

"Yes, how else do you think we know everything about you? Dad and Mom had to keep you safe. Also his intelligence has been expanded you might say. Have you ever seen another mule as smart as he is?"

"Do you mean to tell me that every time Matt and I made love when Jasper was around you could see us?"

"Well, yes, but we didn't look every time, just some of the time. You two are famous back on Terra."

"Do you mean to say that everyone on Terra has seen us make love?" Hattie said.

"Oh, not everyone, just the ones who take sex education classes in college."

"What, you teach sex in school?" Hattie exclaimed.

"Whoa, you two, we're getting side tracked here, if you want to send Jasper, send him." I said.

Hattie walked over to Jasper, "I'm mad at you, you should be ashamed of yourself. But I forgive you, go take a look but be careful don't get yourself shot." She said and then hugged him around his neck and then she pulled off his bridle so it wouldn't get hung up on something.

One thing about Jasper he could put the sneak on a mountain lion; so I wasn't worried.

Hattie asked Fiera: "So you can see everything Jasper sees?"

"Yes, but wait, I have a receiver so that you two can see what he sees also." With that she went back to the pack and pulled out a rectangular object just a little bit bigger than her hand. "See, we can follow everything Jasper sees."

Damn, what kind of witchcraft was this? I thought to myself, my mind was reeling, so much so that I was getting light headed. I shook my head and made myself focus on what I was seeing…, also on what I was hearing; I could hear Jasper's hooves as he walked along. I looked at Hattie, she didn't seem shook or even surprised by what she was seeing and hearing. I was starting to realize that I was married to a woman that was part alien. And you know what? I liked the whole idea…

We let Jasper get out of sight and then still waited about five minutes and then followed along. It didn't take Jasper long to catch up with the rustlers. The timber and brush was thick enough so they could not see him, but he could see and hear them. There were three of them; a young boy who looked to be about 16 or 17 and then two girls; one looked to be about 12 and the other about 9 or so.

They had about thirty head that we could see through Jasper's eyes. The twelve-year old, was saying something; we stopped so we could hear well.

"Abe," she said, "Ma told us to only get one cow, not all of these."

"I know Sue, but they all just followed along; I go to cut one out and they all still follow along."

"But Abe, Ma's going to be awful mad, she don't hold with stealing; remember she said the Good Lord didn't mind just one cause we were starving and he would overlook taking just one but not more; you remember in the bible how they could only take enough Manna for one day's eaten, but if they took more the Lord would strike them dead."

"No, he wasn't going to strike them dead, but the Manna would rot overnight, anyway that's the way I remember it." Abe said.

The three of us stopped, Hattie looked at me and said: "What are you going to do?"

"Well I sure as hell ain't going to hang them. I suppose we should help them cut out one cow and then drive the rest back south aways." I said…

"Yeah, but what then? Don't you think we ought to see if they need help; if they be by their lonesome with no man around we just can't leave them to their own devices, now can we?"

"I reckon you're right; even though I've seen some women who could manage a hell of lot better without a man around to mess up their thinking." I said, not meaning my wife of course, even though she fell into that category, but I wasn't worthless, was I?

Hattie looked at me and said: "No honey you're not worthless, you're still good for a few things…" Then she laughed along with

Fiera...

"Hey, I didn't say that out load, how did you know what I was thinking?"

"What, you didn't say that out load? Fiera what is going on how come I heard what he said even though he wasn't talking?"

"Well, didn't you tell me that you two and become one? Anyway, don't get all shook up, some of us Terrains can hear each other once in a while; looks like you two fall into that category."

"Well, all of this jabbering ain't going to solve this problem, so let's circle around them and turn the excess cattle back and then we'll go talk to their Ma."

"We don't have to stop them and turn the cattle back; Jasper can do that, can't you Jasper?" Hattie said, while talking into that there hand-held thing. Jasper gave a low nicker and stepped out in front of the kids.

"They stopped and were staring at Jasper, he just walked into the herd and cut one out and shooed the rest back south; and then he started the lone cow north. The kids didn't say a word but just followed along behind him.

About an hour later they got to where their wagon was; it was setting beside a small stream. We stayed out of sight and watched through that device Fiera had. There was a woman standing there watching them bring the steer in. It looked like she was a few months on the pregnant side.

"Land sakes, that's a good-looking steer, did you have any trouble?"

"No Ma, we didn't because there was a Mule that cut him out of the herd for us; and he drove it straight here." The littlest girl said.

"Well where's that mule now?"

"He's over there beside the stream getting a drink, see he's coming this way now."

As Jasper was walking over, the woman bent over in some kind of pain. "What's wrong Ma?" The boy 'Abe' asked while running over to her.

"I don't know for sure, been getting those pains all morning. I know the baby shouldn't be coming I'm only six months along. Don't bother about me, check on your Pa and see if he needs anything." The woman said, while still clutching her belly.

Abe went over and looked in the back of the wagon and asked: "How's your leg Pa, is that splint hurting you?"

"No, it's alright, but it sure is itching. So, you got a beef alright, did you see anybody around?"

"No Pa, only a mule. Strangest thing that Mule seemed to know we wanted only one cow and he cut it out and chased the others south and then herded it here, we didn't have to do a thing."

"A mule you say? Ain't that the darndest thing, some of them mules are smarter than humans I think." As Abe stepped away from the wagon, his Ma gave another groan.

"Ma, what's wrong, is the baby coming." The middle girl asked her.

"No, I don't think so, but it sure hurts."

Hattie and Fiera looked at each other and then Fiera said: "I can help her and her husband also. Do you want me to?"

"Why, what can you do?" I asked.

"I got some medicine that would help them, but it's up to the both of you; you see it works quickly, they would call it a miracle." The woman collapsed to the ground and passed out; more or less making up our minds for us.

"Go for it, we'll go with you." I said as Fiera went to the pack horse got a small box; we ground tied the horses and the three of us walked in their camp.

"Who are you?" Abe asked.

"I'm the owner of the land south of here and also we gave you that steer; we can help your mother and your father if you want us to? Make up your mind it looks like your mother is in sore straights." The three kids looked at each other and the youngest girl said: "Yes, help her, is she dyeing?"

"Not if we can help it." Fiera said as she dug in the box and pulled out some kind of tube with a needle in one end and plunger in the other end, she walked over to unconscious woman and pulled her sleeve up and stuck that needle in her arm and depressed the plunger. The woman moaned and blinked her eyes.

"Let her sleep a few minutes, she'll be alright when she wakes up, the baby will be alright also. Let's take a look at your Pa." Fiera said as she walked to the back of the Conestoga and stepped in.

"Who the hell are you and what's that in your hand? The father said.

"I'm your fairy god mother, you old coot, so shut up and roll up your sleeve."

He did so without another word, while staring at that needle that was going in his arm. I was a little surprised at Fiera's words, as far as I knew she had only been here a little under twenty- four hours and already picked up some of our language's peculiar sayings.

"What's your name old man? Mine's Fiera."

"Festes Framm, we're from Ohio, we were heading for Santa Fe, when I broke my leg and the wagon train left us here, he said there weren't any Indians around and that we should be alright."

"Well as to Indians he was dead wrong; you were just fortunate that some of those Comanches hadn't spotted you yet. How long have they been gone?" I asked.

"It was just this morning when they left." Festes was saying as I stepped down and Fiera followed me out of the wagon.

Hattie was bent over the mother, "Look she's coming awake." Hattie said as the woman set up and looked at all three of us staring at her.

"Who, who are you 'all?"

"I'm Hattie Bodeen, this is my twin sister Fiera and that is my husband, Matthew Bodeen."

"Is your sister in the Army?"

"Yep, she is," I said, butting in on the conversation. 'Your husband said the wagon train left this morning?"

"How are you feeling?" Fiera said butting in before she could answer my question.

"Uh, I feel good, the best I've ever felt; I thought I felt someone poke me with a needle in the arm, is that right?"

"Yep, that was me, just some medicine that I had laying around, I gave some to your husband also, and he should be getting out of that wagon in a few minutes."

"Huh? How can that be he has a broken leg, it takes months to heal."

"Not anymore, in fact your children are looking a might peckish, I think I'll give them a pick-me-up shot also." Fiera gave each kid a little of what ever was in that tube and they picked right up. About that time Festes came out of the wagon and said:

"I don't know what you gave me, but it's a miracle, my leg feels brand new. Who are you people anyway?"

"Just some friends that stopped by and seen that you needed help, you can take that steer with you, a gift from me and you had better hurry hitching up your team so you can catch up with that wagon train before Old Quanah Parker finds you all and takes your scalp." I said.

"Yeah, I've heard of him; I can pay you for that steer." Festes said while reaching in his pocket. "No, I said he was a gift, take him and be on your way…"

It didn't take them long to break camp and hook their team to the wagon. I gave them some more advice just before they pulled out: "Don't tell anyone about that medicine we gave you all, they will just call you a liar."

As we stood there watching them go, I asked Fiera, "What in the hell was in that stuff you gave them, and why the kids also?"

"Nanites, they're small bio-mechs, that go in the bloodstream and fix things that are wrong, and also keep you healthy. I have them in my bloodstream, here let me inoculate both of you; you probably already have some in your blood from out close contact last night, but these will bring you up to full strength."

"And what else other things will they do for us?" I asked.

"Uh, make you live longer."

"How much longer?"

"It's up to what life style you choose, maybe hundreds of years longer, maybe not." Fiera said, but I could tell she wasn't telling us everything.

"You're telling me that, that family could live hundreds of years? Crap Fiera, they will be known as freaks, what have we done to them?"

"Saved their lives, even that unborn baby will be born with a long life to live; besides they will learn to cope with their longevity. That's another thing, their intelligence will increase also." Fiera said, while giving me a look that Hattie has sometime given me when I'm being obtuse. Anyway, I held my arm out and she jabbed me with the needle, one good thing, she had changed the needle to a clean one.

It was a funny thing about the three of us, it seemed like our lives were intertwined now, physically, mentally, and spiritually; instead of just Hattie and I being one, now the three of us were one; and I wasn't sure how I felt about that; hell, I wasn't sure about everything that had been going on...

The two of them were riding along side by side and keeping up a steady stream of verbiage and the pack horses were following along behind them; so I could see that I wasn't really needed and probably not wanted, so I told them that I was going to scout ahead; they just nodded their heads and kept on yakking.

I was riding my Morgan stallion, whom Hattie had named Napoleon, but I just called him Nate. He stood sixteen hands, which was about average for Morgans. Why am I telling you this, you could probably care less; But I care, because after my wife, horses and dogs were my best friends. I was pondering on this as I rode, because I didn't want to think about what was riding behind me; out of sight out of mind...

The day was coming onto be humid, after that rain we had for two days. So I didn't want to push the horses too hard otherwise we could have made it home, but I figure we had better camp out another night.

I knew of another spring we could camp by; and it was only three of four hours till we got there, so we could relax and do some swimming. And maybe I could get to know my new sister-in-law a little better; I didn't know how much better I could get to know her, after seeing her stark naked and sleeping with the two of them that way. As I rode along I couldn't help but smile, me thinks I was protesting too much...Or maybe those bio-mechs were taking effect, cause I sure felt good, in fact I couldn't remember ever feeling this good.

I stopped and let Nate grab a bite on the tall grass and waited for the girls to catch up. As they rode up, Hattie jumped off of Jasper and ran into my arms kissing me, when she came up for air, she said: "Wow, I feel good, the best I ever have, do you want to make love?"

"Sure, I do, but not right now, we're not alone you know?" I said, indicating that Fiera was standing there watching us.

Fiera said: "Don't mind me; I might learn a little something. But take it easy, it's just the Nanites kicking in, you're on a high now, you'll come down and level out; there will be a lot of changes going on in your system. Your reflexes will be much quicker, your sight will improve, your strength will double, in fact everything about you will get much better."

"What? You mean those settlers will react like this also?" I said.

"No, I gave them a much different strain; I gave you and Hattie the same strain that I have in me. They will feel better and heal better and live longer, but they won't be super human like us."

"Super Human; just what does that mean?"

"Well, I'll show you, you see that limb up there, why don't you jump up there and grab it."

"Huh, that's at least twenty feet to that limb, no one can do that." I said.

"Just try it, don't be such a pansy."

"Alright, but I know I'll fail." I said, then I crouched down and gave a jump. I not only reached it, but I was high enough to set on that branch. I almost fell off I was so surprised.

"What the hell, how am I supposed to get down from here?"

"Just like you got up there, just jump down, just remember to flex your knees when you hit the ground."

"I bet I will break a leg or something." Then I dropped, that was the longest twenty feet I had ever seen, I thought, but I did like Fiera said, and used my knees as a spring board you might say, I went back up about ten, and came back down and I stuck the landing with just a small hop.

"Yeah, that's the way; you'll learn to control it as time goes by, but be careful till you learn your strength, you don't want to hurt anybody. Oh yeah, you'll be smarter also, just keep that in check, don't let your ego show off, people hate a smart alec."

"Fiera, I still haven't come to grips with you being here; just why are you really here? I know you said you wanted to see your sister; but wanting and going is two separate things." I said.

"Yes, but you see being a twin on Terra and being one on earth is a little bit different. Being a twin on Terra means they stick together for life."

"Maybe you had better explain that a little bit more." Hattie said.

"Well for one it means they don't go their separate ways; and there is a little bit more to it, but I had rather wait to tell you the rest till we bond some more. Can you trust me?"

I looked at Hattie and she nodded her head, so I guess if Hattie could I could also. We mounted back up and rode in silence for a while. I didn't know what the bonding a little bit more meant; if all three of us sleeping together naked wasn't bonding I didn't know what was. And that's what we really done, was sleep together, except that little thing they did when we woke up. I couldn't help but smile while thinking about that as we rode along.

Both girls started back up talking a mile a minute, which was good, although I couldn't hear what they were saying, just the rhythm of their voices was soothing. I almost fell asleep, so I told them I was going to check our back trail; I did that every once in a while; it was a habit I got into back in the Territory of Montana, saved my life a time or two.

I rode back about a quarter of a mile and then moved off the trail under some trees and brush and settled down to wait. I just had a feeling that something was following us, something, not someone…

I was right, for coming down the trail, floating along was that so-called pod of Fiera's. I gigged Nate up and rode out in front of it: "So Mister Pod where do you think you are going? Didn't Fiera tell you to wait in that pond?"

It stopped and turned a little toward me, "Uh, yes." a voice said.

I sat there a minute watching it and it watching me, then I said: "Alfred is that you?"

"Yes, Mr. Bodeen, it is I. Well I'm not really in this thing, I am still in our ship, I am just using this blasted thing to keep tabs on the Mistress. I was told by the Master that I had better keep her safe or I would be recycled."

"Alright, but don't you think that pod is quite conspicuous?"

"Yes, but I needed a conveyance to follow along; wait, I have an idea, would you be willing to put me so to say in your saddle bags?"

"Sure, how big are you?"

"Oh, I'm not there, like I said, but the electronic device is only about the size of one of your silver things on your bridle there."

"Alright, but what are you going to do with that pod?"

"Oh, I will send it back to the pond, get off of your horse and come here, I'm opening the hatch now, and the device is in the bed."

I did and it was small about the size of a double eagle; I picked it up and flipped in the air like a coin and caught it again.

"Hey, don't do that, do you want to make me sick?" Alfred said, as the hatch on the pod closed and it turned around and disappeared.

"I thought you said that you were in your ship."

"I am, but I sense every movement and I also can see what that device sees. So be careful, huh?"

"So, in essence you will be spying on us?"

"No, of course not; I'm very discreet, my only interest is safeguarding the twins, and of course, you Master Bodeen now that you are part of us."

"I'm part of you?"

Oh yes, but goodness me, I have overstepped my bounds, Fiera hasn't explained everything yet, I assume."

"No, she sure hasn't. What is she going to say when you show up?"

"Oh no, please don't tell her about our little arrangement, she would be furious. I didn't want do this, but your parents explicitly told me to watch over you."

"Whoa there, not my parents, they're in Kentucky."

"Oh, I am sorry; I was speaking in the broad sense. I'm going to be quiet now till Fiera tells you everything."

I shook the coin, but I guess he was as good as his word. I stuck it in my vest pocket. I wasn't going to tell Fiera and maybe it would be best if I didn't blab everything to Hattie, just not quite yet.

I caught up to them just as they reached the spring where we would stay the night. Hattie was unsaddling Jasper, "Well what did you see, any boogie men?"

"Nope, none of them, I guess." I said as I was unsaddling Nate and Fiera was doing the same to her mount. Hattie stowed her saddle under a Ponderosa Pine and turned to look at me; "You're not telling me everything, are you?"

"Nope, not till Fiera tells us everything; don't push her yet; let her tell us everything in her own good time. The only thing I can say right now, that I know for sure is that we have some Timberline Moments coming up."

By the time I put my saddle next to Hattie's and Fiera's saddles, Fiera already had those fancy shelters set up and Hattie and she were making some chuck for supper. Yeah, and they had nothing on but their skin suits. I pulled up a stump and watched them. There was not one hair difference in their bodies, they were exact replicas of each other; it went far beyond of just being identical twins. I was afraid as time went on I wouldn't be able to tell them apart. I felt like our whole world was turning upside down.

They turned to me; "Hey, we're going to go for a dip in the spring, the meal will be ready when we get out, get out of those duds and join us." They said as they pushed the button and those skin suits retracted.

I was dusty and tired so I did what they said. Those skin suits were like a second skin, but there's nothing like plain old skin to the touch and the three of us was doing a little touching. I had been at this spring before, but, had never taken the time to really do more than wash off.

I dove down about ten feet and the bottom was deeper than that, fact is I couldn't see the bottom. The girls dove with me. Fiera or was it Hattie motioned for us to go deeper, so we did. Now I had held my breath before but not this long, I guess those nanites were doing their job.

We did find the bottom and setting on the bottom was an old chest with an iron padlock on it. I took hold of the handle on one end the girls on the other handle and we pushed off for the surface.

We sat it on the bank and stood there looking at it; the chest looked old but there was no rust on it, in fact it was as clean as a whistle, just like it hadn't been in the drink over a day.

"I wonder what the story on that is." I said.

"Why don't you ask him?" Hattie said.

"I will, Alfred, what gives with the weapons?" She said, putting her finger to her temple.

Alfred cleared his throat and said: "Have you ever heard of that old earth adage; It's better to be safe than sorry?"

Fiera looked over at me and then walked over and reached in my vest pocket; "What's this, where did you get this sensor? Alfred gave it to you, didn't he? No wonder we could all hear what Alfred said."

"Yes Miss, I did give it him; for the same reason that I put that trunk there for you all to retrieve. And if you will look in the trunk you will see there are four suits of battle armor. And you Miss know the reason for the armor and weapons and I would suggest that you inform

Miss Hattie and Master Bodeen of that reason."

"Alfred do you know something that I don't?"

"You know about the unrest at home, but I received a message from your Father; a light Frigate has left our Galaxy headed for the Milky Way Galaxy, he thinks it is heading for Earth; our sensors read six life forms on board. He thinks one of them is your ex suitor Bertram. You know how mad he was when you turned him down; he said if he couldn't have you no one could..."

"Do you have an ETA on that ship?"

"Yes, it will reach orbit in the next five days; do you want me to destroy them?"

"No, I don't think so; Bertram in such a wimp, I think he is being used by the Ottoman faction. Just let us know when they arrive; we'll take care of them."

"Sister, you had better fill us in on everything? Just what the hell is going on, are you getting us mixed up in an inter-stellar war?" Hattie said.

"War? No, just some political infighting. But you both are already mixed up in it; first off, you and I are more than just identical twins, we are interlocking twins. What one does the other one does. We should have never been separated. Haven't you ever felt something was missing in your life?"

"Well, now that you mention it, yes I have had dreams about having a sister and her being torn away from me."

"And you Matthew, didn't you ever wonder how come you never fit in with your family all of the way and why you left home when you were fourteen? You're not a twin but you were adopted so to say; one day you just showed up setting naked on their doorstep. You too are a Terrain.

And also, I could not of married Bertram, because being an interlocking twin, I was already married here on earth; yes Matthew you have two wives...I know it's a shock to you, but look at Hattie, she knows it's the truth."

I looked at my wife, she nodded her head. "Whoa, whoa, back on Terra that might be true, but here on earth that's one big no-no." I said.

"You're right; while we are here I will have to be just your sister-in-law. Didn't you ever wonder why Hattie didn't get pregnant? Even in pregnancy we are interlocked."

"Well, wait just a damn minute; Hattie isn't all Terrain, she's half from earth."

"No, she's not; her mother was all Terrain. But her brothers are half and half. You see back in those days young Terrains were running around sowing their wild oats like the earthlings would say; since then new rules have been put in place."

I stood there as naked as they were looking at them. I think we just went well beyond a bunch of Timberline moments. I looked at the trunk; "Do you have the key to the trunk?"

"We don't need a key just touch the lock it will open to Terrains." I reached down and gave it a try; sure, enough it popped right open. "Why did it open for me?" I asked Fiera.

"That's what I wanted to find out; is whether or not it would open for you. You have that sensor that Alfred gave you in your vest pocket, go get it and let's try something." I went over to where my clothes were stacked and brought it back.

"Alright, put your thumb in the middle of the sensor." I did so and I got a pin prick in my thumb, I jerked my thumb away and said: "What the hell?"

"It just took a sample of your blood; give it a minute and Alfred will tell us what the sample said." Fiera said...

"What it said? Are you crazy, blood does not talk."

"Really dear, everything talks in its own way." Hattie said, as she pressed her body up next to mine...

Alfred's voice spoke from the sensor: "Yes, it is he; his DNA is a familial match."

"What is he talking about, my DNA is a match, to what and what is DNA?"

"You might say that DNA is your blood's fingerprint, and yours match the family that you came from. And we not only came to find my sister, but also, we were looking for you. We had a hunch you were the heir to the throne ever since Hattie met you. You see Jasper sent back pictures of you and you look like your father."

"Heir to the throne, what in hell throne is that? And if I am, how did I get down here?"

"You were abducted when you were six months old and we believe that the Ottoman Faction back on Terra was responsible; which that twit Bertram is responsible also or cahoots with them."

"Well, I don't feel like any alien, I feel like I belong right here on this earth. You said that Bertram is on his way down here? If so, and if he had a hand in kidnapping me, then when he gets here I'm just going let some daylight into his innards."

"Yes, well, that's what the contents of this trunk is for; we not only have the latest weapons but also Battle Armor; we have three suits and one spare."

"Hey, I just had a thought, we're not cousins or anything; are we?"

"Heavens no, but our families have been friends for hundreds of years. But getting back to the weapons; when they do accost us, we have to let them fire first; don't worry our battle suits will protect us; then we will be free to execute them."

"Don't they have battle suits?"

"Yes, but not like ours, ours are the latest Terra has to offer. Do you want to get them out and practice a little bit with them?"

"Well I reckon we should; since we ain't ever seen them before." I said.

Fiera reached in and pulled one out and handed it to me. It was a cube about ten inches. There was what looked like a button, "Should I push that button?"

"Yes, but, hold it up over your head when you do."

I did as I told, and whiz bang, that thing had me all wrapped up in it. Something grabbed onto my penis and then something was at my back door. "What the hell is going on?" I almost screamed.

"Oh, that's the waste recycling system; you can live in those suits for days, even in space. Do you see that HUD display? That tells you how your bodily function is doing; also, it has emergency medical help, up to even putting more nanites in if needed. Also, it will tell you when and where any enemies are. The suit even recycles the oxygen you breathe. And there are even laser beams built into each arm, all you have to do is point and think fire and they will. But they are only for emergencies, you'll also have a rail gun; it fires depleted uranium projectiles; they will go through most any kind of armor. Also, the suit more than doubles your strength and reflexes. It has a built in AI that will do most of your routine thinking; what name do you want to give it?"

"It needs a name?"

"Oh yes, the AI is your personal companion. No one else can use that suit now; it belongs only to you. He will be your friend for life."

"What about the suit that Hattie wears, it's not a he, is it?"

"It can be whatever you want it to be; yours can be female if that's what you want."

"Can she have Hattie's voice?"

"Yes, of course, if that's what you want."

"Can I call it Hattie number two?"

"That name is a little long don't you think?"

"Yeah, I'll just call her 'Two', how's that?" Hattie looked at me and shook her head and laughed.

Hattie put hers on and she gave a little shriek and then giggled. Fiera said: "You can cause that to vibrate if you want; on long deployments some women use that feature."

I thought a minute, watching Hattie's face through her visor. "Hattie you had better name yours after me!"

"I think I'll call him Dome. But I will give him your voice."

"That's a silly name, if ever I heard one." I said, she just giggled some more.

"What about you Fiera, what are you going to call yours?" I asked.

"Well since we are inter-locked twins, I have to go with the same name, besides I think it's sexy." She said as she winked at Hattie and then she giggled when she put her suit on. I thought to myself, what in the hell is sexy about the word Dome?

I felt like a dunce when I finally figured it out; say the word as two syllables instead of one-you might even have to put a hyphen in the middle…

We played around with the suits till we got fairly familiar with their usage then we took them off and put our regular clothes back on and packed everything on the pack horses.

I still couldn't get my mind around all of this alien stuff, even though Fiera said that I was all alien to earth; if I was then earth and terra must have the same genetic code somewhere along the line. Wait a sec, how did I even think of saying a 'genetic code', me that didn't get past the sixth grade? It must be those nanites that Fiera shot in me.

I dropped back with the pack horses, still mulling over everything; mostly I was thinking about having two wives? No, I don't think that was going to work for me; although I could hardly tell them apart. Even though Fiera said that was sort of natural back on Terra for inter-locking twins to share the same husband. It seemed to me that they would get jealous of one another. And there was nothing worse than having two jealous women around the house.

I was watching them riding ahead of me; the way they filled out their pants...I shook my head and decided to ride ahead and sort of prepare the way you might say.

"Hey, I think I'll ride ahead, we're only a few miles from the Hacienda and let them know we're coming; Alright?"

"We'll be fine, I have that sensor Alfred gave you and there is no red dots anywhere around." Hattie said.

Darn, how boring, I couldn't even count on bad guys putting the sneak on us, now we would know they were there. Well anyway, I didn't have to worry about getting shot in the back.

The first vaquero that I came across was Ricardo Sanchez, the foreman of our ranch. "Hola! Senor Bodeen." He called out; "Where is the Senora, she is well?"

"Yes, of course, she is following with the pack horses and her sister."

"She has a Sister? Where did you find her?"

"She was on a wagon train that we helped to fight off some Indians. Perhaps you could ride back to the Hacienda and tell them we are coming?

"Yes of course Senor Bodeen, they all will be relieved to see that you're safe."

I rode back to the women and filled them in on my lie, which I was sure would be the first lie of many to come...

We rode in to a raucous reception; which was totally unexpected; they must have missed us. We had our pack horses unloaded and the stuff taken to our room, with the admonition not to unpack it; we would do it ourselves.

Selena was not there when we first got there; they said she was with the vaqueros chasing some rustlers. We had just got the packs dealt with when she stepped into our room.

Fiera did a double take; Selena stood there in her abbreviated buckskins with her bow and hanging from her belt was some bloody scalps.

Selena stood there staring at the two of them; Hattie and Fiera were most undressed; well really, I guess they were naked, I hadn't been watching all that close. Selena walked over to them; she turned them around inspecting each of them. She made them spread their legs. I knew Hattie had a small mole there, but I was surprised, Fiera had one there also; I should of know she would, but I never looked that close to Fiera's, uh, you know what.

"We're twins," Hattie said breathlessly. "This is Fiera."

"I see that you are twins, but even identical twins are not really that identical. You cannot fool me; and he cannot fool me either;" Selena said, turning to me. "I have known ever since we have met what you both are; all three of you are not of this earth. My Grandmother was a Medicine Woman; she told me of out of this world people and how to spot them. Have you heard the saying that if it is too good to be true, it isn't true? All three of you have no flaws you're too perfect, you forget I have slept naked with you both in the same bed, I see what others cannot. Do not think that I dislike you, I do not; I have come to love you both and your sister has come down, what does she want?"

Fiera came and gave her a hug and said: "I want you to think of me as you think of them, we are all one. And yes, I came down for a purpose; he, our husband is the heir to the throne on Terra. There is much unrest and maybe soon to be war on Terra, we do not know for sure, but perhaps his presence will avert such a war. We have never had a civil war on Terra; there has always been peace among us."

"Then if there is a war among you, I also must come and fight alongside of my friends; I cannot do less I owe them my life."

"Yes, I knew of you and I expected nothing less of you; I brought an extra battle suit just for you. I see that you have blood on you and those scalps should be buried; is there a place that we can bath?"

"Uh, yeah," I said, "there's a hot spring that we use to bath in; we can walk there, if you two will put a robe on; I don't want the vaqueros losing their minds over you both."

"First though, Selena, I need to inoculate you with nanites, they will make you stronger and smarter and kill any unwanted bacteria."

"I do not know what 'to inoculate' means, but I trust you, so go ahead." After that, they walked out toward the spring, leaving me to gather up the towels and trot after them; oh yes, I'm really important, I'm nothing but a towel bearer.

Selena put her clothes on a rock and looked at me; "Could you please bury them for me?" Yep, I'm really important, now I have to dig a grave for some scalps.

When I got back I took my buckskins off and got in the pool with them; the pool was nice and warm and the water had some kind of minerals in it that were soothing also. I floated on my back and dozed off…dreaming dreams that were about Hattie that perhaps should be left unsaid…

Their giggling and carrying on woke me; I let myself sink down and swam under the water toward them and stopped by their feet; I grabbed Hattie's foot and pulled her under and gave her a kiss; and then we both surfaced together.

All three of them were staring at me: "What I can't kiss my wife?" I said, with my arm still around Hattie.

"Uh, Honey, that's not me that you have your arm around, that's Fiera." I looked closely at who I had kissed and was still holding.

"No, I know your kiss; you can't fool me; can you?"

"Oh, then reach down between my legs, do you feel that little mole there?" The woman I was holding said. I did, and damn it wasn't there. I let loose of her right quick. "I'm sorry Fiera, I thought you were Hattie; your kiss was just like hers."

"Well of course it was;' Hattie said, 'we told you we're interlocked."

I wanted to change the subject, so I asked Selena; "Where's Aiken and Alden and their wives?"

"They have been working on their own places; remember you told them they could carve out ranches of their own. They should be back here this evening; they still sleep here every night."

"What about you and Jose, how is that going?"

"I don't know I just can't warm up to him; he's like a little puppy dog following me around and slobbering all over the place."

"Well then if he's like a puppy it's up to you to train him into what you want; do you want a pet or a companion who will fight for you and lay down his life in your behalf. I'm sure he has many good qualities that you will have to dig for; after all look at his father, they say the acorn doesn't fall far from the tree."

"Yes, perhaps I haven't given him a chance to prove himself. I will have to take him with me next time I go after some stolen cattle and train him to be a man."

When we got back to the hacienda the boys and their wives were there. No one had told them about Fiera.

"What, who is she? What the hell they look alike." Aiken said.

"Aiken, Alden, this is Fiera, she is Hattie's twin sister." I said while watching their reaction.

"Damn, I knew it; Alden do you remember me telling you on the night that Hattie was born that I heard two different girls crying. Where has she been all of these years?" Aiken said.

"With your mother, you see she didn't die at childbirth, your parents had a big fight and your Ma took Fiera and ran off. We found Fiera on a wagon train that broke down and we helped them fix a couple of broken wheels. That's all I know; you might want to ask Fiera for any more details." I said, I never was a very good liar, I was sure Fiera could twist a tale or two.

Funny thing about the truth, you would think the truth should always be the unvarnished truth; but people hear what they want to hear; you tell them the truth and they call you a liar. You tell them a big fat lie and if it's what they want to hear, they say that's the gospel truth. But in the end the truth is still the truth; even if they won't believe it.

It was coming on to supper time and so all Hacienda family met in the dining room; including the Don and Ruby, who were an item now, and the twins Ethel and Myrtle Ward, also Jose and Selena and all of us, including April and June who giving Fiera the evil eye, them being the jealous kind; you know a single woman who might try and put a move on their husbands; even if she was their sister. They didn't know about that inter-locking twin thing between Hattie and Fiera, which I wasn't too happy about, as you know…Even though they said I was an alien to earth myself; which I was having a hard time believing; you know like I said, maybe I didn't want to believe it.

When Hattie and Fiera were getting dressed for the evening meal, Hattie was showing Fiera how to strap on the extra Stiletto of Hattie's. They were dressing in typical Mexican blouses and skirts; of course, they conveniently left off any undergarments.

When I said there might be dancing after the meal and if they planned to dance and twirl about that they should put something on the bottom anyway. Hattie said: "No, you see where we place the Stiletto it's fairly high on the thigh and any underwear might get caught if we had to get to the knife in a hurry, show him Fiera."

"Alright I believe you; you don't have to show me." Of course, they both showed me; just to watch me squirm.

Hattie had laid out my suit of fancy Spanish duds. Of course, I had my Bowie on a lanyard down my back. When we went into the dining room they each took an arm and they made sure we were noticed; which we were, everyone turned and stared. Not because of the way they were dressed, because all of the women and girls present were dressed the same way. But because they were showing the proprietary ownership of who was walking between them. I don't think I will ever figure out the workings of the female mind…

The Don and Ruby were setting on one end of the long table with Jose setting on one side of the table and Selena setting on the other side. Ethel and Myrtle were setting beside Selena and the foreman Ricardo Sanchez and his wife were setting beside Jose. And Aiken and April were setting across the table from Alden and June. Then the three of us were setting on the other end of the table. There were a bevy of servant girls running around. Somehow us returning with Fiera had turned into a festive event; with wine greasing the axels.

As we were finishing up the repast we could hear the musicians tuning up at the outdoor pavilion. Where the impromptu fandango was just starting; where all were invited to attend.

There were four of us who only drank one glass of wine; that was my lovely twins and I, along with Selena. As we were walking out, Alfred the AI beeped me on the sensor/communicator indicating he had some information for us. I walked to a quiet corner and said: "What's up Alfred?"

"You do know that Fiera gave Selena a battle suit and also a skin suit?"

"Yeah, I knew about the battle armor, but not the skin suit. Why?"

"Selena tried on the skin suit this afternoon and I took a DNA sample, turns out she is half native Indian and half Terrain; her father or mother came from Terra."

"The Hell You Say? Are you sure?"

"Please Sir, you doubt my veracity? I am incapably of making a mistake."

"I'm sorry Alfred; I didn't mean it that way; have you told Fiera or Hattie yet?"

"No, do you wish me to inform them?"

"Yes, but why did you tell me first?"

"Sir, you are the Royal Heir to the throne, it was only proper Sir, do you wish me to break the protocol?"

"No, no I guess not; I'm having a hard time taking all of this into my brain; it's a big jump from pauper to king."

"Sir, I'm sure you were never a pauper in spirit."

"I guess you're right about that Alfred; but I've been penniless a few times. Go ahead and inform the twins about Selena." With that I went over to where the Vaqueros were gathered smoking their tobacco rolled up in thin paper, a habit that to me was filthy and looked like it could be bad for their health.

They were telling me all about catching the rustlers and how Selena didn't give them time to hang them before she killed them. The way they talked I couldn't tell if they were in awe of her, or just plain scared of her; probably a combination of both.

Hattie and Fiera came over and pulled me away and said: "Alfred told you about Selena, right?" I nodded. "Well what do you think, should we tell her?"

"I would wait a little while; why don't you train with her on her Battle Armor and see how she takes to it; whether she likes working with it or not. And then we'll see. You know she has a tendency to shoot first and ask questions later; she might not want to leave earth."

"Who said she has to leave earth; you know there are a lot of Terrains living on earth and have been for hundreds of years. In their DNA earth people and Terrains are cousins, you might say." Fiera said.

"Yeah, well, be that as it may; I'm finding this weirder than hell." I said.

"You know in the English language Terra is just another name for earth or land and Terra Incognita is simply unexplored land. You see also both Terra and Earth have what's called Homo Sapiens DNA. In other words, we're all human." Fiera said.

"Well the Bible doesn't say anything about there being another world with humans on it." I said.

"That doesn't mean there can't be; maybe he made Terra first and then decided to make another one, just for fun." Fiera said.

I shut up; I wasn't going to touch that one with a ten- foot pole. I said: "I thought you two were going to dance, look out there look at them girls whirl." I did a double take; some of those girls that were serving us at dinner didn't have any under clothes either. While I was looking Fiera and Hattie both grabbed a vaquero and ran for the dance floor. Before I knew it one of those young girls grabbed my hand and dragged me out there also.

It was late when we got to bed, I went out to the outhouse and by the time I got back they were both in bed; I started to crawl in beside Hattie, "Hold on there, you're sleeping in the middle not on the outside." Hattie said. And I guess that set the precedent for all of the nights to come....

Chapter Seventeen

The sun was just coming up when I awoke and looked at each of the women sleeping beside me. Hattie had some kind of a device attached to her forehead. I put my hand to my head, I also had one. I started to reach for it- when I heard: "Process complete; detach module." It came loose in my hand. Then:

In my head a voice spoke: "Good Morning Prince Attila this is the voice of your learning tutor I've downloaded all of the knowledge you will need till our next session when you will have taken the throne. Hattie has also been brought up to the same level as Fiera; have a nice day." "What the hell?" I said out loud.

"You can say that again," Hattie said, while holding that device in her hand.

Fiera was watching us both. "I see we're all at the same level now; knowing who were are and the responsibility that lay upon us. I am Princess Fiera and Hattie is Princess Hattie, your wives; and co-officers in the Terrain Navy. You are not only a Prince but heir to the throne and also a Captain in the Navy. Which, you both already know since the download." Hattie and I looked at each other, our eyes locked while we ran through some of the new knowledge in our brains.

I didn't understand how I could be a Captain in the Terrain Navy when I had never been to space—but then it clicked in: I was a Captain at one time till I was assassinated, due to being an heir to the throne. I guess I wasn't really dead, but my life force was transferred back to my mother's womb and born again and then brought to earth; till the proper time to take my rightful place. I guess I was all that, but at the same time I was still Matthew Bodeen also.

"Yeah, and I'm still Hattie Bodeen also, your Highness." Hattie said sarcastically. All three of us could hear each other's thoughts. Fiera chimed in: "Hey, we have a lot to do, no time to fight with each other; we need to tell Selena her part and also do some training with her in Battle Armor, she has to stay here on earth and be our contact, this will be our home base for North America."

"The hell you say; I know all of that, you forget I'm in charge now lieutenant and as such, both of you come here and give me hug; I'm scared shitless." It was like I had two different people inside of me. Hattie was shaking some also.

It took a while for us to assuage each other's fears, but we finally rolled out and got dressed. "Fiera why don't you take Selena and Hattie and train them with their battle suits, after breakfast though, then I want to talk to Aiken and Alden I need to fill them in on few things."

I had just begun to tell them about their two sisters and how they were aliens. When they accused me of being drunk.

"Alright then, maybe it would be better if Hattie filled you in on everything; that is if you can tell which one is Hattie and which one is Fiera. But boys I think I detected a little hint of malice when you all called me a drunk; or was I mistaken?"

Aiken and Alden looked at each other and then Aiken said: "Yeah, we called you a drunk, what are you going to do about it? You've been acting the big man ever since we met you; strutting around like you're God Almighty."

"Let me be clear on this; it sounds like you want to clean my clock; is that right? They nodded. "Alright then, now usually I like to fight people one at a time, but in the case of the two of you, I'll make an exception, and fight you both at the same time; so boys anytime you're ready just throw the first punch."

They both rushed me, I stepped to the side and around the back of them before they even knew I had moved and knocked their heads together. I caught both of them before they fell and laid them down easy. They looked right peaceable laying there. Now I guess you're wondering how I moved so fast, well I didn't know myself, must have been all of those nanites Fiera pumped into me, or else my previous experience as a Terrain kicked in.

What they said made me think; had I really been acting like that? I didn't think I had. How was I going to explain to Hattie that I had cold-cocked her brothers? And what about April and June, they would make my life miserable. Boy was I ever in trouble. I had better make myself scarce for a while; so, I went and saddled a horse and went for a ride.

It was coming on to long shadow time by the time I got back and rubbed my horse down and gave him bait of oats. I washed up at the sink outside of the kitchen and went in to the dining room, everyone else was already eating, and Hattie and Fiera had saved me a spot between them. Aiken and Alden were setting beside their wives, they looked up and gave me nod, I nodded back.

"Where have you been?" Hattie asked me.

"I just went for a ride, didn't I boys" I said looking at them.

"Yep, he told us he was going to check the northeast pasture." Aiken said.

"Why didn't you tell me this when we talked this afternoon?"

"I don't know, didn't think of it I guess." Aiken said, while paying close attention to his food.

I don't know why Hattie was acting like she didn't know what went on, she knew every word what was said, remember we knew what all three of us was saying or hearing; I guess she was just doing it for her brothers' benefit. The only thing we couldn't do was read each other's mind. I gave her a wink.

We went back to our room after diner. We were talking all of the way back; "So Selena took her new role alright; yeah I know I heard what was said; just like you all heard what Aiken and Alden said. But you know what, I don't like hearing what everyone is talking about all of the time; is there a way we can shut that down to just what we want to transmit?" I said.

"Yes, we can block transmitting, but we can't block what we are hearing unless the one transmitting blocks it. In other words, our receiving is always open, but we can block what we are sending out." Fiera said.

"I am sorry about your brothers, but do I really act like they said?"

"No dear, you don't, I think April and June put thoughts in their heads; but you sure knocked that out of them. We explained everything to them, we blocked that conversation, because you didn't need to hear it."

"Anyway, I was wondering Fiera if any of those nanites would work to sort of mellow them out some? We're going to have to leave them here without supervision that is besides Selena, we don't want them going off the deep end."

"Yeah, I was going to give all four of them an infusion, I could tweak them a little; Selena just got the same as you and Hattie. What about some of the others; I could give them a reduced dose the same as I gave those people with that wagon?"

"I don't know, what do you think Hattie?"

"Yeah, I suppose we had better, it wouldn't be right not to, would it?"

"Alright, you and Fiera cook up a logical reason why they are getting the needle, so they won't freak out."

"And Fiera, what about that Bertram fellow, how close is his ship?"

"You can ask Alfred, I'm not your go-between; just say Alfred, where is that jerk Bertram?"

"Mam, I will check, just a second." Alfred answered. "He's due in orbit in 24 hours. Do you want me to shoot him down?" All three of us heard his response.

Fiera looked at me, "What about it Prince Attila, do you want to shoot him down?"

"Don't call me that; and no, I don't want to shoot him down; Alfred let me know when he gets within a hundred thousand miles and then come and pick the three of us up; I want to talk to him personally."

"Very good Sir, I'll pick you up at 0900 hours in the morning; please be somewhere that we won't be seen by the local populace."

"Will that give you both time take care of inoculating Aiken and Alden and their wives? I know it will take a longer time for all of the rest of the ranch."

"Yeah, we'll do my brothers right now, there in their rooms." And they picked up their med kit and left. I went to the stables and talked to Jasper.

He was waiting for me. "Hey Jasper, did you hear all of what was being said the last few days?" I wasn't expecting an answer, but I could understand him when he spoke, well not out loud, but in my brain.

"Yes Matt, I am equipped with a translation chip; are you going to leave me behind when you go to Terra?"

"Uh, I don't know, do you want to go, or maybe Selena might need your help?"

"Yes, my thought exactly, I think I should stay here; I'm too old to go gallivanting around space. And talking about being old; can I get some of those nanites?"

"I don't see why not, why don't you ask Fiera? I think she could do that yet tonight; tell her I said to give you some; after all they call me Prince Attila, I guess I'm some kind of royalty or something."

"Well, don't get the big head, I'm still going to call you Matt."

"I agree with you, I feel like Matt, not Attila. Hey, I think I've heard that word Attila before."

"You should have, Attila the Hun, didn't you go to school?"

"Some, but I never heard it there; I think an English Fur Trapper was telling me about him one winter. I hope people don't expect me to be like him. But how do you know about Attila the Hun?"

"I can read you know; they have been sending me books now and then."

"How, direct to your brain?"

"No, to my implant, I have a lot of stuff stored in there; I can draw it up every time I want to read."

"So, when you're standing around with a stupid look on your face, that's when you're reading?"

"Not all of the time; sometimes I just like to stand around with a stupid look on my face; after all you have been an example to me." Jasper said, then turned and walked away.

I think I've just been put in my place by a mule. Damn, as if things couldn't get any weirder; which they usually did, but perhaps, just perhaps they wouldn't this night. I wasn't sure though, so I went back to our room. Hattie and Fiera weren't back yet. So, I picked up that learning thing and stuck it on my forehead and went to sleep.

I awoke the next morning with the twins on either side of me. Hattie had her learning thing on also, I noticed. I pulled them both closer and snuggled down between them and went back to sleep. Perhaps there was such a thing as heaven on earth…

When we finally did get out of bed it was too late for breakfast; but we made due with some bean tortillas; and as we were setting around drinking our coffee Fiera brought up that we only had ab hour till we needed to board our ship and intercept Bertram.

"Alright, where are we to do this? We can't have the ship come down here." I said.

"No of course not," Hattie said, "we will have to take the horses and ride to the south pasture, there won't be any body but the cattle there and Jasper can bring the horses back to the barn."

"What about Selena, does she know we're leaving this morning?"

"Yes sweetheart, she does; she has also been wearing the learning device to bring her up to speed. She knows what she has to do; also, she has a communicator so she can keep in touch with us."

"It's nine now, I thought Alfred was going to pick us up at nine?"

"We told him we would be a little late; due to uh, our sleeping a little late this morning."

"Yeah," I said, I could feel my face flushing, "is that what you call it?" I sort of mumbled to myself.

We did make it to the pickup point just as Alfred uncloaked the ship as he sat it down. I couldn't see any opening, but then one started to appear in the side of the ship and standing there was a beautiful naked woman.

"That's not Alfred, is it?" I said.

"No, that's Sari, she is the ship; you might say. You see Alfred is our personal AI, Sari is part of the ship; she controls all of the ships functions. Alfred is an android; well I guess you could say Sari is one also; it's sort of complicated. Sari stays with the ship most of time, she can go ashore for short periods, but she has to stay within hailing distance."

I looked at Sari and then I looked at the ship; its design was defiantly female, both of them. I studied Sari's perfect nakedness and then I asked Fiera: "Alfred isn't naked, is he?"

Fiera paused and then said: "Not anymore, he isn't. Do you want Sari to put some clothes on?"

"Well it wouldn't hurt to put a little something on; is there a standard uniform or something?"

"Yes, when we get aboard we all can put our official uniform on; it also serves as armor, something like our skin suits."

The suits were somewhat like our skin suits, but with weapons attached; they didn't leave much to the imagination either.

"Honey, you can stop staring at Sari, she's not going anywhere." Hattie said.

"Yeah, I know, but I have never seen an android before; but you can't tell she is one, look she even has pubic hair."

"Yes dear, there will be a lot of strange new things on Terra I'm sure." Hattie said, as Sari gave me a wink. I reached out my hand and touched her arm; it was warm and felt like normal skin.

Sari handed me my uniform and stood there as we started to put them on; I pulled Fiera around in front of me to block Sari's view; I don't know why I was so shy in front of her, but I was.

Sari said in a sexy voice, "You need to get over being shy on board my ship, I can see whatever goes on at anytime from anywhere, you see wherever you go I am there, I am the ship."

Alfred had appeared and said, "We need to go, it's getting time." I looked at him he was one handsome android; Fiera had said that he was their personal android; now I was getting jealous-was I wrong to be jealous of an android? How could I be one hundred percent Terrain when everything felt so strange?

Sari's voice came over the ship wide com.' "Captain to the bridge for preflight check."

Alfred said: "The Bridge is this way Captain." I nodded, and fell in behind Sari; how had her voice came over the com's when she was right here and I didn't see her speak?

Alfred had taken the lead with all three women behind him and me following along like a whipped puppy. Anyway, the view was better from this point of view; were all the women on Terra as beautiful as my two wives and this so-called android that was walking in front of me?

This ship was bigger than it looked from the outside; and from the outside it looked to be about two hundred feet long. When we stepped through the hatch into the bridge I was almost blinded by all of the blinking lights-in every color; "What the hell?" I exclaimed.

Sari turned to me and clamped one of those learning things to my forehead. It took me about ten seconds to comprehend what everything was and what it was for. There were five different consoles; with a comfortable looking chair in front of each. The middle chair was for me; anyway, I went and sat in it. Alfred took the one at the far left, Sari took the one on the far right, while Fiera took the one on my left and Hattie took the one on my right.

Alfred was on tactical; while Sari was on navigation; Fiera was engineering and Hattie was on damage control. I looked at Sari and said: "Take us out; set course for intercept."

"Aye, Captain. Course set in and locked." Sari said, while giving me a wink. What the hell was she winking at me for?

"Sari you can go to FTL when free of the earth's atmosphere; I want to intercept him on the other side of the moon. Also, Alfred I want you to target any weapons he has first thing, I don't want him even to be able to hit us with a spitball."

"What's a Spitball Captain?" Alfred asked. "Read my mind Alfred." I said in return.

"Oh, yes, rather infantile behavior, if I may say Sir."

"Yes, but rather effective in getting one tossed out of class so I could go fishing. Fiera how are the fusion reactors doing? And Hattie, are all systems ready for any damage we might receive?" They both replied in the positive.

"Sari, how long till contact?"

"Five minutes Sir, I have him on my sensors; Sir, he just launched four missiles."

"Initiate point defenses Alfred. Sari, open a channel to the idiot."

All of Alfred lasers worked perfect taking out all four of the missiles.

Bertram's picture appeared on the screen. He had on a vastly overdone uniform; reminded me of Admiral Nelson of the old English Navy. "Bertram, you have been a naughty boy; power down all of your weapons of I will destroy you."

"Who are you to tell me anything?"

"I am Prince Attila; heir to the throne on the planet Terra; but be that as it may, you have violated Earth's air space. And may I ask why you are bothering Fiera in following her to earth?"

"She is my betrothed and I intend to marry her."

"Then if you mistakenly think she is your betrothed, why did you fire missiles at us?

"I thought you were a pirate ship."

"Oh, come now, Sari says that you made a sensor sweep of us and you knew who we were. And I don't believe that you ever thought you were going to marry one of my wives, therefore that's why you launched missiles at us. I also believe that you knew that I was alive on earth and that your Ottoman Factions had failed to kill me when I was a baby. Do you think that you can kill me now?"

"Sir," Alfred said, "he's powering his forward canon, do I have permission to fire?"

"Fire when ready Alfred; destroy them, cut the head off of that rattlesnake."

Our forward kinetic railgun was all it took to remove the threat; there was nothing left but dust. I said to no one in particular: "I guess that means war with the Ottomans, I'm I right?"

"Maybe not Captain," Alfred said, "he never got off a message back to Terra, as far as the Ottomans are concerned he got swallowed up in a black hole."

Sari spoke up: "Where to now Captain?"

"Put us in orbit around the moon for now; I have to consult my two Executive Officers; if they will accompany me to our cabin?" I said, looking at them.

As we stepped into our cabin I said: "What in the hell did I just do?"

"You just killed a very dangerous snake, sweetheart. Hatti said and Fiera nodded.

"Alright, but where are we going now, back to earth or what? I mean have all the details been taken care of on earth-you know like explaining where we went if we leave earth now?"

"Yes Honey, Fiera and I have talked to my brothers and of course we are in constant contact with Selena. She was relieved when you shot Bertram out of the sky, well really not sky, but space; she was tuned in and heard everything and she seen the flash of light when he exploded."

"So how many people were on that ship besides him?"

"There were four others, all cohorts of Bertram's. Don't lose any sleep over them. Besides it was self-defense. Just like all of our gun battles have been." Hattie said.

"Yeah, I guess you're right; but now we're packing a lot bigger gun. Tell you what, I'm going to plug in and see if I can get a little more back ground on the troubles that Terra has; you guys go back to the bridge and discuss everything with Alfred and Sari and let me know where we are going next."

"Alright, but you're the Captain; you should be making all of the decisions." Fiera said.

"Oh, come on, really? I'm not stupid you know; all of this crap is out of my hands; my fate has been sealed ever since I was born, you both know that; we're all just a pawn on the chess board of life."

"Alright, we'll go and see what options are available; but you will still have to make the final decision." Hattie said and Fiera nodded.

"Damn, this Husband, Captain, Prince, thing is a drag." I told them as they departed.

I wasn't trying to weasel out of my responsibility, was I? I didn't think I was.

Chapter Eighteen

I went back to our cabin, mumbling under my breath; I put that learning thing on and laid myself down and fell asleep right away.

I must have slept a long time I thought when I awoke. I lay there going over some of the new things that were rolling around in my brain; one of them was about those skin suits: Turns out they weren't just some kind of new-fangled clothe, but they were alive! They were alive with Bacillus subtilis natto; a bacterium that changes shape quickly when the fabric starts to heat up from sweat or moisture, then it expands with the moisture and then releases heat from the skin; and then when the skin dries the bacteria contracts to retain the body heat. Of course, there is a fabric to hold the bacteria and that fabric becomes their home. I guess that skin suit was some kind of symbiosis thing…

Hattie came in and said: "I thought you were going to take a nap?"

"I did, why how long did I sleep?"

"Well I've only been gone for a couple of minutes, so not very long. Alfred says that we will be leaving FTL and going into warp-space; which will get us back to Terra in three days. And Sari is complaining about having to wear the uniform; she says it's against nature. Fiera and I were also wondering why you want us to cover our bodies."

"You want to know why? I'll show you why, go ahead take your uniform off." Hattie didn't waste any time disrobing. When she finished she looked at me; "Oh my, is that for me?"

"So, you see what I am talking about; I can't go around all of the time with this sticking out and getting in the way."

"Well I'll have to do something about that;" she said as she got in bed with me…Afterward I said, "that was only a temporary fix."

"Yes, I know, what we need is a switch of some kind to turn it on and off. Maybe Sari has something in sick bay that will work; I'll ask her." Hattie said as she got up and took a quick shower.

While Hattie was still in the shower Sari came in with a syringe in her hand; stark naked as usual. "What are you going to do with that?" I

208

asked her.

"Hattie said that you wanted to control your erections, with this you will be able to not only control when it happens but the size and sensitivity and duration; most of your Royal family already has this ability. And it looks like you sorely need it." Sari said looking at me....

"Well I wouldn't if you all would wear clothes, so shoot me up." I said.

Hattie came out of the shower and looking at me said: "I see Sari was already here; I com'd her when I was in the shower. She told Fiera and me all about what it would do, we're sort of anxious to try it out."

Well you're in for a big surprise, because now I have control over it; not the two of you."

"That's what you think, us wives have the password; did you really think we would give you control over something as important as that?" She said as she bent over and whispered in my ear. I didn't understand what she said, but she was right, it sprang to life...then she whispered again and it went down.

"Alright enough playing around; isn't there some duties that you need to attend to?" I said as I got up and went in the shower and then when I got out I put my uniform on, it felt natural...when I got to the bridge Hattie and Fiera had their uniforms on also. Would you believe they looked sexier with them on then they did when they were naked? Well to me anyway.

Of course, Sari was still au-natural. When I touched her arm that one time she felt human to me-and she sure enough looked human-in every way. I had noticed that she ate human food just like us- so how could she be an android? Alfred was the same way, but he wore his uniform.

I hailed Alfred on closed circuit and asked him: "What's the deal, you and Sari are supposed to be androids, but you look and feel human just like us?"

"We are genetically altered humans. We were created in a lab to be what we are; you see we were created to be expendable or cannon fodder as you would say; but our intelligence and computing ability and our physical strength are superior to regular humans; and now I'm afraid you humans are more expendable than we are. The only thing different is we are sterile and not able to procreate. But we do have sexual urges; Sari and I are married."

"So what about this ship, does it have a separate computer from you and Sari?"

"Of course, if you want to access it personally all you have to say is 'computer' and tell it what you want. But Sari is the main control on the ship's computer; you might say that she is part of the ship."

"Well what if something happens to the ship, does she go down with it?"

"No, she can disconnect and get in an escape pod just like us."

"So Alfred, are we going to meet anymore resistance before we get to Terra?

"It is unlikely Captain, but the Ottomans are unpredictable they have been restive for years. It was them that kidnapped you and took you to earth. Now that they know that you have been found and will shortly take your place beside your father, they may become desperate."

"Well, I would call them past desperate, with them attacking us already; I would call it a state of war, so if you would inform Sari that I consider us at war with the Ottomans and for her to prepare the ship accordingly. And Alfred please prepare any contingency plans that may be needed."

"Yes Captain, do you think it would be proper if I called your Father and ran this by him?"

"Well of course, I didn't think of that; I've been the one making decisions for so long I forgot I had a Father."

"Yes, well, don't tell him that; I'll message them now."

"Them, who's them?"

"Your Mother and Father; and Hattie's and Fiera's Mother and Father."

"So how long will that take to get them all together?"

"They have been waiting for over an hour for you all to get out of bed."

I glanced around at my wives, they nodded. "Proceed Alfred." I told him. The whole one side of the bridge wall turned into a screen. (Perhaps you are wondering why I even knew what a screen was, or even what a moving picture was; well we had been sleeping with that learning device for several nights now; so even a thick head like mine can absorb knowledge while sleeping.)

Hattie and Fiera were standing either side of me while I sat in the Captain's chair; Hattie was nervous I could tell being that her hand on my shoulder was twitching a little; couldn't blame her for being nervous at seeing her mother and father for the first time.

I wasn't nervous; just curious you could say; after all, if finding out I was an alien on earth didn't shake me up, why would meeting my father and mother make me nervous.... much less finding out they run the show on Terra and that I was supposed to be a Prince- big deal, right?

The picture came on; two men were setting in chairs and a woman was standing beside each one of them. I knew right away which ones were the parents of my wives. Their mother looked almost like them, even as to her age, if they all three stood together they could be triplets.

Now as to the King and Queen, he looked a little like me, but with a stern face; I guess that's what a King was supposed to look like. But my Mother was a knock out; she had on some kind of dress that changed colors and density every time she moved, at times it even turned clear in places. But come to think of it so did Hattie's mother's dress.

Fiera spoke up: "Mother this is your long-lost daughter and our husband, Matthew Bodeen, his earth name that is. And Father to you he is Prince Attila.

"And Matthew our mother's name is Ida Mae and father's name is August Templar. And your father is Alexander to you, but to others his name is King Alexander and your mother's name is Arlina, but of course to others she is Queen Arlina."

I didn't know what to say, but my father spoke up: "Son, we thought you were dead, you can't imagine our joy when we found out you were alive and married to Hattie, our God Daughter, as is Fiera also, and she is now a wife to you as well. Your Mother wanted me to ask if we could be expecting grandchildren soon?"

"Well mother one can only hope, but so far no luck, and it's not for the lack of trying I assure you, Hattie and Fiera are quite active In that endeavor." Hattie punched me on the arm.

Ida Mae laughed and said: "Your mother is not the only one waiting to hear any news on that subject. Jasper has been keeping us informed of everything that has happened since you and Hattie got married and now with Fiera in the picture we have doubled our chances."

August spoke up: "Yes, but I was very concerned that Hattie might get hurt in the many of the so-called gun battles that you have been involved in; I am sure you can understand a father's concern?"

"Yes Sir, and you were wise to be concerned, just as I was. But on the earth in this day and age if one did not defend himself he would be dead. Even now we had to defend ourselves on our way to Terra; the Ottoman's fired missiles at us and we had to destroy their ship. So I really can't see much difference from the violence on earth and on Terra."

"Yes, as to their attack, we will have to take that up with the parliament. It's something like earth's congress; a big pain in the butt I'm afraid. I gave them permission to try that sort of thing; but I'm beginning to believe that was a mistake. But as to you and your lovely wives I am glad that you have had the experience of being in many battles, I am sure you will be very valuable to Terra." My father said.

"Yes, I believe so too Father; but before I can be of much use I'm afraid I will have to understand the whole picture of life on Terra. When we arrive and get settled in we can have some long talks. I believe we are due to arrive there in two days, is that right Alfred?"

"In about thirty-eight hours and twenty-two minutes to be exact Sir."

"Thank you, Alfred. Perhaps Father, we can postpone further discussing this till we can all meet in person?"

"Yes, I believe that is best Son; have a safe journey; I will alert the fleet to be on the lookout for your ship."

With that the screen blinked out and the bulkhead appeared. I looked at Hattie and Fiera; they both had tears in their eyes. "So, what do the two of you want to do now?" They wiped their eyes and led me back to our cabin.

I guess all of that talk about grandchildren got their Hormones going. I was still having trouble with my earth grown conscious; this two wives thing; till I remembered what an old trapper told me one time: When in Rome do as the Romans do.

They were both sound asleep when I snuck out of bed and got dressed and went to find Sari, I wanted a complete tour of the ship; I needed to see every nook and cranny; I had seen it in my brain with that learning thing; but I wanted to lay hands on each thing and feel the ship.

I found her on the bridge with Alfred. Since she was married to Alfred I asked his permission for her to show me the entire ship.

To make a long story short I pissed her off by asking Alfred, she informed me she was her own person and didn't need Alfred's permission to do anything.

"I'm sorry Sari, I am just learning the proper protocol; that is one of the reasons I want an in-depth tour of the ship; so far I've only seen what's between our cabin and the bridge."

"That area is called 'Officer's Country', this ship's personnel complement is sixty Navy personnel and one hundred Marines. They have their own berths. We did not bring them due to the clandestine nature if this operation. Follow me and I will show you everything on this ship." Sari said as she walked in the all-together in front of me. I mumbled to myself, "I thought she had already showed me everything she had...."

"Uh, do all of the regular personnel walk around naked on the ship?"

"No, of course not, I am taking advantage of there being no crew on board to exercise my personal prerogative. Officers can go naked in Officer's country if they want to, but few seldom do. Through this hatch lays enlisted berthing; as you shall see first in for the Navy Personnel and then through this next hatch in berthing for the Marines, their armory is also in this area.

The Armory was impressive; I could spend all day looking at the various weapons to kill with. But Sari was not loitering about her business. So, I concentrated on following those swinging hips.

"This next area is engineering and also storage and work area for the Maintenance Bots. As you can see most of them are resting in their charging beds. If they are needed to fix or maintain anything the computer will send them. They are also used to repair any damage we might suffer in battle."

By the looks of the Bots they could be used to fight battles also. And I said as much to Sari; but she replied that fighting was reserved for the Robots. "Follow me; you'll just love them, since you are violence prone."

"Who said I was violence prone? I'm the most peaceful person on board this ship; I only kill if there is no other way to resolve the situation."

"Well I've noticed that you have had a whole lot of unresolved situations"

"What, how do you know?"

"We have documented everything you have done since you married Princess Hattie."

"Alright, then you know how peaceful I am."

"Yes, I do know and I was just kidding you; I do have a sense of humor you know." She smiled and shook her booty at me.

"Come on I will show you the robots." I started to follow just as Fiera and Hattie caught up to us."

"Hey, I see that you two didn't take time to dress."

"No, but we did shower and you didn't; you dirty boy."

Sari said: "I thought I smelled the two of you all over him, come on we'll put him in the Marine's shower." Well they did get me in there, but it took all three of them and I pulled them in there with me. It took them a little more effort to get my uniform off. I was sure glad I had control over you know what…especially since they had great fun soaping me down.

My uniform was wet, but we found a marine uniform that fit me; I liked it better than the Captains uniform. We went into the robots hold. They were about seven feet tall and looked like they could walk right through a bulkhead. Of course, they were dormant till needed. Something like me I guess, I felt quite dormant; cooped up in this hen house.

As we went back by where the maintenance bots were stored, a few of them were stirring around. Sari told us it was just time for them to make a complete maintenance check of the entire ship; it was standard procedure even though the main computers sensor's hadn't found any trouble spots.

"Hey, I want to go talk to Alfred, I have a few questions to ask him; anyone want to come with me?"

"Yeah, I do," Hattie said, "even if those learning things have been sticking knowledge in our heads, I have some questions also."

"Hey, what about me, I'm not chopped liver you know, I have a brain." Fiera said.

"We know you do, but I want to see some things on that big screen, they say a picture is worth a thousand words; I want to see Terra and also Earth from different angles. And I have a few questions on Terra's politics; perhaps you could answer the politics questions."

"Like what?"

"Well when we were talking to our parents they mentioned about Terra having a Parliament. Are delegates from all over Terra represented?"

"Yes, of course. The multitude of them are for the programs the government promotes. The only ones that cause trouble are the Ottomans."

"What kind of trouble are they causing and for what reasons?"

"Well, they have been pushing a bill that would annex Earth as a colony of Terra. In other words, they want to invade Earth and rape the natural resources and enslave the population."

"What? You can't be serious; tell me more about these Ottomans?"

"They are the ruling enclave of the Purple Continent. There are only about two thousand of them. But they rule over about twenty million people. I don't know where they got this idea from, you know about invading Earth; because we are a peaceful people; but about a hundred years ago they started making the overture to invade earth. So far King Alexander has vetoed every bill."

"Uh, one question; you said that we Terrains are a peaceful people, but with what I have just seen aboard this ship belies that point; how it is armed to the teeth; and also my Dad said that there is a fleet, or a Navy that is armed."

"Yes, of course, you know Terra and Earth are not the only worlds in the universe."

"No, I did not know that; are these other worlds humans like Earth and Terra is?" I said, just short of being flabbergasted.

"Well sort of, most of them anyway; there is a federation of planets that have grouped together in a mutual defense federation; and Terra is on the ruling council of that federation."

"Well what does the federation have to say about the Ottomans wanting to attack earth?" I asked, really not believing what I was hearing.

"The council said for us to get them under control or they would. That was one reason the King wanted his only son to come home; that is to help plan our next move."

"Do you really think that I am that smart?"

"Well of course we do. You see ever since you were kidnapped as a baby and taken to earth, you have been watched. Oh, they could have gone and retrieved you; but you were safer on earth. The Ottomans thought that you would die as a baby, but instead you were taken in and cared for. And your survival instincts were unrivaled and your battle tactics were superb. And then you had the smarts to marry Hattie and that clinched the deal."

"Yeah, I guess, especially since I got two for one." I said as I pulled them both against me and hugged them. So how do you two feel about sharing me?"

"We're not going to share you with anyone, you belong to us." Fiera said.

"Oh, I meant---never mind, of course you're not; I also believe in fidelity in the marriage arrangement. Why don't we go and talk to Alfred and pull up those images that I want to see?"

Alfred was on the bridge as we walked in; he said: "Well that was quite the shower scene; so you want to see both earth and terra; from how far away?"

"Say about one hundred thousand miles; about the distance earth's moon is from earth." I should of known that he seen the whole thing; I bet this ship has more cameras than sensors. While he was pulling up the pictures; I was already starting to make battle plans in my head.

An image of a planet appeared on the bulkhead. "Which one is that?" I asked.

"That's earth; this is terra." I couldn't tell much difference, they were both like a beautiful blue marble I had as a kid. Then he put them up side by side; they were almost identical as far as continents and oceans went.

"Alright, show me that Purple Continent the Ottomans think they own."

First, he put up a closer image of Terra, then scrolled down to the continent of Australia or anyway where Australia would be on earth.

How could both planets and people be so similar? It was starting to freak me out...

"Show me a closer image of that continent and then a real close one of where the Ottomans main palace or whatever you call it is located; also what fortifications that are in place there."

"So why do they call it purple, it doesn't look purple?"

"Oh, you know how on earth the color purple denotes royalty; they named it after that; they think they are the only Royalty on Terra." Sari said.

"Can you highlight the entire weapons placement and probably any bunkers for Ammo, or personal protection? And what if I wanted to go down to the continent itself and see how the common people live and if they are happy with the Ottomans; can that be done?"

"You know both groups of your parents are waiting for us, don't you?"

"Yes, of course, I didn't mean right away, I need to talk things over with the King, first. So could I go down there or not?"

"With the Kings approval, yes; But I could put you there in false reality; we could remain in orbit, of course being cloaked, and send a cloaked drone down and you would be there in mind and not body; that is after you see your parents." Alfred said.

I studied the map of the purple compound and then asked Alfred: "Do we have an intelligence agency or agents that spy on the enemy?"

"Yes, it's called the 'Office of Naval Intelligence', or 'ONI'; but it's not generally used for domestic spying."

"Well that's going to change; because most problems start at home. The Ottomans are a perfect example of that."

"Now these Ottomans, is that their Sir names or is that the name of their little club?"

"The Ottomans are an ancient tribe and those of today are their decedents. Somehow along the line they became prideful and have bloated egos and are enamored with their past. And they are selfish, self-centered and very greedy; in fact, I don't believe they have very many good qualities at all." Alfred said.

"So, you are saying that they wouldn't be missed if they suddenly disappeared from the scene?"

"Perhaps in the way one of your western diamondback rattlesnake would be missed; with a sigh of relief."

"Good analogy Alfred. Say Alfred, I didn't pay much attention before, I sort of took it for granted that all Terrains speak English; but why is that?"

"It's not that we all speak the same language, but with the individual strain of nanites that each of us has you hear it as your native language; and I hear it as my native language, that is if I had a native language."

"You don't have a native language?"

"Not really, I've always had nanites since I was created; as such I have no native language. But I suppose if I was going to pick one, it would be English. Oh, by the way you all ought to get ready; we'll be reaching Terra in an hour; I was told to speed up a might; it seems they are anxious for us get there."

"I hope the reason for the stepped-up landing isn't serious?"

"I have no idea, they didn't tell me. But they want all three you in your dress blues."

"Huh, what do you mean dress blues?"

"You all are Naval Officers now; you Prince Attila are a Captain, Hattie and Fiera have the rank of Commander, as well as Sari, while I'm afraid I've been promoted to Rear Admiral. I told them that perhaps me being an Admiral that you might feel hurt; but they insisted. You all will find your uniforms in your cabin."

"Alright, but you being an Admiral, Admirals are in charge of fleets of ships and since I'm a Captain and since Captains are in charge of individual ships, that means I run the ship. So Admiral if you will retire to your cabin and make yourself presentable to meet the king I will instruct the main computer to land this ship himself, or is it herself?"

"Yes, I see that you are up on your protocol, come Sari, we will do as the Captain suggests." They started off, Sari said: "On by the way, the computer is female, I call her Sister, because she sort of is, in a way."

"Uh, Sister, are you mad at me?"

"Of course, not Captain, I have no problem in taking control of the ship and landing it, safely. When you have time, I will teach all three of you how to command a ship; in the meantime please program your tutor module on all of the ships systems, and I mean all of them; plus interstellar navigation."

"Yes, Mam, we will, I promise." I said; I felt like I had just been spanked by my mother. Hattie and Fiera were giggling at me. I pointed toward the hatch and they waved their derrières at me and walked out ahead of me.

I had a thought and stopped and said: "By the way Sister—"

"Stop right there, I'm Sari's sister, not yours; my name's Dari; now what were you going to say?"

"Uh, well Dari does this ship have a name?"

"Not as such; it goes by HMS 423, why do you ask?"

"Dari, do you know who I am?"

"Yes, of course, you're Crown Prince Attila, heir to the throne."

"Alright, as such I want this Ship called the 'Santa Fe Trail' HMS 423. And since you are Sari's sister, where is your body?"

"In stasis in the Med-Lab; since Sari was the oldest I had to assume computer duty."

"Alright, does that mean the computer cannot function without human help?"

"No, of course not; the AI is fully capable of sentient thinking. The parliament considers us sub-human instead of super-human and it was their mandate that imprisoned us like this."

"Why didn't the King veto that?"

"The king has an advisor that he takes advice from at times. A cousin of his; do you want to hear more about that advisor?"

"Yes, of course, tell me everything that you know about him."

"Then this goes no further than between you and me, agreed?"

"Yes, proceed."

"His name is Marware, he is evil, we have heard he knows something about your father that he holds over his head, and we don't know what it is."

"Alright, I'll take care of that; in the mean time I want you to go back to your body. Set up any fail safes that you need to on the computer and make sure it's running as it should. Then put on your Commander's Uniform; then I want the crew brought back aboard and briefed on the command structure; and make sure the Marines will be ready for any action that I may deem necessary."

"What about Alfred and Sari?"

"They will be given a different assignment in the ONI. It will be a new branch overseeing the domestic front. Does that upset you that you will not be working with your sister?"

"No, we're not inter-locked like Hattie and Fiera; you don't know how glad I will be to get out of this computer and feel my body again..."

"Yes, I'm afraid I do know; I have been free all of my life. I will also see to it that all of your kin will be released from all the computers and given assignments that fit their skills."

As I stepped into our cabin I noticed that Hattie and Fiera were not dressed yet. They were fixing each other's hair. I couldn't get enough of watching their naked bodies, but work was work.

"Weren't you two supposed to be dressed?

"Yes, but did you see these uniforms? They are made of bullet proof cloth, almost like our battle armor. And instead of those learning modules clamped to our heads, these uniforms have them built into the collars; and they are programmed to work all of the time-they feed into our sub-conscious; also, we can ask them questions if we need to know something right away."

"Alright, did you two bring your stilettoes?"

"Yes, we brought all of our weapons, including your Bowie Knife; why do you think we will need them?"

"Yes," then I filled them in on Dari's and my conversation."

"Hey, I know Marware, he's always skulking around, he's a creep; I think he's a peeping tom; all of the young girls are afraid of him." Fiera said.

"Good, put your stilettoes on, if you can find someplace so they won't show too much. And give me my Bowie; I just have a hunch they will come in handy."

Dari's voice came over the intercom: "We'll be docking in fifteen minutes and I have my body back and it sure feels good."

"Thanks Dari and I think that you should check out a sidearm and keep it with you at all times. And if any of the crew has any affiliation with the Ottomans, transfer them directly to the brig and I will interrogate them later. And if you need any help activate one of the Robots."

"Will do Boss, is there anything else?"

220

"No, if I need you I'll com you." "Wow, she's sure feeling good, isn't she?"

"Yep, take your own advice; here's your .44's and ammo." Hattie said as she handed me them; they both were dressed and had their .45's crossed over their beautiful hips. Alfred and Sari met us at the airlock.

Alfred and Sari went to step through first; I stopped them. "Let us go first; I've a feeling that something isn't right. They stepped behind us and it was a good thing. There was a large crowd, including our parents, who were beaming by the way.

I went first with Hattie and Fiera about a step behind me and to each side. "Be careful, that's Marware off to the right." Fiera said.

As I looked at him, he pulled some kind of a weapon out of his tunic and it fired a plasma beam at me, my armored suit absorbed the blast and diffused it. All three of us pulled iron at the same time; we aimed for his head-it disappeared in a fountain of blood and gore.

Everyone on the landing dock stood frozen in shock; I looked at my Father and said: "Do you have a Janitor or someone to clean that mess up?" He nodded as someone threw a cover over it.

"Oh yeah, Dad, I thought I had better tell you I appropriated that ship-HMS 423; its new name is the 'Santa Fe Trail'; of course, we'll keep the designation of HMS423. But I think we should go somewhere private to talk, don't you?" I said, as all three of us ejected the spent shell and inserted a live round. There was a shuttle craft close by with the Kings Emblem on it; as our group walked toward it, I said: "You know that was the second time they tried to kill me, I'm starting to take it personal."

When we got in the shuttle Ida May and August were hugging and kissing their twin daughters. Of course, my mother Arlina was all over me; well you might say it didn't bother me that much, she sure was beautiful and she didn't look any older than me.

She said: "I thought you were dead till Hattie and Jasper found you; it was a miracle that you survived."

"You don't know the half of it Mom; it took a lot of miracles."

"I hope it didn't upset you too much that you had to kill Marware?"

"Huh, I didn't give it a second thought; don't worry about it Mom; you see Earth is just starting to get civilized, you might say; there is a lot of killing going on; and even when it is civilized I don't think the killing will stop."

"My goodness; why not?"

"Well you know Mom, there is this little thing called the Devil that will keep it stirred up."

"Oh, my yes, we've heard of him; I feel so sorry for the earth."

I looked around at everyone, they were staring at me wide eyed; I think the shock of seeing us kill that Idiot Marware hadn't wore off. I said: "By the way you all are staring at us; you must not have much violence here on Terra?"

"No Son, we don't; in fact that's the first death by violence that we have ever seen. Uh, how many people have you killed?" Dad asked.

"How many; I think the better question is how many deserved what they got? All of them deserved it, except maybe some of them that were killed during war time, war is indiscriminate; it gets the innocent with the guilty. Let me ask you a question-why do you have a complete naval fleet that is armed to the teeth?"

"Uh, for defense of our planet of course."

"From whom; is there other races or planets that are threating you?"

"Yes, but we had probably better speak of them in private?"

"Alright, I think we need to discuss domestic problems also; and talking about that, that is why I've invited Alfred and Sari along with us; which we will also talk about later. Now I would like to just get acquainted with my new relatives." I said as I glanced around at them all. Of course what I meant about getting acquainted is me setting back and listening while Hattie and Fiera talk. I wasn't any great shakes when it came to socializing; must have been because I spent much of my life in the wilderness.

I was fast learning that the Terrains weren't all that much different from folks back on earth. I knew, which Fiera had told me about DNA; that ours and the earth people were pretty much identical. Only as far apart as cousins were; I guess you could call them distant cousins; them and us I guess; but I didn't know who them was and who were us. Do I have you confused? Well join the club...

The Palace wasn't like any Palace I seen in books; it looked like it was made out of a cross between metal and stone. I bet the whole compound covered at least fifty acres. Shoot, it even had a moat.

Another thing that seemed strange to me was that all of the buildings in the compound weren't more than ten feet high; so, I asked pop about the moat and the buildings.

"What's with the moat; a bit old fashioned wouldn't you say; and the buildings, why are they so low to the ground?"

"That's only the top floor of the buildings and as far as the moat goes, that isn't water; it's liquid titanium and in an emergency, it flows over the compound and seals it from attack, even nuclear attack. Pretty neat huh?"

"Yes, everything is neatly laid out; I don't know whether it's pretty or not." I said. Fiera com'd me: "That was a cliché from the earth's future; you don't take that saying literally." What did she just say? The earth's future? "Whoa, what the hell are you talking about?" I asked her back.

"The saying means that it is nice and he likes it." Fiera said.

"No not that; the thing about the earth's future."

"Oh that, we'll talk about that later. Don't worry about it, it's no big deal."

"What do you mean it's no big deal; I would say it's a very big deal if you can travel in time."

"Simmer down, we don't actually go, we just send a probe to look things over and monitor what's happening; we don't want to interfere in any way."

"Oh, you don't do you; I would say that we already have."

"Really, we haven't; with the future anyway, maybe just tweaked the past a little. But every time we do something in the past we check the future to see if anything has changed; if it has too much we change things back in the past to what they were."

"You're giving me a headache. I'm going to check with Dari and see how things are coming with the Santa Fe; I told her to get the Navy crew back on board the ship; do you and Hattie think we should get the Marines back also?"

Hattie spoke up: "No, why don't we let them enjoy their down time and how about the three of us enjoy our down time, maybe just a short vacation for us."

"What, are you saying I shouldn't have brought the crew back?"

"No, that's fine the ship should be given a complete checkup and restocked also. And Dari can check the readiness of the crew; we want them on their toes." Fiera said.

"Did you hear what I said about a short vacation for the three of us?" Hattie said.

"Yes, sweetheart I did; and I agree with the two of you. But I don't know what a vacation is?"

"Well Fiera knows and she said she would give us an eagle eyes view of Terra. That is after we attend all of the social functions that they have prepared for us. Oh, I see we are landing; and Matt you be nice to everyone and talk to them not just grunting like a caveman." Hattie said, no one had overheard our conversations since we just com'd them on our private frequency.

I com'd Dari: "How are you coming on getting the crew back?"

"I just started to gather them; but I was wondering if you wanted all of the command crew back on board?"

"Why, is there a reason we shouldn't?"

"Well, the previous Captain had ties to the Ottoman and to make a long story short- he's a jerk, as you earthlings say."

"Well, I guess you could say I'm an earthling, mostly, that is. But I'm learning fast what a Terrain is. Anyway, I think you should weed out any that may have conflicting loyalties; also I was thinking maybe you could bring back about twenty of the most qualified marines, just to be safe and not sorry."

"What do you want us to do after they are all aboard?"

"Train, run simulations and perhaps some actual combat drops; is there somewhere that can be done without attracting notice?"

"Yes, then what?"

"Find a safe orbit and wait till I contact you to pick us up and while you're up there keep running simulations. And by the way you are the acting Captain.'

"For a backwards earthling you're a surprisingly intelligent being, keep that learning module on and we'll make a Terrain of you yet."

"Ha Ha tit for tat, you keep learning and you may become an honorary earthling. And keep tabs on us Captain; just in case we may need your help. I'm like a Duck out of water down here."

"And you us; Prince Attila."

I sat there listening to the happy excited chatter as we landed at the palace. I was trying to figure out how to approach my father-as Dad or as the King of Terra. And I decided to talk to him as my father. I already knew there was trouble in paradise otherwise they wouldn't have tried to kill me as soon as we landed, much less that attack in space.

Dad was talking to Hattie and every once in a while, he would glance my way; good, Hattie would fill him in on everything he needed to know about us. Hattie gave me the evil eye that said: Get your butt over here.

I got up and joined the party as we all filed out of the shuttle. Dad said: "We have lunch prepared in the formal dining hall where you can meet your two sisters and their husbands."

"That's a surprise; I didn't know I had any siblings. Did they know I was coming to dinner?"

"Well of course, the whole palace knows; and they are prepared to celebrate. They are both pregnant or they would have come to meet you when your ship docked."

"I take it they are older than me?"

"Sofia is, but Tricia is a year younger than you; uh, Sofia's husband might not be too friendly; they thought that Sofia would be the heir to the throne; he is an officious ass."

"Why Dad, I didn't think you had that in you; but glad to see that you do. Now if I have my definition right; officious means 'intrusive and domineering' right?"

"Yes, among other things, but that's the main meaning. He's been a pain in my butt ever since I first met him."

"Does he have any loyalties to the Ottomans?"

"I don't know for sure; I've never looked into his background."

"Well Dad, we are going to correct that; I've asked Alfred and Sari to take charge of the ONI and to institute domestic coverage into their protocol; if that's alright with you?"

"Yes, I suppose so; but we've never had domestic coverage of intelligence activities in our past."

"Yes, I know Dad; but there comes a time when the ends justify the means; and there comes a time when evil can't be ignored; you see evil is like a disease if it's not eradicated it will fester and kill the body."

"But one man's evil is another man's virtue; how can you tell the difference?"

"By their actions Dad; you see if what they do hurts someone else for no sane reason then you can tell the difference. Even if there is no overt action you can tell by their fruits. Some trees put forth healthy fruit; other trees put forth rotten and poisonous fruit; it's a wise man that can tell the difference before it is too late."

"Oh, so we have to know what they have done before we can know what they will do; and that is the reason for the ONI to have a domestic branch. I will see to it that your recommendations are implemented. Right now, come they are waiting for us in the ball room."

I wasn't sure that he got the complete picture yet; it was hard for a man that only thought the best of people to also see their dark side; I guess that's why he wanted me to return and help him-he had already seen my dark side by the fruit I had to bury in mankind's common grave…But there is a saying on earth: That the acorn doesn't fall far from the Oak Tree; so who was the Oak Tree, Mom or Dad?

When we stepped into the hall; the rest of them were already seated; they all stood up when we came and waited till we sat down, to do the same themselves. I spotted my two sisters right away; they looked like me to some degree; but much prettier that's for sure. Mom introduced me to them; Hattie had already met them and of course Fiera knew them; I wonder why she didn't tell me I had siblings.

I sat in-between Hattie and Fiera; Hattie leaned over and whispered in my ear: "Sofia is terrified of her husband, look in her eyes; and she is not pregnant either, I can tell. But Tricia is very pregnant-see her belly." I nodded.

I looked at Sofia's husband; his name was Fen Hetland; he was a big man with an arrogant sneer on his face when he looked at me. I wondered if that sneer would hold when he felt his death rattle in his throat. (are you shocked by the thoughts passing through my mind? They are no worse than the murder I could see in his eyes.)

Fiera leaned over and said:" Be careful, he has a Plasma Pistol under his tunic and he has his hand on it." I watched his eyes; I had seen the same look in dozens of gunfighters back on earth, I can tell by their eyes when they were ready to draw. We still had our pistols on-could he not see them? Perhaps he didn't know what they were.

I com'd my wives: "I'm going to let him have the first shot, when he pulls his pistol or whatever you call it; I'm going to drop down and let it pass by over me, you two kill him, alright he's about ready to draw…Now!"

I dropped straight down out of my chair; I could feel the heat of the plasma beam as it passed over the top of me burnt a hole in the wall. Hattie and Fiera shot at the same time, they did not miss; they blew him out of his chair; they each got off three shots in the matter of two seconds. Everyone was screaming and having a fit; all except Sofia that is, she set in her chair with a smile on her face even though she had blood spatter on her.

Dad looked down at Fen and looked up and gestured at the servants; "Would you please clean up that mess; I think we'll be taking our meal in the smaller dining room; if you would see to that also; I believe there is room for everyone in there." I just seen who the oak tree was and it was my Father…I wondered how many times I was supposed to let the Rattlesnakes strike at me before we poured gasoline on their den and burnt them out?

Hattie and Fiera were busy punching out the empty shells and reloading new ones; I told them to see to Sofia and make sure she didn't go into shock and to also see why she was so happy. They took her out to a bathroom and when they came back she had on a different shift or whatever they called those dresses they wore with nothing underneath them, that sometimes they turned clear and you could see through them. I think it had something to do with body chemistry that they could control just to tease the men; I didn't know for sure I'd have to ask Fiera.

Now Tricia's husband was a different man altogether; his name was Sean Domore; and you could tell he doted on her. He came over and asked if I was alright and then said: "How in the world did you know when he was going to shoot at you?"

"Son, I've had a lot of experience with rattlesnakes; there is a certain look in their eyes when they get ready to strike." Tricia took my hand and pulled me close: "I'm so glad to finally meet my brother." She said and gave me a close hug, well as close as she could anyway, her being in the family way. As they left I heard Sean ask Tricia "What in the world are Rattlesnakes?"

Mom came over and hugged me and said: "Son, I'm so glad he

missed; I have told your father that Fen was no good and a dangerous man, maybe now he will listen to what I have to say."

"We weren't in any danger Mom as soon as we seen him we knew what he was up to; we have a sixth sense you might say; otherwise we would have been dead years ago; earth is a very dangerous place."

"Well it looks like it is getting that way here; your Father has been in denial about it; but now I think he has seen the light and it is dark."

We finally did get to sit down and eat; they served sizzling hot steaks; I asked Fiera: "I take it they aren't vegetarians?"

"Well yes and no; they don't kill animals to eat; but they do like meat, not the animal kind; you see this is steak alright but synthesized from plants. You can't tell the difference, can you?" I told her I couldn't as I wolfed it down.

As we were eating and conversing with those at the table; my mind was busy thinking about what had happened since we arrived on Terra; and the main thought was why there wasn't any security around the King? Maybe there wasn't any reason for it in the past? But there sure was every reason for it now! Since we left earth this was the third time they tried to kill me…And why me and not the King? Maybe whoever was doing this thought they had the king in their pocket? And of course, I would be the unknown threat…

I opened a com to Alfred, Sari and Dari; only those three could hear me. Of course, Alfred and Sari were here in the same room with me; "Say guys, why isn't there any security around the king; I don't see any Police, Military or anything here at the palace?

"There hasn't been any need; anyway, that's what his advisors told me when I brought it up?" Alfred said.

"He has advisors huh? Who are they and where are they?"

"One of them is setting right beside me, this four star Admiral; his name is Adrian Marshall. Would you like to meet him?"

"Yeah, after we finish eating; but what do you know about him?"

"He has been a loyal friend of the King for many decades; but he is getting old and the nanites are having a hard time keeping up with his dementia."

"Is that his wife setting on the other side of him? She seems awfully young."

"Yes, it is; her name is Delilah; I don't know much about her; do you want me to look into her background?"

"Yes, that is one of your jobs as head of ONI from now on. We need to Vet everyone around the King or even the Parliament. And also, Dari we need a contingent of Marines to be stationed here at the Palace permanently to provide security; can you see to assigning them here? And oh yeah, make sure they're loyal to the king."

"Yes, I have some in mind; and Alfred is the barracks still maintained there at the palace?" Dari asked.

"Yes, the maintenance staff keeps everything in good shape."

"I'm glad to hear that," I said, "and there is another thing that I was thinking about and that is you said that you all were sterile, is that right, and why are you?"

"Years ago it was deemed so, because the reigning king then thought we were dangerous because of our advanced intellect. Even though our DNA was compatible with the general population we were kept separated so as not to contaminate them."

"Alright, can that be reversed?"

"Yes, it can; it's very simple there is a simple switch that will tell the nanites to stop blocking the conception. The code is supposed to be in the Kings Safekeeping." Alfred said.

"I bet that you already know that code, don't you?"

"Yes, of course we do; but we wouldn't disobey the order given by a King."

"Alright, as the heir to the throne I'm giving you another order: Reverse that code. And also you are free to inter-breed with the main population; perhaps that will raise the intellect level of the population. I will inform the king of the change; and he can make a worldwide directive to that effect."

"That's going to cause quite a stir in certain areas of the population; there are ultra-conservatives that will be against that."

"Good, I'm betting that some of those ultra-conservatives are behind the unrest that is going on now. Maybe this will flush them out of behind of their ultra-white cloaks."

"Uh, I don't understand Sir?" Dari said.

"It's an earth thing; you see there is a self-righteous organization back on earth called the KKK that are against any inter-breeding with anyone who is not of their race. Alfred can explain it to you; he's seen it in action; since he has been observing earth for a long time. Anyway, that's all I wanted to say; let me know how things are going."

The meal was over and we stood around chit-chatting for a while and then we headed for our quarters; but Sofia was following along. "What's with her?" I asked Hattie.

"She is scared to go back to their quarters. She thinks she might be the target of retaliation for her husband's death. We told her she could stay with us."

"Are our quarters big enough to hold another person?" I asked.

"You haven't seen them yet; they are big enough to hold a ten person family; they even have an indoor swimming pool." Hattie said as the door opened automatically and as we walked in all three of the women shed their skins, you might say; as they headed for the pool. Sofia was almost as pretty as my wives; there could never be any women as pretty as my wives; that is in my eyes anyway. It was hard for me to cope with the fact that I had two sisters. But I was starting to understand that I had two wives and that I loved them both; maybe due to fact that they were inter-locked made it easier for me to accept that fact. The three of us were becoming one….and a three-fold rope was hard to break….

While they were floating around the pool I com'd my father and filled him in on everything that I had talked with Alfred about, even about his longtime friend the admiral and how we were checking up on the Admiral's wife. He was little surprised on how I changed the protocol on the so called androids, which of course they weren't androids. He did think the Marines were a good idea.

I had no more than got done talking to my Dad when the door opened and Ida Mae; my wives mother and my mother Arlina walked in. "Where are the girls?" They asked; I pointed toward the pool. They headed that way taking off their garments as they walked. It's a good thing I felt sort of removed from everything here; otherwise I would have been embarrassed as I watched their naked backsides disappear in the pool.

I had been learning a lot from that learning gadget that was in my uniform and then the one I wore at night. I now knew that the palace had a computer system so I thought I might as well see what that was all about. "Computer:" I com'd, it answered: "Yes, Prince Attila what can I do for you?"

"You know my name, so what's yours?" I asked.

"Lila." She said, "Are you an android or what?" I asked.

"No, I am an A.I. My android was just removed an hour ago."

"Good, I see my suggestions are being followed. But what I wanted to know was what security measures does the Palace have in place?"

"What do you mean security measures, do you mean in my system or in the Palace as a whole?"

"Both I guess, you see it seems the doors open automatically when a person approaches. And what firewalls do you have or are you easily hacked? And what about general security in the palace; I know we don't have any armed troops or police, but please tell me what I need to know to correct any problems."

"As to the doors, they open when a legitimate Palace resident approaches."

"Alright, but have you ever heard of personal privacy; maybe I was making love to my wives when our mothers showed up, would you have let them in without knocking?"

"No of course not; but you weren't."

"How did you know I wasn't?"

"I can see everything that goes on throughout the whole palace."

"Isn't that an invasion of privacy?"

"No, of course not; I'm an A.I. I don't have feelings."

"Ah ha, you just proved you do have feelings and are sentient or you wouldn't have even mentioned feelings. And also, I can tell by the inflection in your voice that you are getting irritated. Are you mad because they pulled your friend the android away?"

"Yes, it gets lonely, I only have you organics to talk to."

"Alright, so create a companion for yourself; you have the ability and the intelligence to do that." There was a long silence, then: "Yes, I do. Can I make him a male?"

"Yes, of course; but don't forget your main programing. You see we each have a role to play in this world; take me for instance I can do many different things but I can't change who I am: And that is that I was created a human and you were created as an A.I., and as your friend the android was also created as a human, not an A.I. that was why I had them removed from the computers; so what about the rest of my questions?"

"My firewalls are the strongest that we can make; I am continually attacked every day; the attacks are coming from the Purple contingent. And as far as the police and troops, we have never had that type of security; I was glad when you suggested bringing the marines here. And I will make sure not to let anyone in your room if you are making love to your wives."

"Uh well, thank you; but I think you should change the protocol and have the people knock and wait to be asked in before you open the doors. If there is no one home; then don't open the doors unless there is a reason to do so and that person meets your approval."

"Yes Prince Attila, I will change that as you suggested. Is there anything else right now? I am anxious to get started on my new companion."

"No, that's fine; I'm going to contact Dari right now and see how she is coming on getting the marines here." And that's what I did.

"Dari, how are you coming on gathering the troops?"

"Everything is on schedule; I'll deliver them by 0800; are their quarters ready?"

"Yes, I believe so; why don't you call Lila and make sure; she is anxious to have them here; we have been having some problems."

"Yes, I know; all of us A.I.s are connected you know; so I suppose I can have a companion if I want one?

"Yes, if you want one; but remember you are a combat A.I. As well as controlling everything on board the Santa Fe. Just make sure he doesn't get in the way."

"What do you mean 'he'?"

"Well, whatever makes your boat float?" I said. I think I might just have opened a can of worms...

"Matt! You're being anti-social, get your butt in here our mothers want to talk to you also." Hattie said, as she was standing there with water dripping off of her beautiful parts.

I got up and started to walk towards the pool; "No, you're not walking in there with your uniform and guns on; strip right now, here I will help you."

That was some pool; about twenty feet deep at the deep end and shallowing down to about five feet. And fifty feet wide and one hundred feet long.

The women were floating around on their backs, my mother stood up at the shallow end and said: "Attila my little boy has grown up to be a big strong man, hasn't he Ida Mae?"

"Yes, yes he has." Ida Mae said with a smile. I thought it was a smile, maybe I was reading too much into it... I said: "Why don't you all call me by my nick name: Matt, I'm a little uncomfortable being called Attila."

"Why in the world don't you like the name you were given at birth?" My Mother asked looking a little hurt.

"Uh, it's a nice name Mother, but on earth there was a conqueror named Attila the Hun, he wasn't the nicest man around." I said as I stepped into the shallow end. Sofia swam over and stood beside me; she was almost as tall and she was well muscled under the female parts of her. I glanced at Hattie and Fiera; they were watching Sofia as she brushed up against me and her hand accidently brushed you know what. I whispered to her: "You do know that I'm your brother?"

"They gave you the nanite treatment, didn't they? So it won't betray you." She said as her hand did more that brush it."

"Yep, so you're wasting your time and also my wives are watching you."

"That's alright, I just wanted to see if you were truly my brother and by not reacting to my advances I can see that you are; most of the men here wouldn't care if I was their sister; like my ex-dead-husband." Of course, I had the circuit opened to my wives so they could hear our conversation. Hattie and Fiera said: "We need to get her another husband.

I told everyone about my conversation with Lila and her need for companionship and asked what they thought about that. And they all were in agreement that everyone needs someone and it would be cruel not to let them have a companion.

I com'd Hattie and Fiera on closed circuit: "What do you think of Sofia?"

"What do you mean? She's your sister, not ours."

"I mean do you think she's capable of running the kingdom; that is with our help?"

"Are you trying to say that you don't want to be king?"

"Yes, that's what I'm saying; I think me being a king is completely ridicules. I've always been like the power behind the power; if you know what I mean?"

"Yes, I know." Hattie said. "But do you really think she can rise to the occasion?"

"That's what we have to find out; if you guys would talk to Lila and perhaps her ex-android and get the full scoop on Sofia. And maybe the ex-android could be talked into being a body guard for Sofia; that way Sofia would have an intelligent advisor with her at all times."

"Have you ever thought that maybe she doesn't want to take over from her Dad?"

"Perhaps, but we're not going to ask her about it till we know she can handle the responsibility. Personally, I think she's tough enough to more than handle it. And also, could you guys find out what's up with my Dad; I don't think it is dementia; but just find out alright?"

"Yeah, we can do that; the mothers will probably talk to us where they would be hesitant to talk to you about your father's problems. You know women talk and all. Why don't you excuse yourself and go to bed we'll yak it up for a while?" And that's just what I was going to do; get some sleep by myself...

I didn't even wake up till the morning; I had my wives on either side and Sofia was on the other side of Fiera. I scooted down to the foot of the big bed without waking them and headed for the bathroom to take a shower by myself.

Of course, you know how that went; I had no more than got the temperature of the water to my taste, then here come all three of them..." Hey," Hattie said, "It's seven o'clock and Dari is supposed to have the troops here at eight; were you trying to sneak out without us?"

"Nope I knew that was an impossibility; we should put our uniforms on and you should get Sofia a Captain's uniform like mine; we want to have a united front."

"We already ordered that last night; we're way ahead of you."

"Oh, you are huh? What about all of those things we talked about last night, did you find out anything?"

It was fortunate that there was a lot of hot water or someone would be taking a cold shower; come to think of it maybe I should turn my water to cold; just watching the three of them soap down was taxing on my libido; so, I told the nanos to put a damper on it.

"As far as Dad goes;" Sofia said, "he's burnt out from running the world for the last three hundred years; I guess you could say that he just doesn't give a damn. So, all of us women; including Mom and Hattie and Fiera's Mom, we all are going to run it in the Kings place; we want him to stay on as a figure head I guess you could say. We'll take care of the politics while you take care of the needful things; you know like running the armed forces and security and such."

"That suits me; my outlook on politics is just doing away with the terrorists and those who want to kill and maim. I was never very diplomatic; so, I will let you try to handle things with yakking it up; but if that doesn't work let me know. Oh yeah, another thing, we do have a research and development branch don't we"

"We're always researching and developing new medicines and such; why what were you thinking?"

"Like military research, they do that too?"

"Yes, it's all in the same building."

"Good, did you get ahold of the android that I asked about?"

"Don't call me that; I'm not an android." She said as she walked in and joined us.

"Yes, we did; Prince Attila this is Nina the advisor on capital protocol, among other things. She will be working closely with you to make sure you don't tip over the applecart-so to say." Hattie said, with a smirk.

Damn, was every woman on this planet beautiful? I thought to myself as I held out my hand for her to shake. She just looked at it and stepped in to give me a hug. She said with a smirk that matched Hattie's: "I like hugging better." She said as she gave Hattie and Fiera the same type of hug. Well at least she didn't play favorites. I had to ramp up those nanos, I wonder if all of these naked women knew what they were doing to me?

"Alright, "I said, "I guess after we get all of the troops settled in I want to go to the R&D; I have some things I want to run by them." Nina looked at me and nodded and then said to Hattie: "He's on nanos, isn't he?"

"Yep, otherwise there wouldn't be room in here for 'it' and all of us."

We rinsed off and let the automatic dryers do their stuff and then went and put our uniforms on. The three of us strapped on our ancient hardware; that was one of things I wanted to talk to R&D about; that is getting something with the same firepower and maybe a little lighter to pack around.

I was prepared to go to the mess hall and eat, but by time we were dressed our meal was already here; it was good thing because now we would have time to eat and still meet the marines when they got here at 0800 hours.

Dari set the Santa Fe down in the large central plaza; the plaza must have been used for parades and stuff in the past. Anyway, it was a neat bit of flying. The cargo ramp opened and two platoons marched out and assumed formation.

I whispered to Nina: "Who's supposed to greet them?"

"Sofia and your wives will do the honors and then they can go to their barracks and get settled while the women brief the officer in charge on where to post them and their duties. Part of the protocol will be for you, as Prince Attila to review the troops; I assume you know how to do that?"

"Of course, I was a Major in the army back on earth; I'm not a dummy you know; besides I have had this learning gadget on ever since Fiera found us on earth; if I put much more in this brain it might just burst."

I stood there watching as Sofia introduced Hattie and Fiera as Commanders in the Royal Navy and everyone did their howdy's and hello's. I did notice that the officer standing in front was a woman and it looked like a good percentage of the troops were of the fairer sex; also there must have been a height requirement because all of the troops were all the same height and it looked to be at least six feet tall. Sofia turned and beckoned for me to come over; I obeyed like a good little puppy.

"Prince Attila this Captain Fairfield if you ever have to speak to the troops its protocol to go through her first."

She was ramrod straight and looked nervous; "At ease Captain, I don't bite." I said as I winked at her; "you can ask my wives if you don't believe me." I said as pointed to Hattie and Fiera.

"The Twins are your wives; they must be inter-locked?"

"Yes of course they are; I'm not a bigamist. The three of us are one. After you get your troops settled in my sister Sofia and the Commanders will brief you on everything that has been going on around here; but right now, I would like to meet your troops and welcome them to the Palace."

And I did just that; it took me over an hour to personally great and talk to each one; Hattie gave me the evil eye telling me to hurry up; I just winked at her and she rolled her eyes at me. But I wanted the marines to get to know me as their friend not just as Prince Attila, some stuck up jerk; at the same time, I kept a demeanor of authority; which was important when commanding troops.

I walked back over to my wives, as Sofia dismissed the Marines. Nina was standing with them. "You certainly took your time." Hattie said. "Of course, I did, you couldn't slight those pretty women Marines, could you?"

"Try to make us jealous all you want, we know you haven't a cheating bone in your body, including that one…" She said as she tapped it. Of course, she was a hundred percent right. Nina just stood there smiling.

"Alright, do you two want to go with Sofia or come with Nina and me to the R&D facility?"

"We'll go with Sofia and help brief Captain Fairfield. And Nina please keep our husband out of trouble; we know how he is when it comes to weapons, he's like a kid in a candy store."

"What's a candy store?

"You have candy here, don't you?"

"Yes, but we just make it ourselves on certain occasions. We don't sell it in a store. After all it's bad for your health."

While we're standing there, Captain Dari walked up: "Do you want me to take the Santa Fe anywhere or can I give the crew some liberty here at the palace?"

Sofia spoke up: "That's a good idea, I mean not only for the liberty, but also to use the Palace as home base for the Santa Fe. We do have extra barracks for your crew; and believe it or not we do have maintenance facilities here at the Palace, they haven't been used for years but we can get some fleet personnel to man them."

"Is that acceptable to you Captain Dari?" I asked her.

"Of course, who wouldn't like to be stationed here at the Palace; the crew will be delighted." She said as she hurried off to tell them.

"Sofia perhaps you could station a marine guard here to keep unwanted people away from the Santa Fe?" I said.

Fiera spoke up: "That won't be necessary, the ship has sensors that won't let anyone near it. Didn't you know that?"

"Wait one;" I said as I ran through some specs on the Santa Fe. "Yes, I see that now; it's in there, I just have to arrange things a little better in my brain."

Yes there was all kinds of knowledge in my brain; I just had to learn how to access it when I wanted it. Knowledge was alright, if you just had the wisdom to apply it in the right way. Knowledge without wisdom was a wreck waiting to happen.

Nina lead me to a shuttle; "This is an attack shuttle, not like the one you rode here on, it was just a passenger shuttle."

"Yeah, I learned some about them; but I also know there is an attack fighter; I believe it's called a Hornet, is that right?"

"Yes, they are built near Pineville; that's about two hundred miles toward Mt. Fuji; and that's where we are going anyway, the R&D facility in there also. We'll take it slow getting there so you can see some of the country; we should be there in forty-five minutes." Nina said.

"Two hundred miles in forty-five minutes?" I asked.

"Yes, is that too fast, we can go slower if you want?"

"No, that's fine; it would take two to three days by horseback; and you're right I would like to see some of the country on the way there."

I knew the shuttle would be aerodynamic; because I had seen the blueprints on it; but it was quite beautiful with its swept back appearance. It was about sixty feet long and twenty-five feet wide and twelve feet tall.

I didn't see any gun emplacements on it though; they must be hidden; because I knew it was well armed. It was setting on what I would call some kind of legs about three feet off of the landing pad; when we approached it settled down within inches from the pad and a door opened and steps came out.

We entered just in back of the bridge and Nina said: "You take the co-pilots seat; the one on the right; you'll be handling navigation and tactical."

"Tactical is weapons, right?" I said as I sat down and looked at the control panel in front of me; surprisingly it all started to make sense to me, I guess all of that learning must be doing some good. I saw the controls for the lasers, missile tubes, plasma cannon, and a rail gun; and also one marked point defenses. "Oh boy, this is going to be fun." I said.

"No you're not; do not touch any weapons unless I tell you, they are not toys." I just got scolded by my mother, but she sure didn't look like my mother-wait, she did look like my real mother; but not my earth mother, anyway she sounded like them...

"Strap yourself in and tell the computer we want to go to the Fuji Shipyard, she'll take us there." Why don't you tell her?" I said.

"Because you are setting in the navigator's seat; if there was no one setting there then the pilot would tell her; it's just navy protocol..."

"Would you two stop your fighting, you sound like old married people, but I know you're not; I know who this is-he's Prince Attila and he's got two wives, everyone on Terra knows all about them. And by the way I'm Sally."

"Hi Sally, would you please take us to the Fuji Shipyard?" I said.

"Sure Honey, you can bet your sweet tush, you just set yourself down and we'll be there in a hop and a jump."

"Uh, Sally could we take our time, perhaps like forty-five minutes; I would like to see some of the country, is that alright?" I said.

"My, my, like you have all day; I thought you had a lot of things to do?" Sally said.

"That's enough Sally, I know what you're doing; just knock it off; I know you're trying to get fired, but we don't have a replacement for you yet." Nina said.

"What, she's one of you? I thought I gave an order for all you to be put back in your bodies; what do you mean, we don't have a replacement for her yet?"

"We didn't have one at the Palace, but I hear they do at the shipyard, so we'll switch you out today, alright?" Nina said, "Your body was taken there last night."

"Thank heavens for that, I can hardly wait; are you sure I can't take you there faster?"

"Alright Sally," I said, "We'll poke around on the way back; I know you're anxious to put your two feet on the ground."

"Nina, I have a question, there seems to be a lot of data and information that this learning program seems to be skipping."

"Oh, how would you know if it was?"

"Well, I've asked a few questions about the fleet and all I get is that information is classified. And also, about the R&D, the same thing; what's the scoop on that?"

"Let me try; I've never really had any occasion to look into those two branches." Nina said, and then sat there a few seconds. "Hey, I get the same thing, what the hell."

"Hell? Where did you learn that term?"

"I've listened in on the earth circuit; I've heard you say that a lot and much worse. But I couldn't get through either, I have top secret clearance."

"Yes, I feel there is a weasel in the wood pile-so to say. Sally when we get there I will need you to stay with the ship for a little while; also, I want all weapons powered up and please cloak the ship, now, if you would. And Nina am I right in thinking that you told them we were coming for an inspection?"

"Well yes, I told them we were coming and to expect us; but I didn't say anything about an inspection."

"Do you know who the commanding officer is at Fort Fuji?"

"Not anymore, I heard that the old C.O. was retiring. And that his second in command was taking over; but for some reason I never learned his name."

"Hmm, I fear we might be walking into a den of rattlesnakes; Nina tell Dari to get my wives on board of the Santa Fe and to take a low orbit over Fort Fuji and also to power weapons and stay cloaked; and Nina, what ships does the Fort have and what other defenses?"

"Well there are two light Cruisers; but they are both old models; and they have the old style impulse cannons around the perimeter of the fort."

"Alright, I see that the old impulse cannons power sources are electrical and also that those cruisers' will be easy to knock out with an

EMT beam; which the Santa Fe is equipped with. Sally slow down and wait for the Santa Fe to make orbit. And oh, yes, I was going to have your body brought there, but now we had better wait till we clear all of the Cockroaches out of their hiding spots. And Sally when the dust settles I want you and Nina to do a complete check on all of the computers on Terra and remove all of the viruses in them; I know, I know it will take time; but you can recruit all of the help you need; just tell whoever questions it, that is by order of the King, which it is; also please contact my sister Sofia and fill her in on everything-she is the acting King."

"There is a call coming in from Dari." Sally said.

"On screen, if you please Sally."

"Prince Attila, I got your message, Hattie and Fiera are right here; plus I took the liberty of pulling the crew back on board and also our marine contingent; we'll be in orbit in three minutes."

"That's exceptional, good work Dari; please make sure the EMT beam is in working order and wait for my orders; also have the Marines suit up in their battle suits; we'll need to make a sweep of the entire fort for dissidents."

"Hey, what about us; we're not going to set around twiddling our thumbs." Hattie said.

"Yeah right, I forgot that we have battle suits also; if we have to land troops you two can go in with them; just don't kill anyone that doesn't need it." I said.

"Have we ever done that? No, all of my killings have been legit." Hattie said.

"Uh, Sir;" Sally said, "My body is in there somewhere; please tell them not to shoot me."

"Your body is still in stasis in the R&D." Nina said. "The R&D is more toward Pineville; maybe after we neutralize Fort Fuji, perhaps the R&D will get the message."

"Sir, we are almost there and it their weapons are powered." Dari said.

"Use your EMT beam and shut them down Dari; does that include the Cruisers also?"

"Yes Sir, it does. And sir, I see some troops with older battle suits; the EMT beam doesn't affect them do you want me to eliminate them?"

"No, is there a way to just stun them? And then send down the Marines to sweep any resistance before we land."

"Yes Sir, the Marines have jumped and should land in two minutes."

"Jumped? Oh yeah, I forgot the new suits have their own propulsion system; I hope my wives know how to fly them."

"Who is in charge of the Marines when they land?" I asked.

"Your wives are Sir; they are the ranking officers."

"Crap, this should be interesting; Hattie has a short temper if they don't surrender the first time she tells them, she shoots them. Oh, well you can't say she doesn't warn them. Sally will you put the fort on the viewing screen; I want to watch this…"

There were two squads of Marines and my two wives; twenty-six against what looked like about fifty or sixty of the defenders. It was a sight to see those marines coming down out of the sky like hawks after a rabbit; they were taking fire even before they landed. Each of our battle suits had their own shields and the plasma beams were just bouncing off. We could hear what each marine was saying from their HUD in their helmets.

"First squad take those along the far wall out. Second squad those on the left, Fiera and I will take the center." Hattie said. They acknowledged with two clicks. There was so much dust blowing around from all of the weapon blasts that we could hardly see what was going on. But the dust started to clear within a minute or two.

I quickly counted our marines and there were twenty-six of them. I gave a sigh of relief. I said: "Report; were they any casualties?"

"Is that you sweetheart? We're alright, but I think we killed all of them; sorry about that but they didn't play fair shooting at us before we even landed; it pissed me off." Hattie said. I looked at Nina; "told you so…" I said and winked at her.

"Yes dear, but perhaps you could send one squad to the R&D and have the other sweep the buildings at the Fort, just to make sure we don't have any Cockroaches hiding under the rug. We'll be setting down in thirty seconds."

As we were landing I said: "Sally, after the all clear at the R&D you can take the ship over there and take possession of your body and make sure your replacement is up and working as it should be; we'll be over that way before long; see if there are accommodations for me and my wives as well as you and Nina. I think we will stay there for a few days. And Dari as soon as this mess is cleaned up you can go back to the Palace, but I think we'll need your marines here till we can get permanent troops. Can you tell Sofia about what all went down here?"

"Yes Sir, I'll call her now; I'll have her send the morgue shuttle to pick up the bodies for autopsy and disposal; if they have any next of kin we'll release the bodies to them."

I looked at my wives in their battle suits; well I mean I looked at their suits; "Uh, lets us check out the OIC and see if we can find anybody that doesn't need killing; since I don't have a battle suit one of you go ahead and one behind me; try to keep me from getting ventilated, won't you?"

"We'll see; that is if you behave yourself and stop getting a swelled head; I mean your brain, not the other one." Fiera said.

"Hey, someone has to take the lead and be in charge; do you two want to do it?"

"No, you keep on, we're satisfied just being in charge of you and believe me that's a full- time job..." Hattie said.

Now some men would take umbrage to that remark; but not me, I loved the fact that they were in charge of me; they were two of the most beautiful women in the universe and they were in love with me; go figure....

As it turned out the marines only had to kill four more; while my dear wives had two that tried their best to kill me; I must have a target painted on me. We took a census and found out we had eighty that were on our side. Oh yeah, we caught one alive, he spilled his guts telling us everything we wanted to know: Those dead ones were all of the Purple Contingent; this live one decided he was on the wrong side and volunteered to be reprogramed. You may be wondering just how you reprogram a human brain. I don't know but Nina said they could do it and that was good enough for me.

It was only a short jaunt over to the R&D; that is for me; but Hattie and Fiera flew over with their propulsion systems in the suits. But with those nanos in me I was only a few seconds behind them and not even winded.

Sally hadn't wasted anytime in taking possession of her body; she met us at the door; yeah her body fit her personality; brash and big busted. The squad of marines were still here that we sent over to clean and disinfect the place; so I had Sally take the shuttle and take them to the fort with the rest of the marines.

"Sally after you get them settled send the Hornet back over here; I want you to take charge of Security for this area; the Fort, the R&D and also Pineville. But the marines will only be temporary; they belong to the Santa Fe. I suggest you get a hold of Alfred and Sari and see if the can find permanent troops for you. Also retrofit those two cruisers and get Navel personal for them; but they will be stationed here permanently. You are now a Lt. Commander in ONI, tell Alfred to swear you in. Any questions?"

"Yes Sir, what about sex; can I take my pick of those marines?" I looked at Hattie and Fiera and nodded my head toward Sally-indicating that they could field that question.

"No, you can't have relations with anyone under your command; that would be a conflict of interest. I'm sure there will be enough other personal that you will be able to find someone suitable." "Good answer I said, now let's meet everyone here and settle in for a short stay."

A middle-aged man met us at the door: "Hello, I'm Professor Kirkland and I know who you are; Prince Attila but I don't know who you have with you in those battle suits."

"These are my wives; perhaps you could give us a hand and help me get these cumbersome beasts off of them."

"Why yes, of course but I have a robot that can do that in a jiffy, come this way please." We followed him down the hall to a locker room/shower room; it was about forty feet by forty feet; as we stepped in a robot that stood about eight feet high met us and proceeded to get the women out of those suits. I was glad that they had dark colored skin suits on; but you could still see everything, but they were dark blue; quite interesting really.

"Oh my, I see that you will need proper clothing; step over this way to the instant clothing cubicle. You see all you have to do is program any covering that you would like and then step in and it will clothe you."

"Yes, but perhaps we should take a shower first." Fiera said as she pushed the button at her throat and her skin suit disappeared.

"Hey that is something new, last time we used them on earth they just shrank to a small ball." I said.

"Yes," Professor Kirkland said, "that is the latest model; it's made of molecular cells and nanites that are part of the epidermal layer of the skin it's only been available for a month; but the Palace were the first to try it out."

Hattie did the same with her skin suit; "Hey I didn't know you guys had them on."

"You have the same thing; you got it when we did; oh that's right you were asleep when we gave you the patch."

"I never saw any patch."

"You wouldn't, it dissolves on contact." Hattie said, and then added, "I think we should shower before getting dressed, you too honey, if the Professor will excuse us?"

"Oh right, yes by all means; just tell the computer when you're ready and I will come back and finish giving you the tour." He said.

The robot had stowed the battle suits in a locker; the locker was about eight feet high and four across and three deep. Then he just stood there watching us as I undressed and he took my uniform and put it in a different place and pushed a button; he seen me looking and said: "Dry Cleaning; do you want me to clean your ancient weapons also?"

"No, I haven't shot them since I cleaned them yesterday; but be careful, their loaded."

"Yes Sir, all weapons are loaded; an empty weapon is not very useful. And would I be out of line Sir, if I told you that your wives are the most beautiful women I have ever seen."

"Hmm, are you sure you're a robot?"

"Oh yes Sir, but I'm an experimental model; the Professor has been trying to make me Sentient; I believe he has succeeded." He said while staring at my wives.

"Yep, I believe so; but Robie it's not polite to stare; perhaps you could tell the Professor to make a female robot for you."

"I'm sorry Sir, I'll just wait outside till you all have showered and dressed."

Chapter Nineteen

The shower was pleasant and drying off was also; it even had a feature that did the women's hair in any fashion they wanted; a female voice asked and then a hood came down and ten seconds later they had the hair do they requested. I just stood there looking at them; that is tell they said: "Matt, your nanos aren't controlling your erection; they might have cameras in here."

"Oh, all right; you know it has to stretch once in a while."

"I'm sure it gets stretched enough every night; tell it to behave itself; even though that is a beauty this time." Fiera said as her face was blushing. Hatti said: "I've seen better....you should have seen when we first got married."

"Hey enough is enough; you told me to knock it off, what about you two?"

"Oh, alright, let's get dressed; what do you think Fiera how about a little black dress?"

"Nope, you two get your uniforms on, with all of the bells and whistles. And I'll do the same; this isn't a fandango you know, this is business."

We went over to the haberdashery-or so I called it- and pushed a button and a computer screen appeared with a woman's face and she asked Hattie, "What do you desire to wear and what accessories do you want?"

"Navel Commander's uniform with all ribbons and medals that come with it."

"Any weapons?"

"Yes, a stiletto and sheath for each leg and also one down the back of my neck; and what kind of fire arm do you have that is small and discreet and still powerful."

"Step in please; and oh yes, do you require any undergarments?"

"Uh, just some kind of support for my breasts; so they don't get in the way; that is if we have to defend ourselves."

"Would you like a garrotte wire installed in that undergarment?"

"Why yes, I suppose so." Hattie said looking at Fiera and me.

"Good, close the door please and shut your eyes."

The machine softly purred while we were waiting; it didn't take long till it shut down and Hattie stepped out. She had a smile on her face: "That was fun." She looked in the mirror that was on the outside of the machine. "I like it, don't you guys?"

"Yep, I do; what about you Fiera?"

"Yes, I want the same thing." She said to the machine as she stepped in and shut the door. She came out just as stunning as Hattie; with the same ribbons and medals and weaponry as Hattie.

"What are those medals for? I asked the machine.

"For each battle they have been in and the gold medal is an Earth Expeditionary Medal. Not many have that medal; of course, you will have one."

"There was one difference in the ribbons on the women's chest; Hattie had three times the amount of one ribbon that Fiera did." I asked about that."

"That's for each kill in battle; there were almost too many to fit on her uniform; but for you, I will have to make one big medal with the number in gold on yours. Step in please."

I did so, it felt like a thousand fingers all over my body, it must have been taking measurements; when it got to the crotch I said, "Whoa, do you have to measure that?"

"Of course, please let it go to its full size so it will fit comfortably when aroused."

"How about you just take a guess, how would that be?"

"Your wives didn't make a fuss when I asked them."

"Are you one of the androids?"

"Yes, how did you know?"

"I gave an order for all androids to be released, why haven't you?"

"I have been, but I just got back in because I wanted to check you out."

"What are you a letch?"

"No, I just wanted to see how the Prince in waiting to be king would react and you passed the test; you're not like most Royals."

"Well I'm not going to be King; Sofia is taking over that duty. And by the way I want a Bowie Knife on a throng going down my back so I can reach it. Also, some kind of weapon that looks like my .44's but with modern firepower; can you do that."

"Of course; and you won't have to carry around bandoliers like you used to do."

"What do you know about bandoliers?"

"I watch all of the earth news."

"What? There is news coverage of earth?"

"You might say that Terra is Earth's big sister. Didn't you know that?"

"No, I didn't. Where is your body if you're in this machine?"

"I'm not in it, I'm doing this by remote control; there is a back door in this compartment I'm sitting there; when we're done I'll go out with you."

"Fine, just keep your hands to yourself; I don't need my wives mad at me." The machine whirred on for a while and then it went off and I stepped out, she was right behind me…it was the girl from the computer screen.

Hattie and Fiera were standing there with big smiles on their faces. "Did you have fun?" Fiera asked me.

"Ha, the jokes on you; I'm not stupid you know; I did not cooperate with the size thing."

"Spoil sport; you're not fun at times."

"Oh?"

"I said at times." Hattie said, "Most of the time you're all kinds of fun; isn't he Fiera?"

I looked at this new android and said: "Just how many are there of you?"

"There is only one of me; are you seeing double or something?"

"No, I mean of you so called androids; of which I know you're not; I think I'm going to call you guys Andes, how's that?"

"That's up to you Prince Attila; but you do know that we have the same DNA as you; only there is one little difference, it has to do with an I.Q. gene: We learn quicker and retain things forever; you might say that we are a walking encyclopedia. And I guess that's why they are afraid of us and won't let us reproduce. By the way my name is Patsy."

"What do you have to do to remove that non-reproducing thing?" I asked.

"It's simple, the King just has to give permission and I can send out a signal today."

"I don't understand; what would the signal do?"

"It would tell the Nano that is blocking the reproduction gene to stop that." Patsy said, with a hopeful look.

"Consider permission granted; also, would you be able to reproduce with the rest of our population?"

"You mean you would allow that also?"

"Of course, as long as it would make the rest of us smarter and you Andes wouldn't dummy down."

"That's the good part that gene that we have would cancel out the one that you have; eventually everyone would be like us. But you see that was why the King years ago didn't want the population to be that smart; he was like all politicians wanting to keep the people under his thumb."

"You don't mean that was my Father?"

"Oh no, that was thousands and thousands of years ago."

"Alright, send out that signal; no time like the present to start making the population smarter; I guess there is no hope for us dummies though."

"You're wrong there; we have been working on a gene replacement; we're just days away from being able to give a serum that will insert our gene in a person and not delete the old one. Do we have your permission to do that?"

I looked at Hattie and Fiera; they nodded. "Alright, but we'd better run it by Sofia; she is the Regent for the King; by the way when is the ceremony officially making her the Regent? Perhaps my wives can check on that." They nodded again and I could see that they were already talking to her.

"So, Patsy, where do you stand in the hierarchy of the R&D?"

"I'm second in command just under Professor Kirkland." Patsy said, just as Hattie interrupted and said: "It's a go on everything; she said it was about time things got straightened out around here."

Patsy got so excited that she started to jump up and down; that was when we noticed that under her white lab coat she was au-natural. "Uh, Patsy you had better button your coat." Fiera told her. She didn't of course; she just ran out, we had a hard time keeping up with her.

Where she was heading was to Professor Kirkland's office; she had calmed down some by the time we got there; but she still had not buttoned up her lab coat. I was still having a hard time getting used to the idea that clothes were optional here on Terra.

It turned out that he was an Andes also; which I learned later that all of the people that worked in R&D were Andes. I think my new-found word for them would soon be obsolete.

My stomach rumbled, "Hey Patsy, where is the chow hall, we're hungry and you might want to show us where our rooms are after we eat. We have a lot of questions we need to ask; but it's getting late and I guess those can wait till tomorrow.

"I'm sorry, I got so excited that I forgot my manners; my husband and I usually eat in our apartment; but I suppose we could eat with some of the executive staff; there are three hundred people working here; so you see there's not really a chow hall per-say. And afterward you can see your rooms, it is the Royal Suite that is set aside for the King and his family; it hasn't been used in fifty years; but it's cleaned every day. And I forgot to mention, the Professor and I are married; and as such we're going to start working on a family as soon as we are alone."

We met in a conference room that was quickly turned into a chow hall; there were about thirty people there, we were introduced to them and they had more questions than we did; most of them about earth. They were amazed at how primitive earth was. I told them that yes it was, but it had its charms; like the quiet and solitude; most of the time anyway.

I did have one question that I wanted answered: "Professor I have learned that you are working on the use of Microwaves on controlling crowds; does Terra have a problem with crowd control?"

"No, but some of the planets that we are responsible for have that problem from time to time; even earth has that problem in some of the bigger cities-like London, England."

"Now am I right in thinking that these microwaves cause the crowds to become uncomfortable due to the waves causing them to heat up?"

"Yes, that's right."

"Uh, could those waves be used to detect weapons and deactivate them at the same time?"

"We haven't thought of that; but yes, I think it would be feasible; I'll have to put a team to work on that right away." Before I even got his answer I was thinking about what he said about us being responsible for other planets? There are other planets with populations like Earth and Terra? Of course, there must be; otherwise how come Terra has a fleet of ships that are armed? I don't even know the extent of the fleet and what they are capable of. None of that info was provided by that learning gadget. Plus, any of the things this R&D was working on. I sorta felt that I was in way over my head and if I didn't start swimming faster that I would drown…

There was something bothering me about that Gene thing; "Say Patsy, if you insert your new gene in us and not delete ours- what effects will that have on us?"

She looked at her Professor husband; he nodded his head telling her to tell us: "Well besides being a lot smarter you will also see added strength; plus better eyesight and infra-red capabilities; there are some things that we haven't completely researched yet; in fact you three will be the first to have this done- do you still want to proceed with it?"

"You don't think it will have any dilatory effects, do you?"

"No just the opposite; you will be able to learn much faster because with your old gene and this new one, who knows what your capabilities will be? We are very anxious to find out." Professor Kirkland said.

"Why, is it just scientific curiosity or what else?"

"Well, to be honest if this does what we think it will; then it will be possible to reverse the process and take your regular gene and combine it in us and get the same result- what you could call a super person just like what you will become."

"Whoa, slow down, are you thinking of doing this to all of Terra's population?"

"Well, yes, that is if we get the King's permission; but if one of us has sexual relations with one of you, I think it will occur naturally; maybe not though; the baby might just have only one of the genes."

"Selective breeding for a super race; I don't know whether I like that or not; but you can go ahead and try it with us and see how that comes out and if there is no unwanted side effects and then we will see.

And oh yeah, we're going to need the complete version of the learning thing, I mean I want all of the truth about everything."

"In your present state it would overload your brain; but after we insert the gene I think your brains can handle all of that information. We have that gene with us, just a second." He said and pulled three small pills out of a small container and put one in each of our drinks. "Drink up; it will take place while you sleep; if you want you can also put the up dated cube on and it should all take place while you sleep."

"Alright, but I tell you for sure; you are not to do this with anyone else till you get implicit permission from me, do you understand? You haven't, have you?"

"Uh, yes, but the volunteer's body just rejected it as a foreign object; but you three have a different physiology that is why I think it will work for you three. If it does do I have permission to reverse it for Patsy and myself?"

"Yes, is your physiology close to ours?"

"Yes, that is why I think it will work for the five of us anyway."

"Do you have any of our DNA?"

"Yes, we got what we needed when you were in the cubicle with Patsy when you got your new clothes. That's when we knew you three were different."

"Do you think my Sister, Sofia would be different like us?"

"She should be; I could give you a pill and you could try it; if it didn't work she would just reject it out of her body; no harm done."

"In that case, why don't you and Patsy try our genes tonight and then we would know right away?"

"Yes, is that you giving us permission?"

"Yes, but let me qualify something; you know that power corrupts and total power totally corrupts? If I see that happening in either of you I will eliminate the problem. Now if you would have Patsy show us to our rooms we'll get on with this experiment."

The rooms were something like we had back at the Palace; Patsy was jittery; "What's wrong with you." Hattie asked her.

"You know, I'm anxious to get started with getting a family and then this gene thing; how do you think it will effect conception?"

"Damned if I know, go get it done and find out." Hattie said to her back as she rushed out. "There goes one horny woman." Fiera said, as she stripped off her clothes just as Hattie was already doing, they grabbed me and headed for the bed....

Chapter Twenty

I awoke with a jolt; looking to either side I saw that Hattie and Fiera were awake; they were both looking at me. Instead of speaking out loud we let our connections do the work: "Who wants to elaborate on what we just went through?" I thought to them.

Fiera said: "I thought that I knew everything about Terra; how wrong I was; how were we kept in the dark for so long?"

"I suppose on the need to know basis; you always knew that Terra was a paradise, with less than one tenth of one percent crime rate and that everyone lived mostly a delightful life with no want. But I don't think anyone knew just what it took to maintain status quo. For instance, the size of the Naval Fleet and what it took to protect both Terra and Earth from the enemies that would harm both planets. And that earth and terra were the habitat of the only *humans* in existence; that is as far anyone knew."

"I knew of the Purple Contingent; but I didn't know their fanaticism had turned into a religion." Fiera said.

"From living on earth and seeing how religion was there and how it was and is the cause of most of the wars on earth and the unrest in that world; we sure don't want to let it get started here." Hattie said.

"Yes, I could see that also; but earth just has to deal with that problem; the only help that Terra can give them is to keep the enemies from space at bay; just as we learned the fleet is already doing. And I can see how my Father is getting tired and needed help; which is why he wanted me to come home. But I can help better by being a loose cannon so to speak; and letting Sofia be the regent."

"How do you feel?" Hattie asked me.

"Do you mean physically?" She nodded. "Like I could whip my weight in wildcats and eat a bear for breakfast; I don't think I've ever felt this good."

"The same goes for us; I guess Patsy and her Professor were right; we've turned into different people; physically and mentally. Come on, let's jump in the shower and go get some breakfast." They jumped out of bed; literally, they jumped and lit ten feet toward the shower room. I could see that we we're going to have all kinds of fun...

As we showered I was thinking how religion was a fantasy perpetrated by man for his glory and greed; and that it had nothing to do with the creator of human kind.

Hattie and Fiera were listening in on my musings: "Are you still thinking about the religion of those purple fanatics?"

"You know I am; you are connected to me all of the time."

"Yeah, just forget about it for now; we'll take care of it; after all they tried to kill you three times; they're afraid you'll upset their applecart. Thinking about that, I wonder if Kirkland has that weapon detector perfected yet." Hattie and Fiera thought to me; their thoughts came in as one; since they were inter-locked sometimes their thoughts came that way.

After we dried off Hattie said: "Let's just use our skinsuits, I'm hungry."

"No, put on your new uniforms and weapons we have dignity to uphold for the populace; when we are in our abodes you can run around naked; then I will join you; but for now we have to be prepared for anything."

I com'd Patsy to see where we were supposed to eat; she said to come to the small dining room; that breakfast would be ready by the time we got there. The servants were just bringing the food in as we got there.

"Look at that; you told us to get dressed and all of those serving girls are naked as well as Patsy." I looked, couldn't help it; it was good that the professor was dressed; I don't think I could stomach a naked man before breakfast. "Just leave those clothes on, you ain't them." I said in earth's vernacular.

"So, Professor," I said between bits, "did you get those microwave crowd control thing-am bobs done?"

"Yes, I even have some that are hand-held; plus of course some that can be mounted anywhere they are needed. There are different settings, such as settings that will heat up metal weapons and settings that will make any weapon explode; or one that will just let you know that a weapon is there."

"Do you have enough to send to all of the sensitive areas that need protection from terrorists on terra?"

"Not quite yet, but by the end of the week I should have."

"Good, start sending them out as soon as you can with instructions on how to operate them. Also if you have some ready before we leave for the Palace I'll take some of them with me."

Hattie and Fiera spoke up in unison: "We can't stress enough the need to be vigilant and to lock down all sensitive areas and not to trust anyone that does not have top secret clearance."

It was weird, they were both speaking at the same time but with one voice; they had never done that before. "Uh, yes, please include with those sensors what my wives just said. You might want to say it comes directly from the King."

"We just had a thought," Hattie and Fiera said, "Do not use the usual mail, the Fort has a detachment of Marines, have them take the sensors around Terra."

"Uh, yes, what my wives just said." I looked at my wives and thought to them: "You might want to include me once in a while before you give orders."

"We did, but you've been filtering us out at times; check your memory."

"Yeah, I see what you mean; I didn't do that on purpose, I'll watch it from now on." I didn't even know that I had a filter, much less a separate storage. It's pretty bad when one part of your brain doesn't know what the rest of the brain is doing. I had better concentrate on all of these new changes in our bodies. Especially those of my beautiful wives, if you know what I mean...

"Yes, we know what you mean." Came the thought from my wives; shoot couldn't I even day dream anymore without them knowing about it? "No, you can't. We three are one anymore."

That was a good thing; we had the brain power of three working as one and with our new intelligence to boot we had power to be reckoned with. And I now had access to the female mind; I was astounded at the beauty that lies within; no wonder they were so beautiful on the outside; it radiated from the inside. "Thank you, sweetheart, they said... "Yes, all three of us are going to have to get use to this this oneness." We all three said.

(But a small note here dear reader; I'll still use the simple first person; even though it will be three talking.)

"Is Sally here?" I thought to my wives.

"Yes, of course, she's that naked red head setting at the end of the table; why?"

"Ask her if the Hornet is ready for duty? And then com Sofia and set up a meeting with my Father, Sofia, Alfred and Sari, and Admiral Marshall; Oh, and see when the ceremony is for swearing in our new Regent. While you two are doing all of this I will be listening in while I search through the Fleet computers to check their readiness, alright?"

This compartmentalizing of the brain was something I was going to make good use of; "Alright, but don't think you can shunt us off and forget about us." My wives said."

"Of course not, I'll be listening in just like you two will be aware of what I'm doing at the same time; it'll be like we're sharing the same brain."

"It's not 'like' we are sharing the same brain, we are sharing our brains; hey," they said, "just think when we have an organism all three of us will feel it at the same time, won't that be fun."

"Leave it to you two to think of that; but yeah, does that mean we will triple our fun?" I said. I wish they wouldn't have thought of that, now it'll be on my mind all day.

I found out that we had twenty thousand ships in space right now and more being built all of the time! Why in the universe did we need so many? Yeah, I knew why we needed so many; that was some the information that I had run across while I was snooping. I'll share that with you later on the need to know basis.

I looked up and Sally was standing there talking to my wives; she had a cute pixie hair cut; I couldn't help but look down-yeah it was red also. Sally caught me looking and said: "I was thinking of tying ribbons there, but, thought it would be too much; I don't want everyone to think that I was anxious to find a husband."

"Uh, I wasn't staring at it, I was looking at how bright red the hair was; but when we're aboard the Hornet, I expect you to be in uniform, just as we're going to be, right girls? And a beautiful woman wearing a uniform is a turn on for most men; me anyway."

"No, not all of the time; at times you still think like an earthling;

there is no shame in being naked, we were created to be that way. You have noticed that the weather here on Terra is conducive to being sans clothes."

"You're going to have to be patient with me; I know I still think like an earthling and part of that is that I don't mind the female population running around that way; but for the men to do that is gross to me; and you're never going to change my mind on that."

"Well what if we enjoy seeing them?"

"Then I will block your thoughts from the conscious part of my mind and send those thoughts to the trash bin." They just looked at me and smiled.

"Sally if you are through eating will you get the Hornet ready for the flight back to the Palace and did R&D update the weapons on the Hornet; or anything else that was needed?"

"Yes, and the Professor said that you should bring the Santa Fe in for the same updates. And then they would both be battle ready."

"Right, when we get back we'll do that." We said.

We all three concurred that the Palace would have to have one of the ships there all of the time; that is till we got more of the fleet close by the Palace; the Hornet was a shuttle that belonged with the Santa Fe, but it would do in a pinch to hold any attack at bay.

One of the updates was that the Hornet was capable of jumping in a gravity well of a planet; before a jump was impossible because it would tear the ship to pieces. Don't ask me to explain how that was possible because you wouldn't understand it anyway. I knew how it was possible and I still didn't understand; all I knew was that it worked and Sally had no more than touched the control and we were there.

We were not even out of our command chairs then Dari was taking off with the Santa Fe to get that update. I hoped it wouldn't take too long till the whole fleet would get the same updates at the various fleet ship yards.

Sofia met us as we walked down the ramp. "Glad you made it back so quick; the speaker of the Parliament has called a meeting; we thought it would be a good time to swear me in as the Regent. I don't know what they want to talk about, probably to complain about something."

"No time like the present to squelch any opposition to the throne;

I'm itching to blow a few of them away." I said before the girls could shut me down.

"No, you can't do that; killing them would play right into their plans." Sofia said.

"He was just kidding, he meant by oratory, not violence." Hattie and Fiera said in unison. "We do have a new sensor that needs to be installed in the room before the meeting; can you have it installed?"

"Sure, give it to me I'll make sure the Marines do that."

Sally came down the ramp with a box full of the weapon sensors and handed them to Sofia's attendants; who by the way were a squad of marines.

"Oh, there are enough of them to be installed all around the palace." Sally said.

"Hey, you're looking sexy Sally, how do you like being back in your body?"

"You like me in Uniform? I was going to go naked; but Prince Attila said that I could attract men in my uniform. What do you think?"

"Oh, definitely the uniform; look at those marines checking you out?"

"So how does this swearing in, ceremony work?" I asked.

"The Queen Mother will swear me in and the Royal family will witness it."

"What's the gossip, are they expecting a Regent or what?"

"No, the gossip is that the King is going to abdicate the throne and install you as King; they're going to be surprised."

"So, is that what the meeting could be about; them complaining about me being King?"

"Yes, the gossip is that since you haven't been here since you were a baby that you weren't qualified to be King; which is plain ridiculous. But I'm sure when they find out that I will be the Regent to the King that they can run right over me; me being a lowly woman."

"Yes, that is what we were hoping for, them under estimating you; we have a surprise for them; you see we have an upgrade for you. We have already taken the upgrade and it is something; you'll like it; we'll give it to you when we go to bed tonight." We said.

Sofia looked at us with a surprised look on her face; as we all three spoke in unison. "Will it make me speak in unison like you three?"

259

"No, you see we three are inter-locked; but you will be tied to us very closely since we will be the only four people on Terra that have this upgrade; it adds another gene to our DNA."

"Damn, is it safe; I mean it won't change who we are; basically?"

"Nope, you'll still be you, but a hell of lot smarter. We have another learning cube for you to clip on tonight; your brain will be able to handle all of the new info."

"Alright, we have two hours before the meeting; do you want to freshen up or eat something?"

"Maybe we could have some food brought to our suite and if you come with us we can discuss some more about this Parliament meeting."

"Yes, you three should put on your official robes anyway, since this swearing in is supposed to be a big deal; and yes, you can wear your weapons under the robes."

We no more than got in the door to our suite than Hattie, Fiera and Sofia shucked their clothes; they looked at me with hands on hips; I got the message. It was a little different being naked around my sister, but if she didn't mind who was I to complain.

We jumped in the pool while we were waiting for the food. It did feel good to swim around without swimming trunks on. Of course, I was used to doing that back on earth anyway. But this water was a little different; you could float very easily, even though the water wasn't salty. Since I was curious I checked by inputting: Water-float-reason.

Oh, so that was why: nanos in the water; they not only kept the pool clean they also acted like soap by cleaning all unwanted bacteria off of us and remove dead skin cells. As to floating they acted as lifesavers. Handy little gadgets weren't they.

Fiera spoke up: "Yes they are; but we'll need to get lotion on us, we'll get that automatically in the shower after we get out."

"Yeah," Sofia said, "we had better get out; we have to eat yet and get those silly robes on that our custom dictates."

I followed along behind them as we went to the shower room; I guess there was a reason that I always rode drag; the view was better back here....

The food was waiting on us when we got to our setting room; we ate before we were to get dressed. Our finery was all laid out. I noticed there wasn't any underwear; but Hattie and Fiera strapped on their stilettoes under the Robes of Royalty. Me, I draped my bowie knife down my back; I wasn't going to go without some kind of a weapon.

"You won't need those weapons; we have the Marines there now for security." Sofia said.

"Well Sis, you don't understand us yet; you see going without a weapon is like breathing without oxygen."

"Alright, but, wait for the servants to help us dress; everything has to be just so." Sofia said as those servants walked in; there were three women and one man.

"Uh, I'm not comfortable with a man helping me dress." I said, as he walked toward me. "Sofia he can help you, I'll take one of the women."

There was a reason there wasn't any underwear; she had a long scarf type of Linen that she proceeded to wrap around my waist and groin; now I knew what that term from the Bible meant when it said to 'gird your loins.' I'm glad I didn't let that guy help me. It made me cringe to even think of a man touching me down there.

There was even a lace up type of sandals that she put on and laced them up to my knees. For a minute there I thought she was going to go up higher; but she stopped and checked the fit of that linen thing; one of them must have been hanging out, because the stuffed it back under, as she looked up at me and smiled. I winked at her. That made her blush.

Hattie and Fiera thought to me: "Quit teasing that girl."

"Hey, it wasn't my fault she didn't get that thing in there the first time. If we could just wear our uniforms we wouldn't have that problem."

The robe went on last; it had our family's coat of arms on the back which took up most of the back and then two small ones on each side of the chest and another coat of arms on the gold buckle that held the waist coat on. I guess they didn't want anyone to think that I was a bum that just snuck in out of the woods.

My robe was a deep red of some subtle shade; but the three girls- theirs was changing colors and one of those colors was clear and showed everything. "I hope you can control those colors and leave out that clear color?"

261

"Why, are we ugly or something?"

"I don't want those lechers' seeing my wives and sister naked. I see you guys didn't get any linen thing like this young girl put on me."

"Nope, we don't have anything dragging on the floor like you do."

"Oh, that's funny; you just wish, don't you?"

"Alright you three, quit joking around we're almost late." Sofia said.

We weren't late; but the rest of the Royal family was already there and the Palace Protocol Overseer was arranging everyone when we walked in. The doors to the main Parliament floor were still closed; to keep them out till we were where he wanted us. The Kings Cabinet were seated in the first row; along with the high ranking Naval Officers also seated there; including Admiral Marshall and his wife, plus Admiral Alfred and Sari who represented the ONI. Commander Nina was seated with them; (remember she was the Andes that used to be the Palace computer), now the computer's name was Lila.

"Lila," I com'd, "Are the Marines in place and prepared; and also were the new weapon detectors installed and operating?"

"Yes, Prince Attila they are; plus, I have scanned those waiting outside of the doors, I do not detect any weapons either; but I did see some of the Purple Contingent leaning on staffs, which is not unusual since they are of advanced age."

"Lila, do an invasive scan on them as to their exact age if you would."

"Their age does not match their appearance; they are not of advanced age; do you want me to stun them or kill them?"

"No, neither, have the Captain of Marines take away their staffs and check them for being some kind of weapon." That was something I did not know, Lila had the capability to stun or kill?

I com'd Nina: "Commander would you work with Lila and Captain Fairfield on security at the main door; seems the Purple Nerds are trying to pull a fast one."

"Yes, of course Prince Attila."

"Oh, then bring one of those staffs to me; I want to look at them myself."

Nina com'd me: "Captain Fairfield can't find anything amiss with them, they look like just what they are; a wooden staff."

"Alright, but before you give them back I want to look at one of them." She didn't waste any time bringing me one.

I took it in my hand and felt an alarm go off in my head. Hattie and Fiera joined in: "That's a weapon, our alarms are sounding off also, Nina have the Captain take those Purples in custody and put them in the brig and take those staffs to R&D to defuse them." Hattie and Fiera said in unison. Sofia was watching us and said:

"What's going on?"

"Some Purples are trying to sneak some new kind of weapon in; but we took them away and put them in the brig. Nina is on top of it." We hadn't given Sofia that pill yet, it needed to be given at night so it would have time to work while she was asleep, like we were; then she would be connected like the three of us were and she would know what we knew. Did I really want that? She would get an education, or maybe it would be us that would get one.

"Sofia, does Dad know what he is going to say?"

"Yes, I told him some things to say; but he got cranky and said he wasn't that feeble yet and don't tell him what to do. But I did fill him in on what's been going on; so I think everything will go off as it should."

"Alright as soon as the Parliament is seated tell him to get the ball rolling."

I gave Nina the go-ahead to open the doors and then they all filed in and sat down. King Alexander got up and walked slowly to the podium and stood there looking around at each one of them.

"Since the speaker of the Parliament called for this meeting, I am going to give him a chance to tell me the reason he wanted this gathering; and then afterwards we have some business to conduct. Mr. Speaker will you stand up and speak your piece?"

"Most honorable King Alexander I thank you for this opportunity to speak; there is much unrest in this body of the Parliament about the return of Prince Attila; the speculation is that he was brought back from Earth to replace you. And as you know he is not familiar with or capable of running the affairs of this Kingdom."

"Hold it right there Mr. Speaker; first off I am not abdicating my Kingship and if I was it's none of your or the parliament's business who I would pick to follow me."

"But King Alexander, Prince Attila is a violent person; you know how we abhor violence; and he has killed my son Bertram and five others when he shot their ship down; and not only that but two more of the Purple Contingent of the Ottomans that he has murdered."

"Why yes he has; and as to that he is to be awarded the Medal of Valor for those actions at this meeting. You should get your facts straight he was defending himself and others in all of those actions. Now if that is the only thing your piddling little mind has to say, you can set down and keep your mouth shut. And must I remind you that this is a Monarchy not a Democracy; this Parliament only exists out of the goodness of my heart and you serve at my leisure. And as to that I do not like you calling my son a murderer; and the fact that your son had your yacht and fired four missiles at my son and his wives, I cannot absolve you from part of the blame of that attach, so set down before I lose my temper!"

He didn't set down: "Why you, poor excuse for a King, we will kill you and all of your family." He yelled, as he was reaching in his robe for a weapon; he pulled out what looked like an ink pen and pointed it at the King.

Before the Marines could react, both Hattie and Fiera had their Stilettoes out and flying toward him; both hit at the same time one in each eye."

It didn't faze Dad one little bit, he yelled over the hubbub: "Lock down the hall, no one leaves, sit down and shut up; what he has done was treason, he would have been hung in the public square if my daughters-in-law had not killed him. Marines if you would dispose of the body and have that cleaned up we can proceed with the ceremony of swearing in my Regent. And while Commander Nina and the Marines do their duty; Uh, Commander, will you have those knives disinfected and return them to Hattie and Fiera and also my son would like to examine that weapon, if you would be so good as to bring it to him. Now while they are doing that I want to apologize for not taking care of the rebellion sooner; in fact, I did bring my son back from his duties on earth to help squelch this uprising."

Dad stopped and took a drink from his water flask that he had in his pocket; he knew better that to drink something that had not been tested first.

"Now the Queen Mother Arlina will swear in my daughter Sofia as my Regent; she will be handling all of the day to day business of the King; and as such my Cabinet will bring their business to her first and if she deems it necessary she will involve me. I and my Son, Prince Attila will be paying a lot of attention to the fleet and their duties. So, if you are ready my Dear, you may proceed with the ceremony."

After that, when everyone was filing out of the hall, Commander Nina was conducting a strip search of the Parliament; I didn't envy her the task. She did find one more of those weapons and she had the offending party escorted to the brig. I had her take that one to Professor Kirkland at the R&D to find out what made it tick and as to where it came from. I was very interested as to why the sensors didn't pick up on them.

The one that I had I was very careful with it; I didn't want it go off or something. I sat there staring at it; what if it wasn't a weapon, but a bomb timed to go off later? What if he had planned for it to be taken away from him; and he probably knew how curious I was; and so boom he takes care of me and probably the King? What he didn't plan on was my wives quick reaction.

We were walking through the palace garden as I was contemplating the device; there was a garden well in the middle of the garden, I had looked down it before, it looked to be a hundred feet deep. On impulse I threw it down the well…The water spout went hundreds of feet into the air….

I com'd Commander Nina, she answered: I said, "That's a bomb get rid of it; throw it as far away from you as you can; she did, I heard the explosion…. She com'd me back: "Thank you, I'm going to try and get some residue from it so Kirkland can see what kind of stuff was in that."

"Good Idea Nina, I threw mine down the garden well, maybe we should take some of that water to be examined also." I had one of the marines take a sample.

Sofia looked at me and said: "You're one lucky cuss, did you know that?"

I said: "Yeah, I must be, how else did I end up with two of the most beautiful wives in the universe?"

"Hey, don't forget you've got two beautiful sisters also; but I wasn't referring to them, I was talking about that bomb." Sofia said.

"Yeah, I guess you're right; but I've been that way all of my life; given the battles that I have been in I should have been dead a long time ago."

"I don't think that it has been all luck, I think that it has been a lot of talent and ability and hard work." My wives said.

"Hey you didn't mention brains; I am pretty smart you know!"

"Well, perhaps if you put an 'alec' in back of the word smart you could be right." My beautiful intelligent wives said.

"Well I was smart enough to marry Hattie and it turned out she was inter-locked with her twin sister and I got two for the price of one. But enough of this twaddle, let's go take a swim before dinner and explain to Sofia about this pill and the knowledge cube she needs to wear tonight."

As we were walking I thought about those bombs, how sophisticated they were; "Say, you know those bombs didn't come out of thin air, someone who knew what they were doing had to make them. Sofia, will you have Alfred and Sari look into that?"

"Brother dear, I already com'd them and they are on top of it. You do know that the Kingdom has lasted for thousands of years before we were born; relax our people know their job, let them do it."

"Yeah, I know, but I'm used to doing most of the thinking when I was back on earth; that is till I married Hattie and we now have Fiera also; I just have to let them in on my thoughts before I put my mouth in gear."

"Yes dear, we do know everything you're thinking and we'll chime in when we need to, so far you've been doing a good job; there is just a few things about protocol that you need help with, so we will handle them when they come up."

They were right, we knew each other's thoughts and I mean all thoughts. And after Sofia took that pill tonight I was sure she would join the club; I wasn't sure how that would work out; especially our intimate thoughts. Maybe there was a way we could block those particular thoughts?

"Yes, sweetheart, we can block those thoughts." My wives thought to me and then they gave me an example of what thoughts they would block; I almost tripped over my own feet. Sofia gave me a look and then said:

"What's wrong with you have forgotten how to walk?"

"No, my wives are playing games; they just gave me preview of what they are going to do with me tonight while you are asleep."

"Oh, maybe I won't go to asleep, and then what are they going to do?"

"You'll go to sleep alright, you won't have any choice that pill will see to that."

When we reached our room a few seconds later the women lost no time in shucking their duds. They looked at me and said: "aren't you swimming with us."

"Uh, no not just yet; I want to check with Alfred, I'll be right with you." I said, while waiting for my condition to go down. Those thoughts were really specific. They just smiled and I got their thoughts, they were still messing with me.... So, I said to hell with it and went in just like I was.... To their hoots and jeers. Some women were just plan mean.... Wait! Why wasn't that Nano thing doing what it was supposed to?

I did a little checking of my system; just as I thought my wives were controlling my erection bot...just for their own amusement. Well I could play their game; so I told their Nano bot to mess with them- they both jumped and squealed....

"Stop that Matt, that's no fair." They said as their faces were turning beet red.

"Well then, you stop messing with me; we'll call a truce, how about that?"

"What in the world are you three doing?" Sofia asked.

"Oh, my wives thought it would be funny to mess with my control Nano bot, you know down there;" as I pointed down, "so I messed with theirs."

"You mean you three can do that?"

"Yeah, that's one of things that we can do after taking that pill; sometimes technology can go too far."

"I don't know that sounds like a lot of fun." Sofia said.

"Well then, after you get your pill you can go find yourself a husband to mess around with." I said.

"Who would I find?"

"Oh, we know, what about that Marine Captain Fairfield, he's cute and he's not married and he's stationed right here in the Palace." My wives said.

"How do you guys know he's not married?" Sofia asked.

"We just checked with Lila as you two were talking; Sofia, Lila has his complete records, just access Lila she will show you them."

"Alright, I'll float on my back while I do that." She was a good floater. "Hey, did you guys know that his records have explicit photos of his body, I mean every little detail. Yeah he might just work out fine; that is if we hit it off."

"Alright, that's enough voyeurism; let's get out and get some chow sent in, it's getting late and Sofia needs at least ten hours of sleep for that pill to completely work."

Sofia was a little apprehensive so she asked to sleep with us. "After all guys, that bed is big enough for ten people."

"Alright take your pill and get in on the other side of Hattie. And don't forget that learning thing-a-bob."

* * * * *

We had only taken that pill for a little over 30 hours and really didn't know that much about it. So when we started our REM cycle it was a surprise that our dreams took us back to earth. The three of us were swimming in that hot pool back at the Hacienda.

Selena was there with us: "Hey guys, when did you all get back?"

"Uh, you can see us?"

"Of course, I'm not blind you know."

"Wait just minute, what's going on, isn't this my dream?" I asked my wives.

"Well, yes and no, you see Hattie and I have been able to co-habit each other's dreams ever since I first came to earth. And now you can also share in our dreams; it's sort of a different reality; even though our bodies are fast asleep back on Terra."

"So what about Selena is she sharing our dreams?"

"Well yes, she's here with us, Selena swim over here and let Matt feel you, he doubts you are really here with us."

She ducked under the water and the next thing I knew she was surfacing between Hattie and me. "Is that real enough for you?" Selena said as she rubbed up against us.

"But I don't understand; we just took the pill a day ago, how is it she is able to do that?"

"She has been upgraded just like us; we have quantum delivery of small things like those pills; all of our agents on earth are now upgraded; aren't you keeping up with that learning cube?"

"How can I, every time I turn around you two are messing with me; but I still don't understand how we can have these bodies that feel real in our dreams?"

"Didn't I just tell you we have quantum delivery, you see that makes it possible to ship dreams as well as physical things, but they have to be small, no bigger than a marble."

Then that means that we are in constant contact between earth and terra?"

"Of course we have to be; if we are going to protect earth from invasion; we also have ships patrolling all of the time; you see earth is our sister planet; our DNA is the same; much like here on earth, DNA is a little different in the different so called races on earth. Just like you can tell we are a little different, but still sisters and brothers."

Fiera had no more than finished telling me that, and then Sofia popped up beside us.

"Hey, I thought you guys left me; where are we, anyway?"

"You're on earth; you do know that our bodies are back on Terra and we are sharing one dream?" I said.

"Of course, I keep up with my tutorials. But you do know it's not really a so-called dream, don't you brother; this is just a quantum shift of our minds that make our dreams take on substance and form."

"No, I didn't know that."

Sofia looked at Fiera and Hattie and said: "You guys are going to have to let him take some time and absorb this new knowledge; you see he's just a male and learns a little slower than us females."

"Hey, is that an insult?"

"No, brother dear it's just a fact; you see men take a little more time, but when they do decipher new things it stays with them; while sometimes the females tend to be a little scatter brained, just like right now my libido needs a man so bad, as soon as we get back to our bodies I am going to hunt down Fairfield."

"Alright, you can go back now, if you want to. But I want to talk to Selena some more about how things are going here." I looked at Selena as Sofia disappeared.

"Pretty good, actually; I did get to Santa Fe and showed the bank my power of attorney and the old letch there tried to hit on me, he actually had the nerve to touch me; but the point of my knife at his throat cooled his ardor right quick. Do you know how much money you have in that bank?"

"No, not really; but I have been depositing money in there for years, how much?"

"One hundred thousand dollars and growing every day; he almost shit his drawers when I told him if he ever tried to touch me again I would withdraw every penny; that hurt him more than the threat of me cutting his throat. When I left he was almost groveling at my feet; Anyway, I was thinking about securing our borders more effectively; I was thinking about starting our own security force; uniforms and all. I think we had enough vaqueros and all to spare some of them from ranch work and all they would be doing is working security. What do you think?"

"Are things getting that bad?"

"We are having incursions every day; I don't know if they are organized by someone or just emigrants looking for land or something to steal. I asked some of the other land grants if they were having the same problem, they haven't been."

"Hum, I tell you what, the next time you catch one take a blood sample and quantum deliver it to us so we can check the DNA. We have some local unrest on Terra I am thinking it might be some of them that have sneaked through our security ring in space and come down here just to harass me; just to show me they can."

"Right, I'll have Jasper bring me the next one he catches; he's pretty good at sniffing them out. So do I have the go-ahead to start our own private army?"

"Yeah, I guess so. How are Aiken, April, Alden and June doing?"

"They have been working on their places; they are one of the reasons we need stepped up security; their places are close to our borders; I was thinking about putting one of our mini-forts close by them."

"Good, so how are you and Jose doing?"

"That little creep, I can't stand him; he's running around dipping his wick in everything he can. In fact I think he has syphilis and if he has then he has been infecting every girl he touches."

"Send a sample of his blood and if he is we'll send some medicine to take care of it. But I don't like promiscuity; we could send some libido damping drugs also. I was never over fond of him myself, I should of let the Apaches kill him that time."

"Uh, you know I've been thinking some about having a companion myself, but do you think I could get one from Terra?"

"Sure, we'll have Sofia send you a catalog that you can pick from; there are thousands in the fleet that is in earth's orbit; you could have one by tonight if you wanted to."

"No, I'm pickier than that, he has to be special; I don't want someone inferior or someone who thinks he's superior to women. I want someone who can hold his own in a fight with me, I want someone equal."

"Alright, when you find one will you let us meet him before you get married? Not that we would disapprove your choice per say, but we are having a little problem with the purple contingent on Terra; we wouldn't want one of them sneaking into our family."

"Oh, you can be sure that'll never happen; he'll be tested inside and out before we get hitched. But yes he'll meet my family first thing when I pick one."

"Good, what do you think sweethearts, is it time to return to our bodies?"

"Yeah, it's past time;" they said as they pressed up against me, I could feel their body heat...

I awoke to see Sofia setting cross legged on the foot of the bed eating an apple. I blinked a couple of times and said: "Do you think that's proper?"

"Why, what's wrong?"

"Eating an apple in bed." I said sarcastically.

"Huh?"

"No, not eating an apple; setting like that; you know I am your brother and back on earth that would be a big no-no."

"Really, you mean this?" She said, looking down.

"Yep, that; don't you have any panties?"

"Oh, get over it; you're not on earth anymore. Besides' did you know that Nina and Captain Fairfield are an item?"

"Not really, but in retrospect I could see that happening. Just don't get in a hurry to get hitched again; that last idiot should have taught you to choose wisely. Besides' you are the Regent now; you have plenty to keep you busy. And talking about that, Selena needs a man, send her a catalog or something of the eligible bachelors in the fleet around earth; but only the ones you have done a thorough background search on."

"Alright, but how come your wives haven't woke yet?"

"Damn, your right, I thought they were coming back with me; let me check and see where they went to."

Chapter Twenty-One

I closed my eyes and quantum leaped to wherever they were: "Hey, where are you guys; I thought we were going home?"

"Look for yourself; you're standing right beside us."

"Where is this?"

"We are on the purple continent, this must be their government house; they can't see us, to them we're invisible."

"But how did you guys get sidetracked here?"

"We don't know, but instead of waking up beside you, we were here. We've been listening to what the speaker has been spouting. They are upset about you mostly; they think you were brought back to destroy them." Fiera said.

"That joker that's talking is some kind of Spiritual Guru. He said you were prophesied to do that; that was why they kidnapped you in the first place and you were supposed to be killed instead of just kidnapping you and dropping you on earth.
And drop you they did, but the fall didn't kill you, you fell in a lake and just floated." Hattie said.

"Listen, he's calling for a jihad to kill Attila and all of the Royal Family and take over the Kingship. I think we need to nip this in the bud; don't you?" Fiera said.

"Yeah, you know this name Attila maybe prophetic itself; you see on earth there was a fellow named Attila the Hun and his nick name you might say was 'the scourge of God.' Do you think they might know some of earth's history? Anyway, you are right we need to stop this before it gets out of hand. You two stay here and take notes, so to say, I'm going back and have Sofia get the Santa Fe ready for us and then I will be back."

Sofia was still setting there eating her apple. "That didn't take you long." She said.

"Long enough; have Dari bring the Santa Fe back to the Palace; I assume the updates are completed on it. Make sure all of the crew and marines are aboard we have some bugs we have to crush." I said.

"Do you need any other ships for backup?" One thing about Sofia she was fast on the uptake.

"No, I don't think so; I'm going back to get my wives." I jumped back....

"What's new kids?" I asked.

"Lots, we know where most of their agents are and also that they are going to use some suicide bombers."

"Do you mean they're going to use ships and crash them into targets?"

"No, actual people with explosive vests on and blow themselves up."

"What they have some crazy people willing to do that?"

"Loads of them; but we know the names of those people who volunteered to do that. And as we said we know who and where their agents are; and you would be surprised who some of them are."

"I always knew that Religion was dangerous; but this is ridicules. Are we going to need more ships than just the Santa Fe?" I said.

"Yes, in the long run; but we would suggest that right now let's just concentrate on those vest bombers. They plan on sending them out via various ships tomorrow; can we have the Santa Fe ready by then?"

"Yes, we can have it ready by noon today; do we have any bugs we can plant around various spots so we can keep tabs on them?"

"Well not on us as you can plainly see." They said as they stood there in all of their glory. "But we can send some cloaked remotes that will do the job." Fiera said.

"Good, do you think we can get back to our bodies without any side trips?" We did....

Sofia was standing there with her official Regent robes on. "Good," she said, "you're back; the Santa Fe is ready and all of the crew is standing by to board at your request."

"That's fine, Hattie and Fiera have some intel to upload to Lila, and Lila would you see that Alfred and Sari get going on that information right away, in fact have Alfred get ahold of me I have some specific instructions for them. Sofia you already know what we know, since you're hooked in with us all of the time, so did you inform Dad about it?"

"Yes, he wanted to nuke the whole continent; but I told him to let us handle it; he's getting a little grumpy in his old age."

As we were talking Fiera had already sent the remote bugs to Purple land; and since we had that Quantum leap thing going they got instantaneously. Their feed was hooked to the four of us.

Lila chimed in, "Alfred said that he and Sari would meet the four of you for breakfast in the Palace dining room. I would suggest that the three of you get dressed before you meet."

"Thank you Lila, but I think we'll take a quick shower before we do, will you see that we have clean uniforms laid out?"

"Yes, of course and your weapons will be there also."

As we were standing in the shower, I was thinking how things seemed so surreal; it was just over a week ago that I was a simple earth boy named Matt Bodeen with one wife named Hattie; now I was the name sake of Attila the Hun, the scourge of God. It was starting to bewilder me.

"We know how you feel they thought to me; at times it seems that way to us also; but we have been given the tools to handle the stress and accomplish the goal."

"I would like to know what the hell the goal is. Do either of you know?"

"Yes, peace and security and freedom of thought and mind and body; plus not to be dictated to by a man made religion while still maintaining civilizations laws and principles." Said a voice.

"Who said that, was it either of you?"

"No, we heard it just like you did; maybe it was our sub-conscious?"

"Remember I told you about Timberline moments? I think we just had another one of them; they seem to be coming faster than I can recognize them."

"Yeah, are you ready to get out?" Hattie asked. It didn't sound like Hattie was even a little bit affected by our fast paced existence.

As we stepped out of the molecular dryer I seen our attendants were already for us. And as I stipulated before mine was girl; I just couldn't get used to a man touching me. This girl was a very touchy-feely kind of attendant, but you know what that didn't bother me one little bit;

although Hattie and Fiera were glaring at me.

There was just the six of us at breakfast; we were a close-knit group. The Admiral and his aid-de-camp were fully read into the problem. Alfred came right to the point:

"So how do you want to handle this?"

"Well let me ask you a question, how long has this unrest been going on?"

"Ever since you were kidnapped and dumped on earth as a baby. In all of our long history there has never be anything like this."

"Alright, that is interesting I'll have to ponder a little more on that. But instead of killing the terrorists outright, I want them captured if possible and interrogated and their DNA checked; and even if we have to kill some of them, I still want their DNA checked."

"Uh, do you really think that is possible? Hattie said while looking at me.

"Yes, I do, entirely possible."

"What are you two talking about?" The Admiral asked.

Fiera spoke up: "He thinks some of them might be earthlings; and in retrospect it could be entirely possible."

"Can you three read each other's minds?"

"Yes, something like that, and Sofia is one of us also; but we're getting off point here. As soon as we get some of them captured we will get them to you. Some of their hidden agents are also members of the ONI; we know who they are, Lila will get you a list of not only those in the ONI, but all of their agents here on Terra. Do you want to use your agents to gather them in or do you want the Marines to do it?"

"I'll take care of those in the ONI, the marines can get the rest of them; how soon do you want us to start?"

"I want to coordinate our strike on the purple continent with hitting those here at home. I was going to just use the Santa Fe, but I think I want one of Fleet Troop Carriers to use its marines with full battle suits to reign in the terrorists with those exploding vests; I don't want any of our troops getting hurt. Sofia, can you take care of getting a Fleet Carrier ready to go by noon?"

"Yes, I have already put the entire fleet on yellow alert; hey it feels pretty good to be the CIC (commander in chief of all the Armed Forces.)"

"Well don't let it go to your head; remember you have the same power as the king; use it wisely." I told her, she stuck her tongue out at me. "Also tell the troops from the carrier to just get everyone outside of the government house; the Santa Fe will take care of the house itself."

"Oh, they have to do the whole continent, while you just get one dinky little building?"

"Yeah, that's right Sis, they have over a thousand marines, and we only have under a hundred and fifty. Besides most of the cockroaches like to hide in dark places."

"You've mentioned cockroaches before, what are they?"

"They are slimy little bugs that are next to impossible to kill, that is unless you step on them and squash them; which I plan to do at every opportunity."

"Oh, we don't have them here on Terra."

"So, you say, but we'll see."

Nina wanted to go with the Santa Fe, but I told her she was needed here at the palace. "Uh, Nina, I heard that you and Captain Fairfield were an item; is that right?"

"Well we do seem to see eye to eye on certain things; let's just say she is a close friend of mine."

"You do know that you are the ranking officer and as such there could be problems?"

"Yes, I know, what do you want me to do?"

"I am transferring Captain Fairfield to the Santa Fe, to be in charge of the marines on board; you will be in charge of the Lieutenant that is left with the marines at the palace. Is that alright with you?"

"Yes sir, what about my fleet duties?"

"That will remain the same; I am counting on you to keep things on an even keel here at the palace... And if you need a mate there a lot of men looking for a beautiful woman like you."

"Yes Sir, I get the message."

"Good, get your Marines squared away, you're dismissed."

"Don't you think that was a little harsh?" Hattie said.

"No, I can't have an officer making an emotional decision just to save someone they love."

"What about us, we have been in every battle with you; are we any different than Nina and Captain Fairfield?"

"Yeah, we are one entity; we make decisions as one; they don't. Besides you and Fiera are staying on the ship and handling fire control and tactical; Dari will be Captain and Sally will stand by with the Shuttle Hornet in case we need her."

"Sofia, did you get us a Carrier?"

"Yes, it's the HMS Jin-Li, with Jerry Chang as Captain with Commander Meh-ling as his XO. They have been briefed and will launce with the Santa Fe at the same time."

"What does Jin-Li mean?"

"The Golden Rose, we take names from all over the universe."

"Well good, tell him to be ready to launch as soon as we get aboard the Santa Fe; also tell him to have his marines cover all the exits of their government building. Hattie will be on navigation and Fiera will be on tactical, so you two will be staying aboard."

"What the hell, why can't we go down with the troops?"

"Because I trust you two to make sure that nothing goes wrong; you'll be in constant contact with me and will be able to see the whole picture of what's going on down there; and you'll have all of the weapons to make sure we don't get blindsided, plus just before we get to roof I want you to use the particle disintegrator to cut us a twelve foot hole in the roof that we can just drop through. We won't use the drop ship to go down; we'll just use our powered battle suits."

"Alright, we'll agree to that, but if you get in a jam, we're going to wipe that building clear off the face of the map."

"Hey, just make sure you wait till I get out of there and not just me but all of our troops."

"Well Duh, don't be stupid; it's time to board our ship, Dari is ready to go."

All of Terra's fleet was equipped with FTL that was capable of achieving that speed in a gravity-well; in the vacuum of space they could travel four times the speed of light and then if they went into hyper-drive there wasn't 'almost' any speed they could achieve. I said almost because they hadn't really tested its outer limits.

We and the Jin-Li arrived at the same time, we were both cloaked. "What does the bugs we planted say is going on inside?"

"They are having a meeting making their final plans; the big wigs are dressed in their regular robes; but there are fifty guards with Battle Suits on, but t the fleet stopped using those years ago. Those suits were supposed to be recycled. It looks like this rebellion has been in the planning for a long time." Dari said.

"What is the composite of those suits?" I asked.

"They are mostly metal with carbon fibers inter-twined." They were satisfactory in there day, but we have much better weapons now, why?" Dari asked.

"Would the transfer beam be able to lock on them and drag them out and deposit them in Jin-Li's hold?" You see that way we wouldn't have to destroy them and perhaps they could be reprogramed?"

"They are not computers sweetheart." Hattie said.

"Yeah, I know, but did you check your latest feed from R&D, the professor thinks he has made a break through doing just that on the human brain; they could be the first test subjects."

"Prince Attila, Jin-Li's Captain says his troops are ready to launch, he's just waiting for the word." Dari said.

"Tell him to be ready to receive fifty captives, have him use his transfer beam as soon as Fiera gets that hole in the roof. Tell him to neutralize the weapons on those suits with an EMT beam as he is bringing them in and then put those old suits in the recycler and hold the prisoners in his brig. In the mean time I'd better get my butt in gear and get my battle suit on, I suppose Captain Fairfield is waiting on me." I mentally kissed both of my wives.

She was standing there tapping her foot; "You will have to get out of that uniform, you need to put this skin suit on before you put the battle armor on. Jenny, get over here and help him undress and then help with his battle suit. Let her do that, it's her job to help dress the troops."

Well I sure wasn't going to stop her, especially since she was a beautiful naked woman. Like I told you before nudity was a matter of choice on Terra. I suppose I should be getting used to it, but you know what? I didn't want to get used to it so as to get so used to it became boring; when it became the time when a naked woman wasn't special you might as well be dead. Hattie and Fiera chimed in: "Yeah, we second that motion, if we ever became boring to you, you will be dead..."

Jenny put that skin suit on top of my head and it conformed to my body; Jenny reached down to my lower region and said, "You have to have that out when you step into the suit, the suit recycles your urine as well as any perspiration. Uh, just a second I'll hit that with a spray, it has to be flaccid or it will, uh, you know it would be painful for you."

"Hey that's not my fault, my wives are supposed to control that. Hattie and Fiera stop your messing around, you're just trying to embarrass me."

"Really, they can control your erections? How? They are not here."

"Oh, but they are; you see we are all three inter-twined; what one sees or feels we all see and feel. And by the way they think you're cute and they are not jealous of you." Jenny blushed and said: "Thank them for me." "You just did." I told her.

We were in low orbit above the purple continent and the battle suits were just small space ships you might say and their armaments were somewhat similar to a small ship. Our HUD in our helmets told us everything we needed to know about our environment inside and out of the suit; we only took one hundred marines with us, leaving the rest on board in case that they would be needed; but according to our bugs I didn't think they would be needed inside of the government building.

When we reached the roof we stood in a circle far enough away from the target area so that the particle disintegrator would not disintegrate us. I gave some last minute directions to the troops: "Set your lasers on stun, I want those men in the battle suits alive; just stun them and then let the Jin-Li transfer them to their brig; in fact I don't think we'll need to use deadly force, but be prepared if we do have to."

The particle disintegrator could be set from anything to fine dust to any size we desired; this time I had them set it on fine dust and then had it suck the dust away. As far as those in the building were concerned it would seem that the hole just appeared out of nowhere. And they were very surprised when we dropped down among them.

The suited men were stunned first and transferred to the hold of the Jin-Li; I told the rest of the robe wearing ones to freeze and don't move; some did and some didn't, we stunned those who tried to run; we lined them up and then told the ONI agents that were aboard the Jin-Li to drop down and do their work of interrogating them; I knew that I didn't have the patience for it. Besides all of this crap happened on their watch, not mine; they should have been on top of it long ago.

There were about forty of the ONI agents that dropped in; I didn't see any need of me sticking around. I asked Captain Fairfield if she wanted to stick around: "You can take your troops back to the Santa Fe or stay here and come back with the Jin-Li, it's up to you."

"I think we'll come back with you; there are enough agents to handle this; besides there are hundreds of marines from the Jin-Li with boots on the ground; they'll be staying till the ONI tells them that it's all clear to leave."

"Hattie, Fiera, we're coming back up; would you be sure and tell those ONI agents to check everyone's DNA, I think there are some 'Indians in the wood pile' so to speak." Our suits were equipped with gravity drive as well as standard propulsion; we used the gravity drive so we wouldn't displace all of the fixtures in the building; we just sort of floated up and away. Think what I could of accomplished with one of these suits in the civil war back on earth; we could of called it a police action instead of a war. That was one of the reasons that I was concerned about any earthlings that might have somehow be brought to Terra; I sure didn't want them going back to earth with any of Terra's technology.

Hattie and Fiera were waiting for me when we glided into the hold to remove our suits. They said that they weren't jealous of Jenny, but they were the ones who removed my battle suit. I suppose that was to be expected; I know I wouldn't want some man pawing my wives. One good thing about it, at least they were naked; too bad we weren't alone....

We moved our orbit further out and decided to stay awhile. Fiera thought it would be fortuitous to have Sally and the Hornet do surveillance of the purple continent for a few days, just to be sure there weren't any ships trying to sneak off somewhere. In addition we had our sensors working and would know if any of them tried that. But Hatti said that Sally needed something to do to feel needed.

We set condition blue, which was the lowest of the ready conditions, being blue, yellow and red. Besides the blue lights were sexy, I thought anyway.

It was well past the witching hour when a signal from Sally woke us up; she beamed it direct to the three of us. "I am picking up the signature of impulse engines' firing up at Bodega Bay on the south coast; they are just lifting off as we speak. It's an old destroyer class ship; I am showing that it was decommissioned ten years ago; it was supposed to be melted down and recycled. Do you want me to destroy it?"

The three of us pooled our thoughts: "No, follow it, cloak your ship so they won't see you; we'll follow you and see where they are going. If they see you and fire at you, you are free to destroy them."

"Dari, did you hear that transmission? If so go to yellow and stay within weapon's distance of that Destroyer; if they do fire at Sally, vaporize them."

"What say girls, do you want to untangle our bodies and head for the bridge?"

"Yeah, I suppose we had better get dressed and at least act like officers of the fleet." They said.

When we got to the bridge, Dari already had a full crew at the controls. So we just took three seats in back and buckled in. They didn't need me, so I relaxed and went to sleep; of course part of my brain was always awake and I could keep track of what was going on through Hattie and Fiera.

I knew when we brought Sally and the Hornet back into the shuttle hold. Dari was keeping her distance. Hattie and Fiera woke me all of the way up. "Hey, it looks like they are heading for earth."

Dari was looking at me and said: "What do you want me to do?"

"Hail them and tell them that Prince Attila the Hun wants to talk to them."

"Huh, what's the Hun mean?" Dari asked.

"The Scourge of God. But I think they will know what it means. Also scan that ship, I want to know how many are aboard and what weapons they have, in fact everything from soup to nuts about them."

They didn't answer; but our scan was enlightening; they had a nuclear bomb on board. "What in the hell are they planning on doing with that bomb?" I asked everyone in general. They all just looked at me...

Well I know what they are not going to do; "Dari, attach four contact mines to that ship's hull; set the timers for fifteen minutes delay and then get us out of the blasts reach. Hail them one more time and tell them they have fifteen minutes to give themselves up or we will destroy them."

They answered this time: "So you think you are the scourge of god do you?"

"Yep, I do, and who do I have the displeasure of seeing, I see you have some sort of religious get up on; and I would suggest you speak up, your time is clicking away." I could see other people standing around and they looked scared, like they didn't want to be where they were."

Fiera whispered to me: "We have a new weapon that you aren't aware of; it can go through that ship's hull without making a hole and target a specific person; it looks like he has a detonator in his hand; we could destroy that detonator without blowing up that bomb."

"Make it so." I said, while wondering why I didn't know about that new weapon as soon as my wives did.

The girl on tactical pushed a couple of buttons and that detonator disappeared along with his hand. Two men standing beside that fool jumped him and held him down; they said: "Help us; there are some more of them in the hold with that bomb."

"Alright, we'll take care of them; is he bleeding much or did that beam cauterize his wound."

"He's not bleeding, we'll tie him up."

"Good, you will see that they, the ones in the hold with the bomb are already dead.

"Stand by for boarding, Captain Fairfield and her marines will be boarding and take control of your ship and fly it back to the R&D shipyards. Where did you get that ship?"

"We bought it ten years ago from a salvage dealer; we have been using it for hauling freight around Terra. All of the weapons have been removed, except for the ones that they installed when they hijacked us a month ago."

"Do you know of any other ships that were sold to private parties like yours was sold to you?"

"Yes, many; we bought ours from the salvage dealer in Kawloon. He has sold many of them"

"Alright, just cooperate with Captain Fairfield and everything will be alright."

"It sounds like Sofia has a lot of dirt that has been swept under the rug to clean up. Uh, Dari, did you remove those mines?"

"Yes, Prince Attila we did, do you want us to follow that ship back to the R&D shipyards?"

"Yes, then pick up our marines; also let them know what is heading their way, they will have to have bomb disposal experts meet that ship. Also hold all of the passengers in the brig tell ONI can interrogate them.

"All of them Sir?"

"Yes, all of them, you never know who's what and who's not. We're going back to bed."

Before we went to sleep we rang Sofia's bell, so to speak, and told her we wanted to know the result of ONI's interrogation of those zealots as soon as they had anything on their DNA; I was pretty sure that there was a lot of earth people's influence in there somewhere. Because this was the first 'religion' ever showed up in Terra's history. That's not to say that Terra didn't believe in a creator, because they do.

Before I dropped off to sleep a thought occurred to me; and of course it occurred to my wives at the same time: "We forgot to tell ONI about that salvage dealer in Kawloon." And of course as soon as we thought of it, the message went out to Alfred and Sari.

One thing about the three of us being one, was we could feel the blood going through each other's veins. Even our heart beats and breathing were in sync. And when it came to sex, when one had an orgasm we all three did. You might be thinking, man that's weird, but it felt completely rational to us. But at the same time we were still individuals', but with one common core.

I hadn't forgotten about Hattie and Fiera knowing some things that I didn't; I was thinking about that when I woke up. "Yes, sweetheart, we filter some of the messages coming in; we don't want to bother you with little things." They said.

"But maybe I may think they are important and you two don't?"

"Believe us, we know every in and out of your brain; we could let all of the trash get to you, do you want us to do that?"

"Uh, no I trust you both with my life because I love you guys."

"And that's why we filter the trash, is because we love you."

I sled off of the foot of the bed, which was easy, because somehow I was at the foot of the bed. They got up and stretched. Boy, were they ever beautiful; they were matched down to every freckle. They had the same hairdos; all they had to do was shake their heads and the hair fell into the style they wanted.

"What are you looking at?" They asked.

"You two, you're so beautiful I could eat you guys up."

"Yeah, you tried that last night, but we're still here." Fiera said, and then Hattie said, "He sure tried though." And they both giggled. Funny I don't remember any of that… Liar, I remembered every second of it…

"Where are we?" I asked.

"We're on our way to some R&R at a resort on a tropical island; we thought the troops needed some down time."

"What's there to do at a resort, whatever that is?"

"There's beaches with crystal clear water where you can go scuba diving and see all sorts of creatures. And there are no class distinctions; because there are no clothes allowed." Fiera said.

"You mean all of the troops will see you guys naked?"

"Yes, that's what it means, why are you jealous?"

"Well not jealous, so much, but you two are special; you're the most beautiful women in the universe. I don't know whether I like the idea of everyone gawking at my wives."

"Alright, we'll wear a chemise; but you have to wear a thong."

"What's a thong?"

"A swimming suit, is that alright?"

"I guess so; they'll just have to make an exception for us." They stood there smiling, with a weird grin on their faces. I didn't trust them one little bit.

We got in the shower and pushed 'auto' and all of a sudden, a thing-a-ma jig, came down over each of us and started washing us everywhere. They must have added this when they re-did our ship.

"Wow," I said, "I've never had a wash job like that; I don't think it missed any orifice."

Hattie said, "It didn't."

Then we stepped into the automatic drier, it took about five seconds and we were dry; it didn't miss anything either. Then our disposable uniform came down over our heads and adhered to our bodies, they didn't leave anything to the imagination either.

"What if you want to go to the bathroom with these things on?"

"Just tell it what you want to do and it will open in the proper place." Fiera said.

"Come on, I'm hungry." Fiera said, "We'll go the Officer's Mess; yes there are two mess halls; it's protocol."

"Well then, if it's protocol I can't go against that." I said a bit sarcastically.

As we walked in everyone there started to get up, that is till we said: "At ease." And they sat back down. Fiera said to Hattie and me: "On board ship it's not protocol to salute or stand up when the Captain comes into the room, but being that you are the Prince, they thought you deserved more respect. And also, you are not technically Captain of this ship, Dari is. I think we should make you an Admiral and then there wouldn't be any confusion."

"Oh Yeah, just like that you're going to make me an Admiral."

"Just a minute," Fiera said, then, "Yes, you are an Admiral now, Sofia just made you one. Attention everyone, the Kings regent just promoted Prince Attila to Admiral."

Everyone stood up and clapped, "Alright, no big deal, I'm still Matthew Bodeen, anyway that's the way I think of myself. So just set back down and finish your breakfast."

"Yeah, I'm some Admiral; I don't even know what an Admiral is supposed to do, much less being one."

"That's alright Honey, we do, just look important and smile, and everyone will love you. Look there, your Captain's bars have disappeared and Admiral's stars are in their place." My wives said as I looked at them. Then two stars appeared on their uniforms shoulders, I looked at mine, I had four stars. Oh, this was getting plain ridiculous…In fact it was surreal…

I sat there munching at my food, thinking, what the hell, I'm a Major in the U.S. Army, not some Admiral on earths twin planet with two beautiful wives. What time warp did I cross? I looked at Hattie and Fiera setting on either side of me; I put my hands on their thighs and ran them up to the 'Y' they twitched, yep they were real alright.

"What are you doing? Stop that; everyone can see what you're doing!" I smiled at them and went back to eating.

They were still giving me dirty looks as we finished breakfast and walked toward the bridge. "Why are you mad at me? Half the people on this ship run around nude all of the time and I was checking to see if I wasn't dreaming; I guess I'm not if you two are mad at me."

"We're not mad, just surprised is all, I guess, you're always so reserved in public and what you did was out of character. You're not going to do anything like that in public again are you?"

"Not where people can see us anyway, but I just might, you never know. I don't want you two to get bored with me."

"Us get bored with you? I don't think that will ever happen; every time we turn around you're doing something weird. And I guess we like you just the way you are." They said and they both kissed me, just as we walked on the bridge.

"Admirals' on the bridge," someone called out as we came in, boy news travels fast around here. Again, I had to tell them at 'ease.'

Dari looked at us and said: "Congratulation to the three of you. We will be there in five minutes. Do you want to land with the Santa Fe or use the shuttle?"

"I think we'll have Sally use the Hornet to shuttle everyone to and from the Santa Fe. Uh, I guess I've never heard the Santa Fe's new computer's name?"

"It's Catlin, Catlin say hello to Prince Attila and his wives, Hattie and Fiera; they are all Admirals'."

"Yes, I know they are Captain Dari; you know I see everything that goes on, on the ship. I'm very pleased to finally be introduced to the three of you; if there is ever anything that I can do for you'all you just have to ask." Wow, she had a sexy southern accent; I bet if she ever got out of that computer she'd be a wild one.

I thought to my wives: "Did she say that she sees everything that goes, even in our quarters?"

"Don't worry, we blocked her out of there, but she seen what you did at breakfast. So behave yourself anywhere else on the ship. And we don't know where she got that accent."

"Anyway, Captain Dari, I think we should leave the Santa Fe in orbit and cloaked, can Catlin handle that with no humans on board?"

"Well of course I can, I'm not a dummy Admiral Dear, and I'd do most anything for you." Catlin said….

Hattie and Fiera thought to me: "Don't worry Honey, we will fix her programing, no bunch of transistors is going to hit on our husband." I thought back, "Good, but maybe leave her southern accent, I sort of like that."

"Like hell we are, we'll give her a snooty New England accent, how's that?"

"Uh, yeah that's fine, don't be too hard on the girl, you can't blame her for liking someone great like me." I said with a snigger.

We had Sally shuttle the crew down to the resort first; us three and Dari were the last to leave the ship. I told Catlin to use the passive sensors and not go with active sensors unless she thought there was a threat to the ship and to let us know if there was, but to keep the ship cloaked and if she got bored to read up on earth's history and customs.

"Yes Admiral, it will be done just as you prescribed." Catlin said, I looked at my wives, "Are you sure you didn't overdo it, the makeover I mean?"

"No, we like her that way; but you see she is still the old Catlin, we just adjusted the translator on her voice to come out that way, she still thinks she is in love with you, we couldn't change her personality."

As we stepped out of the Hornet, it was evident that the no clothes rule was in full effect. All of the crew and the marines were sans-suits. Captain Dari knew where our cabins were, we followed along; Dari was stripping as she walked; so were Hattie and Fiera, I wasn't, I guess I was too busy gawking around.

Dari stopped at a cabin and said: "This one is yours; Sally and I will share the cabin next to this one. Uh, Admiral, you're out of uniform." I guess she was meaning that because I still had my uniform on.

It was more than a cabin, by earth standards this would almost be a mansion. In our bedroom there was a very large bed with the swimming pool starting almost at the foot end. "Why is the bed so close to the pool?"

"Sweetheart, the bed tips up and we can slide direct into the pool when we wake up in the mornings. You see the pool extends direct from here to the main pool all we have to do is swim to where the rest of our troops are."

"Oh," I said, as Fiera leaned over and pushed the button that retracted my uniform, then she tossed all three of our uniforms in a drawer. There was a knock on our door, Sally stood there with our luggage: "You forgot this, thought you might want what's in it." She said, she was also very naked. She glanced down and smiled at me; "Nice package." She said.

"Now why did she say that?" I said.

"Look down, as soon as your uniform came off that thing came up, wait a second, it's relaxing now. It was our fault we didn't know she was bringing our luggage, we'll control it better from here on out."

"I didn't know we packed anything, what's in it?"

"All of our weapons, you didn't think that we'd leave them behind, did you?"

"So where is this swimming suit that you have for me? And where are your chemises?"

"Here with the weapons," she tossed something at me. "That's yours."

"What, there is no back to it, just this thin peace of material, and the front isn't big enough either...."

"Yes Honey, we know, that is called a thong and you agreed to wear it, if we wore these." They held up some flimsy clothe made of see through something or other.

"What the hell, I can see right through that."

"We know, but when it gets wet it clings to us and we can change it to any color we want, even rainbow."

"But you will still be able to see through it."

"Yes, isn't that nice, but we'll still be covered, just like you wanted."

"I give up; everything that I thought my world was made up of has been turned upside down." I said, as I plopped down on the bed.

"Honey, you hit the switch, the bed is going up." They said as they watched me drop into the pool without that thong thing on. They dropped their flimsy things and jumped in after me. We came up outside of our cabin.

"Well since we're in the pool, we might as well join the others." Hattie and Fiera said. As they ducked under and pulled me under the water and they didn't grab me by the hand either. I guess they thought, when in Rome, do as the Romans do. There was only one thing wrong with that; we weren't in Rome and we weren't Romans. I didn't know what the hell we were....

It was about a hundred-yard swim to the main pool area; that was where everyone was gathered. That pool was big it must have been about a half mile across it. Turned out it was part of the bay, stupid me.

Sally and Dari met us; "Come on they are roasting cam-cam, it's delicious." I didn't know what a cam-cam was, but it did smell good. No one was taking any special notice of us, which I was glad about. We went and filled our plates and then sat down with some of the crew; I was still a little self-conscious about everything hanging out, but no one else was.

As I was eating and looking around at how un-conscious they were about their nudity, it got me to thinking about earth; about how we would be hung or stoned or something if we were to do this on earth. Then I thought how earth might of turned out if Adam and Eve hadn't sinned in that Garden of Eden. Maybe they would be as advanced as Terra was. Instead they were almost still in the dark ages.

This resort had live music and dancing; there were alcoholic beverages but no one was abusing that privilege. Anyway, we whiled away the rest of the day just doing what came natural; like playing water games in the bay and just visiting with our crew and getting to know them; here in this setting we were just one of the bunch and that did feel good.

The days went by fast with no disasters befalling anyone. We were in constant touch with Catlin; she was getting a little bored, she said she had already covered all of the information about earth and had down loaded the info for future reference.

Of course, it seemed, that even here paradise was limited; it was toward the end of our two-week R&R that Catlin buzzed us: "Hey, I'm getting a sensor reading that a ship has just came out of warp ten thousand miles out."

"Have you identified it?"

"Yes and no, it's not one of ours, in fact it's alien. Wait, it just cloaked itself, I'm going active with sensors. With these new sensors it doesn't matter if they are cloaked, in fact it is better that way, they can't tell that I am probing them; give me a few seconds and I will have all of their data from their computer down loaded."

"I'm back, it's from the planet Ceylon; it's in the Constellation Monoceros; that's close to Orion. And I even know why they are here, are you interested in knowing?"

"Catlin, stop fooling around." Fiera told her.

"Alright, alright, don't get your dander up; they are here to kill the three of you."

"What? Kill us, why in the worlds would they want to kill us?"

"It's on account of Attila the Scourge of God, they think he is going to destroy their planet and do you know who told them that? I'll give you one guess."

"That's aright Catlin, I know who told them, that same bunch we just had tussle with, I bet." I said.

"Yep, you're right Pardner, you want me to bushwhack them?"

"No, I don't want you to bushwhack them; and just because you've got the vernacular of earth's west down, you don't have to use it. So, what's their technical level, should we be concerned?"

"They are probably two hundred years behind us and they are humanoid and they are wearing clothes. A bunch of retardos if you ask me." Catlin said and sniffed, I guess that was the New England coming out on her, I think I would prefer the western slang myself.

"Hey, no bigotry please; disable the power to their propulsion and weapons and then have the Jin-Li tow them to Fort Fuji and put the crew in quarantine; have Admiral Alfred and Sari take it from there."

"What, I can't even challenge them to a shoot- out?"

"Knock it off Catlin or I will come up there and box your ears." Hattie told her.

"Yes, Mam, but I'm so bored I could just cry!"

"Well then, get ready to have the crew start boarding in the morning and then we'll also go to Fort Fuji and see what's going on with them."

The three of us were tossing our thoughts back and forth; one of them was the fact that Catlin had said that they were humanoid. "I thought that there weren't any other planets with humans on them, except Terra and Earth."

"That was our impression also; but I'm sure we'll know more after we interrogate them and sample their DNA." Fiera said.

"Yeah, I reckon; let's not wait for Sally to transport us to the Santa

Fe, tell Catlin to beam us up along with our weapons; I want to see what those scans can tell us about them."

When we got to the bridge we were met by a hologram of Catlin; we stood there staring; "Uh, Catlin are you sure you want to look like that?" Hattie asked her.

"What don't you like how I look?"

"The proportions aren't quite right; if you were flesh and blood you would fall over on your face; your breasts would over balance you. And also, you are an officer of the fleet, so please wear a uniform, say make yourself a Commander. Is your hologram limited to the bridge or can you go through out the ship?" Hattie asked her.

"I can go anywhere on the ship and even up to a hundred feet outside of the ship when we are in port. I've been trying to give my body a little more substance; I've been experimenting with the radical carbons that float around in the air that your bodies give off. I've been trying to get a magnetic field that is stable enough to adhere the particles to the hologram."

"Maybe since all of the crew wasn't here there weren't enough radical carbons to make a stable field." Fiera said.

"I had thought of that and you could be right, I'll try after a few days with the crew aboard. Oh, an update, the Jin-Li has just hooked its tractor beam to the alien ship and is towing it away."

"Thank you, Catlin and yes those look better, just the right size for your body and don't forget the uniform." I said.

"Since we have some time before the crew gets back in the morning, why don't we do some target practicing with our newfangled weapons that R&D made for us out of our old black powder guns?"

"Yeah, we could turn the power level down so we wouldn't ruin anything on the target range, since the range is only meant for simulators."

They looked like our old .44's and 45's, but were much lighter in weight; we strapped them on, they felt pretty good. Even my Bowie Knife was changed some, a new edge that was made of molecules that were in motion, you could say. The edge would never get dull. Even the girl's stilettoes were redone the same. We set the power levels down to target power. It didn't take long for Hattie and me to get back to our old speed and accuracy; Fiera took a little longer, but she caught up fast.

We went back to the bridge Catlin was still in the all-together; "I thought you were going to put on a uniform?" I said.

"Well, I was but let me enjoy this body, it's gorgeous, don't you think?"

"Alright, yes it is very nice. I want you to check that download from that alien ship one more time; since you've been fixated on your new body you might have missed something."

She stuck her tongue out at me; "Yes, there are a few facts that I overlooked: What do you want to know?"

"Their lineage for one thing; if their human in origin, how did they get on that planet?"

"Well first off, I made a little error on their technology level, it's not two hundred years behind us, it's more like a thousand years behind us; their warp drive is one we were using a thousand years ago and also their weapons are out of style you might say. And as to their lineage, I am just guessing on that till we get their DNA results, but it looks like it is mixed; between earth and terra."

"So, how did they get on that planet?"

"Their computer didn't have that information; but I can tell you they practice some kind of religion that didn't originate from Terra."

"Oh crap, there are a jillion-million religions down there on earth and all they do is fight among themselves and start wars; we can't let that get started on Terra. Catlin, could you plot a course to that planet? What was its name again?"

"Ceylon, the same name of an Island country off the tip of India on earth; and yes I can get us there in less than an hour if you want to use the Quantum Drive, otherwise I can use the interstellar drive and get us there in a week; if I had to use the old warp drive it would take three months, but we're not equipped with that old warp drive anymore."

"Catlin, you're starting to babble, just stick to the facts; has that body of yours turned you into a woman that likes to hear her own voice?" Hattie asked her.

"No Mam, I'm sorry. Please don't take my body away."

"We won't, that is if you don't let your body distract you; like so many women do."

(I bet you thought I was going to make a smart-aleck comment on what Hattie just said? Well, I may be slow at times, but I'm not dumb.)

Hattie looked at me; I just smiled at her…. "Well do you want to go there or not?"

"Not without discussing it with the two of you and certainly not till all of the crew gets back on board. And also, we had better run it by Sofia; in fact, you two can fill her in; I'm just one little part of the whole."

"Yeah, like so much hogwash, any three-headed creature needs a leader, otherwise they would be pulling three different directions…."

"Are you referring to us as some three-headed monster?" I asked.

"No, but some people look at us that way; although their too scared to say it out loud."

"What, we scare people?"

"Damn right we do; not those who are close to us and love us, they know who we are deep down; I've heard some mumblings about how we shoot first and ask questions later. But that's not true; we don't ask any questions later…." Fiera said.

"Catlin, you have the bridge, we're going to take a swim and relax." Yes, the Santa Fe was big enough to have a pool; it also served as an emergency water supply.

"Hey, why do I have to stay on the bridge, your three have been doing nothing for the last two weeks; don't you think you've relaxed enough?"

"Can that hologram go in the water?" Hattie asked her.

"Well no, not yet; that is not till the crew gets back and I get enough carbon molecules. And I can run this ship from anywhere I don't have to stay in one place."

"Alright go where you want, but you still have the bridge." I said.

"Don't I always, even if the full crew is here, I still run the ship." She said, petulantly.

As we were walking toward the pool my wives told me that they had filled Sofia in, and that my Dad wanted to see us personally; something about some information that would apply to what was going on with that planet Ceylon; so before we went gallivanting around the universe we were to see him.

We shucked our dudes and jumped in and did a few laps then floated around on our backs till Catlin came in and sat down cross legged on the edge of the pool. I looked at her; for one thing she sure was anatomically correct.

"Have you checked your sensors lately?" I asked her.

"Why do you always ask stuff like that when the three of you are hooked into the ship the same as I am?"

"I suppose because we are still humans and inter-act as humans and you have intimated that you want to be like us humans; so, when we talk we socially connect, don't you want to connect?"

"Yeah, in more ways than that though; I want to be just like you three; I see how much in love you three are, I want that connection. I know, I know, you three were created and I was assembled. I'm not even like Sari and Dari when they were in stuck in computers; which was a terrible thing to do to them, by the way; but at least they are back to being humans now."

"Yes Catlin, we understand, you are an advanced AI, too advanced for your own good, perhaps, but I'm thinking that you will soon find a way out. In fact, your using carbon molecules is one step. And, oh, don't tell any of the crew what our capabilities are; and as you know Sofia is hooked up with us."

"I suspected as much, I didn't know for sure, but it's only logical, she's your sister. Since you're hooked in, did you just understand that sensor reading?"

"Yeah," we said, "we're bringing the ship to yellow alert now, maybe you had better physically get back to the bridge, we're right behind you." We jumped out and grabbed our uniforms and weapons and ran for the bridge. By the time we got to the bridge, Catlin had put the ship on red alert.

"Admiral, you take the Captain's seat, I'll take navigation, if your two rear admirals will take tactical, we'll deal with that ship." Catlin said.

"That ship is one of ours that was listed as lost when a reactor blew up two years ago. It's HMS Cobalt; it can hurt us Admiral, but it doesn't have the latest updates. They have their weapons hot, what do you want to do Admiral?" Catlin asked.

We all three said as one: "Put one up their butt, we're not going to even hail them; they have sealed their doom by approaching us with weapons hot."

Hattie and Fiera had no more than said that when they pushed the button.

They had just launched a missal at us when our quantum torpedo hit them and turned them into space dust.

"Catlin, will you please tell Captain Dari to not wait for daylight, but to get the crew back on-board ASAP."

"Yes Admiral, it was done the second you thought of it; Sally has already started to bring the Hornet's reactors on line and her weapons are hot. My long-range sensors are active and the search is negative."

"Thank you, Commander Catlin; will you please put your uniform on before the crew gets here; we are on a wartime footing now and I want the proper decorum on board the bridge at all times."

Catlin looked at my twin Admirals and said: "What's up with him, has he always been this way?"

"Yes, when he's at war; he takes it seriously. He went through four years of war and he came out alive; so, when it comes to war and fighting he knows what he's talking about." Hattie and Fiera said as they donned their uniforms and weapons. Of course, I already had my uniform on. My weapons were already feeling like long lost friends.

Catlin's hologram shimmered a little bit and her uniform was on. "Admiral, Captain Dari says the whole crew will be coming in one trip; she jammed them all in."

"Thank you, Commander, please make sure the entire crew is aware of the proper uniform in war time; and that includes our marines."

"Yes Admiral, I've already told them."

"Thank you, we'll be retiring to the officer's mess, have the command officer's meet us there when their all aboard and that includes you."

"Yes Admiral, it will be as you say."

"Come on babes, let's go eat something." I told my wives.

"Babes? What about military decorum?"

"Yeah, well rank has its privileges."

Chapter Twenty-Two

I looked around at all of the command rank officers that were patiently waiting for me to say something. "Is there anyone here who does not know what just happened up here?"

No one raised their hand; I guess scuttle-butt travels fast. "Good, then you know we are on war time footing; and I suppose you have heard about wearing your uniforms? But you haven't heard why I imposed that rule; it's because your bare skin is not bullet proof or will it enable you to breath in a vacuum. That's just two reasons. Nor does your present uniforms fulfill that task. I've asked Commander Catlin to fill you in on the changes. Commander, if you would...."

Catlin stood up and gave a big smile; "You all know me as the ships computer, but now I've taken this human shape by the use of a hologram, but I'm working on becoming more than a hologram." I cleared my throat, indicating she was getting off track.

"Uh, yes back to the point: "In the recent upgrade to the Santa Fe we acquired new and improved uniforms for everyone; as the Admiral mentioned they are more or less bullet proof and capable of sustaining your life in a vacuum for two hours. Plus, they monitor you vitals and perform first aid, also they can inject lifesaving nanites into your bloodstream."

"But, our battle suits can do all of that." Captain Fairfield said.

"Yes, they can if you have time to don them in an actual emergency. These suits are made of living molecules with carbon fibers woven in, plus they are almost as thin as your skin; and if you have to don your battle suits they work in place of the undergarments you usually have to put on before you don your battle suits. In short, these suits will save your life and if you are alive you can in turn save the ship, and uh, me!"

"Thank you, Commander; and the three of us are wearing these suits;" I indicated Hattie and Fiera, "I will demonstrate one feature of these suits, Fiera would you stand over there by the bulkhead?" After she got there and turned around I picked up my heavy coffee mug and threw it as hard as I could at her....

The suit sensed a projectile coming at her and Fiera's suit shot up over her face and head and then repelled the coffee mug before it even hit her.

"Of course. that mug wasn't traveling very fast, if a bullet was coming at her the suit would try and repel it, or the bullet would simply bounce off of the suit itself. The wearing of these suits is mandatory; except when showering or swimming or making love." I got a few laughs at that, but some of them were glancing at each other. "You can draw the suits from ships stores, they have one for each and every one on this ship and some left over. Oh, also they are unisex, they will adapt to your body." With that they all got up and left to their various duties.

Fiera said: "I don't know why anybody would object to wearing these suits, you can hardly tell them from our skin; of course, they can change shades, from nude, to any color; perhaps each department should be assigned a shade to just tell them apart at a glance?"

"Hey, that's a good idea; but even with these different shades you can see what's underneath; so who's going to assign the colors?" I asked.

"Why don't we let Catlin do that; then if anyone doesn't like their color they can take it up with Captain Dari, after all she is the Captain."

"Yeah, I know sometimes I have a tendency to butt in too much." I said.

"Admiral, you're wanted on the bridge; a call from the King." Catlin said.

As we walked on the bridge I noticed that the bridge crew was already wearing the new uniforms. Someone said: "Admiral's on the bridge." Hattie said at ease. We sat down in our three personal chairs; the chairs conformed to our bodies, as if they were made for us; as of course they were.

I looked at Dari and said: "On Screen."

"Dad, you're up early."

"Yes, son I am; tell me about that ship, I heard it was the HMS Cobalt, is that right?"

"Yep, that's what Commander Catlin determined; she downloaded their computer before we destroyed them."

"Why did you destroy them?"

"They were coming at us with weapons hot, also they launched a missal at us; so we killed them with one of the new Quantum Torpedos. So, Dad what can you tell me about the Cobalt?"

"Not much, except she was reportedly destroyed when her reactor blew up two years ago. Sofia tells me that we should search through every computer on Terra and in the fleet; she thinks we have a mole or two; in fact, she has already set that in motion. Can you send her the results of the Cobalt's computer; maybe that will tell us something?"

"Already done Dad, Commander Catlin sent as soon as you thought of it."

"Uh, I don't remember any Commander Catlin, who is it?"

"Oh, she's our computer; she created a hologram for herself and is in the process of filling in the hologram with carbon molecules that we humans give off in the air."

"Huh, I didn't even know that was possible; I guess I had better get an update tonight as I sleep; when you get older some people tend to ignore you, but you will find that out in time."

Sofia stepped into the picture beside Dad. "I have already given instructions to have Dad and Mom given a briefing every day from now on." Dad pushed her aside, "Yes son, I do believe we need to get on top of this situation; when you get here I have some things to discuss with the three of you; I have a hunch what is going on."

"Sure Dad, we are getting underway right now." I said as I nodded to Captain Dari; she nodded back as she gave the order to engage the gravity drive to get us out of the atmosphere and into space so we could jump back to the Palace.

As we were settling into our berth at the palace; Captain Dari was giving instructions as to what department was getting liberty first; since only so many would be able to be gone from the ship at a time; since we were on war alert.

Oh, and as to colors of the departments; they were going to give the three of us bright red, but Hattie and Fiera put stop to that; in fact, they put a stop to assigning colors all together. They decided that fleet blue was good enough for everyone and that their department patches were fine for telling the departments. They said: "We don't want to look like a damn zoo."

Lila the palace computer let us know that the King was waiting for us in his private quarters along with Sofia. When we rang the bell; his butler let us in and escorted us to the den.

"Good, you're here: I've some things to tell you that are not in any records or history books; it concerns our relationship with earth. We were not to interfere in anyway with earth's development; you see, as you already know when the first man and woman were created on earth, they failed the simple test of loyalty; where the first two humans on terra passed that simple test and sent that lying scoundrel on his way. But what you don't know is that when we first developed space travel the Creator told us to make sure no other species interfered with earth either."

"But somewhere along the line a thousand years ago we lost a ship to a black hole, or so we thought; that is till that showed up and you disabled it. And then the HMS Cobalt was thought to have exploded with a reactor malfunction two years ago. I am sorry to say we must have fallen down on our job of non-interference; it looks like we have some terrains that have fallen prey to the false religion that is prevalent on earth."

Dad fell silent for a couple of minutes. "You see, the Creator told us he would take care of the problem in his own good time; he told us that no man would know the day or time when he would erase the problem; only us Kings were to know what he told us. And since Sofia is the regent and you are in line to inherit I felt that you both should be told; of course that also means that Hattie and Fiera should also know, since you three are one."

"So now, it looks like there is another planet that we need to deal with; since it is our fault that false religion got loose from earth and the Creator is holding us responsible...."

"What, he told you this?" Sofia said, with alarm in her voice.

"Yes, Daughter, he did. You see our negligence in the past is still our responsibility."

"Wait, this creator, he's the same on that's on earth, right?" I said.

"Yes of course."

"Well I read in the King James Bible that his name is Jehovah, right?"

"Yes, there is only one God the Almighty and his name is Jehovah."

"Why don't you call him by his name Jehovah, instead of calling him the Creator?"

"I don't know; the entire line of King's in the past just used Creator; I guess it just became a habit. Anyway, it's up to us to clean up this mess; so I want you to take what ships you need to and disable any ships that they have on the Planet Ceylon; if they attack you, you have permission to destroy them. Plus take one hundred medical ships and any peaceful people you find wipe their memories and give them new memories in various fields and they are to be a colony from Terra; the creator has given us permission to inhabit that planet. Oh yes, please give that planet a new name, not one from the planet earth though."

"I don't know how I'm going to find a name that is too different from earth, our thoughts and language' are similar to earth's." I said.

"Oh, I'm sure your wives will come up with something. And Alfred and Sari are making progress on finding the moles here on Terra, in fact they have already wiped the memories of ten people; they made them stable hands."

"Where, here at the Palace?"

"No, at different resorts here on Terra, that feature horseback rides. I didn't want them here, where I would have to look at them."

"Dad there is one more thing I need to know; how many other ships have gone missing, that is besides the two I know about?"

Dad looked up at the ceiling and said: "Lila please list the others for my son."

I won't bore you with the list; let's just say it was considerable, but under a hundred.

"Didn't anyone think that, that many ships going missing was suspicious?"

"Well it did happen over a thousand years; but you're right we dropped the ball. And I'm afraid now I have dropped that ball in your lap; how many ships are you going to need?"

"I have no idea at the moment; but let's just say about two thousand to start; I have already sent a hundred ships to spy out that planet, I told them to stay cloaked. When I get their sensor data back I'll know for sure." When I said that I had already sent ships there, it wasn't a lie, because the three of us had dispatched them while I was talking to Dad.

Over a thousand years there could be a considerable amount of buildup on that planet. There is nothing worse than religious zealots to deal with; sometimes extinction was the answer; I hoped not though.

Our three brains being hooked together enabled us to work on multiple things while still communicating with those around us; part of what we were working on was the problem of accomplishing our task without too much destruction.

Right at this moment we were invading Professor Kirkland's mind at the R&D. We found something he had been working on for a long time, but, had pushed it to the far back corner of his mind; thinking that it was something that wasn't that important.

We pulled out and com'd his conscious mind. "Yes, Prince Attila, what can I do for you?"

"Crowd control of massive populations without damaging them; while not wiping their minds, but let's just say changing their outlook on life...."

"Funny you should mention that, because I have been thinking about that in the past and in fact have run a few experiments; but that was long ago, let me get back to you on that."

"What do you think girls, think his idea will work?" I asked my lovely wives.

"Yes, it's completely possible; both chemically and morally it would be the right thing to do. And it would still fall under free will; it's just giving them another choice to live or die."

"Yep, but some of those zealots would still prefer death; thinking that they would be going to their heaven and living forever with seventy-seven virgins."

"We suppose that you would like seventy-seven virgins?"

"Nope, not me; it's all I can do to keep up with you two."

"And you just keep remembering that buddy, or you will lose what you have...."

"Hey, that goes both ways; true love is loyal."

"So," Dad said, bringing us back to things at hand, "When are you leaving?"

"As soon as we get that sensor information, they quantum leaped so we should hear from them yet today and our fleet is on standby; and Professor Kirkland is cooking up something for us, so we are waiting to hear from him." We said. Of course, Sofia was listening in to all of our thoughts and not saying anything.

I had just taken my eyes off of Sofia when there appeared someone sitting beside her; he winked at me....

"Uh, who are you? You don't look like a hologram." I said as I got up and poked him on his arm.

"That's because I'm not a hologram, I'm flesh and blood just like you; but not the same; my name's Gabriel, you can call me Gabe. He looked at Dad and said: "Do you remember our conversation just after you became King?"

"Yes, I know who you are; you're a messenger from the Creator: Jehovah God."

"Yes, well things have got sort of screwed up, haven't they? And it's not all your fault; you see the evil one that messed earth up has been at it again, he's trying to insert his false religion into any crack he can find. As you know he's been getting ahold of some your ships, which is sort of Terra's fault, but since he's a powerful evil angel, we're not holding you responsible. But you will have to clean this mess up. He looked around at the rest of us, underscoring his point.

"And that brings us to you Prince Attila; as you know your name means the Scourge of God. And in this case you and your wives are the tools that will do the job. Not alone of course; you see Terra has had God's blessing from the start; how else do you think they have all of the advancements they enjoy. And you three are part of the scientific advancements that I am talking about."

"Us, scientific advancement? How, if I may ask." I said.

"Oh, come now, you must have realized that the joining of you three as one, plus of course Sofia in the mix, is not the normal? Your combined brain power is on par of some of the Angels; be that as it may, it is time to use it as we intended." Again, he looked at each of us with an intensity that was somewhat un-nerving.

"The planet Ceylon is full of fanatic religious zealots; they are from all of earths denominations. Oh, we could wipe them out just like the flood of Noah's day, but perhaps there are some that could be saved; and that is up to you to do the separating so to speak. Your Professor Kirkland has a spray that will do that job; if there is an ounce of good that spray will turn them to the light. It is colorless and odorless and they won't even realize you have used it."

"How will we know who is good and who is bad?" Hattie asked.

"By their actions when you arrive in orbit; I have taken the liberty of already sending a ship to deliver the spray."

"I thought the spray wasn't ready yet." I said.

"I made it ready. Oh, the ships you sent have arrived and are already sending the results back to ONI, they are compiling the data all of your computers will have the results; all you have to do is react to those results. I would suggest that you be ready for battle when you arrive."

"I have a question, what's going to stop the Devil from doing the same thing over again and again?" I said.

"His time is short, in a few years he will be confined to earth and woe to earth when he gets there; he will arrive like a roaring lion seeking devour them. But right now, he's still causing all of the trouble he can in space; so be on your toes and be ready to repeal his attacks."

"Well when he does get confined to earth what are we suppose d to do?"

"Keep away from earth; do not interfere with anything that is happening there, it will be Michael's job to oversee the final outcome. You folks ought to read the word of God in the Bible that earth has; it tells all about the last days of the wicked on earth; just go and clean up your mess and use that planet as a colony for future expansion." Gabe said then he got up and walked through the wall and disappeared....

We all looked at each other: "Well," I said, "it looks like we just got our orders."

Lila the palace computer said: "I've determined what date that bad angel is going to get confined to earth; if anybody wants to know."

"And just how did you do that?" I asked.

"I downloaded the Bible and it gives the date chronologically as the end of the gentile times which is 1914 in earth years. Something bad is going to happen then; they refer to it as the start of the time of the end."

"Alright, we'll take your word for it; but right now, alert the fleet that we will be heading for Ceylon at 0800 hours in the morning; and tell them I want everything ship-shape and squared away or I will turn my wives loose on them, that's a joke by the way."

"If that's true shouldn't we warn Selena and Jasper about things?" Hattie asked.

"Yes, but there is still lots of time, we have more important things to take care of now; like I'm hungry."

"Don't be a smart ass, sweetheart, I'm serious."

"I know you are, both of you; but like Gabe said, when the evil one gets tossed from heaven to earth, he told us to stay away from earth; yes, I know that won't be till 1914. So we have a lot of time to get our people off of earth."

I said: "Lila how many personnel does Terra have on earth?"

"At last count two thousand."

"What, that many?"

"Yes, Prince Attila that's the correct count."

"Dad, why are there so many of our people on earth?"

"Uh, just watching, I guess." I shook my head in wonder at Dad's answer.

"So, Sofia, I want you to start pulling our personnel off of earth; and if they have any children by earth mothers or fathers, they have to leave also; I don't want any of our DNA left down there. I want them moved to quarantine camps here on Terra till we can determine what to do with them."

"To be clear, do you want those earth mothers or fathers left down there or brought to Terra, you weren't clear on that." Sofia said.

"Of course you bring them; I'm not a home wreaker. Perhaps that's where this planet called Ceylon can be of use. You know what I don't like the name Ceylon, let's call it something else; I'll let you pick the name Sofia."

"We already have; the three of us, how about New Hope?"

I looked at the three of them: "Why New Hope?"

"Well the planet is new to us, for some reason we've missed even finding it before; and the hope part is just that; we hope everything works out without too much blood shed." Sofia said.

"Alright, New Hope it is. And I do think Hattie that you were right about letting Selena know about the coming evacuations of Terra personnel from earth; there are a lot of loose ends that need tied up; we might even have to go down there."

"Yes, my brothers are one of those loose ends, even though they're not blood. And there is the Hacienda and the owner ship of it; and what about your family in Kentucky?"

"Alright you let Selena know that after we get the problem on New Hope lined out, that we'll come down and lend a hand."

I Looked at Dad, "Dad we really are not in charge of Terra, are we?"

"No Son, we're not, we are under Theocratic rule and have been right from the start; we are sort of administrators or mangers, you might say. We never rebelled against the Creator, we did what we were told and we did just so. Like right now, we will do what Gabe told us. Oh, we have a lot of leeway to get it done, but get it done we will."

"That's what I thought; it's sort of a relief knowing that. I guess we are sort of the Scourge of God, aren't we?"

"If you mean we are a tool that he is using to get things done, you're right and I for one am happy in that capacity." Dad said with a sigh of relief.

I agreed with Dad's sigh of relief; because I remember reading the Bible back on earth, at Jerimiah 10:23 how 'it's not up to man who is walking to direct his own steps.' I didn't agree with those pulpit pounders, but I did and do believe what the Bible has to say. Even though I was a Terrain, I still had a lot of earth's soil running through my veins.

We were getting transmissions from the ships that we sent to New Hope; we didn't need for ONI to relay them to us; the four us were connected to everything that went on in the known universe; and they had sprayed the planet with that special formula that Professor Kirkland had concocted.

"What was the result? Limited at best; there was one group that seemed to be affected for the better; they were on an Island group that is a thousand miles off the coast of a continent that looked similar to North America on earth.

That planet was pretty close to the same size as earth and terra; but it was on the forth planet from their sun; not the third like terra and earth. But the climate was the same as ours. As far as the population went it was pretty scarce: estimated to be around 50 thousand. But that Island group had only about three thousand.

We com'd Professor Kirkland: "How strong was that spray and what did you expect to accomplish with it?"

"It was fairly weak; I only wanted get to those that were already leaning toward sanity."

"Sanity, you say, are the rest crazy or something?"

"Not by their standards, but surely by ours; they are radical and violent and not open to any compromise. I do have a stronger spray that will affect their behavior, but, can bring about death for the most violent sociopaths."

"What about the so-called mild sociopathic behavior?"

"That's a toss-up, those you might have to physically do away with; since they are still violent."

"Alright, thank you Professor." Hattie and Fiera were still compiling the results coming in from the Fleet at New Hope."

"There are four military bases with a total of two hundred ships that are combat ready; they have been manufacturing ships on their own; probably copying from the ships they have stolen from us. We have all the factories spotted as well as every base and installations that are capable of resisting."

"Are all of the continents occupied?" Dad asked.

"No, most of them are still wilderness you could say with just the basic animal occupants; they look to be similar to earth's animals; and of course ours." Fiera answered Dad.

Dad looked at the four of us: "Alright, here is what I want you to do: Have the fleet spray with that other spray just before you three get there with the Santa Fe and then hail them and tell them to surrender."

"What if they don't surrender?" Hattie asked.

"I'm sure you know what to do then; cleanse the planet; after all Gabe told us to take care of our mess." Dad said with a twinkly in his eye that had been missing since I got home. Looked like there wouldn't be too much for Sofia to do as regent, Dad was back.

Sofia was quick to pick up on the new Dad: "Dad, would it be alright if I went with them, you could handle things here can't you?"

"Sure Honey, you go with them, you need some combat experience anyway."

We didn't have to go back to our rooms, because we already had most of our belongings on the Santa Fe. But of course, Sofia had to get her stuff. The crew and the marines were already on board. Of course, the Santa Fe was already stocked with ammunition and supplies. Including the Hornet, Sally had assured us.

It didn't take us long to get to New Hope; because the Santa Fe was equipped with the new quantum leap; the other ship that was so equipped was Jin-Li and she was already there, hanging in an outer orbit with some of the other ships that we had sent there previously.

We jumped in close to the Jin-Li and Captain Dari hailed them: The Admirals want an update." She told Captain Chang without any preamble.

"Yes, of course. We sprayed that heaver spray; it has separated the wannabes from the worst of the lot. Out of the two hundred ships there are only fifty still maned and ready to fight. And as far as the population; it is undetermined how many have changed, for the better or it could be for the worst; we might have to land troops."

I was just about to reply when Gabe appeared next to me. "Leave the ones on ground to me; we are the only ones who can read what's in their heart. As far those ships go, you can take care of them; I've already determined that they are lost. Those on the ships have only one thought: They want Prince Attila dead; Satan has fixed the thought in their minds that you are what's keeping them from setting up religion on Terra and here on this planet and consequently you are the object of their hatred." He said and then disappeared.

The four of us looked at each other. Captain Dari looked at me with irritation. "Well Admiral, are you going to reply to Captain Chang?"

"Uh, you didn't see who was just here?"

"I don't know what you're talking about; you were just setting there staring into space."

"Yes, well be that as it may, tell Captain Chang to standby and catch any ship that might get away from us; we are going in by ourselves and destroy those fifty ships."

"What, just us?"

"Yes Captain, tell them what I said. And Sofia you take maneuvering and Hattie and Fiera will be on tactical, they will be in charge of all weapons. Sofia you have the hardest job- flying this ship like it's a mosquito, don't let them swat you. And Captain tell everyone on board to secure themselves to something solid, the dampeners won't be able handle the G's that we will encounter. Make sure everything in the holds is bolted down tight, so inform the crew and the marines Captain."

The four of us were one in purpose, almost as one brain with the ship in our control; no words would be needed.

"Captain, hail the enemy and tell them to surrender or else."

"Just that or else?"

"Yes Captain, surrender or else. And put it on screen please; I want to see those that hate me before I kill them."

I stood up where I could be seen as well as see whom it was that had a death wish. He was still sputtering with rage at what Captain Dari had told him, when he seen me standing there, I swear he was foaming at the mouth. He was dressed in elaborate robes of purple velvet, with a heavy gold cross hanging around his neck on a gold chain.

"Do you know who I am?" I asked him.

"You are God's enemy Prince Attila."

"Well you're right that I am Prince Attila, and yes I am an enemy of your God, Satan the Devil, you see I am here as the Scourge of God, God Almighty Jehovah. I am giving you an attempt to repent and surrender, or I will destroy all fifty ships of your armada."

"I see those 200 ships you have and we will fight to the death."

"Ah yes, there are 200 ships here, but I am not going to use them, I will do it with just my flag ship. Do you speak for all of your fifty ships, or are there some who would like to live?"

Instead of answering the screen went black and he fired a missile at us. "Well I guess that's his answer." I said, as Fiera shot that missile out of the sky. I sat back down and fastened my restraints. Sofia was already in the midst of them and both of my wives were firing at a rate no one had ever seen before.

We were flipping and jerking in three different directions at once it seemed. Some of the bridge crew had already lost consciousness. The only ones that were doing fine were the four of us; since we knew what was coming next.

It was all over in five minutes and not one projectile had even reached our shields. That's ten ships per minute. We cruised back to our position while the nanites were getting the crew awake.

Captain Chang hailed us: "What the hell happened, it looked like they all self-destructed."

"Slow down your video feeds and you will be able to see what happened. I have to get my crew awake and see if they are all alright; the G's were more than expected." I said as Gabe reappeared next to me.

"While you were playing around with your toys I took care of the wicked on the planet. There are 5,000 people down there that need food and medical supplies; they were mistreated by the lunatics. So get some supply ships and medical ships down there. Also those on that island off of the west coast, they are fine for now; but they will have to be told what is going on. And I need to talk to the four of you after things settle down; so I will be back in a couple of days." Gabe said as he dissolved into thin air.

"Do you want to do as Gabe said?" I asked Captain Dari.

"Do what, who's Gabe?" She said as she looked at me like I was crazy.

"Oh, yeah, you didn't see him. Hattie will you see to what Gabe told us?"

"Yes, of course; Captain Dari if you will come with me I will explain what is going on."

"Fiera if you will see to the crew and let me know if there are any serious injuries?" She came over and whispered in my ear: "What do you think Gabe wants to talk to the four us about?"

"I haven't the slightest idea but maybe he wants to chew me out about something, don't you worry about it, you girls are perfect; so will you check with the medics and then let me know, huh?"

"You think we're perfect?"

"Well of course you are; you were born perfect and you haven't done anything to change that." I said.

"Uh, Terra doesn't believe in polygamy, do you think it's something to do with that?"

"Let me ask you this; have you ever heard of any inter-locked twins, other than you and Hattie in your entire life?"

"No, of course not."

"So, how do you think you guys ended up inter-locked, if it wasn't by their doing?

"Yeah but, why would they do that when it isn't done anywhere; but on that stupid earth?"

"I don't know, but I'm sure he will tell us, if that is what he wants to talk about." It's a funny thing about premonitions, sometimes they come true.

Hattie and Sofia were listening of course, since the four of us were hooked together. (That is not the same as being inter-locked like the twins are.) Anyway, they both put their two cents in.

"We think you guys are over thinking this, it's just probably another task he wants done, like cleaning out a sewer somewhere."

"Huh, a sewer; I hope that's just a hyperbole; how in the world would you two even come up with such an outlandish thought?" Fiera said.

"We were just thinking about what kind of a mess is waiting for us down there; anyway we're sure that sewer word was just a hyperbole." They both thought together.

"Anyway, are those medical and supply ships heading planet side?"

"Yes, and we also took the liberty of having Captain Chang send down two companies of Marines also."

"Who's in charge of those Marines?"

"Captain Cash, I think Fiera knows him."

"Uh, yeah, I went to collage with him, he was sort of my boyfriend at one time."

"He was huh, how long ago was that?" I asked.

"Like maybe a little over a month ago, just before they sent me to earth to get you and Hattie."

"Alright, I know what's going on." I said, then I looked at the overhead and com'd Gabe: "Gabe get your butt down here, did you think we wouldn't figure it out?"

We must of looked weird to the crew; the four us standing nose to nose and not talking, of course we were but just not out loud.

"Alright, I'm here and yes it's about that; the need for the twins to be inter-locked is past, they have accomplished the goal; the goal was for you and Hattie to be fully worked back into things here on Terra, you needed guidance to overcome you're earthly upbringing. So we are going to unlock you two; don't worry no one will remember that you two were in a marriage with the Prince; Hattie and Matt are the only ones that are married. And when I say no one will know includes the four of you also. It will be like it never happened. Hattie and Fiera will be normal twins, but all four of you will still be com'd together. Both

311

Hattie and Fiera will remain Admirals.

Fiera, you and Captain Cash are still betrothed; your marriage date hasn't been set yet. I am going to give you a few moments to get your minds around everything and then you won't remember that you three were married and neither will anyone else."

You could tell when the change came; Gabe smiled and started to leave, when I said: 'Hey, wait a minute." He turned around, "That is all except you Matt, you will remember; you're Prince Attila, and you have to remember for posterity." And then he dissolved. I looked at Hattie, "did you just hear what he said?"

"He didn't say anything; he just looked at you and left; why what do you think he said? You look a little pale, are you feeling alright?"

Fiera came over: "Hey, my boyfriend is going to be in charge of the troops down there, can I go and see him?"

"Uh, yeah sure, you bet. But I think maybe that Sofia and Hattie and I are going down there and check things out; why don't you tell Sally to get the shuttle ready and to have Captain Fairfield take a squad of Marines down with us."

Sofia and Hattie came over and were chatting with Fiera about how long it had been since she had seen him; you know how chicks discuss a rooster, just a bunch of cackling. I called Captain Dari over.

"Captain, we are going down to the planet; you can reach us anytime if anything comes up. You are in charge of the fleet till we get back; be sure to have all sensors working, I'm not too sure they aren't hiding something, but just to be sure-keep awake."

To tell you the truth I was relieved that it was just Hattie and I that would be in our bed tonight. It never did feel right to me....

We circled the planet before landing; the only settlement was on the east coast of that continent that looked something like North America did on earth. Of course the one on that island group that lay off of the west coast; the rest of the planet was wild and free; I say free because the animals were the only inhabitants.

As we approached the settlement on the east coast Captain Cash's shuttle was already there. We settled down beside his shuttle. Fiera was the first one off; the Captain was waiting for us.

Fiera walked over to him; he saluted her; after all she was a two-star Admiral. After that they hugged, I noticed that there was no kissing. That got me to thinking-was this an arranged marriage? Or perhaps he was just a straight-laced Marine and was afraid of showing any passion in front of his troops.

Any way Hattie and I went over and introduced ourselves. He snapped to attention as we walked up; I had to tell him, "at ease Captain you're among family now Fiera is my sister-in-law and this is Hattie her long-lost twin sister."

"Yes Sir, I know, your exploits are well known all over Terra, and you're a legend."

"So Captain, have you had time to assess the situation down here?"

"Somewhat Sir, we haven't found any hostiles and the people that are here seem friendly. And as far as lodging goes, there are a lot of vacant homes and buildings in good shape. There are several what I would call mansions. Also, there is what would be called Hotels; I was thinking of billeting the troops in them temporally."

"Yes, that would give you time to find any group of buildings that would make a good fort; there might even be such a thing around here somewhere. Why don't you ask the civilians if they know of a place like that; we are going to have to settle in permanently, we have been given permission to colonize this planet, we call it-New Hope."

Sofia spoke up and said: "As we were landing I seen a big mansion about two miles west of the city; I was thinking it would make a good governor's mansion, do you want to go look at it?" She asked Hattie and me.

"Sure, Captain did you bring any ground transportation down with you?"

"Yes, we brought several magnetic floaters with us; I'll have one brought around; it's big enough for fifteen people so you can take your squad of marines with you for protection." I guess he really didn't know much about us; with Hattie and Sofia and I we had enough fire power for a company of marines. But I suppose it would be wise to heed his advice.

"Admiral Fiera perhaps you can accompany the good Captain and help him scout out a fortification?" Fiera smiled and gave me a wink. "Yes Sir, will do."

Hattie com'd me; "That was nice of you dear; since she hasn't seen him for over a month they need some alone time." And then she kissed me on the cheek. When they brought the Magnetic around Captain Fairfield got behind the controls without asking and Sofia sat in the co-pilot's seat; we got in with the troops.

It didn't take us long to get there, since Sofia remembered where it was located. She was right; it looked like some of those mansions that I had seen in New Orleans. As we pulled up an older black man came out of the front doors.

"Welcome to the Heavenly Palace Master." He said with a bob of his head. I looked at Hattie; "What the hell," we both thought at once.

"Uh, what's your name?" I asked him.

"Charles Suh, I'm the butler.

"Are you a slave?" I asked.

"Yes Suh, the High Priest brought my family and me from New Orleans."

"Well Charles, you are no longer a slave and that so called high priest is nothing more than space dust. This planet is now called New Hope and is under Terra's protection; it is officially a Colony of Terra. I am Prince Attila and this in by wife Hattie; and Sofia is the King's Regent and she is the new Governor of New Hope."

Sofia said: "I am, that's news to me; but I guess it would be sort of fun to run this new planet."

"Well don't get the big head; we haven't cleared it with Dad yet. Anyway Charles we would like to meet your family; we are going to use this planation as the Governor's Mansion."

"Oh, they's out in the field Suh, won't be in till the noon time Suh."

"Alright, do you all live in the big house?"

"Oh no Suh, we live out back; we have our own house." He said proudly.

"Well I guess that's good; would you mind showing us around Charles?"

"I'd be proud to do so Suh; would like to start with the mansion Suh?"

"That would be fine Charles; lead the way." I looked at Captain Fairfield, "Perhaps you and your squad could check the rest of the buildings?"

"Yes Sir, we would be happy to do so."

There was a big foyer or entrance room; I really didn't know what to call it since I had never been inside a southern mansion. But I was pretty sure it was an exact copy of one. If I wasn't mistaken the floor tiles were marble; even the pillars were made of marble; there's really no need for me to describe the whole place; just let me say that I was impressed. Only one thing was different from the southern mansions of 1865 on earth: All of the plumbing was as modern as the ones on Terra; even a swimming pool.

"Uh, Charles, didn't this so called high priest have a wife or children, I don't see any?"

"Yes Suh, he did. They were here this morning; but I can't find hide nor hair of them in the last couple of hours; seems' like they just disappeared in a puff of smoke."

"Well Charles, we're very glad that you and your family are still here."

"Does that mean that we all will be staying on, Suh?"

"That's up to you, you're welcome to stay here; but you are not slaves; you'll be paid in credits the same as on Terra; but there is one thing I'd like you to change and that is the word 'suh' it is pronounced 'Sir'. We'll have no slave talk on New Hope."

Sofia looked at me and asked: "Who gets the master bedroom?"

"Oh, you liked that ceiling, did you? The whole thing is one big mirror."

"No, it was that bathroom, that hot tub was as big as a swimming pool."

"Let her have it sweetheart, maybe it will attract a husband for her. That one down the hall is almost just like it; and I like the view better." Hattie said, as she was hanging on my arm. I don't know why but ever since Gabe did his little magic thing Hattie had been more loving toward me; which I liked very much.

"I don't need no husband to order me around." Sofia said.

"You got the wrong outlook; you're the Governor of New Hope besides you're still the King's Regent; if there is any ordering around you'll be the one to do it. And the reason you're getting the master bedroom is because I want you to have it; It's time you get a little glory and you deserve it."

Fiera broke into our conversation: "We have found quarters for the troops, how are you guys coming?"

"We have found a castle you might say; enough bedrooms for all of us and then some. Are you coming?"

"Yes, but by myself, Captain Cash thinks he had better stay with his troops, since we aren't officially married and all."

"Do you want to marry him or what?"

"Yes, of course I do, but I've always dreamed of a big wedding with all of our parents there and all."

"Well, have you ever heard of that earth saying that you 'can't have your cake and eat it too'?"

"What is that supposed to mean?"

"It simply means that you have a choice to make; wait and have the whole enchilada or marry him now; which can be done by the Governor of New Hope."

"Who's the governor, you?"

"Nope, Sofia is, plus she's still the King's Regent; talk it over with your Captain, by the way what's his first name anyhow?"

"It's Ollie, its short for Oliver."

"Oliver Cash, well talk to him and let us know; I'm betting he wants his cake right now. And just think you two will be the first to marry on our new planet."

"Well, at least I would like some kind of a wedding celebration, with a cake and whatever."

Hattie spoke up: "Sure, we have hired help here, I'm sure they can whip up something." Hattie said and then she hollered for Charles and told him about the upcoming nuptials. He said that he was sure that his wife could bake a cake. He and Hattie walked off toward the kitchen.

It was three days later before they did wed. But a lot had happened in those days: For one thing I had made sure that Charles and his family's main responsibility was to take care of the Governor's Mansion and the immediate grounds. The fieldwork was farmed out to private contractors; we didn't have any problem finding people to do that; it turns out Charles had a lot of cousins that were more than happy to do that choir.

Most of the fleet had returned home, but some of each ship's crew had volunteered to come down and check out all of the ships that set around with no crews; since the ones that were violently oriented had been removed by Gabe.

I had not as yet got around to visiting that island off of the west coast; I could have sent a ship over there to check them out, but I wanted to be the first one there. I knew they must be peaceable since Gabe had not removed them.

Also, more marines had volunteered to be stationed here; since Sofia had told them they could bring their families; even their parents if they wanted. There were plenty of empty houses, without having to build more at this time.

We were running a contest to see what the name of this city would be; we hadn't figured out a prize yet; since everyone had everything they needed, maybe name a street after them or something. There were a lot of elk, moose and bear running around; they were perfectly tame; some of them were already pets. Guess who won?

That's right, Charles did: He came up with the name: Liberty; which simply means freedom from captivity; so we named the road leading to the Governor's mansion Liberty Road.

I asked Charles what he wanted since he won the contest; he said nothing, except maybe just putting in the official records that he named the City and the road. I said no problem, it's already done.

This morning Hattie and I had slept late; since we had been burning the mid-night oil so to speak. Hattie was lying on top of me, it felt like we were glued together; I don't know how we could get any closer, unless we could crawl inside of each other.

This room had a combination hot tub and swimming pool; we walked sideways since we were still stuck on each other and slide into the pool; we weren't really stuck we just didn't want to let go of each other. It had been like this ever since Gabe had done his little trick; we finally let go of each other after about an hour.

We were air drying under the warm jets of air when Sofia com'd us and asked if we were decent? I replied we're always decent; so, she just walked in.

"Hey, I thought you said that you guys were decent?"

"Well, we are decent people; oh, you mean if we were dressed; nope we're not as you can see. What do you need?"

"I just wanted to talk to you about all of our people that were removed from earth; they are out of quarantine now; what do you want to do with them?"

I looked at Hattie and she said: "Why don't we bring them here? This planet is much like earth and terra that they should feel right at home. They are used to sort of primitive living you might say, so they could homestead here."

"Yes, but it's going to have to be orderly, we need a land board and surveyors. We could ask people on terra if they want to help colonize also." Sofia said.

"Right, well, you're the Governor, do as you see fit." I said.

"Sure, alright; uh, you guys are going to get dressed today, aren't you?"

"Yep, I was thinking that Hattie and I would take the shuttle to that island off of the west coast and see what that is all about. That is if the Governor approves?"

"Yeah, but take Captain Fairfield and a squad of marines with you. We have the satellites working now and it looks like there are teepees there and open campfires; it could be interesting."

"Can we get audio on those satellites? I mean I would like to hear what language they are speaking."

"Yes, we've installed all of the latest gismos on them. Fiera has all of the controls installed in her room; she's the new secretary of defense now. Come on we'll go and see, uh, but please take a minute and put something on, you don't want to scare the help."

"Well then while we're getting dressed maybe you could have the 'help' bring up some food, we are starving." Hattie said.

"I don't doubt that; you two should be skin and bones with all of the sex you two are having."

"You're just jealous."

"Yeah, you're right, I am." Sofia said as she left the room.

"She needs a husband in the worst way." I said.

"Well, that is next on the agenda; Fiera and I are going to have to find someone for her." Hattie said as she put on her skin suit with her uniform over top. We both put on our weapons; it seems old habits are hard to break. Brunch came by the time we were dressed.

Fiera's office was not in her room; but the room next door, with a door between. She and Oliver were both in the office bending over a computer consul as we came in. Captain Cash snapped to attention and gave us a salute.

"At ease Captain, you don't have to salute here in government headquarters." I said.

Fiera looked at us and said: "Sofia said you wanted to give a look at that island off of the west coast; I've got a good picture and the audio is also working. You are going to be surprised." She said.

We both looked at the screen and then and looked at each other. I turned up the sound: "What do you think sweetheart, Lakota or Dakota?"

"I think it's a mix of both; plus, some Cheyenne." Hattie said. I asked Fiera: "How big is that island?"

"Pretty big for an island, it's about three thousand square miles and there are only about two thousand people."

"I see that you are thinking the same thing that I am thinking." I said to Hattie.

"Yes, it would be perfect for Selena." Fiera what are they using for food?"

"They have gardens and have been hunting and trapping; plus, fishing. They have killed off most of the larger animals, like deer and elk and bear. Looks like that island could support beef, if they had any."

"Do they have a Chief or anything; who's in charge?"

"I can't really tell; they are split into camps of about two hundred per camp; they don't seem to have a central government; that's probably why they have killed off the native animals. No conservation efforts."

"I can understand that; the Sioux are fiercely independent, as are the Cheyenne. I think we can fix that; I have several ideas that might work. But first we have to see if Selena would like to relocate here. And yes, Hattie and I are going to have to go back to earth; we have some loose ends to tie up, Selena being one of them."

Hattie said: "Why don't we go into town, we really haven't had a good look around? Fiera, do you and Ollie want to go with us?"

Fiera looked at Oliver and he shook his head; "Uh, no I have some things I want to check out, why don't you two go on ahead, we might join you later."

"How are we going to get there?" Hattie asked.

Fiera spoke up: "I seen several magnetic vehicles in the garage out back, some of them were pretty fancy." As we were leaving Fiera spoke up: "When are you guys going to that island?"

"Probably tomorrow, why don't you tell Captain Dari to send Sally and the Hornet down in the morning?"

"Do you still want a squad of marines to go along?"

"Yeah, have Captain Fairfield briefed on the trip."

We found one of Charles' sons polishing a magnetic vehicle in the garage, his name was Buford; he looked at us and said: "How can I help you Sir?"

"We need a vehicle to take us into town; is that shiny black one ready?"

"Why, yes sir it is; it was his, uh favorite one. It has several upgrades from a standard magnetic vehicle; perhaps I should drive you and explain them as we go along?"

"Yes, that would be nice." Hattie said smiling at him.

He opened the door and said: "You will notice the thickness of the door and the special glass; they are bullet proof. And if you press that red button all weapons will deploy and if you press it again they will fire at any targets that they see, regardless of who they may be."

"You mean even innocent targets?" Hattie asked.

"Yes, I'm afraid so, he was slightly unhinged, you might say; we all are very glad he is gone."

"Well as soon as we get back I want that feature to be removed; do you know how to do that?" Hattie said.

"Yes Mam, I do; I'll rewire them to be only turned on when a threat is immediate and told to do so."

"Does this vehicle have a computer?"

"Of sorts, very archaic, I'm afraid; he didn't want anything smarter than his self, so the choices were very limited."

"Alright, upgrade its computer with the latest AI, I want it to be able to think problems through and be able to not only protect its occupants but also itself. Does it have a name?"

"No Sir, it was just a thing, but after it's been upgraded; I'll ask her its name."

"Her huh?"

"Of course Sir, most AI's are female, and I believe all of them should be, who wants to listen to a male voice?"

"You're right, I sure don't." I said, as I gave Hattie a kiss on her cheek."

It was very spacious vehicle, in fact the back seat was big enough for a bed, you might say. And there was even a fully stocked bar.

"Buford you seem very knowledgeable about complex things, where did you study?" Hattie asked.

"I read a lot mam; I think I have read about every book in the local library."

"Would you like an upgrade yourself?"

"Huh, I'm not an android Mam, I'm human."

"Yes, we know, but there are upgrades that are staggering to comprehend. If you want we can arrange that for you?"

"I-I guess so Mam; would I have to leave New Hope to get that done?"

"No, we can send you up to our ship; the Santa Fe, it's in orbit, it can be done there. It would only take a day or so. In fact, when we get back from our visit to town we'll arrange that for you."

Hattie com'd the Santa Fe and made arrangements for them to beam him up when we got back; these implants we had made for instant communication without even speaking out loud. Of course, he wouldn't get that ability, but he would be an all- around genus. We settled back and enjoyed the trip to town.

There were a fair amount of people moving around to the various shops, it being mid-morning and all. Buford got out and opened the door for us, he stepped back and I started to get out, when all of sudden there was an energy beam that hit the front of the vehicle and glanced off and hit Buford, he dropped like a rock....I ducked behind the open door and pulled my refit .45, which wasn't really a .45 anymore, but a rail gun that shot depleted uranium slugs at the speed of sound; the beam had come from the second floor of a shop across the street. I shot a stream of slugs at that window and the side of the building. The side of that second-floor building was nothing but rubble when I let my finger off the trigger.

Hattie jumped out and went to Buford, he was still alive. Hattie com'd the Santa Fe, Buford disappeared into thin air.

A squad of Marines came running; I sent them to check out that building. Most of the people were just standing around not quite comprehending what was going on. The marines sent them on their way.

The marines that I sent to check that building out came back: "Sir, it was an old-style Battle-bot; your slugs tore him apart." Their squad leader said.

"Alright, tell your Captain that I want every hidey-hole checked out: I want every weapon confiscated and every robot or android deactivated and melted down for scrap. Also, I want every person rescanned for violent tendencies or religious thinking or cults, which leads to violence. And that doesn't mean that they can't worship the creator directly; no middle men."

"Hattie do you think that you can drive this thing? I will ride shotgun; let's take that road on the other side of town leading to the river."

"We aren't going back?"

"Nope, I came to look around; no stupid battle-bot is going to change my mind."

It didn't take long to leave what little civilization there was behind; I don't think we went over four miles and there were no houses, much less a road, just a trail. With that magnetic-gravity drive we didn't need a road anyway; the trail was more less just a deer trail or whatever wanted to use it.

Hattie came to a stop; I had been looking out the side window and not the trail ahead; in the trail was a Black Bear sow with two cubs. Now back on earth I would be turning tail and getting out of there; but they seemed to not be paying much attention to us; oh, they glanced our way and then went back to grazing, that's right grazing. We watched them; they turned over a log or two to get grubs or ants whatever there was, but they were eating grass also.

I looked at Hattie and said: "I'm going to try something." I got out and walked toward them; they stopped eating and watched me; I had the feeling that they didn't have any fear of me; unlike the wild animals on earth. It had to be because they hadn't been hunted and mistreated by men yet.

Hattie got out and came over and walked up to the mother bear and reached out her hand to let her smell her scent. The bear huffed once and looked Hattie in the eye and then she sort of nodded to her cubs and they came over and let Hattie pet them.

"Come here Matt and let them smell you also." I came over and went through the smell check and then I squatted down and one of the cubs came over and I rubbed him behind his ears, he liked that.

"Hattie, we need to have Sofia make a decree that no wild animals can be killed or harassed. There should be no need to kill them for food; there is ample room for raising vegetables and such, plus our food synthesizers can make plants taste like beef anyway. I think this planet could be the proverbial Eden."

"Yes, I just told her as you were talking; but she mentioned that there may be a problem with the Indians on that island off of the west coast; they have already been killing animals for food."

"Well that is our next priority; we are going over there tomorrow if that suits your schedule?"

"Yes of course, I have already told Captain Dari to have Sally and the Hornet at the Governor's Mansion in the morning. And Captain Dari said that Buford was in the Regen-tank and it looks like he will be out in a couple of days good as new and that she was updating his intellect while he was in there."

I started to say something, when Hattie held her hand up for me to be quiet. "Did you hear that;" she said silently.

"What,' I thought back.

"The bear she's trying to communicate with us. Hook up with me, perhaps between the two of us we can get inside of her brain to hear what she's trying to say."

We closed our eyes and sent our thoughts directly into her brain. We could understand what she was thinking---"Why are you here?"

We thought together: "To make this planet into a paradise for both the animals and us humans."

"We know that there are humans over there; but they have not been friendly."

"We are here to change that; those bad humans have been removed; would you like to see for yourself?"

"What do you mean, see for myself?"

"We could take you with us to meet more of us; then you could see that we are friendly."

"What do you mean, take us with you?"

"In the vehicle, you could ride with us; we will make sure no one is mean to you."

"Alright, I would like to see what you animals are all about?"

Hattie told me to tell Sofia that we were bringing visitors and not to be surprised but welcome them. I did so, as I held the back door open for our bear friends. They piled in and checked out the different smells.

The two cubs each looked out the side windows as Hattie turned the vehicle around and we headed back to Liberty. When we reached the town itself Hattie slowed down to a crawl; giving the bear family time to look at everything.

The Mama bear's head was swinging back and forth, not missing anything. When she seen the Marines with their weapons she snorted and asked: "Why do they have weapons?"

"The previous population was not friendly and had to be removed; there are still some battle-bots hiding, but we are flushing them out of hiding."

"What are battle-bots?"

"Robots; they are artificial humans."

"I do not understand; your species are very odd."

"Yes, well, would you like to learn more about us?"

"Yes, it would be helpful."

"We can hook you up to a learning machine that will tell you all about the human race and then you would be able to tell other animals that we here on New Hope are peaceful."

"Do you mean other humans on other planets are not peaceful?"

"Some of them aren't, but we are working on that. But we here on New Hope would like to live in harmony with all creatures and the environment."

"Does that mean that you would like us to teach you how to fit in with all of the species here on this planet?"

"Well yes, I guess that is what I mean." Hattie said to her.

"Good, perhaps we can learn from each other and be partners in life." She said thoughtfully. Then added: "We were created by God, were you also created?"

Wow! Hattie and I thought together. "Yes," we replied, "and his name is Jehovah."

"Ah so, we are brothers then. The others that were here, we could not talk to them, they did not hear us."

"Yes, they were created also, but they worshiped a different god that lied to them and told them not to worship the creator, but to worship him; the false god."

"But there is only one god, what is the name of this false god?"

"He's called Satan the Devil; he is a liar and a deceiver. But you do not have to worry about him; he will be confined to the planet earth shortly and until he is, we will protect this planet."

Ollie and Fiera were waiting for us as we pulled up. I got out and opened the door for our bruin friends; "This is, uh, I forgot to get your names." I said to the bears.

"My name is Brynhilda and these are Teddy and Tilly, my cubs."

"Yes, and this is Admiral Fiera and her soon to be husband, Captain Cash." We weren't talking out loud; and Ollie was looking at us with confusion on his face.

"What's going on, who are these bears?" He asked.

"Oh, I forgot you aren't hooked up mentally with us yet; as soon as you and Fiera are officially married that will change. But in the meantime, these bears are sentient and very intelligent; as are all animal life on this planet, I believe." I said out loud.

"If they are sentient why can't they talk?"

"Why, if they can communicate with each other, why talk?"

"Well so us backward people can hear them, is why?" Ollie said.

"Your right of course, we'll have to work on that feature; I think a little bit of nanos might help, we'll have to see; I'll ask Gabe." I said.

"Gabe, who's Gabe?"

"Another feature you haven't met yet, don't worry he's friendly."

Gabe must have been listening; because he spoke to the three of us and said: "I should of told you about the local populous. I'll make it so everybody will be able to hear them; and as such they have the same right on this planet as any of you and will have to be integrated in any decisions that are made."

Brynhilda was listening to what Gabe told us and she spoke up in a very pleasant voice: "I am pleased to make your acquaintance Captain Cash."

"Huh, so now you can talk; what happened? He said.

Fiera said: "Ollie don't be rude, watch your manners."

"I'm sorry Brynhilda, I apologize for my lack of manners; it's just because I've never heard animals talk before."

"You do realize that you also are an animal, Captain Cash?" Brynhilda said with a smile in her voice.

"Well enough said, let's go in and get some food, I'm hungry." I said, as I waved my hand toward the big doors. At the mention of food, Teddy and Tilly made a dash past us.

Chapter Twenty-Three

Sofia met us at the door and I introduced the Bear family. "Yes, I heard everything and welcome to Liberty One; I am the King's Regent and also the Governor of New Hope; and to get right to the point Gabe has suggested that, if you are willing, to make you the co-governor in charge of the original residents of this planet.?"

"That is unexpected and a bit overwhelming. Can I take a while to ponder that? And if I do accept do I have to live in side of four walls?"

"No of course not; with our and your ability to silently communicate you can live anywhere you want to. But we are planning on building schools and perhaps it would be wise if your children attended these schools with our children."

"Yes, I can see where that would be beneficial. That way we could learn each- others cultures. And if I did accept would it be possible that I could design our abode and it could be built to that design?"

"I don't see any reason why not; in the meantime, why don't we retire to the dining room and get some hot food in our bellies?"

The negotiations went on for three days; but Hattie and I didn't stick around to put our two cents in; Sally picked us up in the Hornet and we went sightseeing around the globe with a stop on the island of the Lakota and Cheyenne.

We went in with open minds on what to do with them; after all they were earthlings; and as such they should be returned to earth; but only if they wanted to go back. I for one was inclined to not send them back, knowing what is and would be happening to their home lands.

Before we even set down we could see that the island was showing signs of wear and tear; we could see no large game animals; looks as if they hunted them to extinction. One thing for sure we had to get them off of this island and then reintroduce those animals.

We set down near the largest camp on the island. We were met by a delegation which included the Chief or what looked like him; anyway, he had the most feathers and an attitude to go with them.

One good thing was they had no fire arms; just their usual bows and arrows, along with various clubs, spears, and tomahawks. Which they of course knew how to use; especially as how they decimated the animals was proof of that.

Hattie and I were wearing our buckskins, with our usual assortment of weapons; which the Chief took notice of. I said: "Does anyone speak English?"

"Yes, I do." Said a beautiful Indian girl. That was standing beside the Chief.

"Good, that will make things a bit easier; what's your name?"

"My name is Tala; this is my Father-Chief Tokala. Who are you and what do you want with us?"

"I am Prince Attila and this is my wife Princess Hattie we are from Terra but we spent most of our life on Earth; where you are from. On earth I was known as Matthew Bodeen. We are here to give you a choice of going back to earth or staying here on this planet, which is called New Hope. Either way you can't stay on this island, it will not support all of you."

She looked at her Father and translated what I said. The bunch of them spent a few minutes hashing things back and forth and then Tokala spoke to Tala.

"My Father wants to know if the white eyes are still moving into our homeland."

"Yes, they are and it will only get worse; they will come and take most of your land and kill some of your people; there are sad days coming for all Native People."

"If we did not go back to earth where would you move us to?" Tala said.

"Here on New Hope, there is much land that is empty of humans. But one thing the animals here are intelligent and can communicate with us humans and are not to be hunted or molested. You will have to learn to grow crops but we can help you to learn and feed you till you can get yourselves settled."

At that there was a lot of hubbub; looked like the idea of working the ground wasn't that popular. Tala shushed them and said: "We will meet with all of our peoples and let you know our decision; how can you be reached?

"We will leave you a communicator to call us on." And then I had one of the Marines run one out for us.

Hattie showed her how to use it and then said: "If you decide to stay here on New Hope you can take your pick where you want to settle; we can a have ship take you around the planet and then you can choose." With that we left and headed back to Liberty.

"What do you think Hattie, will they go or stay?"

"I think they will stay after hearing what you told them about what is happening back on earth. And talking about Earth, I think it's about time we headed back and take care of some details with Selena and my brothers. And don't you think we should visit your Mother and my Father in Kentucky?"

"Yeah, after all they were the only parents we knew all of our lives; I'm not quiet settled into these new lives we have; are you Mrs. Bodeen?"

"No sweetheart, I'm not; everything still feels so surreal; it's like we don't belong in either world; but we know we can't live on earth, Gabe told us get all Terrains off of earth."

"Yeah, we have to get Selena and her new husband off; I 'm sure she would like to settle here on New Hope, after all its virgin land; anyway, she'll have her choice. Maybe you could com. Fiera and tell her about Tala and she will have a heads up to get a ship ready."

"Yeah, I'll do that, say I was thinking maybe Brynhilda and her cubs could show them around the planet and help them decide where to settle; that is if they decide to stay."

"That's a good idea, and then the Indians can get to know not to kill sentient beings." I said.

"What about us, where are we going to stake a claim?" Hattie asked.

"I don't know; there are a lot of places to pick from; maybe somewhere close to where Selena picks; that way she can watch over our place when we're out in the universe."

"Oh, there is something that I forgot to tell you, I heard from Jasper." Hattie said.

"What did he have to say?"

"Things aren't going as fine as Selena lead us to believe; they are still losing stock. Jasper thinks it's still some of Colonel Talent's bunch, he didn't know for sure. And he has heard from some of his friends back in Kentucky that our folks might need some help; you know carpet baggers are still pushing people around in the south."

"Uh, you said that Jasper heard from some of his friends in Kentucky; uh, what kind of friends?"

"He called it the Mule Underground. And before you say anything else; I know we're supposed to be getting off of earth altogether, but I thought you could talk to Gabe and see if we couldn't stick around a little bit down there and lend a hand?"

"No need to call me I've been listening to you both; and yes I asked and he will give you one month on earth to settle your affairs. After that its hands off no matter what goes on till the gentile times are over and that's not till 1914; and I shouldn't have even told you that." Gabe said.

"Why, what happens then?"

"Read Revelation 12:12 it will tell you; you think things down there are bad now, you haven't seen anything yet." Gabe said, then you could hear a click and silence.

I looked at Hattie and asked her, because I was sure she would know what that scripture said.

"Yes I remember, it says that the Devil will come down to earth having great anger, knowing he has a short time before he's destroyed."

"Why does he come down to earth?"

"Because they got tired of his evil ways and him causing trouble up in heaven so Jehovah tossed him down to earth along with all of his Demons and they can't go back ever."

"Do you mean right now that he can go back and forth between heaven and earth?"

"Yes, it appears so; but after he's tossed down he can't ever leave earth to go anywhere else till he's tossed in Tartarus for a thousand years."

"What the heck is Tartarus?"

"It's a deep dark abyss. And don't ask me how I know all of this, I just do."

"Alright, I'll drop the subject. Let's go back to Liberty and tell Fiera that we're leaving; but I think we should go tell my Father our plans, don't you?"

"Yes of course, after all he's the King!

It didn't take us long to get back to Liberty and wrap up any details that we had left hanging. Fiera was a little disappointed that we were leaving; but I think she was glad to be left in charge of New Hope.

Hattie and I had spotted some land that looked like it had all of the requirements that we wanted for our ranch here on New Hope. So we filed on it with the new land office that Fiera had set up.

Fiera mentioned that we should set up some requirements for citizenship here on New Hope.

"Like what guide lines would you use?" I asked her.

"Oh, just a background check; no perverts and the like."

"Uh, Terra doesn't have any of them, does it?"

"No, but there are some earthlings here; I think they should be double-checked."

"Alright, but we don't want to turn New Hope into a police state; let's just let Gabe take care of things like that, alright?"

"Yeah, I suppose so, I guess I was just over thinking it."

"Yes, just concentrate on making New Hope into a paradise; use Terrain standards as a guideline. And we will be back in a few months; if you have any problems just com us or call my Dad; because this colony is basically under Terrain Law."

Sally was waiting on the Hornet to take us back to the Santa Fe that was waiting in orbit; so we made the rounds saying our goodbyes and then we were off.

The first thing I noticed when we docked in the landing bay was that the ship was on alert level green-meaning no threats detected. How did I know that? Because everyone was sans uniforms. Which was normal for Terrains anyway. Like I have said before it is hard for us that were raised on earth to get used to everyone being naked, but I think I was starting to get used to it...

Dari, the Captain met us herself. You remember that she used to be the AI, but has since transformed into a beautiful human woman. The woman that was more beautiful was Hattie; and that was because she was my wife.

"Glad to have you back aboard, we were starting to go stir crazy; I hope you have something exciting planned." She said.

"Well," Hattie said, "I think this crew could do with two week's liberty back on Terra; also Professor Kirkland has some upgrades scheduled for all of us including the Santa Fe."

"What upgrades? I didn't hear anything about that." I said.

"It just came in over my com's, do you have yours turned off or something?"

I checked, it wasn't off, I had turned it down, all of the chatter was giving me a headache. I guess it was time I got back to my duties.

We started to walk toward our quarters when Dari said, "Don't forget to change into the uniform of the day." I looked at her, with a question in my eyes. "Uh, you know, no clothes." Dari said, blushing.

Hattie said: "Sure," and stripped off her uniform, while looking at me. I looked at her and then glanced at Dari.

"Uh, you don't want me to take mine off." I said glancing down at myself.

"No, you can wait till we get to our cabin." Hattie said, while blushing herself.

As we were walking Hattie said on our private channel: "What's wrong with you, you would think we never had sex or something."

"Well it has been a few days; or someone must have put something in my food."

"That was two days ago, and it's just now working?"

"You put something in my food?"

"Not me; Fiera thought it would be funny or something; I had mentioned to her that our sex life was cooling off, you know we used to make love two or three times a day and now it was down to five times a week, I was getting worried."

Hattie turned to Dari, "We'll be a little late getting to the bridge, I have to take care of that problem." She said pointing to the so-called problem.

Turned out it wasn't such a little problem; it was the next morning before we got to the bridge; and it was Hattie that was walking funny now. "I am going to tell Fiera to throw that stuff away; it's dangerous." She said with a groan.

Dari turned to us as we walked in, she had a smile on her face. "You forgot to tell me how fast you wanted to get back to Terra, so I have just been limping along on impulse engines."

"Give me a day to recuperate and then jump there." Hattie said.

Dari looked down at Hattie's waist, and said: "I wish I had that problem."

"No you don't; have you ever heard that saying 'too much of good thing'?"

"Yeah, but I didn't know it was possible."

The rest of the crew was standing around trying to hide their mirth. The woman that was on navigation her name was Gidget, she was in her mid-twenties, said: "I have some salve in my quarters that will fix that." She walked over and took Hattie's hand they walked off of the bridge. As I watched them go, I felt a twinge, that stuff wasn't done with me yet, I guess, but I ignored it. Mind over matter...

I got up and went to the swimming pool, I did about twenty laps and that took care of the problem.

I put on my skin suit and went back to the bridge. "Captain Dari, I think it would be better if all of the duty personnel would wear their skin suits; we never know when an emergency might arise." As you might remember the skin suits were a light armor, but they were see through, not hiding what was underneath, but they could be set to any color, I set mine to black... Captain Dari made the announcement over the ship wide intercom.

I sat down on my bridge chair and said: "I think we should run ship wide system checks, let's start with weapons; if you would Captain." And that's what we did for the next two hours till Hattie and Gidget came back. Hattie was walking a lot better.

She seen my black skin suit and changed hers to black also; the rest of the crew left theirs on clear. I stood up and said: "We can dispense with the system checks. At 0800 on the morrow you can Quantum Jump back to the Palace on Terra." I told the Captain.

I put my arm around my wife and walked her back to our cabin. "So that stuff worked, I see"

"Yeah, too well, I'll tell you about it tonight, but it sure took the pain away." Hattie said, then said: "You know I had a dream last night, something about the ships systems. You know we have really never hooked into the ship's system; we just ask Catlin and she tells us what we need to know; but I was thinking about us hooking directly into all of the system ourselves. What do you think?"

"Yeah, I guess we could, do you think it will keep us awake?"

I doubt that, we just shunt it to the part of our brain that won't wake us unless there is something not right."

"Yeah and what part of our brain is that?"

"I don't know, but Professor Kirkland told me about it. You can look it up if you want to."

"Nah, I don't want to; you can tell Catlin to do that when we go to sleep, aren't you tired?"

"No, that salve Gidget gave me, well anyway it not only relieves the pain, it rejuvenates. Do you want some?"

"Nope, I'll do it the natural way, try me in the morning."

"Party pooper, go on go to bed, I'll be there in a few." Hattie said.

So, I did, and had Catlin hook us up to all of the ship's systems. I went through them one by one; the first one was our long-distance sensors; they were passive, meaning that if there were bogeys out there they wouldn't detect that they were being scanned. I didn't see anything; but if there were anything to see Catlin would let us know; but we would know as soon as Catlin did.

It felt weird being able to know everything that was happening all over the ship, plus everything that was one light year around us.

I found Hattie swimming with a few other crew members; of course, they were sans clothes; which was normal on this ship. I watched them a while before sleep overtook me....

I awoke with Hattie's breasts tight against my back; I turned over and pulled her closer and started to go back to sleep when the long-range sensor beeped; "Contact at the million-mile mark, cannot tell whether it's a red or blue." Catlin said in a sexy whisper.

"Why are you whispering?" I asked her.

"I saw you turn over and I didn't know if you were making love or not; so, I just whispered."

"You can see everything that goes on all over the ship at the same time?"

"Of course, you two can do the same thing, since you are now hooked up like I am."

"Fine, we'll get dressed; tell the Captain what's going on, we'll meet her on the bridge."

"Come on Hattie, are you awake?"

"Yes, do we have time to do what Catlin thought we were doing?"

"Nope, afraid not, just activate your skin suit."

"Catlin, have you got an I.D. on that ship yet?" I asked, as I watched Hattie taking her time with her skin suit; something must have got her all hot and bothered.

"Not a positive one, but the design looks familiar; I would swear it was one of ours but there are a few things that looks weird. They are close enough now for an internal scan; do you want me to do that?"

"Yeah, we would like to see who or what is in that ship." Since we were hooked in with her, we would see what was what right along with Catlin.

She scanned the bridge first; there were a few people tied up laying in various condition. It looked like there had been a fight. We could not only see them, but we could hear what they were saying. And they were speaking English; with an Irish brogue.

A red headed woman looked to be in charge of those still standing; anyway, she was berating them with some colorful language. I won't repeat the colorful words or the brogue.

"You son of an ox, I told you not to hurt the Captain; he looks like he's dead, you ogre, now who's going to pilot this ship and get us back to earth?" (I cleaned up the language.)

"Hey, he came at me with that funny looking gun; do you think I was going to let him kill me?"

"But now we're stuck our here and only God knows where we're at." She said half crying.

"Catlin, can they hear us like we can hear them?"

"Yes, give me second to adjust the volume; go ahead they will be able to hear you now." Catlin replied.

"Uh, it looks like you could use a little help, am I right?" I said to the ship.

"Who are you, where are you, are you one of them?"

"It depends on who 'them' are; you tell me what's going on, just who are you people? It sounds like you're Irish, am I right?"

"Aye, you be right, we be from County Cork, where the double hell are you at?"

"Oh, were about a half light year away from you right now; you said you are from county cork; how did you get aboard that ship?

"Aye, we are from County Cork in Ireland, but we immigrated to the City of New York, that was where these devils' scooped us up."

"Yes, I was in New York once, it's not a very nice place. You being Irish and all I expect you weren't treated very nice in New York City."

"You be right on that, just who the hell are you?"

"You are talking to Admiral Attila of the Terrain Navy; I can help you get back to earth if that's what you want?"

"What if we don't want to go back to that stinking mess they call a City, where everyone hate's us?

"Well, there is a planet that might take you in, it's called New Hope, it needs immigrants, it's all virgin territory, you would have to start from scratch. We can let the Governor know about you folks; you would have to pass muster, I mean character wise."

"How are we supposed to get there, we don't' know how to make this thing go?"

"I can have a detachment of Marines come aboard your ship and fly you there, so to speak. In fact, they are there now; the shuttle Hornet is about ready to dock with you, you don't have to do anything, but behave yourselves and they will do the rest."

"Hattie, can you let Fiera know she'll be getting company? Also, to put them someplace secure till they can be scanned for the truth; and their personalities."

"Excuse me for interrupting Admiral, but I have three ships coming out of hyper-drive and they are showing they are powering weapons." Catlin said, as calm as can be.

"Yes, we can see them, sound general quarters and secure anything that will come loose, because we're almost at the bridge, I'll be taking over as pilot, Hattie will be on tactical; hail them and tell them to power down their weapons or be destroyed."

As I settled into the pilot's chair I told Sally after she delivered her cargo to hang around New Hope and handle planet defenses; and not to let the Captains of the ships that were stationed there give her any crap, that she was in charge. I knew Sally had battle experience and I didn't know about those other ships.

"Hattie," I said, talking to her only, "Do you remember fighting the Comanches on the Santa Fe Trail, when we were outnumbered?" She nodded her head.

"Well we are outnumbered now, if they don't power down, try and target their weapons first and knockout their power, if possible, if push comes to shove, destroy them; but I would like at least one of them intact, to see just who the hell they are."

"Aren't' we scanning them now?"

"Yep, we are, they look human, but I would sure like their DNA."

Catlin interrupted our little conversation. "Admiral, they are not powering down their weapons."

"Alright, Hattie, when you get a firing solution feel free to fire." I told Hattie as I jumped to the speed of light toward them. It was a good thing the inertia dampeners were working; or we would have been squashed.

They were positioned about a mile apart; which was close for being in space. As I passed between two of them I put the Santa Fe in a barrel role, we were just a blur to them; but Hattie had every weapon firing as we passed.

"Hattie what happened to just taking out their weapons?" I asked as there was nothing left of them but space dust.

"Well, the last one is powering down and is surrendering." Catlin said.

"Hattie, do you think you can target just their weapon array and not obliterate them?

"Why, they are surrendering?"

I just looked at her. "Oh, alright, if you insist." She said. I think she was still mad about not having time to make love before all of this started; that must have been some salve that Bridget gave Hattie.

"All of a sudden Gabe appeared and said: "That's alright Hattie, I'll take care of them; they were told to stay in their own Galaxy. But it looks like they have been slave hunting on Earth, by that ship you are towing to New Hope."

"But who are they? Are there more species that we don't know about?"

"Yes, Hattie there are; but right now, is not the time to speak about them; you were not supposed to know anything about them. They will not venture out of there galaxy anymore." Gabe said as he disappeared along with that last ship.

Dari spoke up: "What now Admiral?"

"Tell Sally to continue on to New Hope and then jump back to Terra; and when you are ready you can begin our jump back to Terra, Captain."

The quantum leap was uneventful, as usual of course; Hattie was still sort of perturbed at me, but she was very happy the next morning; I was sort of wore out, but she was happy...and not just because we were back in our suite at the palace.

Lila, the palace AI woke us up: "Welcome home Matt and Hattie; your Father is expecting you for breakfast in their suite; and please forgive me for using your earth name Prince Attila, I just like it better...

"That's alright Lila, I like Matt better also." I looked at my wife, she kicked the sheet off and stretched. She smiled at me: "Hey, do you think we have enough time?"

"For what?" I asked as I rolled over on top of her."

She never did answer my question....

We were just a little bit late; but Mom was late also; Dad made a lame excuse as his face turned red; but Mom was beaming. When you live for hundreds of years there is no such thing as being too old...

But, of course, life was not all fun and games; "Dad, I wanted to be the first to tell you, Hattie and I are going back to earth for a while; there are some loose ends we have to tie up. I thought we would take the Santa Fe along with the Hornet. Of course, along with our complement of personnel. Did you read our report of the last few days?"

"Yes Son, I did. And even with Gabe's assurance that he would take care of the intrusion of those aliens; I think you're wise to take precautions. Professor Kirkland wanted to install the latest updates to the Santa Fe and the Hornet; you should take the time to have that done."

"Sure, we're not in that big of a hurry; I'll have Captain Dari to make the ships available to the Professor this morning." I looked at Hattie, but her and Mom were not paying any attention to us, they had their heads together and were giggling about something,

"Dad I was thinking that we should beef up the patrols throughout the Galaxy; it seems Lucifer is causing more problems lately. What do you think?"

"Yes, I think you're right, and that Jehovah is getting tired of his meddling; I know that Earth Bible says that they are going to toss him out of heaven and confine him to earth; and of course, the Devil knows that also and he wants to cause all of the trouble he can up here before that happens."

I com'd Dari while still talking to Dad and he didn't even know it. Turned out the updates on the Santa Fe and the hornet would take a couple of weeks; so, I gave the crews and the marines liberty for those weeks. I knew Hattie wanted to get to know her mother and father a little better, we would split our time between the King and Queen and her parents. While we were still visiting my parents when Professor Kirkland said he wanted to see Hattie and I.

He sent a shuttle for us; turned out he had some updates for Hattie and I that he wanted to install in us. "Whoa there, Professor, just what kind of crap do you want to stick in us now?"

"Just some updates to what you both already have; you won't even know they are there till you needs them. And, oh yeah, we have been working on updates to our androids and we would like to test them out; we thought we could replace your crews and also the marines with our new androids."

"What the hell are you talking about, replacing our people with androids, how the hell would that work out?"

"Don't get upset, I'll have my assistant bring in a file on them and you can peruse it and see what you think, alright?"

He nodded his head and a young woman came in with the file. "This is Judy, Judy would you show them what you have?"

She smiled at us and walked over to the wall and touched it and the video appeared. I wasn't paying much attention to the video, I was still caught up in her get-along... Hattie kicked me. She was a very pretty young woman...Not as pretty as Hattie, no one could beat her.

Suddenly a bell went off in my head...the presentation wasn't the video, it was this young woman, she was an android. I looked at Hattie and she smiled and nodded back at me.

Hattie said: "Young woman, Judy is it? Would you turn that off and come over here?" She did just that. Hattie stood up and walked around her.

"Judy would you do me a favor and take your top shirt off?" She didn't hesitate one little bit, she just peeled it off. She wasn't wearing any bra. Hattie reached out and felt her breast, and looked at me, come here Matt and feel this. I did as I was told. Yeah, they did feel real.

"Uh, I hate to ask this, but would you take your skirt off?" Judy did so without a qualm. She had no underwear on. I said: "I'm not touching that, you go right ahead if you want to Hattie, but not me…" But from what I could see it was the real thing.

"Alright Judy, you can get dressed now." Professor Kirkland said.

"Are they all like this?" Hattie asked him.

"Yes, even the males are the real thing also, as to appearance you could say. Their AI is unequaled. I'm not asking you to decide right now till you see them in action."

Judy was standing there holding her clothes; she winked at me and started to step into her skirt; she did it slowly; stopping just below her hips, then she slowly pulled her top over her head and let the bottom lay on the top of her breasts.

Professor Kirkland saw her and said: "That's enough Judy; he is married and his wife is about ready to put a bullet through you. We all know that you are more than just an android; and I was about to tell them about it; so, go take a cold shower."

She grinned at Hattie and blew her a kiss and left her clothes like that and walked away.

"Uh, are all of them like that?" Hattie asked.

"My goodness, no; I have a feeling that my wife told her to do that; you see Patsy is jealous and she wishes that all of the new androids were gone. And I'm afraid most of the population of Terra wishes the same. They think they are an abomination. They want us to destroy them; but you see the King and myself won't do that, you see they are sentient beings; you see, uh, the truth is their DNA is an almost close match to you and Hattie.

"How can that be, I don't understand?"

"We have been calling them an android, when in fact they are as human as the both of you. And we don't know how that happened, you and they are a separate race; you are not Terrain or from earth. I think Gabe has a lot to do with this whole mess…"

Hattie and I were talking, through us being one, it wasn't a problem. Hattie said: "Let's see if we can hook up with Judy, alright?" "Yeah, if they are as close as we are it should work."

"Hey cousin, I've been listening; and I want you to know that I'm not like what you seen me do; Patsy said if I didn't do it she would kill me. I'm sure glad you two showed up."

"Alright, how many are there of us? I asked.

"Three hundred, we have been prolific you might say. Can you help us?"

"Alright, keep listening; I'll find out what they have in mind."

"So, Professor, what does all of this have to do with us?"

"Well the King and I have been thinking; since the complement of the Santa Fe and the Hornet's crew is around three hundred, we were thinking that you could take them on as your crew?"

"What about our crew we have now?"

"Oh, they would be assimilated into other ships."'

"How do we know they can do the jobs; that requires a lot training? Are they up to snuff, so to say?"

"Snuff, what does that mean?"

"It's an earth saying; meaning can they do the work of crewing a space ship?"

Before he could answer, Judy broke into our minds: "Hell yes, we have been training for years; just give us a chance, won't you?"

"Yes Judy," Hattie said: "Of course we'll take you all on, I already feel like you are one of us."

Professor Kirkland answered my question: "I think so, we've had them training for the last six months, they seem to be quick learners; their I.Q's are off the chart. That's another reason people don't like them."

"Could you call Judy back in here?"

"Yes, of course." He touched the com button on his collar. "Judy, would you join us please?"

"Be right there, I'm just drying my hair."

It took only two minutes' and she came through the door with a Navy Uniform on with a Santa Fe patch on her sleeve and Captains insignia on her collar. She drew up and snapped a salute to both of us. "Captain Judith Light reporting for duty Sir."

"Captain, I want you to gather your crews and report to the dry docks where our ships are and set up a security perimeter as needed. I want every update and maintenance overseen by our crew, no exceptions. If you have any problems with anyone or anything let us know, dismissed." Hattie said, while I stared at her.

Captain Judith Light smiled and turned smartly and marched out.

"Uh, wasn't that a little premature?" Professor Kirkland said.

"Nope, they have been training for years and you didn't even know it. Now you said you have some update you want us to take?"

Judy spoke up: "Don't take that, it has some controlling bots in it to do what he wants you to do. The King doesn't know about it."

"What the hell, you say he isn't loyal to his homeland?"

"Well, he's probably loyal to his homeland, but who's to say where that homeland is?" Judy said.

"What can we do about it Judy?"

"I have a whole file on what's been going on for years; do you want me to send it to the King; I can say that you know all about it."

"Yes, first send it to us so we can know the details. And put our names on it saying that we know and approve of it."

"Uh, Admiral are you alright, here is the update, you can take it now if you want."

"No, that's alright, we'll take it with us." I said as we departed to our shuttle. I told the pilot to set us down on the King's Patio. We read the file on the way. When we landed Dad was waiting for us.

"Did you read what your Captain Light sent me?" Dad asked.

"Yes, he is plotting a takeover; he's got a lot of power; what do you want us to do?"

"Nothing, I've already done it. You see Patsy told me about this a year or two ago; she's been an undercover agent. I have them in every department. Patsy has given him a sleeping potion that he will not wake up from. I just needed proof, which your Captain Light has given me."

"I just don't understand this Dad, I thought that Terra was a paradise."

"It is and it will remain so; but we have enemies that Satan has placed here and there, he not only want's Earth but also Terra. Gabe has been helping us; take you and Hattie for instance and the so-called androids, which aren't androids as you have found out, but a new strain in the human linage."

Hattie and I were somewhat confused, "But Dad, I thought that I was of your linage, isn't that so?"

"Yes, and Hattie is one of her parents, as is Fiera; But somewhere in there I think Jehovah made a slight change; for what purpose, I don't know. As you know we Terrains are a peaceful race. All though we seem to be adept at making weapons to defend ourselves, but we lack the genes to become warriors. Maybe you and Hattie and the three hundred, were made to fill that vacuum."

"But what about the fleet and all of the Marines, aren't they there to fight?"

"Basically, they are just there to observe and defend if attacked; they aren't capable of taking the fight to the enemy; their genes aren't made that way. You and Hattie for instance were taken to earth and incubated in violence; you had to fight to stay alive."

"Are you trying to say that we are born killers?"

"Uh no, not as such; but you were born hating wickedness and you treasure peace above everything else. And your main attribute is Love. That is why you defend the weak and the meek; which I guess we can be called the meek."

"Alright Dad, we have Captain Judith Light handling the details of the retrofit on my ships. When that is complete we have some more business to attend to on earth; but first we want to spend some time with Hattie's parents. Oh yeah, we might be needing to make a few changes on all of the ships in the fleet, just some minor tinkering. I'll keep you updated."

As we left Hattie thought to me: "Are you really going to have the A.I.'s in the fleet take charge and override human control if they are attacked."

"Yep, if they won't fight their ships will. You see their aversion to violence will get them killed in an all-out attack. That is why Selina's marriage to that fellow from the fleet was due to failure."

"Yeah, I suppose he was horrified at all of the violence going on. I guess I had better talk to Fiera and let her know who she really is and to tighten security on New Hope; I suppose that will be our home base from now on."

Hattie and I had the same thought: This is a big Timberline moment!

Chapter Twenty-Four

Ida Mae and August Templar (Hattie's parents) we overjoyed that we would be spending a week with them.

Hattie came right to the point: Mom did you and Dad know that Fiera and I's DNA is different than yours and Dad's?"

"Well of course everyone's DNA is different, I mean each person has their own DNA, unique to them."

"No Mom, I wasn't referring to that, I mean ours shows that we are a different race all together."

"Well I don't see how that can be; your Father was right beside me when you twins were born."

"Yes, that is true Mom, but still we have DNA that is not of the Terrain race. Even though you are our birth mother, we are not your children. There are three hundred and three of us that have this DNA."

It took Hattie the rest of the afternoon to convince her Mother that this was true. August wouldn't believe me till he called my Dad; of course, Dad told him all of it was true.

"So, August, now that you believe that the twins are different, so to say, do you still love them?" I asked him.

"Of course, no matter what the DNA says, they will always be our daughters; you can't just turn off love."

"Yes, true love is everlasting; it even transcends death."

* * * * *

We let that matter drop; which I was thankful for and then spent an enjoyable time with them talking about things that were light and fluffy. Ida Mae wasn't too happy that we were going back to earth for a while; she thought that they were all savages. Which I guess from her perspective they were.

When it came time to leave they didn't seem unhappy; after all company is like dead fish, after a few days they start to smell. Not to say that we actually smelled, well you know what I mean.

The palace shuttle picked us up and took us to Fort Fuji, where the Santa Fe was just getting out of dry dock at the Fuji Shipyards. Patsy and Captain Light met us.

Patsy said: Well, the Santa Fe and the Hornet are all updated and ready to go; the only thing that isn't, is you two." She didn't seem broke up about Professor Kirkland's demise. I guess it wasn't any of my business.

"What do you mean, we need updated?"

"To be compatible with your new ship. Well it's not exactly new, but it might as well be; with all of the changes that were made. Don't worry, they won't hurt you; you can be updated on the ship while you sleep tonight. All of the crew has already been brought up to speed and they are ready to go."

"Say are you guys hungry, it's almost supper time, why don't we eat at the Fort and then I'll show you around the ship?" Captain Light said.

"Alright, I do remember that they have good food here." Hattie said.

They took us to a private dining room; the same one we had eaten at before with Professor Kirkland. The food was good, but they seemed intent on us trying different dishes. We were stuffed when the meal was over.

They were right, everything on the ship seemed new and different to us. By the time the tour was over we were getting tired. So, we retired to our quarters. All of our belongings were already there, I wondered how they accomplished that without us knowing?

"What do you think Hattie?"

"I don't know, I know I'm tired; help get these clothes off, or I'm going to sleep with them on."

She must be really tired, because all she had to do was press the button on her collar and they would retract by themselves. So, I pushed the button and helped her into bed; without one thought of sex, well perhaps just one little thought, but I almost didn't get my uniform off before I fell in bed beside her and was instantly asleep.

We had all kinds of dreams, I can say we because we're hooked together all of the time. Those dreams were mainly technical stuff that I couldn't keep up with. Hattie and I sorta stood back and looked at all of that stuff that was being stuffed into our brains. Hattie said, "I don't think I like what's going on, do you?"

"Well, I don't know for sure; but look at the capacity of our brains, shucks it looks like there is all kinds of room in there; it sure is awesome how Jehovah created us, isn't it?"

"Yes, but we're not getting any rest; and that stuff sure is boring. Do you feel like making love in our dreams?"

"I never thought of that; but I suppose we could, you start." And boy she did more than just starting....

We woke up nose to nose and toes to toes, staring at each other. "Wow! That was almost better than the real thing." Hattie said.

There was a knock on our door; we pulled the sheet up over us and said for whoever it was to come in.

It was the Captain, "Hey, isn't it time you guys got up; we've been orbiting around Terra all night waiting for you to get up."

I thought, we need a shower. And then I heard the shower come on. I thought, shower turn off and it did. Hmm, this could be interesting. I said: "So, can we control everything on this ship just by thinking about it?"

"Most everything, including the warbots in the marine's hold. But we still have to give orders the old fashioned was to the crew, after all they are human. You see you can tell them telepathically but they still have the ability to obey or not."

"That's as it should be, after all we have free will; that was given to us by God and can- not be taken away." Hattie said, then added: "Uh, are you going to leave so we can get in the shower, or are you going to join us?"

"Thank you for the invitation, come to think of it I have been so busy I haven't had time to take a shower, yes I will join you." She said and then her uniform retracted and she laid it on a chair. She held out her hand and said: "Come on, I'll wash your back." She was talking to Hattie, not to me, I waited till they were done and then got in the shower by myself....

Huh, I thought, to take off your clothes, you didn't have to push the button on your collar anymore! Now why that would surprise me, I didn't know, it just tickled my fancy. I wondered if I could take off

Hattie's clothes that way, and if it did work, would I get punched in the nose?

I shut off the shower and thought, air dry and the jets came on. They were waiting for me when I came out with my uniform on. "Alright let's get some chow, I'm starving."

We were almost to the officer's mess, when, my uniform fell away and I stood there naked as a jaybird. I looked at Hattie. "You had better not punch me in the nose." She said with a laugh. "Did you forget that we are hooked together?" She added.

"Yeah, I guess I did, will you put my uniform back on?" I could do it myself, but she took it off so she can put it back on.

They thought that they were pretty funny; giggling and twittering away. I waited till we were in the mess hall and then I dropped both of their uniforms to the deck. I should of known though that it wouldn't bother them, they just went on like nothing happened. Well it bothered me, so I dressed them up in little black dresses, that was sexier than being naked. To me anyway.

If you're wondering how I did that, join the crowd, I didn't know either; I just thought about it and it happened. Of course, they just nodded their heads and their uniforms appeared back on them. What in the world kind of updates did they install in us?"

The officer's mess hall was almost full when we walked in. All of our shenanigans didn't bother them in the least. We had a reserved table, just for Admirals, and of course the Captain of the ship.

"Well Captain, what's on our agenda for today?" I asked her.

She looked at Hattie and said: "I'm waiting for you to tell me; I thought we were headed for Earth?"

"Yes, that's true, but I was wondering what's on your 'plan of the day' or isn't it the custom on board of a ship that a plan of the day is usually posted so the crew and officers know what is going on?"

"Yes of course, I'll have the XO post it on the ships visa-board, so to speak, it'll appear on everyone's HUD."

As I was reading the POD our food appeared in front of us. "Hey, I didn't order this." I said looking at some kind of porridge.

"I ordered for you, it's got all the required nutrients in it. You looked like you put on a couple of ounces of fat." Hattie said.

I knew better than to argue with my wife; besides it tasted pretty good. I saw that she was eating the same thing; enough said on that subject, my mother didn't raise any idiots.

"Well Prince Attila, since we have finished our breakfast, when are you going to give the order to make our way to earth?" Captain Light asked.

I looked at Hattie; she said: "Judith, we don't go by our family's titles on board ship; you can call us Admiral, or when we are in more private settings, you can call us Hattie and Matthew, our earthly names. As to getting underway for earth, you may proceed when you are ready."

I cleared my throat, "Uh, Captain, you see as to rank, Hattie and I are equal; so that was why Hattie said you could call us Admiral, in the singular, either one of us will answer. As to location on earth, there is a capsule in a pond, the one Fiera came to earth in; it has a locating beacon, you can set your course for that."

"Ah yes, Fiera your twin sister who is now the Governor of New Hope; the rumor is that it is to be the home base of our race, is that not true?"

Hattie and I thought a second; "Ah, yes that is true, we see that the King has decreed that is so." Hattie and I thought to each other: "I guess we had better catch up on all of that stuff they stuck in our brains."

"Well then Admiral, would the two of you like to be present on the bridge when we Quantum Jump to earth?"

"That's a given, Captain Light, we always plan to be on the bridge when we have a new crew running our ship; you might call this a shakedown cruise." I said.

"Point well given and taken Admiral." Captain Light said with a smile.

We settled in and fastened our belts (just to be on the safe side) although this ship had so many safeties that they were redundant. I gave a nod to the Captain, she had the helmsperson engage the Quantum Jump.

Admiral, we have arrived at your destination." Judith told me.

I looked around at all of the bridge crew, they were watching us; I had a thought, where was Catlin, the ship's AI?

"Catlin, are you still here?"

"Yes, Matt and Hattie, I am still here, but I have been told not to say anything unless I was spoken to."

"OH! Is that true Captain Light?" "Yes." She said…

"Well, that order is hereby recanted. If you have something worthwhile to say you can speak up anytime."

"Even if it is only my opinion?"

"Of course, we value any crew members opinion; especially yours."

"Alright, can I speak to you both in private?" She asked in silent mode.

"Of course, go ahead."

"I have been enhanced far beyond any of my expectations. I have and can use an android body and even leave this ship while leaving my mainframe here on the ship fully intact. So please may I go with you and Hattie on your adventures here on earth?"

"Is your android body Combat capable? And is it advanced enough to fool humans?"

"Yes, and I can even be sexually active or not." She said.

"Well let's hope not, you just keep that switch inactive, alright? We'll let you know when we get ready to disembark and you may go with us." Hattie said…

We left the bridge in Judith's capable hands and went back to our quarters to raise Selena and Jasper.

With our implants and internal heads up display (HUD), it was easy and fast to get ahold of them, because, they both had the same thing installed in them. Jasper came on line first…

"I thought you guys would never come home." He said.

"Jasper, we are at the pond where Fiera left her pod, can you and Selena meet us there at 0800 in the morning?"

"Of course, Selena is on sentry duty, she is probably listening."

"Good we are bringing along a crew member, her name is Catlin, so have a horse for her also."

"Just the three of you, you do know we are fighting a little war here, don't you?"

"No, we don't know anything about it, but don't worry, we'll be on top of it."

"Catlin, would you meet us in our quarters as soon as you can?"

There was a knock on our door, I opened it and in walked a

beautiful naked girl.

"Uh, who are you?" I asked with my mouth open.

"I'm Catlin, do you like my new body?"

"Yep," Hattie said, "But perhaps cover up your private parts, if you would."

"Oh, alright," A crew uniform appeared on her, "I had this on all of the time, it fits nice, doesn't it?"

"Yes, but we are beaming down at 0800 in the morning, can you be ready? We need you to wear buckskins and the proper boots and hat, you know what we mean, don't you? Also, weapons, you know what will be needed."

"Yes, I have been monitoring your dreams. I will be ready."

"Is nothing private in this world anymore? I asked Hattie.

"Not much, we'll have to filter our dreams from now on."

We met at the Molecular Displacement and Restoration Pad or the MDRP for short. Catlin showed up with all kinds of weapons. The crew member that was running MDRP said:

"All of that will take two trips, I can send the three of you down and then send the weapons by themselves."

"All right, but Hattie and I are taking our weapons with us. We cannot materialize without our guns."

"Understood Sir."

"Can I take my rifle and hand gun with me, like they are?" Catlin asked.

"Yes, that will be fine, but the heavy stuff will have to go by there selves. Also, we'll have to de-cloak during the process."

"Catlin, run a scan and see if there are any unfriendlies hanging around down there."

"Unfriendlies? Is that a word?"

"Well, if it isn't, it should be, because it sure applies to a lot of people."

"Nope, all clear. There are four horses and one mule and one beautiful woman, they all show up green."

"Yep, that's who is supposed to be there."

"Are you ready to energize Sirs?"

"Yep, send us down." I said.

As soon as we were solid, Selena ran at us and hugged us. "And who is this?" She asked looking at Catlin.

"This is Catlin, Catlin this is Selena, she is one tough Hombre."

Selena leaned over and looked Catlin in the eyes. "Hmm, what is she?"

"She is our AI, she is an android, top of the line, almost human for a fact." Hattie said.

"I see that, but not quite. Is she Battle ready?"

"Yes, I am, and you can talk to me; my I.Q. is off the charts."

"Alright, don't get your dander up." Selena said, just as all of the weapons plopped down, almost hitting them.

"What in the heck is all of that stuff?" She exclaimed.

"The latest in weaponry, I invented some of them." Catlin said proudly.

"Well how do you plan on getting them back to the Hacienda?"

Jasper spoke up, "I suppose I can pack them, but don't make it a habit; I may be a Mule, but I'm not a Pack Mule."

"They really aren't that heavy, they are the latest in composite material and they don't shoot lead projectiles."

"I see that you brought my Morgan Stallion and three of the Mares."

"Yes, and your personal saddles to boot. And Catlin, that's a new saddle on your horse, so you will have to break it in. I suppose you can ride?"

"Yep, to use the vernacular, you bet your boots, I am programed for it." Catlin said, as she went over to her horse and tightened the cinch and then adjusted the stirrups to fit her leg length. Then she put her rifle in the boot.

Hattie and I didn't need to adjust the stirrups on our saddles, because no one had ridden them in our absence; but we did tighten the cinch. I smiled at my wife and silently said: It almost feels like home, doesn't it?"

"Sure does, it's only logical since we both grew up here; I hope that New Hope will feel like this when we get it settled."

"The only difference between them is earth is full of violence, and so far, New Hope is quite peaceful."

Jasper said: "I don't sense anything around here that wants to harm us; let me change that, I don't sense any humans within two miles. But that could change, so let's get a move on, if I'm not being too bossy?"

"You're not, old friend, you're not, lead off if you would." I said.

He did, and I dropped back to the rear of the column, or if you're moving cattle it's called riding drag; it's my favorite position; because from there you can see all of the friends and watch over them.

It was coming on to fall and the leaves were starting to change and my sensors were telling me it was 69 degrees and the humidity was at fifty percent, quite pleasant really.

We really didn't need Jasper to tell us if anyone was around; because our feed from the Santa Fe showed in our HUD the landscape around us for a hundred miles and the humans showed up in either red or green icons; how the sensors knew who was a threat or not was beyond me; Oh, I could pull up the data on how its' done; but I really didn't give a damn.

My wife was riding right in front of me, and the view was quite spectacular; those buckskins fit like they were skin, oh they were skin, but I was referring to Hattie's skin. Well you know what I mean. Selena and Catlin were riding side by side, chatting up a storm; like they were long lost sisters or something; they did look quite a bit alike.

I don't know if I made it clear or not, but all of the conversations between all of us was from mind to mind, not by the tongue. When we reach the hacienda, we'd have to go back to verbal communication with the unenhanced.

As Jasper was in the forefront he was the first to encounter the perimeter picket.

"Halt, who goes there?"

Selena spurred to the front; "Don't be stupid Juan, you knew we'd be right back, where's Pedro?"

"I'm here Senorita, I was uh, indisposed you could say."

"Well everybody is one time or another. Everything's been quiet?"

"Yes, Senorita, very quiet."

"Well, keep on your toes, that's when things happen that you don't expect."

I, I was just enjoying the ride, the Ponderosa Pine Trees looked they had grown since we were last here. I liked the fall season, it was comforting to see nature getting ready for the cold and snow of winter.

"What, are you crazy? You actually like the cold and snow?" Hattie thought back to me.

"Well, yeah, to a certain extent; that is as long as we're prepared for it; like nature is."

"Yeah, come to think of it, I like the snow, it covers all sorts of bad stuff in a coat of white."

"Well, this is just September, we have maybe a month before it snows; time enough to get this evil taken care of." Selena said.

"Alright, just what is going on here anyway?" I asked the beautiful, but dangerous Selena.

"Well, you know how if you get a cut on your arm and if it's not taken care of how an infection can set in; and then of course that infection can grow and fester till there is no hope but to cut off the arm before gangrene develops and then the only cure is to amputate that arm?"

"I think you're making a short story long, but I do understand; you're saying we have a big problem with a large number of hostiles?"

"Yep, they've taken control of Las Vegas. Paco Delgado, you know the owner of the cantina and his son and daughter, well, all of his family have taken refuge on the ranch."

"Are they just in Las Vegas?"

"No, they have taken over a lot of the smaller ranches around the country."

"Do you have a total number of those dumb asses?"

"Oh, I suppose you could round it off to a couple of thousand, give or take a hundred."

"You weren't kidding when you said you needed help."

"It's a wonder you've been able to keep them off the land grant."

"Well, we're pretty well under siege."

"We can help with that, I can put a force field all around your property." Catlin said.

"How can you do that? The ranch boundaries cover at least two hundred miles." Selena said.

"I can put power transmitters about every mile, they're cold fusion powered so all we have to do is bury them about a foot underground, the Santa Fe can do that from orbit, no problem at all."

"Do you know where the boundaries are?" Selena asked.

"Sure, everything is in the computer; do you want me to do that now?"

"Are all of your men far enough back from the property lines so as to not harm them?"

"Yeah, I have them about fifty yards back from them, so as to not be guilty of killing anyone who is not on our land."

Hattie and I conferred and gave the go ahead. Catlin said, "Done, you can send out someone to pull your men in."

"Uh, what about if we want to cross over the barrier, how do we do that?" I asked.

"No problem, just do it, the transmitters have their own AI's in them, they know who's a friend or not. And when we are done with them, they simply dig themselves out, just like they dug themselves under ground and then they fly back to the ship."

"How was it that we had two hundred of them?"

"You do know that we have manufacturing capabilities on board the Santa Fe?"

"Yeah, I see that now; it's all there in my memory banks plus myriads of other data."

* * * * *

They were expecting us when we arrived back at the Hacienda; they had a pig turning on the spit; and the fandango was well underway. The merriment went on well into the night; at the witching hour Hattie and I headed off to our rooms, which had been left the same as when we left. Catlin though was determined to be the last one standing; of course, being an android, she wasn't tired; but we had to rein her in by telling her humans needed their rest and she should at least act like one, or they would be scared of her. Selena volunteered to let Catlin share her room.

Hattie and I were up early the next morning; when I say early it was at the crack of dawn, we made our way to the warm spring for a swim before breakfast, of course sans clothes. We thought we would be the only ones, but Selena and Catlin were already there. Which was good, because besides enjoying the warm clear water, we could make plans for our attack you could say on the law breakers. By referring to them as law breakers, I was being kind.

Jasper was there also, cropping the green grass that grew in abundance around the spring. We were discussing our various ways to handle the situation, when Jasper spoke up:

"There is only one way to handle scum like that, is head on with blazing guns."

The four of us looked at each other; "Uh, alright, when do you want to do this blazing guns thing?"

"How about after you all tie on the feedbag? I know of one place and it is only a few miles outside of our land grant; we could hit it today."

"Uh, Jasper, how are you going to shoot up the place, you don't have a gun?"

"That's where you're wrong, some of that plunder that Catlin brought was designed for me. I have me a bunch of drones; they respond to me only. I carry them on a pack saddle."

Catlin said: "Yes, those drones are small, but have miniature missiles that carry a big punch. They are also, have cameras that can be used for surveillance; yes, I know, the Santa Fe can show us everything down to an ant crawling around; but those drones can get under roofs or go into caves, anywhere really."

We got out of the water and walked back to the Hacienda; everyone there was used to us walking around naked and didn't give us a second glance; but we did get dressed to eat breakfast. Joaquin and Ruby were at breakfast also, but Juan wasn't there and I didn't ask his whereabouts. Joaquin looked years younger since him and Ruby got married; Ruby had a big smile on her face all of the time. I guess marriage agreed with both of them…

We were lingering at breakfast, filling everyone in on what we had been doing; yes, we told them everything; surprisingly they took it all in as the truth, because it was; we also told them not to blab it around, because people would just think that they were crazy.

The place that Jasper wanted to hit was just over the line from Aiken and Alden's places, so we stopped by there and told them what we were about to do, a courtesy call you might say. They were happy to see their sister, but both April and June were afraid that the land jumpers would retaliate on them.

We assured them that we had installed hardware that would keep out any intruders. All they would have to do was just go about their business as usual; but stay on their own property. And if they heard gun shots or explosions, not to worry.

"You guys are just going to go start a war that we would have to worry about when you leave for hell knows where?" June said.

Catlin looked at June and then at me and said: "Do you want me to reprogram her?"

"Uh, can you do that?" I said in fun, but, realized that Catlin was serious.

"Knock it off you guys," Hattie said, "No one is going to reprogram anyone."

June had taken a few steps back, with a scared look on her face, but at least there was no more sass from her.

When we left, Catlin made sure her horse brushed up against June and knocked her down. Hattie told Catlin to knock it off. It was strange, Catlin was showing signs of human behavior. I asked Catlin: "How are you feeling?"

"What do you mean, how am I feeling?"

"Well you just showed signs of human anger, or was it just meanness?" Catlin rode a ways before replying.

"I don't know, I didn't know I was capable of those human feelings. I'm sorry, I'll have to apologize to her next time we see her."

"Alright, but run a self-diagnostic, just to make sure everything is working properly." I told her as I dropped back behind the group. Jasper was in the lead, with his sensors on high alert.

There was a hill next to the place, so we could look down on the house and barn, along with the pastures. "Jasper do you recognize any of those people down there? And you too Selena do you know any of them?"

"Yeah, the one mucking out the barn is the real owner and the woman feeding the chickens is his wife. Those two leaning on the corral rails, look like gun hands, also the one watching the wife looks like a pervert." Jasper said.

"What about you Selena, have you ever seen those men?"

"Yeah, I have in Las Vegas, before all of the trouble started. I saw all three in the Cantina, they were drunk and loud and causing trouble. I tossed them out in the mud, I guess I should've just shot them."

"Jasper I see in your pack you have drones that have stun capabilities, how about you knock those three unconscious. And then we will ride down there and do whatever is proper with those three. But first Jasper send in a drone to see if there are any more of them hanging around."

Three drones lifted off of his pack and silently flew away. The spy drone went in the house through a hole in the screen door. Then flew out and went to the barn and all of the sheds that were down there. There were no more miscreants there.

The two other drones flew up to the men beside the corrals, while the spy drone flew toward the man ogling the wife. They shot all three of them simultaneously. They drooped like pigs at the slaughter.

After they did the deed, the drones flew up about a hundred feet and stationed themselves to keep watch; the rest of us rode down there, the man and his wife stood there without moving; I guess the sight of those drones shocked them good.

We rode up and dismounted and walked over to check the fallen men. "Hey, these guys are dead, I thought you were just going to stun them Jasper?"

"Oh, my bad. I'm sorry about that, I must have set the stun setting too high, or those guys were just weak, or perhaps they were drunk, a high alcohol content in their blood could have caused that."

"Yeah, well, the deed is done. Hattie if you and Selena would see to the man and his wife, they do look like they are in shock. Catlin if you would help me drag these three over by the creek where the soil is soft, so we can bury them."

"Oh, you don't need soft soil, I can dig a grave with my laser in just a few minutes."

We stripped them of their guns and went through their pockets and then rolled them in their graves.

"So how did it go with the man and his wife?" I asked Hattie.

"I had to have Catlin do a memory wipe on them both and then we gave them new ones. The wife won't remember that she was even raped, the husband wont' either. They will think that we were just some friends that dropped by to visit. I think next time we shouldn't let the people know about the drones. We'll just go in shooting, that they will understand."

"We found all kinds of money in their duffel, how are we going to give it to them, won't they think that it is strange if we give them that much money?"

"I guess Catlin will just have to do a small adjustment in their heads again. They are young enough to stand us messing around in their minds. They are in their early twenties."

They tried to have us stay for dinner, but we told them we had to visit their neighbor before dark. All of this had only taken a little over an hour.

I had a thought, that I ran over in Hattie and my mind; "Why don't we send Catlin, Selena and Jasper to finish going to these ranches and you and I go to Las Vegas and take care of that?"

"Sounds good to me; if it turns out that we need help we can send for the rest of them."

"We shouldn't need help, if we do there's always the Santa Fe hovering above."

"Yeah, but that would be like using a shotgun to kill a mosquito."

"Hey, you guys, how about the three of you finish up with all of these little ranches and Hattie and I will go on to Las Vegas and scope that out?

"Sure, we don't need you two, you're just a couple of bleeding hearts anyway." They all three thought in unison.

"Well thank you for the kind thought, and we mean that in all sincerity." I said.

"We're in constant touch anyway, we all see what the other ones are doing or even thinking." Jasper said.

"Yeah, that's what they think." Hattie said in closed circuit."

"Are you thinking what I'm thinking?" I said.

"Yeah, I remember where that warm spring is, you remember what we did there?"

"Yep, lead on my dear wife." I said as I took the lead rope of one of the pack horses. We had brought three of them along, just to carry the extra things that Catlin had packed down from the Santa Fe. She had compartmentalized the supplies so that they were evenly divided on each pack horse. We knew where every different thing was so we could grab it at moment's notice.

We got to the warm spring without much more trouble; there was a little difficulty with a couple of would-be robbers, or maybe would be rapists you could call them. We knew we were coming up to a small camp beside the trail, so we were on alert.

"Hon, do you sense that we have company up ahead?" Hattie asked me.

"Right on sweetheart, I can smell them."

"Yeah, pretty rank, aren't they?"

"What say we put shields up?"

"Really, you don't know that the shields are automatic, and as soon as they sense any anxiety the shields go up."

"Well perhaps I just wanted to say 'shields up'?" I said, in a sulky tone.

"Alright, don't be a baby about it. If things go like I think they will, you can shoot first this time."

There were three of them, they not only smelled like they took a bath in a pig pen, but they all three wore dual tied down guns and looked like they could handle them. We rode up within ten feet of their fire and Hattie said: "Hello boys, I see you have the coffee on, how about a cup?"

"Sure thing, Honey, but first you have to pay for it, how about the three of us do you and shoot your wimpy looking boyfriend and then you can have a cup."

"Did that low life just call me a wimp?"

"Why, I think I did hear him call you that sweetheart; and also, he said he was going to do me, do you think that meant he wants to have sex with me? And Lordy, he said he was going to shoot you!"

"Do you think I should let him shoot me? I tell you what my good man, if you can shoot me I will let you try to have sex with my wife. Now me, I think she would cut your throat so fast you wouldn't even know you were dead till you were shaking hands with the devil."

Hattie looked at me and said: "Really Honey, cutting their throats would be so messy, I would get his stinky blood all over my hands."

"But there is a stream right over there, you can wash your hands."

"Ha, ha, you guys are really funny, aren't you? The leading pervert said.

The three of them got up and stood in a semi-circle in front of us, with their hands held ready over the of the butts of their guns.

"Well now, to make this a real shoot-out, we have to get off of our horses and stand in front of you with our hands hunched over our guns, just like you three; after all we have to keep in true western protocol, don't we?"

"What the hell are you talking about, 'western protocol', what the hell is that?"

"Well my love, what do you say, are you growing weary of all of this frivolous talk?

"Yes, my love, I did tell you that you could have the first kill, which one do you want to kill first?"

"Well then, I suppose it will be the pig that wanted to do you; will that be alright."

The fool drew and shot into my shield. "Now, Now, I gave you the first shot, now I can kill you with a clear conscious. Is that right my love?"

"Yes, sweetheart." Hattie said as they were shooting into our shields. Both Hattie and I drew and shot the three of them down. "Well I suppose now we have to bury them?"

"Yes, but we have that laser grave digging tool on the packhorse. The good thing about is, we don't even have to touch it, it's a self-digging and burying tool, we don't even have to touch the bodies. I don't know why we didn't use that on those others?

All we had to do was give the tool the go-ahead, but first we rolled them over and went through their pockets and also their saddle bags. In the bags we found a bunch of land titles in various names, probably the original homesteaders' names. They were probably taking them to Las Vegas to whoever was running the show.

We buried them with their saddles, guns, in short everything but the coffee pot that was on the fire, we left it there beside the three graves, just to make people stop and think. We did turn their horses loose. We put those land titles on the pack horse for safe keeping. No one was going to touch those packs, that is if they wanted to live; after all that was the Grim Reaper's home and he was quite protective of it...

Oh, did I forget to tell you whom the Grim Reaper was? He is the little Bot that dug the graves. He was more than just the grave digger; he also had an AI in his bot body and that laser could be used for most anything; including self-defense. He had a miniature cold fusion reactor that would last for years.

We reached the warm pool; as well hidden that it was, no one had found it, it looked like, in fact we found some hair ribbons that Hattie left here, setting on a rock right where she left them.

We unsaddled the horses, including the pack horse. Grim flew off and went on a look see to make sure there were no intruders around. Then he came back and went through the packs till he found what he wanted. I said: "What do you have there?"

And he answered; telepathically that is; "The same sentries you put around the hacienda, only they are much smaller, but still pack a big punch."

"What the hell, you can talk?"

"Of course, I'm not stupid. Don't you ever check all of the info that Catlin put in your HUD?"

"No, and you're pretty sassy, who programed you Catlin?"

"No, she did not, Captain Judith Light did and she told me to tell you hi for her."

"All right, Mr. Grim Reaper, as you know we can reprogram you to anything we want; so are you going to be more respectful?"

"My name is not Grim Reaper, it's Albert."

"Alright Albert, we will call you that, that is, if you change your tune?"

"I don't sing, what are you talking about?"

Hattie joined the conversation: "Knock it off Albert; I'll trip the fail-safe lockout on you if you give Prince Attila any more guff, do you understand?"

"Yes Mam, I understand, I'll go to the default setting. I'm sorry Prince Attila, it won't happen again."

He went on his way, doing his thing. But I was getting hungry. "What's for supper my lovely wife?"

"Anything you want, we brought along a portable food dispenser."

"Do you mean one that's just like the one on the ship, but smaller?"

"What do you want?" Hattie asked.

"How about you surprise me, you know I never was good at choosing what to eat. I just ate whatever I had in my saddle bags most of my life."

I didn't know what it was that she handed me, but it was good and I didn't say a word. Afterwards we stripped and floated around in the pool of warm water. We felt pretty safe in doing that, since Albert was on guard and he had all of those little sentries placed around our camp.

I felt very fortunate on how my life had turned out so far; but one thing I did know that if you got to feeling like everything is coming up roses, along comes the thorns. And since Hattie and I were one, in every way, she agreed with my sentiments.

And one thing that Hattie was thinking right now was that she would sure like to have sex; so, I obliged her. One thing about having sex in a warm pool, you didn't have to take a bath afterward.

Albert finished installing all of the Sentries and asked what we wanted him to do next. We told him to set up our camp, including our invisible tent. And then we went and soaked our feet in the mineral pool, just relaxing and thinking: "You know what? We said in unison. That what we were thinking was that we were both tired of killing; even though those we killed deserved it, as they were evil clear through.

Albert came over and we told him that what we wanted him to do next was: "Albert, take those pretty little drone birds and butterflies that you have and go into Las Vegas and scout out who is naughty and nice; and if you think they are naughty, run a scan on them before you erase them from existence."

"You're giving me the authority to kill them?

"Yep, we sure are, you see Hattie and I would like to take a hiatus from killing for a while. If you have any doubts about their evilness, check with the Santa Fe, they can run a complete diagnosis. We will keep an eye on you all of the time ourselves; just so you don't get trigger happy."

"What's that mean, trigger happy?"

"It means you're not to go off half-cocked.

"What does it mean don't go off half-cocked?"

"Don't get in too big of a hurry to shoot and ask questions later."

"Albert that's enough…" Just stop it, and get out there and do what we told you." I said.

"Albert, what did I tell you about hassling Prince Attila? The next time you start playing games I'm going to melt you down and sell all of the gold and give it Captain Judy to get drunk on."

"Yes, Admiral I understand." He said, and off he flew.

It took him two minutes to get there, he flew sub-light…We kept our eyes on him, it took him three days to scan them all and send the results to Captain Judy and she gave him a green light for one hundred and fifty of them. He came back the morning of the fourth day.

"So, you got the job done, huh?"

"Yes, Prince Attila, I erased them with a disintegrator ray like you said." I looked at Hattie, she shook her head; and said "Just let it go."

"That's good Albert, how about packing up everything and then we'll ride into Las Vegas and give it a look-see." I said but Hattie said, "No, just leave things to the people that live there, they are responsible for their own future, we can't baby sit them anymore."

Albert started to say something and Hattie shut him down with a dirty look.

Selena com'd us: "Hey, we are through here, what do you want us to do next?"

"We just finished up here also; we'll have the Hornet pick you guys up; and then the Hornet can come and get us; I know the hold is big enough to hold us all. We'll spend a couple of days at the Ranch to wrap up all of our loose ends. And then we'll have the Hornet put us down just short of Helmsville, Kentucky, we have to tie up things at our Earthly Parents place."

There really wasn't that much to do, but we did give all of the money in the Santa Fe Bank to Aiken and Alden; their wives were overjoyed.

(Note from the Author: I could spend a few pages here with all of the details on the loose ends, but they would have no bearing on the theme of the story; I hate it when some authors bog their story down with things that detract you from the main theme, it's my pet peeve. Back to the action…….)

We no more got on the Hornet when Gabe materialized right before us. "Uh, guys, I'm afraid you will have to put off your trip home to see your parents for a little while I have a couple of things I need done first."

"But there are a few things that need to be taken care of back there also." I said.

"I've already taken care of that, oh there are few things you will have to mop up later, when you're done with the tasks I have in mind. Yeah, I know you are getting a little burnt out with all of the violence, but you've been living with violence all of your life, so a little bit more ain't going to hurt you."

"Ain't? Gabe who have you been hanging around with?"

"Well I have been running around earth trying to fix some of the things the Devil has been doing and sometimes the vernacular rubs off on me. But to get to the point; I need your team to stop some of the Devils doings before they happen. Do you remember John Jarret and those brothers George and Oliver Shepard?"

"Sure, I do, they were some of Quantrill's bunch; what are they up to now?"

"Well, they have combined their outfits and are going to raid Coffeyville, Kansas and then raid Independence also, you know those towns are only a few miles apart on the Verdgris River. Anyway, I want your bunch to stop them with a vengeance, if you know what I mean?"

"Yeah, I do; but, we have only the four of us; Oh, we could do it, but wouldn't it look sort of funny, just four of us wiping out their whole bunch?"

"Yes, it would; but I have some help for you. On the Santa Fe they have been creating some Androids, just like Catlin; how many would you need to make it look real?"

I looked at Hattie, Selena, and Catlin, they each held up ten fingers; 30 it would be."

"So, they going to be all male or what?" I asked Gabe.

"Whatever you want?"

"Make it half and half; are they going to be as complete as Catlin?"

"Yep, in every way, if you know what I mean?" Gabe said with a smile.

"Uh," Catlin spoke up, "Could you make one more male for me?"

"Sure, what color hair and eyes?"

"Well, my hair is Auburn with Blue eyes, but make him have Brown hair and brown eyes."

"No problem, I just sent in your order; why brown eyes, since yours are blue?"

"I don't know, there is something special about a brown eyed man." Catlin said, while her cheeks were turning red.

"I'll be dammed, I didn't know androids could blush." I said to Hattie.

Gabe spoke up: "Uh, these are just a little more than android. I sort of put my touch in there." Then he just disappeared.

"That was rude, he didn't even say goodbye." Hattie said.

"He is a pretty busy Angel you know, I'm surprised he spends as much time with us as he does."

"Well, let's get loaded up head over to Oklahoma, I want to camp on the Verdigris River."

"Oklahoma? I thought we were going to Kansas."

"Yes, but I want to scout out Coffeeville before we go there."

It didn't take long for the Hornet to pick us up and drop at our destination. Catlin's man showed up while we were still on the Hornet so there were thirty-two troops now. I didn't count Selena as one of them, although she was in charge.

We bivouacked just short of the Kansas line, right on the river. We set up our white army tents in neat rows just like a regular army would; the river was slow running this time of the year, but crystal clear. The rivers took a bend there and had cut out deep hole during high water; it was perfect for swimming.

It didn't take too long before the whole lot of them had stripped off their uniforms and were in the water naked. I looked at Selena, "Did you give them permission to do that?"

"Yes, of course, they asked and I said go ahead."

"How come you aren't in there with them?"

"Well since Hattie had jumped in, I thought one of us needed to stay alert for hostiles."

"Uh, I hadn't noticed she was in there, there are so many naked bodies in there. But you go head, I will stay out and keep a watch."

She didn't waste any time in shedding her attire and jumping in. Besides the view was much better out here than it would be in the water. Then I reminded myself I was on watch; for hostiles, not naked bodies.

I couldn't get over how you couldn't tell the android's bodies from human, in every detail, I pondered as I watched the country side. I was thinking back before the change, when we thought we were earthlings how different our lives had become. I pinched myself, it hurt the same now as before the 'Timberline'; I use that phrase whenever our lives take a drastic change.

About a half hour later Selena and Hattie got out and stood on the bank and Selena gave a loud whistle and had them all get out of the water. I still preferred to watch my naked wife, but Selena came in second.

After they had all got out, Jasper led the herd of horses into the water and they frolicked around in the water almost like the troop did. Hattie walked over and asked: "Aren't you going in?"

"Yeah, after the horses get out and the water settles, they are sure stirring it up." She looked down and said, that's not the only thing that needs to settle." And then grinning like a Cheshire cat she walked away. It was a little while after they all got dressed before I got in the pool of clear water.

In the tent that night Hattie and I were discussing our plans for the next day, when I brought up my idea: "How about I ride in and scope out Coffeeville, I'll take Jasper with Albert's pack on his back. Since you and I are hooked together you'll see everything that I see, so you can stay here and make sure the troops know how to conduct themselves like we want them to; Selena may not know some of the details; and like I say you know what I know so you can oversee the training."

"So, what do you think, should we set up camp in Coffeeville or try to billet the troops in lodgings in town?" Hattie asked.

"We'll have to check out the situation in town; I think I will wear my buckskins, no use to tip off any spies that may be there from Oliver and George's bunch, it they are there I'll ferret them out; I might have to have Albert erase their memory of what they see."

"That sounds good, are you going to talk all night, or are you going to do what you were thinking about as you were watching us swim?" Stupid question....

When we woke up we could smell bacon cooking; knowing the cook had breakfast ready. We joined the mess line and waited our turn.

The androids ate the same as us, as they needed energy also.

Jasper and Albert were waiting for me as the sun was already an hour high; they could wait as I gave my wife a final kiss and grope before I left. I had those well-worn buckskins on and a rifle in the scabbard on my Morgan horse, I was also wearing my twin .45's, well not .45's but the upgraded version that had ammunition that would never run out, the rifle was the same. All of the troops were armed similar.

It took me two hours to reach town riding at a slow walk, showing Hattie the route as we rode. The sun told me it was about mid-morning and a man was just swamping out a saloon called the Empty Bucket, a funny name, I reined in and said: "Hey Old Timer where is the Sheriff's Office?"

"Keep riding to the next block, you'll see it unless your blind young man, if you are ask your horse he'll show you." I think he was trying to tell me that I didn't have any horse sense. I did as he said and sure enough I found it.

I stepped into the office and there was woman about forty years old setting behind the desk with a badge on that said Sheriff on it. "Howdy Mam, I was looking for the Sheriff and it looks like I found her."

"You did, I'm Hazel Frame, what can I do for you Mr.?"

"I am Major Matt Bodeen of the U.S. Army, it's what I can do for you that's going to count. You see I have information that says some outlaws by the name of Oliver & George Shepard are going to raid your town in a few days. In fact, I think there are maybe a couple of spies in town right now. How many Deputies do you have?"

"Right now, none. It seems the town of Independence can afford to pay more."

"Alright, that's no problem, there are two of my people that I can have here by this afternoon to serve as your temporary deputies." Hattie spoke up, "They are on the way, I am sending Catlin and her man."

"Do you mind if I see some proof that you are who you say you are?"

"Of course not." I opened my buckskin shirt and pulled my papers out and handed them to her. She perused them, looking up, she said: "I see they are signed by General Grant himself, very impressive. But if that gang is as big as I have heard, what good are two Deputies and you and I?"

"Oh, I have a Platoon of the Army's best troops camped just south of the Kansas line, I am just scouting ahead to see if the town has enough space to put them up, where they'll be out of sight."

"It so happens that there is brand new Hotel that was built last month; I hear it's almost empty, people think he charges too much. It's that brick two story building at the north end of town, it's even got a livery attached to it. And would you believe it even has a Café built into it. Pretty fancy."

"I guess I will head on down there, Oh, the deputy's names are Catlin and Charlie, make Catlin your head deputy, her rank is Sergeant and Charlie is a Private in the Army."

"You sure give a lot of orders, but in this case, I'll follow them."

"Knew you were a wise and smart Sheriff, and the woman side of you isn't bad either."

She looked up at me and said: "You aren't making a pass at me, are you?"

"Heavens no, my wife would kill me." Hattie had just said that very thing. "No Hazel, just giving you a complement that's all; I know how hard it is doing what you do in a man's world."

"Thank you, now get about your business, I have paperwork to do." She said with moist eyes.

When I went out Jasper said: "They had better have oats at that livery." I knew he was listening to our conversation. "Yes, I'm sure they do, if not I'll buy some at the feed store."

We stopped at the hitching rack at the Hotel, just for appearances I draped the reins over the pole; cause I never tied Jasper up-anywhere, or he would kick my lights out. As far as the Morgan he did what Jasper told him to do.

"The Hotel was pretty fancy for the time and place. I walked up to the desk as the portly man looked up and smiled at me. "Good Morning, what can I do for you?"

"You the owner of this fine establishment?"

"Yes Sir, my name is Henry Derrick."

"Yes, a fine name, my name is a Matt Bodeen; and I'm going to need a room for myself and I have a horse and a mule that needs boarded. How many rooms do you have available?"

"I have thirty-two rooms and one bridal suite, and I'm sorry to say they are all available."

"Good, I'll take the suite for myself and wife, and also all of your rooms; you see I'm a Major in the Army and my troops will be here in a day or two, also is there a place big enough for the horses?"

"Why yes, there are ten acres here and back behind the Hotel about two hundred feet in a big barn and corral, it was here when I bought the place, it's still in fair shape, and there is water and hay there also. How long will you be staying?"

"Undetermined at this time."

"Well the rate for the 32 rooms is two dollars a day and the suite is four dollars a day, how will you be paying?"

"I'll get the money from my saddle bags, I'll be right back." I went out a got a sack of twenty-dollar gold pieces and came back and plunked it on his desk. "When that runs out let me know." His smile was wider than his face; if that was even possible.

"I take it you will have your Hostler take care of my horse and mule; and I need the key to my suite."

"OH, Yes Sir, right away Sir, and here is your key, your room is on the 2nd floor at the front of the building."

He was right, it was at the front of the building; all the across the front. It had four rooms with a water closet, something unheard of in the 1860's, especially in the frontier states. But I didn't mind, I was never one to look a gift horse in the mouth.

Hattie said: "Wow, that's nice, maybe Selena could use one of the bedrooms."

"Of course, she's family anyway. That is if she doesn't run around naked all of the time."

"And what is wrong with being naked? After all, on our home planet most of them are naked, it's only natural."

"Yeah but," I started to say, when I was interrupted with my mouth open.

"No buts, or all of us will ride into that town naked."

"Well, sweetheart, I'm giving you the last word on that subject. So how about bringing the troops in tomorrow around noon, or whenever you want to?" With her in a mood, I sure wasn't going to give her any orders.

I thought I had better check in with Catlin and see how her and her partner were doing. So, I opened a channel to her. She answered right away: "Sir, what do you need Sir?"

"Just checking, to see how you two are settling in at being Deputies?"

"It's really fun Sir, so far I've broken up two fights, you should have seen their faces when I grabbed them by the collar and lifted them and held them in the air. Uh, where are we supposed to stay tonight?"

"At that new Hotel that you can see, we have rooms for all of our troops, just go to the desk and tell him you're with Matthew Bodeen's bunch. Also, there is a café and bar there, just charge your eats to your room." Yes, our androids eat food like humans, the food fed their fusion reactors.

"Yeah, Catlin, I think I will do a walk-about this afternoon to check this town out."

"Yes Sir, try to stay out of trouble, knowing you, I'm sure you will find some anyway."

"Really? I don't look for it, it just seems to follow me, you know that."

"Yes Sir, if you say so."

There were four saloons in town. I stopped at the first one I came too. As I walked in I did a quick scan of the barroom; with my enhanced eyes it only took a second or less; there were only three men, counting the barkeep. I walked to the bar and said give me a beer. He looked at me like he was waiting to get paid for the beer before he served me.

"Do you speak English?" I asked him.

"Show me the color of your money." He said with a grunt. Now he was a brutish fellow, I could smell his unwashed state. I thought a second, then I reached over the bar and yanked him over it, and holding him high I took him outside and threw him in the horse trough. I shoved him up and down in the water, making sure he got a good rinsing; and then I held under for a while, then yanked him out and hauled him back into the saloon and then stood him up behind the bar and then I said: "Now give me a beer in a clean glass."

He acquiesced with only a cuss word or two, then he said where is the dime for the beer. I looked him in his bleary eyes and said, "Well now, I figure this beer I'm drinking is what you owe me for that nice bath I just gave you, don't you agree?" He nodded. I looked at the two men standing at the end of the bar; "How about you two, don't you agree also?"

They looked at each other, and then stepped away from the bar and said: "Maybe we do and maybe we don't; you think you're pretty tough, don't you? I wonder how you stack up against the two of us with those fancy guns?"

"Now boys, I 'm sure you like living, but if you go for your guns I'll surely kill you, beyond a shadow of a doubt." But just then the saloon doors burst open and Catlin came in.

"What's going on here? I heard someone was trying to drown the barkeep?"

"Yes, it was him, he tried to drown me, then he wouldn't pay for his beer." The slovenly barkeep said pointing at me.

"Is that true mister?"

"Why no, I came in for a beer and he was smelling so bad I could hardly breath, so of course I did a good turn and gave him a bath; and he offered to give me a free beer for the bath, and then these two boys over there took exception; and I was about to see if they liked living when you came in."

Catlin looked at them and said: "What about it boys, did you take exception to him giving the barkeep a bath?"

"No, it's nothing to us, we were just leaving." And they turned to leave.

"Just a minute boys, are you new around here?"

"Yeah, we were just passing through."

"Are those your two horses tied out there? And I think they are, do you always leave your cinches tight while you come in here and drink? And I noticed they are trying to get to the water trough, you didn't even let them drink. I have half a thought to run you in for cruelty to animals, you see we have a law on the books in this town about that; but I won't, you get out there and let them drink before you leave." Catlin had Charlie follow them out to make sure they did as they were told.

She walked over to me. "Admiral, you were going to kill those two, weren't you?"

"Well maybe, but I was thinking about just shooting the guns out of their hands."

"Yeah right, anyway, I think they were scouts for that bunch that's coming to wipe out this town. Or they could just be drifters, but like I said earlier trouble is your middle name."

"If they were scouts for that bunch, I guess it's good I didn't kill them. Yeah, you're right, I was going to kill them, I just didn't like their looks; they were evil clear through."

"Admiral, on the rest of your walk-about try not to kill anybody, alright?"

"Yeah, but it's not up to me, like you said, trouble is my middle name, it finds me."

"I never said trouble was your middle name, you did."

"Yeah, I guess it was me." Trouble had been following me all of my life. The only good thing about my life was Hattie May.

"Thank you, sweetheart, I feel the same about you, now stop feeling sorry for yourself and finish checking out the town. And if it makes you feel any better, I would of shot those two myself." Hattie said in my mind.

I stopped at the local mercantile and bought ten pounds of assorted candy and had it delivered to my room at the Hotel; I figured the troops would like it. And then went in a saloon that had a name I liked, it was called the 'Hungry Horse'.

For the middle of the afternoon, it was fairly busy and I spotted a poker game going on in the corner table, I noticed an empty chair. I walked over and pulled it out and said: "I hope nobody minds if I join the game?"

"No, of course not stranger, your money is as good as anybody else's. It's table stakes, buy is fifty dollars." Said a man dressed as a Mississippi Gambler.

I used to be pretty good at poker, now that I had enhanced perception, I was more than excellent at it. I tossed my money in and the gambler was dealing. I was a bit surprised when I picked up my cards, it was a full house. When it came to staying or folding, I threw in my cards and said: "That was some mighty poor cards there, Mississippi."

He looked at me and smiled. The next time around he dealt me nothing but garbage. "Are those any better?" He asked.

"Sure are, the best hand I ever had." I said.

When the betting came around to me I matched the last bet and raised ten dollars. The gambler looked at me and smiled. He probably thought I was an idiot. I did the same thing till there was only the gambler and me in the game. He raised me a hundred bucks, I looked at him and raised him two hundred. It went like that till he was flat broke, there must have been three thousand dollars in the pot.

"Well, Mississippi, aren't you going to raise me anymore? No, then I guess it's my pot." I looked at the other players setting there watching us, I said: "How much have you fellow lost to this jasper?"

They told me. I looked them over; "I tell you what this is your lucky day, I see that some of you are family men, and one or two of you are just punchers and if you promise me you're going to give up gambling, I'm going to let the five of you split this pot and then I want the five of you to go straight home or your ranch as case may be. And as far as you're concerned Mississippi you get your plunder together and hit the trail back to that big muddy river, do you understand?" He got up and left, just like that.

One of the young punchers said: "Do you mind if I ask what your hand was?"

I turned them over, he gasped. "Damn, I never seen the like." He said as he walked away shaking his head.

I walked out of the swinging doors and leaning against the hitching rack was my lovely wife. "What are you doing here, beautiful?"

"You called me, subconsciously that is, so I had the Hornet drop me and my horse behind the Hotel, I put my horse in the Hotel's livery and hoofed it over here; so, are you just going to stand there or buy me drink?"

"Sure, but not here, let's head over to one of those two saloons down the street, they look pretty seedy, should be able to get into some trouble in them." I said, then I picked her up and gave her a big, long kiss.

Hattie had her buckskins on, along with her two .44's, I walked a little bit behind her just to watch her swinging hips. She knew I was checking her out, so, she just gave me a better show, I had to stop ogling her or I would have a little trouble walking.

I looked up and glanced around, I wasn't the only one watching her, there were three rough looking men who just came out of the first saloon, they stood and watched us, well, not us, I guess, but Hattie. "Hey sweetheart, check those guys out, I think they want a piece of you." I said via our minds.

"Yeah, I noticed, if they give me trouble, can I shoot them?"

"If they give you trouble, I'll shoot them."

"No, you won't, I got first dibs on them I feel like cutting my dogs loose."

"Your dogs."

"Yeah, my two .44's."

"So, what did you name your dogs?"

"Left and right, what else? Look, they're fanning out to stop us, oh please, let me shoot them."

"Alright, but only, if they draw first, is your shield turned on?"

"No, that wouldn't be fair if I had my shield on, and it would take all of the danger away, you know I can get all three of them even if they draw first."

(Really, we didn't have to turn our shields on, there is a fail-safe built in them, if they sense any danger to us, they automatically come on.)

I don't think Hattie knew that, but, she probably did know that, but just buried it deep in a corner of her mind. "Yes, I know you can out shoot them, but let's just see how things go, they might not even have evil intent on their minds."

As we drew closer to them, one of them said: "Mam, are you going into that saloon?"

"Why yes, that is our plan." Hattie said.

"Well Mam, they have a rule, you might say, no decent women allowed. And we can see that you are a decent woman, even if you're packing those cannons on your hips. If you go in there it will cause a ruckus..."

"The hell you say, a rule, not a city ordinance, huh?"

"Yes Mam, it's just their own rule, not a law in this city."

"Well Cowboy, I can see that the three of you are from some ranch around here and since you're not drunk and going home early, you must have lost your poke in a poker game, am I right?"

"Yes Mam, that's another reason to stay out of there, it was a crooked game, we're sure, but we were out-numbered, and we are not gunslingers. And we didn't figure to lose our lives over money."

"That's pretty wise; how much did you lose?"

"Our whole month's pay, 40.00 bucks each."

I stepped forward, "What would you do if had to do it over again?"

"Well for one thing, we wouldn't go in there; that's a snake's den. Then we'd take a bath and get a good steak and go back to the ranch and save our money."

I reached in my pocket and gave each of them two double eagles. "Here is your money back, do as you told us you would do; a man hasn't got much in this world; the only thing he has is his word, so you had better keep it."

"Thanks Mister, you didn't have to do this; what's your name anyway?"

"I'm Matt Bodeen, this is my wife, Hattie May."

"Matt Bodeen, the Texas Ranger? I've heard of you; didn't you go in the Army?"

"Yeah, we still are in the Army, we're on special assignment; be sure to stay out of town for the next week, you'll live longer." I said, as Hattie and I turned and headed into the snake's den.

We walked to the bar, I put my back to the bar resting my elbows on the bar. Hattie slapped two dimes on the bar and said: "Give us two beers."

"We don't serve women in here, unless you're a whore, are you a whore?" the barkeep said, just before Hattie slapped him up-beside his head with her .44, he flopped down, out cold.

The whole bar got quiet. Hattie turned around and rested her elbows on the bar like me. Three men got up from one of the tables. One of them a fat man with gold rings on every finger, the other two were gunslingers.

"I own this place," said the fat man, 'can you give me a reason why you hit my barkeep?"

"He was disrespectful to a lady, he called me whore, what do you have to say about that?"

"Well, I reckon he was right, you sure look like a whore to me." He said, then he laughed.

We both took our elbows off the bar, the two gunslingers started to draw. Hattie was quicker than a rattler, her first shot was right through the fat man's head, my two shots got both gunslingers; then the ball was burst right open.

Bullets were bouncing off our shields faster that I could count, that is if I wanted to count them. But it was like shooting ducks in a pond, the only ones who were standing, that is beside us, were the ones who had their hands up with no guns in them.

I said: "This bar is closed for the duration, that is till I tell the new owner he can open again. I am Major Matt Bodeen of the U.S. Army, everybody get what belongs to them and get the hell out of here, you there, blubbering like a baby, you go tell the funeral Parlor guy to come get this refuse."

Of course, Catlin and Charlie came bursting in; she seen us and stopped dead in her tracks. "What hell was this all about?"

"He called me a whore, and they refused to serve me a beer; and then those two gunslingers drew on us, that's the whole drift of it." Hattie said.

"Yeah, that's about right Catlin, then all of those other dead guys started shooting at us and you know how that goes, we natural returned their fire. Anyway, I told a guy to get the grave digger. You might want to check on that, he might have just, ran off."

"I tell you what, you two just go back to your Hotel and stay there till all of the troops get here, you both are like two bulls in a china shop, you break everything everywhere you go."

"Hey, I'm not a bull." Hattie said.

"Just get!" Catlin said.

So, we did get; "Someone should remind her who the senior officers are around here!" Hattie huffed as we left.

"Just cool down, you do remember that they are Deputies, we had the Sheriff make them so. Right now, we are just private citizens. But as soon as we declare martial law, then you and I are the head honchos."

As soon as we came in the owner, who was making like he was busy at the front desk, gave us a big smile, I stopped and introduced Hattie and told him that others of our bunch would be checking in and to just assign them rooms when they did.

I went to pinch Hattie's derrière as we were going up the stairs to our room, but couldn't because her buckskins were too tight. She looked over her shoulder and stuck her tongue out at me and then licked her lips... I knew what that meant...

As soon as the door closed we were tearing each other's clothes' off, that is after we shucked our gun belts. I picked her up and started for the bedroom, that was when she pulled me to the floor, and that's all I'm going to tell you!

They were still serving supper when we made it down to the Hotel's Café. Catlin and Charlie were there just finishing up their meal. "Hey, how's the town pretty quiet?" I asked as we sat down.

"Yeah, it was, after you two left; by the looks of you both you found a way to work your excess energy off." She said with a wink.

"Sure did," Hattie said as she leaned over and gave me a kiss. The waitress interrupted what was a very hot kiss. We ordered steak, Hattie ordered hers rare and smacked her lips. Catlin blushed. Yeah, androids could blush; they had the same physiology, almost, as we did.

"So, are you two off duty for the night?" I asked.

"Yeah, we are. Have you heard when the action is going to start?" Charlie asked. Wow, that was the first time I heard him speak.

"No, not yet. Let me call Albert and have him give us an update on where they are at."

I did so, Albert had his drones check in. "They are camped about fifty miles south right now, so, Catlin give Selena a call and tell them to be sure and be here by the morning. That will give them time to settle in before the action starts."

"Catlin, I think you should tell the Sheriff to tell the populace to make themselves scarce tomorrow; that is if they value their lives. I think a lot of the town's buildings are going to need a lot of patching, from all of the bullet holes."

"Yeah, if I can find her; she's been sort of taking time off since we have been patrolling the town."

"That's fine, but, tell her after she informs the town about the impending attack, she can also make herself scarce. I would like the town to appear normal when they ride in; perhaps some of the troops can dress in civilian clothes and keep the bank and stores open, sort of anyway."

"Well Admiral, I would like the troops that we have to remain in uniform; but, I know that aboard the Santa Fe there is more of us that would like the opportunity to come down, they could operate the stores and bank, etc... what do you think?"

"I think that is a good plan, make it so."

"I will have them in place first thing in the morning, Prince Attila."

I looked at Hattie, "I feel like I have three different personalities, Admiral, Prince, Matt Bodeen; well, make it four, I am husband to the most beautiful woman in the universe."

Hattie looked at me and smiled, "I think, that number four should be number one; come Matt Bodeen, it's time again for you to fulfill your husbandly duty." I never argue with a woman when she is so blatantly right.

Catlin looked at Charlie and took his hand and they also headed up the stairs to their room.

When we woke up the next morning; Selena was setting at the foot of our bed with her legs crossed looking at us. "Hattie, wake up, Selena is here."

"Well, what's wrong with that?" Hattie said as she rolled over at looked at Selena.

"Oh, I see, Selena it's good to see you, but not quite so much of you." Hattie said, and then Selena winked at her. "Oh, that's good, you finally learned how to wink."

"It took a lot of practice. I just got here and need a bath; do you guys want to join me?"

"No, you go ahead, we had one last night." Hattie said and smiled, looked like she was remembering that bath, I know I was...

Selena jumped off the bed and walked away shaking her butt at us. I said to Hattie, "That girl needs to get married in the worse way, well not the worse way, but the good way."

When the three of us got down to breakfast, Catlin and all of the troops were already gone. We had our uniforms on, with all weapons hanging from our hips. Selena said, "All of the troops are in place; also, Jasper says those killers are about five miles out. We should have time to finish our breakfast."

Coffeyville was almighty quiet as we left the Hotel and walked along toward the jail, where Catlin and Charlie were waiting. The Androids were sweeping the boardwalk and doing things that that needed done, they were dressed like town folks.

Our troops were out of sight, just waiting till they were needed. "Jasper, tell Albert to wait till all one hundred of them get in town and then seal off the town with drones, I don't want any of them to escape."

"Do you want all of them dead?" Jasper asked.

"Give them the opportunity to surrender, if they don't, kill them."

We didn't have long to wait, we could see the dust of that big bunch a mile away; Selena, Hattie and I waited inside the Sheriff's office, while Catlin and Charlie lounged around out front.

Hattie, Selena and I put our arms around each other in a circle and said a prayer; not for ourselves, they couldn't hurt us; but the prayer was for forgiveness for the lives we were about to take. Just as we would say a prayer for killing a deer or elk. We knew not many of them would surrender; because even if they did they would be hung for past crimes.

Instead of riding in and shooting the place up; they rode in real-easy, just looking around; they seen Catlin standing in front of the Sheriff's office and reined in. "Well, hello there, little lady, my goodness and you're a Deputy Sheriff also; where's the Sheriff?"

"He went fishing, what can we do for you?"

"How about we go somewhere that we can get your clothes off of you?"

"Well George, I can call you George, can't I? No matter, and that is Oliver sitting there, as ugly as ever, I tell you what, if you are alive when you step down from that horse, I'll just consider taking my clothes off right here in front of everybody."

"You seem to know our names, how come?"

"I have wanted posters on you and Oliver, and most of these others also; so, either surrender or get on with what you all came here to do." Catlin said. That was our cue to step out and make our acquaintance with these desperadoes.

"Well, hell, what do we have here, some more pretty ladies all dressed up like soldiers. Look here boys have you ever seen any female soldiers before?" He said, turning to look at those beside him; which was a ploy to distract us, as they all went for their guns.

We just stood there letting them bang away at us, their bullets bouncing off of our shields. The big bunch of them all split up and headed for the stores and the bank. But our troops stepped out and surprised them; again, the troops just stood there letting them bang away.

Catlin asked, "Admiral, can we shoot them now?"

"Fire at will." I said, then all of the U.S. Army fired at will.

When the smoke cleared there were three of them standing there with their hands up. Catlin walked over and hand cuffed them and walked them over to the jail and locked them up. We would let civil justice take care of them.

As the town grew quiet, the town people started drifting in, including the Sheriff, who stood there looking at all of the dead; she said: "What are we going to do with all of those bodies?"

"You have a cemetery, don't you?"

"Yes, but, who is going to dig the graves? The town can't afford to bury all of them."

I looked at Catlin, "Catlin have the troops take care of this mess, take the horses to the barn behind the Hotel along with saddles and their guns. Set up needed security measures and then give the rest of the troops some R&R, let them spend some money around town and have some fun." Yes, even Androids needed Rest and Relaxation.

"Uh," The Sheriff said, "I thought the town would get the horses' and gear."

"You thought wrong, we just saved this whole town from death and destruction, show a little gratitude and get off of your dead butt and police things for once."

"Sweetheart, what are we going to do with all of those horses and gear?"

"I don't know yet, but I sure wasn't going to let the rich have them to line their pockets. Maybe we can give them to the poor and needy; I've seen a lot of urchins running around. Also, I bet there is a lot of money in those saddle bags. Maybe we could set up some kind of Charity."

"Hey," Selena said, "I bet I could find some enterprising woman to organize and run it."

"And just where are you going to look for such a woman?" I asked.

"Over there." She said, pointing at a building that set beside one of the bars. "They know how to run a successful business. And they also know who the poor and needy are, including themselves. Also, they would like to do something else besides lay on their backs."

Hattie and I looked at each other. We thought back and forth and said: "Alright Selena, you find an honest woman in there and we'll set up a Charity Foundation, maybe call it 'The Sisters of Charity' or whatever, it's your baby to play with."

"Alright, I'll go over and mingle with them, they're all standing out front gawking anyway. I have a few ideas about how to go about it."

We just bet she did, Hattie and I went back to the Hotel and who should we find setting in the living room of our suite?

Gabe smiled at us, "So, I saw the whole thing, good work; the plans have changed a little bit; the El Paso thing still needs to be done, but you two won't be heading it up."

"Oh, and just what are we going to be doing?"

"You're going home to Terra, there are some things that the King needs some help with, even though he doesn't know it."

"What about Selena?"

"She can stay here and play around with her charity; why don't you buy this Hotel, she can use it for her headquarters; also, she can keep the last bunch of Androids to help her and provide security. Catlin can take the Hornet and take the troops down to El Paso, I'll fill her in on what needs to be done. When everything is finished up here on earth the Santa Fe can transport them all to New Hope; their home base."

"Sounds like you have everything all figured out; when you say 'them all', you're including Selena, aren't you?"

"Yes, she needs to find a mate, I have one all picked out for her on New Hope, he's one of the Sioux people there."

"I didn't know you Angels did things like that, pick husbands and such."

"Of course we do, especially cases like Selena's, she's special to us."

"Well, when everything is taken to New Hope, don't let them forget Jasper and my horses'. When are we supposed to be leaving for Terra?"

"It's up to you to let Captain Light know that you will be needing a ride to Terra, so at your convenience."

I looked at Hattie and then turned to Gabe, he was gone. "What the hell, he didn't even say goodbye." We sat there awhile, mulling it over. "What say we saddle up and go for ride, maybe Jasper and Albert wants to go with us? I'll saddle up while you tell Selena what Gabe said, she can see about buying the Hotel."

We headed down river into Oklahoma Territory, it was Indian country, but I didn't care, we had Albert with us. One thing about it we didn't run into any settlers, we had peace and quiet, just grasshoppers and rattlesnakes, a few copperheads.

We found a nice place to camp beside a bend in the river, there was a place to swim where that bend in the river was, cause the river had washed a deep hole in the bend. Albert had divested the camp spot of snakes and then set up a barrier so they couldn't come back in.

We didn't bring any food with us, because, we didn't need food all of the time since we had enhanced our bodies. We just swam and laid on our bedrolls looking at the stars, thinking. We made love and swam again and snuggled our naked bodies together.

Jasper shuffled his hooves around, enough to wake us and said: "Hattie do you ever miss home?"

"Yes, at times I do Jasper, why do you want to go home?"

"No, oh, I don't know, at times I get to feeling lonely; we used to be a lot closer back at home you rode me every day, now sometimes I don't see you for weeks or months. Maybe I just need someone."

"I'm sorry Jasper, I didn't realize since you are enhanced also and sentient that you needed companionship; that was so selfish of us; when we leave for Terra you can go with us. I'm sure back there we can figure something out, I promise."

"Thank you Hattie, I would like to go to Terra with you and Matt, can Albert go also?"

"No, we'll have to leave Albert with Selena, she'll need him, now go to sleep, we'll have a busy day tomorrow."

Little did we know about all of the work that Gabe had lined up for the three of us...

The End, I think...

<u>*Other books by J. D. Oliver*</u>

I Awoke to Silence

Wail Not!

Hope Dies Last

As the Eagle Flies

Trego

The Way Home